E. V. Thompson was born in London. After spending nine years in the Royal Navy, he served as a Vice Squad policeman in Bristol, became an investigator for British Overseas Airways (during which time he was seconded to the Hong Kong Police Narcotics Bureau), then headed Rhodesia's Department of Civil Aviation Security Section. While in Rhodesia, he published over two hundred short stories before moving back to England to become a full-time award-winning writer.

His first novel, *Chase the Wind*, the opening book in the Retallick saga, won the Best Historical Novel Award, and since then more than thirty novels have won him thousands of admirers around the world. *Brothers in War* is the ninth volume in the Retallick saga.

Praise for E. V. Thompson

'With settings that stretch from China to Cornwall, these romantic sagas delight'
Independent

'E. V. Thompson is, as always, an extremely good storyteller'
Historical Novels Review

'His many fans won't be disappointed'
Bristol Evening News

Brothers in War

E. V. Thompson

SPHERE

First published in Great Britain in 2006 by Sphere
This paperback edition published in 2007 by Sphere
Reprinted 2008, 2009, 2012, 2013

Copyright © E. V. Thompson 2006

A CIP catalogue record for this book
is available from the British Library.

ISBN 978-0-7515-4592-0

Typeset in Palatino by Palimpsest Book Production Limited,
Grangemouth, Stirlingshire
Printed and bound in Great Britain by
Clays Ltd, St Ives plc

Papers used by Sphere are from well-managed forests
and other responsible sources.

MIX
Paper from
responsible sources
FSC
www.fsc.org FSC® C104740

Sphere
An imprint of
Little, Brown Book Group
100 Victoria Embankment
London EC4Y 0DY

An Hachette UK Company
www.hachette.co.uk

www.littlebrown.co.uk

Brothers in War

1

I

'You may have a Cornish name, Retallick, but you are *not* a Cornishman and never will be, not if you live to be a hundred, so I suggest you stop trying to tell Cornishmen what to do with a business that some of us have been in for much of our lives.'

The speaker was Brigadier General (retired) Sir Robert Grove, and he was so angry that his drink-induced ruddy complexion had taken on a purple hue.

Ben Retallick had seen such outbursts from the irascible old man before, but he was taken aback by the present paroxysm. It had been brought about by Ben's suggestion that the owners of the Cornish china clay works should supply their product to the British government at the lowest possible price as a gesture of support during the difficult months of 1915. The days when treated clay was used solely for the manufacture of pottery and porcelain were long past. It

1

now had a great many uses, many vital to the war effort.

As the owner of Ruddlemoor, the largest clay workings in Cornwall, Ben had called a meeting of the other clay works owners, thinking they would agree with his suggestion – in principle, at least. Instead, he had met unexpected opposition from Sir Robert, a man whose army career had brought him a great many rewards, including a knighthood, and who might have been expected to be more patriotic than any other man in the room.

Hiding his surprise, Ben replied to the personal attack. 'I don't think my Cornishness has anything to do with the issue under discussion, Sir Robert. I am merely suggesting that we make a joint gesture of support for the war effort. It would certainly be appreciated by the families of men who are risking their lives in Europe . . . many of whom are Cornishmen.'

'You can *think* what you like, Retallick . . . suggest what you like too. I have done my duty to this country and have nothing to prove, so I'm damned if I'm going to risk bankrupting myself by making a gesture of support for this government. The best thing we can all do is ensure that our companies remain in profit in order to provide work for men when they return from the war.'

'I am not suggesting we sacrifice our companies, Sir Robert, merely that we do not take advantage of the difficult times in which we live in order to make an excessive profit.' Ben spoke with a patience he did not feel.

His anger unabated, the retired brigadier brushed Ben's argument aside. 'Profit is the life-blood of business, Retallick. No company can exist without it. Times are just as difficult for the clay business as for the government. There is no sense in shooting ourselves in the foot by cutting prices.'

There was agreement from many of the assembled works owners and Ben was almost ready to concede defeat when the door to the meeting room opened unexpectedly and one of the girls who worked in the Ruddlemoor office appeared in the doorway.

'I'm sorry to trouble you, Mr Retallick, but there's a telegram for you.'

Irritated by the interruption, Ben said, 'You take it for me, Millie. Tell the telegram boy I'm in the middle of a meeting.'

'The telegram's been brought here by postmaster Williams, Mr Retallick. He says he should give it to you himself. He says it's from Switzerland.'

Ben's attitude changed immediately. His wife Lily was a patient in a Swiss clinic. Suffering from a serious lung complaint, she had been there since before the war erupted in Europe in 1914. Although there had been initial cause for great anxiety, she had eventually begun to make steady progress. Recent reports from the clinic had been optimistic.

'All right, Millie, I'll come right away . . .' Turning to the others in the room, he said, 'If you will excuse me, gentlemen, I believe the telegram contains news of my wife.'

The men in the room knew of Lily's illness, and

3

although they were in disagreement with him about business affairs murmurs of sympathy followed Ben from the meeting room.

Postmaster Henry Williams waited in Ben's office, a yellow telegram envelope in his hand. Holding it out towards Ben, he said, 'This just came for you, Mr Retallick. I knew you would want to see it right away. As both our boys are out delivering messages I thought I should bring it to you myself.'

'Thank you, Henry.' Even as he spoke, Ben was ripping open the envelope. Reading the message, he tried unsuccessfully not to allow his elation to show, aware that the postmaster was watching him closely.

'I am pleased to be the bearer of happy tidings, Mr Retallick,' the postmaster beamed. 'I am sorry to have interrupted your meeting, but I know you have been waiting for such news for a very long time . . . will there be any reply?'

'No . . . yes.' Ben contradicted himself very quickly. 'Send a reply to Lily saying, "Wonderful news. Will come as soon as I can. Love, Ben."'

As the St Austell postmaster left, Ben stepped to one of the windows and looked out. He remained at the window for a long time, until one of the older women who had worked at Ruddlemoor for many years and knew his wife well came into the room from the outer office. Approaching Ben, she said, 'The telegram, Mr Retallick . . . is it bad news about Lily?'

Turning towards her, he broke into a happy smile. 'No, Ruth, it's good news . . . very good news. The doctor says she's made such excellent progress that I

4

can go to Switzerland and bring her home as soon as it's convenient for me to make the journey.'

'That's wonderful! Oh, the staff in the office will be absolutely delighted for you. It's what we have been waiting to hear for so long. When do you think you'll be leaving?'

'I've been trying for more than a month to get permission to go to see her, but without success. The British government has banned all civilian travel across the Channel for the time being and they've said they cannot make an exception for me. But I'll try even harder now. They've *got* to let me go and fetch her.' Ben was silent for a few moments, then he said, 'I'm going home now to telephone the Foreign Office and try to persuade them to change their minds. Send someone up to the meeting to tell them what's happening. I don't want to go back and discuss business matters just now.'

With that, Ben turned away and strode from the office.

Riding home to Tregarrick, his home in the Pentewan valley, Ben wondered what could possibly be done to obtain the necessary permission to travel to Switzerland.

He could understand the government's policy about civilian travel to the Continent. Every available vessel was being used to carry soldiers and essential supplies to the battle front. Unfortunately, they were suffering heavy losses. German submarines – the dreaded U-boats – were sinking any vessel found in British waters, regardless of its nationality. By this tactic the German High Command hoped to prevent urgent supplies and reinforcements from reaching the battle lines that stretched across the breadth of France, at the same time starving Great Britain into submission.

Already almost half a million tons of merchant shipping had been sunk, including a number of ships flying the flags of countries not involved in the conflict between the warring nations. So far Germany had ignored the protests of the neutral countries.

Whether or not such a policy might eventually succeed, it was certainly hitting Britain hard – and affecting the clay industry too. The Cornish china clay companies had always sold much of their product to overseas buyers, but ships were no longer coming in to the tiny undefended harbour at nearby Charlestown. It was just one of many problems that had convinced Ben that the china clay producers should be working together.

Suddenly, Ben's thoughts were interrupted and he brought his horse to an abrupt halt in the narrow main street of St Austell town. A party of wounded and disabled soldiers was crossing the road in front of him. Their loose blue jackets identified them as convalescents from the nearby hospital.

It was late May, and the British army was locked in battle with its German counterpart in the trenches of France and Belgium – and suffering appalling casualties. The numbers were such that when they were sent back to England the military hospitals were unable to cope and many thousands of wounded soldiers were being treated in civilian hospitals throughout the land.

Ben drew in his breath sharply as a wounded soldier supporting his weight on crutches slipped on a cobbled section of road. He would have fallen to the ground had not a uniformed medical orderly walking beside him reacted quickly and caught him.

Escorting his charge to the pavement, the orderly turned and came back to where Ben sat on his horse. 'Thank you for your patience, sir. Some of the men find it difficult to manage.' He spoke with a strong Irish accent.

Nodding acknowledgement of the orderly's words, Ben asked, 'Where are you taking them?'

'To the public house just up by the church, sir. The landlord lost his son at Ypres and he makes us welcome. Regrettably, not all landlords show the same understanding of the needs of wounded men.'

Reaching inside a pocket, Ben pulled out his wallet. Extracting all the banknotes it contained, he handed them down to the surprised orderly. 'Here, see that the men need to pay for nothing. If the money runs out tell the landlord that Ben Retallick will settle his bill. He knows who I am. I wish your charges a speedy recovery.'

Ben rode on while the orderly was still calling down the blessings of the Almighty upon him. The plight of the soldiers had brought home to him once again how Lily had suffered under the illness that had affected her for so long. He had desperately wished that she too might one day be a convalescent. Now she was fit enough to return home and he hoped that many of the soldiers he had just seen might soon be declared fit too.

7

Unfortunately, those who made a full recovery would immediately be sent back to the battle front, to risk their lives once more.

Thoughts of Lily and what the future held for them took the place of concerns about Ruddlemoor for the remainder of the ride to Tregarrick. She was still on his mind when he rode up the tree-lined driveway to the house and saw a motor car parked on the gravel outside the main entrance. It was a dull green coloured Vauxhall staff car with a military number plate.

Ben could think of no one who would come to visit him in such a vehicle. After delivering his horse into the care of a groom he was met at the doorway to the house by his housekeeper, the ageing Mrs Rodda.

'You have a visitor, sir,' she said. 'He's been here for an hour or more. I suggested that he came to see you at Ruddlemoor, but he said he would prefer to wait for you here and speak to you in private.'

'What sort of visitor, Mrs Rodda? Is he a soldier?'

'Yes sir, and a very important one I'd say. I've put him in your study with a cup of tea and some cake. His driver is being looked after by Cook, in the kitchen.'

'An army officer to see *me*?' Ben was puzzled. 'Did he give you a name, or say why he is here?'

'He did say who he was, sir, but I was that flummoxed that I really can't remember who he said he was – except that he introduced himself as a general, or something similar.'

'Well, I suppose there's only one way I can find out who he is and why he's here. Have some tea sent to my study for me please, Mrs Rodda.'

8

As the housekeeper hurried off to the kitchen, Ben made his way to the study. When he entered the room a tall, distinguished-looking man wearing a tailored army uniform rose to his feet. He seemed vaguely familiar, but Ben was unable to place him immediately.

As his guest advanced across the room, Ben observed that he walked with a noticeable limp, but he greeted Ben with a warm smile and, extending his hand, said, 'Ben! Please accept my apologies for descending upon you without notice, but it's good to see you again. Time has been very kind to you.'

Still at a loss about the identity of his unexpected visitor, Ben shook the extended hand. 'I'm sorry, sir, I'm afraid you have the advantage. Your face is familiar, but . . .'

'There is no need to apologise, Ben; it has been many years. About thirteen, I believe. You were no more than a lad then. We met at Insimo. I am Carey Hamilton.'

Ben was taken aback by mention of Insimo, his family home in Matabeleland, now part of the country recently named Rhodesia in honour of its founder, Cecil Rhodes. But he was now able to identify his visitor.

'Of course! Forgive me for not recognising you immediately. As I recall, you were a captain when we first met – and a lieutenant colonel when you finally left Africa. But, as my housekeeper was quick to observe, you have become a very important man now.' He indicated the red tabs on the lapels of Carey's uniform jacket, each decorated with a plaited cord of gold braid.

'Well . . . I am a lieutenant general, it's true, but thanks to an encounter with a German shell last year I am now in charge of nothing more exciting than a desk in the War Office, where generals are more common than orderlies.'

The sympathy expressed by Ben in response to his visitor's words was genuine. He had known Carey Hamilton during the Anglo-Boer war, when the officer's skill and daring had won him rapid promotion. Ben had been too young to be involved in actual fighting during that African war, but Adam and Nat, his two brothers, had taken part in the conflict, Nat, the older of the two, acting as a scout for Carey Hamilton and other senior British officers in South Africa. When the war ended Nat had returned to Matabeleland to take charge of Insimo once more. Adam, younger and wilder than his brother, had fought against the British as a member of a Boer commando, eventually marrying an Afrikaans girl and settling down to farm in South Africa when hostilities had ceased.

Ben assumed that Carey Hamilton's War Office duties had brought him to Cornwall and he was delighted when the officer agreed to stay the night at Tregarrick. It meant the two men would be able to spend the evening chatting of old times and of the men and women they had both known in Africa, including Carey's sister Thomasina, widow of an officer who died in South Africa during the Boer war.

Ben had once believed Thomasina would marry his brother Nat – and he believed Nat had thought so too. Instead, Thomasina had become the wife of a titled diplomat and Nat had married a girl who was almost as wild as his brother Adam. Indeed, she had herself been shot and severely wounded whilst riding with a Boer commando. It was Nat who had helped to save her life.

But Ben had some urgent private business of his own to attend to first. While a meal was being prepared for them both he told Carey about Lily, and the telegram he had received at Ruddlemoor that day.

Expressing his delight with the news of Lily's recovery, Carey asked, 'Do you expect to be successful in obtaining a permit to travel to France, Ben?'

'I would like to say yes, Carey,' Ben replied, 'but experience has taught me that when dealing with government departments rules and regulations take precedence over personal problems.'

Carey Hamilton was seated in a leather chair in Ben's comfortable study. Suddenly he leaned forward, his relaxed air disappearing. 'I have a confession to make to you, Ben. My visit is not entirely social – even though I am delighted to be able to share your company in this beautiful house. I am here to ask a favour of you – a favour that, I hope, will make a very significant contribution to the war. Now I can see a way of repaying you. If you agree to come with me to London for a couple of days and speak to some of my colleagues in the War Office, I will guarantee to obtain a pass for you to travel to Switzerland to bring your wife home. Indeed, if you come to London prepared for the journey, you can carry on to Switzerland from there and so save yourself a great deal of time.'

For a moment Ben was speechless with surprise, but

he decided he would leave his questions unasked for now. All that was important was obtaining the necessary permission to travel to Switzerland.

'I don't know what you could possibly want from me, Carey, but whatever it is it is yours if you can arrange for me to go to Lily. When do we leave for London?'

II

Carey was prevented from giving Ben any more details of what would be required from him in exchange for the permit to go to fetch Lily home by the arrival of a maid to say that dinner was ready. It was not until after the meal, when the two men were once more in the study, that Ben asked his companion for an explanation.

'I can't think why I should suddenly be of such importance to you,' he said. 'Is it something to do with the china clay industry – or do you want me to turn my works over to manufacturing munitions?'

'Neither, Ben. It is your knowledge of Africa that I, and senior members of the War Office, urgently need. But before I say any more I must swear you to absolute secrecy about what I am going to tell you.'

Thoroughly intrigued, Ben said, 'Of course, but I can't imagine what knowledge I possess that can be of such significance to you and the War Office. After all, I have been away from Africa for some years now.'

'That may be so, Ben, but before I say any more am I correct in thinking that you have travelled northwards from Matabeleland through Northern Rhodesia and the Belgian Congo, as far as Lake Tanganyika?'

'Yes, I once took a party of Matabele warriors with me and spent a season hunting in the area – but surely there's no fighting going on up there?'

'Not yet, but Lake Tanganyika forms much of the border between German East Africa on one side and the Belgian Congo and part of Northern Rhodesia on the other. Unfortunately, we have allowed the Germans to build gunboats and station them there. As a result, they control the lake – and with it the tribes who depend upon it for their livelihood. It is making life very difficult for us. Recently, someone came to us with a plan that we hope might change the situation – and it has become very important that we do so. Somehow or other we must wrest East Africa from the Germans, but without control of the lake it will not only prove extremely difficult, but be likely to cost the lives of a great many of our soldiers.'

Still uncertain what Carey Hamilton wanted from him, Ben said, 'I'll do anything I can to help you, of course, but I still don't know how . . .'

'You have already told me that you *can* help, Ben. You've spent time in the Congo – and the Belgians have done very little to change it in the years since your visit. We are particularly interested in the country between the Southern African railhead at Fungurume, and Sankisia, where the Belgians have built a short stretch of railway line going to a river that is navigable almost to the lake. We are told there is another very small length of railway track linking the two, but the Belgians are unable to provide us with reliable maps and it is of vital importance to us that we obtain the fullest possible details of the terrain. Do you recall anything about that particular area?'

'I remember it very well indeed,' Ben replied confidently. 'While I was there something stirred up the tribes and as a result I spent far more time there than I had intended, finding ways through the country that would keep us out of trouble. By the time I was done I felt I knew the area almost as well as I know Insimo.'

His reply delighted Carey Hamilton. 'I *knew* you were the man to speak to us at the War Office, Ben. If you can spare us a few days in London we will be able to fill in some details on the very sketchy maps given to us by the Belgians. As they are at present they are virtually useless. You can also give us first-hand knowledge of what our men can expect to come up against along the way.'

'I'll be happy to come to London with you – especially as you have promised I can travel to Lily afterwards – but things are rather difficult at Ruddlemoor at the moment – indeed, for the clay industry as a whole – so I don't want to be away for too long. However, Lily is more important to me than business. Before we go to the War Office I'd like you to tell me what you are planning and how many men will be going up to Lake Tanganyika. I might be able to give you some idea of the number of native carriers you'll need and the amount of food and water that will be required for the journey between Fungurume and Sankisia. Getting that right will be of vital importance to any expedition. The country we're talking about can throw just about everything at

14

you. Mountains, rivers, dense bush, grass tall enough to hide an elephant . . . not to mention snakes, crocodiles, mosquitoes and tsetse flies.'

'But *you* reached the lake?' Carey Hamilton queried. Ben nodded.

'Do you think you could have got there if you were taking something with you that was both heavy and bulky?'

'That would depend very much on what it was,' Ben replied. Reaching a decision, he said, 'Look, why don't you tell me exactly what it is you intend doing, Carey? If you do, perhaps I can tell you what you need to know and we can stop playing mysterious games.'

After only a moment more of hesitation, Carey Hamilton capitulated. 'I'm talking of boats, Ben . . . gunboats. We intend shipping two of them from London to Cape Town, then carrying them overland to Lake Tanganyika where they will be launched to tackle the German vessels.'

Ben looked at his companion in disbelief. 'Take two boats overland from Cape Town to Lake Tanganyika?' he said, echoing Hamilton's words. 'That's almost three thousand miles. How large are these gunboats?'

'Each one is about forty feet long, with a beam of eight feet – and they will be fitted with three-pounder guns and Maxims. But when you come up to London you can see them for yourself and get a far better idea of the problems we are likely to encounter with them.'

Ben's incredulity was so evident that Carey Hamilton said, almost apologetically, 'I realise it must sound something of a madcap venture, Ben, and it probably is, but Lord Fisher, the First Sea Lord, will be providing the naval personnel to transport and man the boats, and he has given it his personal seal of approval. Despite my own initial misgivings, I too believe it can be achieved – if sufficient planning is done beforehand. Indeed, it *must* be done. We have to take control of Lake Tanganyika at all costs and in order to do that we need craft on the lake capable of outgunning the German boats. While we are at the War Office I'd like you to listen to what is being planned and tell us how best to get there and what we can expect along the way.'

As Ben had already mentioned to Carey Hamilton, it was not a good time to be leaving Ruddlemoor, but by going to London he might be able to help the army and navy avert total disaster in what would seem to be an impossible mission – and also gain something for himself. Something he desperately wanted.

'I'll speak to my works captains first thing in the morning, write out some orders for them, and we should be able to get away to London by midday. Before then I would like you to tell me everything you can about this crazy expedition.'

III

Seated beside Carey Hamilton in the staff car as they were being driven through central London to the War Office, Ben thought that men – and women – dressed in uniform outnumbered those dressed in civilian clothes in the streets of the capital city. When he

16

commented on his observation to his companion, the lieutenant general said, 'There are likely to be even more in the near future, Ben. At the moment all the servicemen you see are volunteers. Unfortunately, things are going so badly for us in France that the government intends bringing in a conscription bill at the earliest opportunity. Once it is in force there will be very few young men to be seen who are *not* wearing uniform.'

'Is the war really going that badly for us, Carey?'

Carey Hamilton thought for a few moments before replying. 'The war is going no better and no worse for us than it is for the Germans. They thought they would take Paris in the course of their initial thrust and that France would capitulate as a result. For our part, we believed we would throw them back to the German borders within a matter of weeks and they would immediately sue for peace. In either event, the war would have been over in a few months. Tragically, neither forecast was correct. It has become a war of attrition with appalling casualties being suffered by both sides. No one talks of an early end to the war any more, only of winning a series of costly battles.'

'Battles such as the one to be fought on Lake Tanganyika?' Ben asked.

'Exactly,' Carey agreed, 'but that is more likely to be similar to the war we waged against the Boers in South Africa. A contest demanding fluidity and innovation.'

'As I recall, you are an expert on that kind of warfare,' Ben commented. 'Will you be going to East Africa yourself?'

17

'That *is* my intention,' Carey admitted, 'but before I do I have a personal battle to fight and win – with the army surgeons. I must persuade them I am fully fit for active service once more. Once I have done that I expect to be calling on the services of another member of the Retallick family. Nat was the finest scout anyone could have had during the Boer war. I hope to persuade him to serve me in the same role once again.'

Letters from Insimo to Cornwall had been few and far between since the outset of the war, due to the fact that a number of ships carrying mail between Southern Africa and the United Kingdom had been sunk by German submarines. Nevertheless, letters had arrived, and they indicated that Nat was no more inclined to involve himself in this conflict than he had been during the early days of the Anglo-Boer war. However, it had been Carey Hamilton who had successfully persuaded Nat to change his mind then. Ben thought he might possibly do the same once again.

At the meeting held in the War Office with senior army and naval officers present, Ben realised that not all of them were enthusiastic about the mission that Carey Hamilton had outlined to Ben in Cornwall. The naval officers in particular were dubious about the feasibility of carrying gunboats overland for such a distance before giving battle to the enemy on a 'lake', even one like Lake Tanganyika, which was more than 400 miles long and up to 30 miles wide.

Their lack of confidence proved well founded that afternoon when Ben accompanied them to a spot on the

River Thames, to the east of London, to watch the launches try out the three-pounder guns that had been mounted on them.

When the first gun was fired, the recoil sent it and its gunner hurtling backwards, depositing both in the river. In the haste to have everything ready in time for the demonstration, the dockyard fitters working on the gunboats had neglected to secure the gun to the launch.

Fortunately, the naval gunner was rescued having suffered no more than a ducking and a loss of dignity. The three-pounder was left to take its place in the mud of the River Thames alongside artefacts spanning thousands of years of the river's history.

Such an accident might well have sounded the death knell for the improbable venture. However, contrary to his earlier misgivings, Ben was captivated by the sheer audacity of the proposed enterprise. Back in the War Office, after poring over the woefully inadequate and often inaccurate maps supplied by the Belgian authorities, he declared that, despite the awesome difficulties that would need to be overcome by such an expedition, in his opinion it could succeed. Furthermore, because of the improbable – not to say fantastic – nature of such a venture, he was convinced it would take the German authorities unawares.

Carey Hamilton was delighted. He had supported the plan from its conception, often against the strong opposition of more conservative senior officers. Others, hitherto undecided, eventually added their support, impressed by Ben's first-hand knowledge of the area and his balanced assessment of the chances of success of the mission. As a result, when a vote was taken on whether or not to go ahead with the mission, it was carried by a majority of two to one.

It was a victory for those who shared Carey Hamilton's belief in the imaginative project. However, although they had won the day, it was now time to face practicalities – and it was here that Ben's knowledge of the terrain to be traversed was put to the test.

First, he needed to correct the frighteningly inaccurate maps supplied by the Belgian authorities. He had told Carey that he believed such a task might prove beyond his capabilities, but once he sat down to study the maps he recalled details that he had believed to be long forgotten. The Belgian maps were similar to those he had acquired before setting forth from Insimo on his hunting trip, many years before. Along the way he had corrected them, adding many of the features he had encountered. Now, looking at the maps, memories of his earlier work returned to him.

Here was the ravine where he had been attacked by a lion. There, a river where only dynamite would disperse the basking crocodiles. On another map, where an apparently unbroken chain of mountains barred the way of an expedition such as the one planned by Carey Hamilton and his fellow generals, Ben pencilled in an uncharted pass, used by him and his Matabele hunters to provide them with a safe route, bypassing the lands of hostile Congolese tribesmen.

Using such knowledge, he was able to trace out what he considered to be a feasible route by which the two gun-carrying launches might be transported from Fungurume to Sankisia.

For part of the route the launches could be floated on a river that was not even marked on the Belgian maps. Unfortunately, at the time when the launches were likely to reach the area the water would be too low for them to risk using their engines, for fear of breaking the propellers. They would need to employ natives with paddles to propel them to their destination.

There were few tracks along the route and a path would need to be carved out of the undergrowth. In addition, it would be necessary to build bridges over numerous small rivers and equally small but deep gullies.

Ben also stated that for part of the route more power would be needed than could possibly be provided by local tribesmen. But he had become excited by the concept of such a mission and, after initial hesitation, he offered to provide two of the traction engines currently in use at Ruddlemoor. Steam-powered, their boilers could be heated by means of wood cut from trees along the way.

He even suggested they might make use of the services of a brilliant young Cornish engineer named Sam Hooper who was currently employed at Ruddlemoor. Hooper was familiar with the traction engines, having been responsible for them from the day they had been brought to the works. He would ensure that the heavy and powerful vehicles were not driven beyond their considerable capabilities. After discussions with the senior officers present at the meeting, Ben put in a telephone call to Ruddlemoor, and was able to persuade

Sam to journey to London immediately in order to discuss details of his proposed participation in the forthcoming operation.

By the end of the second full day in London the maps had been drawn up, Ben had given the War Office all the information he could – and Sam Hooper had received official approval for the part he would play in the imaginative venture.

A quiet but confident and assured young man, Sam had not visited the capital city before. After listening to details of the proposed plan and the part that would be played by steam, he agreed to accompany the expedition to Lake Tanganyika and assume responsibility for the Ruddlemoor traction engines.

A delighted Carey Hamilton declared that to celebrate Ben and Sam's participation he would take them to one of London's top restaurants before Sam returned to Cornwall and Ben began his journey to bring Lily home from Switzerland. He explained that the restaurant was a favourite with senior officers of the army and navy. Its reputation was such that it was also frequented by members of the government and the staffs of London's many foreign embassies.

The table to which they were shown was covered with an immaculate white cloth and laid with gleaming silver cutlery. It was the first time Sam had been inside such a restaurant – indeed, inside any restaurant. When Carey left the table to pay a visit to the cloakroom, Ben, aware of his young companion's uncertainty, tried to make the Cornishman feel more at ease.

'This is quite a place, Sam, but I must admit that I find it a little awesome. I'm going to order some of the simplest things on the menu – why don't you do the same? I'm also a bit baffled by all this cutlery. I know we're supposed to start at the outside and work our way inwards, but let's just follow what Carey does.'

By the time Carey returned Ben and Sam had decided what they were going to eat. Carey began scanning the menu, breaking off occasionally to point out some of the interesting fellow-diners.

'There are many military men from the foreign armies in London too,' he said, 'and some of their uniforms put ours to shame. Take that worn by the young man coming through the door right now, for instance. I saw him only a week or so ago at a party given by the Portuguese ambassador. He is a newly appointed assistant military attaché at the Portuguese embassy but his uniform might have been designed for an operetta.'

Looking towards the restaurant entrance, Ben saw a young man of perhaps twenty-six or seven, wearing a colourful uniform adorned with a liberal amount of gold braid. He was accompanied by a very attractive olive-skinned young woman who was perhaps a year or two younger than her companion.

Carey Hamilton was startled when Ben sprang to his feet, his chair almost crashing to the ground in his haste. 'I know that young man,' he declared, 'and that must be his sister with him. It's Philippe St Anna and his sister Antonia. You must have met them too, Carey . . . though you probably don't remember. They spent a great deal of time at Insimo – we practically grew up together. I must go and greet them.'

'Of course,' Carey replied. 'Invite them to join us for dinner, Ben. It will be a great pleasure. It has been a very long time since I shared my table with someone as attractive as the young lady . . .'

IV

Captain Philippe St Anna was a very personable young man and, as Carey had commented, his colourful Portuguese army uniform stood out in a restaurant where most of the male guests were dressed in uniforms of dull khaki. Antonia too attracted a great deal of attention, her beauty outshining all the other women present.

Once they had recovered from their initial surprise and delight at seeing him, the young couple readily accepted Ben's invitation to join him and his companions for dinner. Ben received many envious glances from male diners as he escorted the Portuguese siblings to the table which was being hurriedly laid for five by the restaurant manager and his staff.

As Ben explained to Carey and Sam, he, Philippe and Antonia had been very close friends in Africa, where their parents had been friends before them. Indeed, Daniel Retallick had once saved the life of the Portuguese couple's father by removing a bullet that was threatening his life, using a hunting knife as a primitive surgical tool, during a particularly turbulent period in the histories of Rhodesia and Mozambique, otherwise known as Portuguese East Africa.

In those days Philippe, Antonia and their parents had looked upon Insimo as their second home, a place of refuge on the frequent occasions when the tribes of the Portuguese colony rose in rebellion against their over-lords.

The introductions over, Ben said, 'You *must* remember them, Carey, even though they were children when you were there. You knew their father and mother.'

'Of course I remember them,' Carey declared. 'I once tried to teach them both how to play cricket. As I recall, Antonia showed rather more aptitude for the game than her brother! But what are you doing in London now, Antonia . . . apart from turning the head of every man in the restaurant?'

Giving him a smile, Antonia replied, 'I am *Doctor* Antonia St Anna now. I am in London visiting Philippe before travelling on to France to work in a hospital treating wounded soldiers. I have been told there is a desperate need of doctors there.'

'Is this where you see your future, Antonia, in British military hospitals?' Once more the question came from Carey.

Antonia shook her head. 'No. I intend eventually to return to my people in Mozambique. There is a great need for medical care there too. But the greatest need for doctors at the moment is in Europe. There is much work to be done treating wounded soldiers.'

'But your country is not involved in the fighting,' Carey persisted. 'Would your presence in a British military hospital not be frowned upon by your government?'

'As a doctor I will treat whoever has most need of

25

me,' Antonia declared firmly, 'and there is much I can learn here.' Glancing briefly at her brother, she added, 'Besides, I do not think Portugal will always remain neutral.'

Carey's military interest was aroused by Antonia's unexpected statement and he asked, 'What makes you think that? Portugal is far removed from the fighting, and with the way the war is going – for everyone involved – I would have thought your leaders would wish to remain outside it.'

'In Europe perhaps.' It was Philippe who replied. 'However, the Germans have attacked the homeland of Antonia and me in Mozambique on more than one occasion. True, they have apologised in each instance, but that will not prevent it from happening again.'

'Portugal is taking the situation there very seriously,' Antonia said. 'Our father has been sent to take charge of our army in Mozambique and prevent further German incursions.' Turning to Ben, she said, 'You know he too is now a general, like his father before him? But let us not talk of war and soldiering this evening. It is such an unexpected pleasure to meet up with you again, Ben. We must catch up on all the news of our families. What of your wife . . . Lily, is it not? When last I had news of her she was not at all well. Is she better now?'

For the remainder of a very enjoyable meal the talk was mainly of the Retallick and St Anna families, with most of whom Carey was familiar. Although Sam knew little about Ben's family life in Africa he was included in the conversation as far as possible, but he did not mind being a listener rather than a participant in the talk. He was a naturally quiet young man and enjoyed learning a great deal more than most Cornishmen knew about Ben Retallick.

Carey Hamilton too was happy to spend much of the evening listening to what was being said. His contact with the young Portuguese military attaché might well prove fruitful in the future and could lead to an eventual meeting with the commander of the Portuguese army in Mozambique. It would certainly strengthen his case for returning to active duty in the East African campaign, especially if Portugal *did* enter the war against Germany – and the fact that the possibility of Portuguese involvement in the war was being discussed would be of considerable interest to British government intelligence.

The five diners left the restaurant in a very happy state of mind, and although it was late they were reluctant to part company with each other. It was decided they would walk together to the Portuguese embassy where Philippe and Antonia were staying, then Ben and Sam would carry on to their hotel leaving Carey to make his way to the London flat provided for him by the War Office.

Guided by Carey, they were taking a short cut through a residential area between two still busy roads when suddenly there was a frighteningly loud explosion just ahead of them. To their horror, a section of one of the houses seemed to rise in the air before masonry began tumbling down into the street. Then they saw the flicker of flames from behind a glassless window.

'What the . . .' Carey uttered the words as Ben thought

27

there must have been a gas leak, but then there was another explosion, this one in the next street. It was followed by a third – and then another, even farther away.

As though the last explosion had triggered a switch, shafts of light from a dozen or so searchlights began to probe the night sky over London and one of them briefly touched upon a slim, silver, cigar-shaped object high above the capital city before it disappeared behind a patch of cloud.

'It's a German Zeppelin,' Carey exclaimed. 'We're being bombed! Quick . . . take cover.'

After what the German bomb had just done to the nearby house, it was difficult to know what might be considered suitable 'cover' from the surprise air raid, the first experienced by London since the war had begun some nine months before.

At that moment Sam cried, 'Listen! There's someone in the bombed house.'

Fire had quickly taken hold on the ruined house, fuelled by a fractured gas pipe, but above the crackling of the flames they could hear the sound of screaming from inside the building.

A number of women and children, together with a few mainly elderly men, had rushed out into the street, but they seemed too dazed by the devastation that confronted them to comprehend what was happening in the damaged building. Tackling an elderly woman who had come from the house next to the one struck by the German bomb, Ben said, 'The bombed house . . . the one on fire,' he added quickly, when the woman seemed not to understand, 'who lives there?'

28

He needed to repeat the question before the woman said, 'Emily . . . Emily Proctor and her three little 'uns. Her husband's in France, with the army . . .'

Waiting to hear no more, Ben ran to the front door of the bombed house with Sam and the others close behind. Despite the damage to the house the door was securely closed, and when kicking it made no impression Sam and Ben charged at it, hitting it simultaneously with their shoulders while a frustrated Carey stood back, his injured leg preventing him from offering any help to them in their efforts.

When the door eventually sprang open, the heat from the fire burning at the far end of a passageway was immediately evident. There were stairs rising to the upper floor from about halfway along the passageway, but a great deal of masonry, including a chimney, had crashed through the roof, carrying away a whole section of stairs and leaving the remainder hanging precariously away from the wall.

It was from somewhere beyond the top of the stairs, where there was a great deal of smoke, that the cries for help were emanating.

Ben stepped on the first stair but it immediately fell to pieces. 'How are we going to get up there?'

Sam slipped past him. 'Let me try. I'm a lot smaller and lighter than you.' Cutting short Ben's protest, he said, 'I'm smallest of all of us and stand more chance of making it to the top without the stairs collapsing. You, the general and Philippe stay here. When I find the children I'll lower them down to you – but keep Antonia outside. If there's fire upstairs she's likely to be needed.'

Before Ben could argue further, Sam was making his way up the shattered staircase. Halfway up, part of it broke away, but he managed to scramble on to the next sagging section, leaving pieces of staircase falling away behind him. It was apparent now that he would make it to the top, but Ben realised he would have great difficulty returning the same way even if the fire had not reached the stairs by then – and it seemed to be devouring everything in its path along the passageway at an alarming rate.

At the top of the stairs there was sufficient black smoke to smart Sam's eyes and set him coughing. But he was close to the frantic voices now – and a terrified child was crying. The sounds came from behind two adjacent doors. From one room a woman was alternately shouting reassurances to her children and calling for help. In the other room he could hear the voices of two children, one of whom was now crying hysterically.

Sam's shouts that help was at hand went unheeded, and when he tried to open the doors, which were partially hidden behind a heap of beams and roof tiles, he realised that the walls of the rooms were distorted and both doors were jammed.

A couple of kicks made no impression on either, although it did bring a halt to the cries of those inside the two bedrooms. Looking about him, Sam saw a crossbeam that had crashed down from the roof. It was heavy, but he was able to lift it and believed it would be solid enough for his purpose.

'Stay back from the doors,' he shouted. 'I'm going to break them down and bring you out of there.'

'Hurry up . . . please! There's smoke coming up through the floor . . . it sounds as though the fire will come through at any moment . . .' cried the woman in the room to his right.

'It's coming up through the floor here too!' The screamed message came from the room containing the children – and Sam decided to attack their door first. If he released their mother now she would be so concerned for them she would probably hamper his rescue attempts.

The first swing at the door splintered some of the woodwork, but it also jarred his shoulders so much he thought for a moment he must have dislocated something. However, feeling quickly returned to them and when he swung the beam once more, harder this time, the door gave way enough for two small boys to squeeze through the opening, emerging from the smoke that escaped with them.

'Good boys! Go and stand at the top of the stairs – but don't try to go down until I have released your ma and come back to you.'

Sam immediately attacked the second door, but it took four attempts before the door crashed open and a young woman emerged clutching a small girl in her arms. Both were coughing and spluttering and this time it was not only smoke but flames which followed them through the door. Sam, his own eyes streaming from the smoke which was by now dense throughout the upper floor, realised the woman's clothing was smouldering.

There was no time to waste trying to tear away the

31

scorched nightdress. Clutching her arm, he said, 'Quick
. . . come with me,' and led her to the top of the stairs
where both boys crouched, whimpering with fright as
she pulled them to her.

Gently prising the youngest of the boys from her, Sam
took him by the hand and said, 'Come with me. The
rest of you stay here, I won't be a minute.'

There was too much smoke filling the house now for
him to be able to see anything well, but he led the boy
down the broken staircase as far as he dared, feeling his
way until his foot found only empty air.

'Mr Retallick . . . Ben, are you still there?'

'I'm here, Sam,' came the hoarse reply, 'but the fire's
very close. Have you found anyone?'

'I've got all of them,' Sam replied. 'If I try to swing
the first young boy down do you think you could take
him from me?'

'Yes, do it now . . . but hurry, the fire is really taking
hold.'

Wasting no more time, Sam took the young boy by
the wrists and ignoring his cry of fright swung him out
and down beyond the stair on which he was standing.

The staircase sagged alarmingly, and it seemed an
age before the weight of the young boy was taken from
him and Ben said, 'I have him. Let go, Sam.'

Releasing his hold, Sam said, 'I'm going back for the
others. Come back here to take them from me, Ben.'

The next young boy was passed down to Ben in the
same way and then it was the young girl's turn. She
proved more difficult because she was terrified and too
young to have it explained to her what was happening.

32

However, Ben took a firm hold on her and quickly passed her back to Carey, who was waiting between the staircase and the front door.

By now the flames had almost reached the staircase and were on the landing above, and as Ben guided the children's mother to the staircase he could feel her trembling as he helped her down. They had almost reached the last stair when their combined weights proved too much for the badly damaged staircase. It collapsed, sending Sam and the woman crashing down into the passageway.

Dazed by the fall, Sam lost all sense of direction, but he was grabbed by two hands and hauled from the building and into the street by Carey Hamilton. Coughing up smoke and at the same time trying to breathe air into his lungs, Sam croaked, 'The woman . . . she fell with me . . .'

'She's all right, Sam, Ben brought her out. Antonia is treating her now. She's been burned a little and has hurt her arm, but she has no life-threatening injuries. Neither have the children . . . thanks to you.'

Relaxing now the rescue was over, Sam realised that his chest and throat were sore from the smoke he had inhaled. He hardly noticed the congratulations of the neighbours of the family he had rescued, but he would never forget the congratulatory kiss he received from Antonia and Ben's handshake and sincere 'Well done!'

The final accolade came from Lieutenant General Carey Hamilton. While Antonia was treating a burn Sam had somehow sustained on his neck during the rescue, the senior officer came to shake him by the hand.

'You were truly magnificent, Sam,' said the senior officer. 'If I ever had any doubts about your taking part in the African expedition, tonight would have dispelled them once and for all. Your presence of mind in the emergency we have just encountered was absolutely superb. The officer commanding the expedition is very fortunate indeed to have you with him – I will ensure he is aware of my high regard for you.'

Before they parted company at Paddington station the following morning, Ben gave letters to Sam to pass on to Captain Bray, who would be in charge of Ruddlemoor during Ben's absence, and also to Lottie, Lily's mother, who lived in St Austell. He had tentatively suggested to Carey Hamilton that she might accompany him to Switzerland, but Carey told him bluntly that they had broken all the rules by granting *him* permission to travel through France. It would not be possible to arrange for Lottie to go with him.

Before the train left the platform Carey had to return to the War Office for a meeting. Saying goodbye to Ben, he said, 'Are you quite certain I cannot persuade you to join the expedition to Lake Tanganyika with Sam? I would be far more confident about its ultimate success if I knew you were there to guide it. I don't doubt that the naval officer in charge of the party will carry out his duties well enough when he and his boats are afloat on the lake, but he has to get there first, and he is something of an oddball. I would like to know there was someone I could trust guiding the party.'

Ben shook his head. 'It's a tempting offer, Carey. There

34

are many times when I feel I want to be back in Africa, but more than anything else I want to get to Switzerland and bring Lily home to Cornwall. We've been apart for far too long. I miss her.'

'Of course,' Carey said, 'I do understand. And having Sam there to take care of your traction engines will be a great help . . . but if ever you change your mind remember that I am only a telephone call away.'

Carey left Paddington station well satisfied that bringing Ben to London had been worthwhile. He also believed that in Sam the commander of the expedition had a man who could be thoroughly relied upon in whatever emergency it might encounter along the way.

When Carey had gone, Ben smiled wryly at Sam. 'There can be few men who have had a more eventful introduction to London, Sam. What are your feelings about it all?'

'Well, it's certainly been exciting and I doubt whether I will ever again meet such a beautiful woman as Antonia, but I could never live in such a place as this. It's too big and full of people who don't know one another.' Suddenly grinning, he added, 'But I've got a fine suit and can look forward to an adventure that most of the men at Ruddlemoor would give their right arm to take part in.' The suit had been bought for him by Ben earlier that morning because the one he had worn to London – his only one – had been ruined in the bombed house.

'Africa is going to be no picnic, Sam – and you mustn't so much as hint to anyone in Cornwall what you'll be

35

doing there. Say the traction engines are being shipped out to Rhodesia to carry out some work on my family's land at Insimo and that I want you to go with them to ensure they stay running well. That reminds me, you'd better make a list of any spares you are likely to need. I'll have Carey Hamilton place a government order for them. That way you'll get them faster.'

The conversation then turned to what Sam was likely to encounter on the long journey through Africa and what to expect from the people he met there, both white men and African tribesmen. Long before Ben had finished telling him, the train guard came along the length of the train ensuring that all the doors were closed. Then a whistle was blown, a flag was waved and the Cornwall-bound train steamed out of the station.

It was now time for Ben to cross London and take a train to the Channel port of Folkestone. He felt he had accomplished a great deal during his visit to the capital. In his pocket he carried a letter authorising him to travel from Britain to Switzerland 'by whatever means deemed to be appropriate'. It also stated that he was travelling for 'compassionate reasons' and would be returning accompanied by his wife. The letter was signed, not by Carey Hamilton, as had been promised, but by the First Sea Lord, Admiral Lord Fisher, who had been given ultimate responsibility for organising the expedition to Lake Tanganyika. As Carey had explained to Ben, a letter signed by such a high-ranking, titled officer would carry far more weight than his own signature.

Once on his train, Ben's thoughts turned to the unexpected meeting with Philippe and Antonia St Anna in the London restaurant. He was not surprised that Philippe was in the army and apparently at the start of a promising career. His father and grandfather had both been generals in the Portuguese army and had seen a great deal of active service in East Africa during the turbulent years of the late nineteenth and early twentieth centuries. The two men had been close friends of Ben's father and of his brother Nathan.

The presence of Antonia had been an additional pleasure. Ben had last seen her more than twelve years before, when she had paid a fleeting visit to Insimo with her mother from their home in Mozambique. She had then been a rather skinny twelve-year-old, with a shy 'crush' on Ben's older brother Nathan, whose exploits as an army scout during the Boer war had always been greatly admired by both her father and her grandfather.

She was now no longer the skinny young girl he had known then, but a very beautiful young woman. It was apparent too, from the talk about the table, that her brother and the other members of her family were very proud of the fact that she had chosen to pursue a career that had few women among its ranks – and none at all from the part of the world where she had been born and brought up.

Then his thoughts returned to Lily once more and he felt a warm glow. How much he would have to tell her when they met up once more!

'I don't like the thought of you being all that way from Cornwall and me not knowing what you're up to, I really don't . . .'

Sam had received a telephone call from Ben asking him to come to London, only a few hours before. In his bedroom in the small granite-built cottage he shared with his mother Betsy, he had been cramming clothes into a suitcase.

As she handed him clean socks, shirts and underwear and criticised his haphazard method of packing, Betsy had expressed the misgivings she had repeated at least half a dozen times since Sam had returned from Ruddlemoor after receiving Ben's telephone call from the War Office saying that he was sending the works' traction engines to Africa and would like Sam to consider travelling with them to keep them maintained in good order. Ben had said nothing about the purpose of sending the machines so far away, and the young Cornish engineer had assumed he would be going to carry out work on the Retallicks' family home in Rhodesia.

When Sam immediately said that he would be delighted to make such a journey, Ben told him to come to London immediately. He would meet Sam at the station and take him to the London hotel where he too was staying, and they would together attend meetings to discuss the work Sam would be required to carry out in Africa.

'London's far enough away from Cornwall,' Betsy had said unhappily, 'but *Africa* . . . ! Why, it's the other side of the world! The Lord alone knows what you'll be given to eat there – and who will do your washing and mending? . . . No, it's no use you saying such things aren't important. I don't like it, Sam, I'm telling you straight. I shall tell Mr Retallick so when I see him. *Africa*, indeed . . .'

'You'll do no such thing, Ma,' Sam said sharply. 'I'm a grown man now and can make up my own mind about such things – and I haven't gone to Africa yet. Besides, think of all those we know who've gone off to war and are being shot at and shelled. I'm going to be a whole lot better off than any of them.'

'That's as may be,' Betsy said, determined not to accept her son's reassurances, 'but they're not in *Africa*.' She spoke the word as though it was akin to being on the moon, adding, 'And what will Muriel think of you going off to the ends of the earth?'

Muriel was a girl he had known all his life and everyone except Sam thought he would one day marry. They were certainly very good friends, but she did not excite him in the way he felt the girl he would one day marry should.

'Muriel will think it's a great adventure, Ma. She'll probably wish that I could take her too.'

'No doubt she will.' Betsy's expression had registered disapproval. 'I really don't know what's the matter with the young people of today. When I was a young girl it was enough for a man to have a good steady job of work and find himself a nice young girl to settle down with and raise a fine healthy family. That was considered enough of an adventure for any young couple.'

Sam knew that nothing he said to his mother would

change her mind. He was aware that she was worried about his proposed journey to Africa – and concerned for herself too, no doubt. Sam's father had died when he was still a boy and life had been hard in the Hooper household until Sam was able to find work in the Ruddlemoor clay works.

His initial employment in the clay industry was as a 'kettle boy', his duties entailing ensuring there was always boiling water for the older men's tea, warming up their pasties ready for 'crib', or meal time, and keeping the rest room clean and tidy. He was also required to run any errands for them.

It had always been the first rung on the ladder for most of the men who worked in the china clay industry. Over the ensuing years their experience and initiative would mean they were gradually given more responsible duties to perform. A few eventually became shift captains; even fewer rose to become works captain. But whatever a man did or did not achieve, he was assured that he had work in the clay industry for the whole of his lifetime.

That would have been Sam's future had Ben not recognised his aptitude for working with machinery and sent him on a course that qualified him to work on the various steam engines in use at Ruddlemoor, including the two traction engines he would be accompanying to Africa. Betsy was extremely proud that her son had been chosen for such work, which would enable him to rise above the station in life that was the lot of so many of his contemporaries.

'You must try not to worry, Ma. I'll be all right. Mr

Retallick has promised that if I go you'll be taken care of while I'm away. Anyway, I haven't said for certain that I will.'

'You'll go, you know you will, and I've no doubt Mr Retallick means what he says – at least, he does now,' Betsy had said pessimistically, 'but he'll have enough on his plate if he intends going off to fetch his wife from that foreign hospital where she's been for so long. Too much to worry about what's happening to you. Still, I suppose she's lucky to have married someone who had the money to send her there in the first place. Her poor brother didn't have the same luck. I remember seeing him only a few weeks before he died. No more than skin and bone, he was . . .'

Sam was quite content to allow his mother to prattle on about the illness of Lily Retallick and her late brother. It took her mind off the journey he hoped he might soon be making. He found the thought of going so far away from home for an unknown period of time very exciting – but not a little daunting.

However, many of his friends were abroad now, most serving in the army, in France. Sam had seriously considered enlisting too, but concern for his mother had held him back. Then his name had been included on a list produced by Ben of those men who were considered essential to the running of Ruddlemoor, and therefore performing duties that were important to the greater war effort.

Ben had told Sam in their telephone conversation that, if he agreed to go with the two traction engines, he could expect to be called upon to set out for Africa in weeks or even days rather than months. In the meantime, after he returned from London, he would be required to ensure that the two vehicles were fully ready for the task ahead of them.

He set off on the train from St Austell station with an increasing sense of excitement bubbling up inside him.

VI

Sam did not meet Muriel until the evening after his return from London. She was a sturdily built girl, pretty in a dark-haired Cornish way, but Sam could not help comparing her with the indelible image he had in his mind of Antonia, who was like no other woman he had ever met.

Muriel worked in a women's hairdressing salon in St Austell. As Sam's mother was fond of pointing out to him at every opportunity, she had learned a trade which would always be in demand and would bring a few extra shillings into the household, even when she was married and had a family.

Sam had been working hard on the Ruddlemoor traction engines all day, determined that they would be in perfect condition when the order came for them to be shipped to Africa. He did not leave the works until dusk, but he found Muriel waiting for him outside the gate. Greeting him warmly, she said, 'Hello, Sam. I've just come from your house. Your ma tells me you've made up your mind to go to Africa with Mr Retallick's traction engines.'

'That's right.' Sam was aware of the need to lie to Muriel, and he found it no easier than deceiving his own mother.

'How long do you expect to be away?'

'I don't know.' At least he was able to give an honest answer to this question. 'Probably for a few months or so, I expect.'

'What are you going to be doing there?'

'I'm not exactly sure.' This was only half a lie. He was not *exactly* certain what was likely to be involved in supervising the hauling of two gunboats through a sketchily charted area of central Africa. It was equally certain that no one else could have given an accurate reply to the question. 'I'll be doing some work for Mr Retallick. His family have a huge farm out there. It's so large it's almost three times the size of Bodmin Moor and surrounded by steep hills. He's got cattle, crops, and even a gold mine on the land. There will be plenty for me to do, I've no doubt.'

'I wish I was coming with you,' Muriel said wistfully. 'I've never been out of Cornwall, not even as far as Plymouth. I don't suppose I'll ever go anywhere.'

When Sam made no reply, Muriel asked, 'What was London like, Sam? Did you see the king while you were there?'

Muriel had no comprehension of London's size. The only city she had ever visited was Truro, probably the smallest city in the whole of Great Britain and hardly larger than a market town.

'No, I never saw the king, but I saw Buckingham Palace, where he lives. It's *huge*, so big that I doubt whether he and the queen can have been into every room.'

'You mean . . . it's nearly as big as Ruddlemoor's new dry?'

The 'dry' was the huge new building recently constructed at Ruddlemoor for use in the final stages of working and storing china clay. It was the largest building Muriel had ever seen.

Sam thought of Antonia St Anna's sophistication and could not help comparing it to the limited knowledge possessed by Muriel. He immediately felt ashamed of himself for making such a comparison. Muriel had been born and brought up in 'clay country'. Antonia had travelled the world. He hoped that, if Antonia had ever thought of him at all, she would not have made any such comparison between himself and some of the more worldly men she undoubtedly knew.

'I shall miss you, Sam.' Muriel's unexpected statement broke into his thoughts and he looked at her in surprise. They had always seen a great deal of each other because they had lived in adjacent houses since they were born, and his mother, and hers too, were in the habit of dropping heavy hints about a joint future for them both, but Muriel had never intimated that she considered him as anything more than a friend.

'I expect I shall miss you,' he said uncertainly. 'I shall miss Ruddlemoor too, and Cornwall. Africa will be very different – but exciting.'

It was not quite the reply that Muriel had been hoping for, but she told herself she should not have been surprised. Sam had always taken it for granted that she would be available whenever he had need of her company, or wanted help with something that needed the skills of a young woman. Muriel had always been happy to have him turn to her on such occasions, although recently she had found herself hoping for more from him.

'Will you try to write to me when you are out there, Sam?' she asked. 'I'd like to go into work and say I'd just had a letter from Africa,' she added hurriedly when she saw his startled expression. He had given no thought to writing directly to her, aware that any letters to his mother would be passed around the small, tightly knit clay country community.

'I doubt if I'll have very much time for writing,' he said, thinking of the nature of his journey through Africa.

Muriel was hurt. 'I'd write to you if I ever went away from Cornwall,' she said unhappily. 'Especially if I was going to somewhere like Africa. I'd want to tell you all about it, especially if you were like me, never likely to go anywhere outside Cornwall.'

Sam was aware that Muriel was far more upset because he was leaving Cornwall than he had imagined she would be. He felt remorse at upsetting her because he was fond of her – albeit in a brotherly way.

'I'll try to find time to write to you,' he said. 'If I can't write to you personally I'll put a note in one of my letters to Ma.'

'No,' Muriel said, unexpectedly firmly. 'If you write I want it to be sent in an envelope addressed to *me*.' Less positively, she added, 'I've never had a letter sent just to me. I'd like the first one to be from you, all the way from Africa.'

Giving her an understanding smile, Sam said, 'In that case, I promise to send a letter just for you as soon as I arrive in Africa.'

When a delighted Muriel hurried away to tell her mother that he would be writing to her from Africa, Sam thought it was a very minor commitment to have made to bring her so much pleasure.

2

The officer in command of the secret expedition to Lake Tanganyika was Lieutenant Commander Spicer-Simson – and he and Sam Hooper got off on the wrong foot the moment they met.

Made up to the temporary rank of acting commander when he assumed command, Spicer-Simson, who preferred to be referred to as Spicer, was a large over-bearing man with a heavy moustache and lightweight beard who was fond of telling outlandish stories about his imagined exploits in many lands. Approaching the end of his naval service, Spicer had been constantly passed over for promotion and had been given charge of the Tanganyika expedition only when it had been turned down by others who thought it had no chance of succeeding.

Sam Hooper was called upon to embark the two Ruddlemoor traction engines on a passenger cargo ship, the *Tamerlane*, moored at Tilbury docks, during the first week of June 1915. He was then to proceed to the Admiralty in London to meet the other members of the expedition.

Accompanying the traction engines on an overnight freight train, Sam satisfied himself that the huge steam-driven vehicles were safely stowed and secured before making his way to London, arriving at the Admiralty in the early afternoon. He was directed to a room where there were already a number of officers and ratings present. Two were ex-army volunteers who had transferred to the navy after hearing of the 'top secret' expedition whilst drinking in a London bar.

Spicer greeted Sam simply as 'Hooper' and made no offer to shake hands with him when he entered the room where the meeting was taking place. His first words to the young Cornishman were, 'Where have you been, Hooper? You were supposed to report to me this morning, when all the others arrived. You are part of a team now – a Royal Navy team – and I expect you to behave as such at all times. Is that understood?'

'I received my orders only forty-eight hours ago,' Sam replied evenly. 'In that time I have accompanied the traction engines by rail to Tilbury overnight and seen them safely stowed on board the ship taking them to Africa. That was completed only a couple of hours ago. I came here as quickly as I could.'

As leader of the expedition, Spicer had no intention of allowing anyone under his command to disagree with him. 'You will not argue with me,' he snapped fiercely. 'You should have reported to me this morning and left the loading of the machines to those who have experience in such things – the dockers.'

Sam was not willing to allow Spicer's admonishment to go unchallenged. 'My sole reason for coming on this expedition is to take care of Ben Retallick's traction engines. That is what I was doing and I will continue to do so until they are returned to Cornwall.'

Angry now, Spicer shouted, 'You will address me as sir when you speak to me and I will have no one on this expedition questioning my authority – especially not a rating. I have designated you petty officer, but I can just as easily reduce you to able seaman.'

'I am quite prepared to call you sir,' Sam replied affably in his soft Cornish voice, 'just as I will respect your position as head of the expedition, but I am neither an able seaman nor a petty officer. I am the engineer responsible for Ben Retallick's engines and transport. I am here to ensure that the company's traction engines carry out all that is required of them and are returned safely to Ruddlemoor. They will not let you down and neither will I . . . sir.'

Spicer realised he had misjudged this young man. Blind obedience was clearly no more acceptable to him than unfair criticism. Nevertheless, he had to be made to understand that this was an expedition subject to the same discipline that was so important to the smooth running of the Senior Service.

'I seem to have been misinformed about your duties and the extent of your engineering experience,' he said. 'Very well, you will be commissioned as a sub-lieutenant, RNVR – the volunteer reserve. It lacks the status of a

49

regular commission, of course, but you will have all the privileges that go with commissioned rank. It also goes without saying that you will accept the duties and responsibilities of a commissioned naval officer.'

Spicer had made his decision reluctantly, but he had been passed over for promotion too many times and was fully aware that this was the final chance to make his mark in what had been for him, at best, a mediocre career. He was determined not to waste the opportunity. However, he had reckoned without Sam's native stubbornness – coupled with the advice given to him by Carey Hamilton. The senior army officer had stressed that in no circumstances should Sam accept a commission in either the army or the navy. Should he do so he would be obliged to carry out whatever duties were required of him by Spicer, a man of whom Carey was somewhat wary. Referring to the naval man he had said, 'I don't doubt that he will do all that is required of him when he reaches Tanganyika, but I fear that command of such an unusual expedition might have gone to his head. He is desperate to prove himself. Should anything go wrong he will be looking for scapegoats. My advice, unprofessional though it may be, is that you retain your independence and, should it prove necessary, be in a position to remind Spicer that your sole duty is to ensure the traction engines perform with maximum efficiency.'

With this in mind, Sam said, 'I thank you for your consideration . . . sir, but I have explained my duties. I will ensure that the Ruddlemoor traction engines are able to do whatever is required of them. Neither they, nor I, will let you down.'

Scarcely able to control the anger he felt, Spicer thundered, 'I will have no one on this expedition who is outside my personal control. If I am to assume responsibility for its success then everyone under my command must be subject to the rigid discipline demanded by the Royal Navy. There can be no exceptions.'

Sam was seated at a large table with all the others looking at him, and had been wondering what he would do if Spicer issued just such an ultimatum. Suddenly standing up, he said, 'I'm sorry to have wasted your time . . . sir. I have no doubt you'll be able to find another couple of traction engines to take with you, although you'll never better those from Ruddlemoor. I must hurry to Tilbury now and make sure they are unloaded before the *Tamerlane* sails.'

Sam was halfway to the door before the commander of the Tanganyika expedition called after him, 'Just a minute, Hooper.'

Spicer had intended that Sam should provide him with an opportunity to remind the members of the expedition of the powers he possessed and was prepared to use if the need arose. His stratagem had backfired on him and he was in serious danger of its having quite the opposite effect from that he intended. He was aware that Sam's employer had influential friends in the War Office and he had glanced briefly at a report written by Lieutenant General Carey Hamilton. In it Hamilton had mentioned that Sam had behaved with extreme coolness and bravery when in the general's company during the recent Zeppelin attack on London. Spicer realised that he needed to tread very carefully.

'Now look here, Hooper, you must be aware that it will be impossible for me to obtain alternative traction engines at such short notice. If you take them away you will be putting the success of my expedition at risk.'

'All I know is that I agreed to take care of Ben Retallick's traction engines – and I can't do that if they're in Africa and I'm in England.'

'You can't take care of them if they are on . . . whatever ship it was you mentioned, while you are on the *Llanstephen Castle* with the rest of the party,' Spicer retorted. A way out of his predicament had just occurred to him. One that would not undermine his authority. 'If you insist on putting yourself and your traction engines outside naval jurisdiction then you have no entitlement to naval privileges. Give me details of the ship on which they are being carried, then take yourself off to Tilbury and join the ship yourself. By the time you get there I will have made arrangements for you to take passage with your precious traction engines – even if you need to make up a bed in the cargo hold!' Spicer smiled at Sam for the first time, believing he had successfully solved the problem to Sam's disadvantage. 'When you arrive in Cape Town you will report to the office of the Senior Naval Officer. He will give you your orders and provide you with the drivers you will need for your machines. I will make it clear in my initial report to the Admiralty that the work carried out by the traction engines is to be a civil operation. As such its success or failure will be down to you. Now you may go.'

On his way out of the building, Sam wondered whether he had taken the right course of action by insisting that he would not accept being placed under naval discipline. He was not particularly concerned about taking passage on the *Tamerlane*; the vessel was, in fact, a passenger cargo ship and the accommodation would be quite comfortable. Besides, he would be much more at ease if he was able to make an occasional check on the well-being of his charges. Nevertheless, he was quite upset at not travelling to South Africa with the others. They would all be working together on their long journey from Cape Town to Lake Tanganyika and he would have welcomed a chance to get to know them before then. He told himself that the lack of such an opportunity would be compensated for by not having to spend the voyage under the eye of Commander Spicer-Simson.

The naval man had extricated himself from a difficult situation without too much loss of authority, but Sam realised that during the course of their journey through Africa Spicer would be waiting for him to do something wrong – and he knew that little he did would be right in the eyes of the other man. He wished it was possible to discuss the turn of events with Ben Retallick, but the Ruddlemoor owner was no longer in England. He had taken the earliest opportunity to set off for Switzerland in order to bring Lily back to their home in Cornwall.

3

I

Walking along the quayside in the Kent coastal town of Folkestone, Ben felt conspicuous dressed in civilian clothes when every man passing by was wearing an army or naval uniform. He had come here to board a ferry bound for Boulogne, but had first to report to the embarkation office – and it was here that he encountered his first major problem.

An army sergeant seated at a desk in the office was inspecting the papers of the service personnel boarding the ferry and he viewed Ben's letter of authority with considerable suspicion. Looking up from it he studied Ben for some moments before asking, 'What's the purpose of your journey to France, sir?'

When Ben replied that he was going to Switzerland with the intention of bringing his wife back to England from the clinic where she had spent many months, the sergeant sniffed derisively. Without a trace of sympathy, he said, 'If everyone in the country who had a loved one in hospital travelled to France to visit them there'd be no room for soldiers on the boats. Can you tell me why *you've* been given permission to do something that the wives and mothers of wounded soldiers can't?'

'No, sergeant, I can't,' Ben replied patiently.

'Can't – or won't?' snapped the sergeant. 'Not that it matters, either way. You certainly won't be catching any ferry to France today – or any other day as far as I'm concerned.'

'Before you make up your mind on that I think you had better speak to your commanding officer, sergeant. I doubt whether he will appreciate being reprimanded by the War Office on account of your actions.'

Ben was trying hard not to lose his temper with the officious non-commissioned officer. It was not easy. Excited at the thought of fetching Lily home he was not prepared to allow anyone to stand in his way in the name of officialdom.

The sergeant hesitated uncertainly. He believed he was performing his duty by refusing to allow a civilian to board a ferry to France, and although a letter signed by the First Lord of the Admiralty sounded important, it did not impress him. Talk of the War Office did. Staffed by generals and government ministers, it was the omnipotent source of authority for all things military.

'I'll have a word with Major Andrews,' he said, 'but don't expect to get any change from him. He had the last two civilians who tried to cross the Channel arrested on suspicion of spying.'

'I suggest you hurry and find him,' Ben retorted. 'I have a ferry to catch.'

Major Andrews's office was a wooden hut on the dockside which he shared with a couple of elderly corporals. A cavalry officer and veteran of the Sudanese and Boer wars, he complained bitterly to all and sundry that he should have been filling the saddle of a charger instead of a wooden, government issue armchair in a shack on the wrong side of the English Channel.

Nevertheless, the ageing warrior knew in his heart that he was too old for a combatant role in this war. As a result of talking to some of the many thousands of casualties passing through the port from the battle front he also realised this was not a cavalryman's war. It was being fought like no war he had known. He would have been out of his depth, totally unable to cope with the rigours of trench warfare. What was more, he had reached an age when creature comforts had become more important to him than military glory.

But this was not the image he projected to others. When his sergeant came to him with the story of a civilian with an unidentified accent who was trying to cross the Channel with the authority of a letter allegedly signed by 'some titled officer in the Navy', the major ordered that the bearer of the letter be brought to his wooden office immediately.

When Ben arrived escorted by an armed soldier, the major snapped, 'What's this my sergeant tells me about you trying to cross to France with a letter of authority signed by a naval officer? *I* am the officer who decides who takes passage on a cross-Channel ferry and my orders are that no civilians are allowed to proceed to France until further notice.'

'I am aware of your orders, major; that is why General Hamilton felt that my authorisation should be signed by someone more senior than himself. I have it here.' Ben handed his letter to the army officer without further comment and saw the startled expression that appeared on his face when he saw the signature.

Looking up at Ben, Major Andrews said, 'Why should Admiral Lord Fisher personally give you permission to cross to France?'

'I am going to Switzerland to bring back my wife who has spent almost a year in a sanatorium there.'

Major Andrews stiffened perceptibly as Ben spoke and when he had ended he snapped, 'I recognise your accent now. You are South African. We recently had South African prisoners pass through here. They had been fighting for the Germans in South West Africa. Whose side are you on?'

'I am not South African,' Ben said. 'I was born in Matabeleland – that's part of Rhodesia now.'

'I am fully aware of where Matabeleland is,' the major retorted, 'but I am not satisfied with the authority of this letter. You will remain here, under guard, while I have it checked.'

The letter lay on the desk between the two men, and before Andrews could prevent him Ben reached across and picked it up. 'I'll keep this, if you don't mind. It's my authority for the return journey through France, not just across the Channel. If you want to check my credentials I will use your telephone to call Lieutenant General

Carey Hamilton at the War Office and you can speak to him. He will tell you all he feels you ought to know.'

Ben's unexpected repossession of the letter had brought the major to his feet and caused the armed soldier who had brought Ben to the hut to take an uncertain step towards him.

The major's order for the guard to take action was left unspoken. Instead, he said to Ben, 'You know General Hamilton personally?'

'Very well. We first met at my Matabele home during the Boer war.'

'You were involved in the Boer war?' Major Andrews wondered whether he might have underestimated Ben's age.

'My brother was General Hamilton's chief scout. I was too young to take part in the war itself, although we did have to fight off a Boer commando when it raided our farm.'

'I thought I had heard your name somewhere before!' The major's manner changed dramatically. 'Of course, your brother is Nat Retallick. We were involved in the battles against Commandant Tromp in the Drakensberg mountains. He was a splendid scout – and saved General Hamilton's life on one occasion, I believe. Well, that puts an entirely different complexion on everything! How is your brother? Is he involved in the war in Africa?'

'The last I heard, he was still at Insimo, but that was a long time ago. The mail hasn't been getting through just lately . . . but the ferry?' Ben was relieved at the major's change of attitude, but was anxious to get away, just in case he changed his mind.

'Of course. I am delighted to be of assistance and will do all I can to help. You must remember me to your brother when next you write . . . but do you mind telling me why your letter of authority is signed by the First Lord of the Admiralty?'

'I had occasion to help him with a highly confidential matter when I was called from my home in Cornwall to the War Office. I found Carey was working there after being wounded in France.'

Ben felt there was sufficient truth in what he said without giving anything away about the Tanganyika Lake venture. It certainly satisfied Major Andrews, who believed he had almost made a grave error of judgement by offending someone who had connections with admirals and generals at the War Office.

'I will take you back to the embarkation sergeant myself and ensure that you enjoy a comfortable crossing to Boulogne. When you get there, make yourself known to Captain York. I will put a telephone call through to him to let him know you are on your way. He organises troop trains and should be able to help with your onward journey to Switzerland.'

II

Walking the streets of Paris in a light drizzle brought back a great many memories for Ben. Some were happy, others were accompanied by a sense of guilt – and there were genuine feelings too of deep sorrow.

On the journey to the Swiss clinic, shortly before the war began, he and Lily had been accompanied by Emma, a young distant relative of both of them. She was heavily involved in the suffragette movement and in Paris they had been met by Tessa, another suffragette who was known to them all and was deeply admired by Lily.

At the time Lily firmly believed herself to be dying and was convinced that Tessa was just the sort of woman who could comfort Ben in the sorrow she knew he would feel when she herself was no longer there to care for him. She had connived to throw them together as much as possible in the city that possessed a reputation for inspiring romance.

Her plans had borne no success at the time, but on the way back to England, lonely and vulnerable, Ben had passed through Paris once more and met Tessa again. Weakened by wine and cognac and fuelled by a mutual attraction, Ben had succumbed.

He and Tessa began a brief but passionate affair that came to a tragic end when war broke out and the German advance through Europe threatened Paris. Tessa and Emma together with other suffragettes became ambulance drivers, carrying wounded soldiers from the battle front to Paris hospitals. One day the ambulance driven by Tessa was struck by a German shell and she was killed.

In Paris now, Ben visited Tessa's grave and was touched to see that it was being kept neat and tidy by the citizens of a grateful city. He placed the bouquet of flowers he had brought beside a similar tribute, put here in recent days.

Later, in the streets of the Left Bank, Ben found a small restaurant that had once been special for them both. It had been his intention to go in and renew his acquaintance with the manager and his family, but wartime Paris was not the city he had known on earlier visits and the morose, drizzly weather dampened more than the city's pavements. The small restaurant seemed somehow drab and forlorn and he turned round and walked away. What had happened with Tessa had been a brief and passionate chapter in his life – but it was over. He had no right to even remember it. It was time to look to the future – and to Lily.

The trenches of the opposing armies cut deep into the body of France like a ghastly, suppurating wound that extended to the very borders of Switzerland. Trains travelling in the vicinity of the battle lines were frequently commandeered to carry troops and bring back the wounded. As a result passenger travel suffered almost total disruption. Ben was obliged to change trains frequently on a devious route to his destination and the journey took him three long and weary days. However, when he stepped from a motor taxi and gazed up at the stark but clean lines of the clinic that had been Lily's home for so long it was worth all the frustrations and tribulations he had suffered.

He knew that Lily's room was at the back of the clinic, so he could not see whether she was out on the small balcony, enjoying the clean air which Dr Bertauld believed contributed so greatly to the recovery of his patients. Paying off the taxi driver, he entered a marble-floored reception area which was as immaculate as the outside of the building suggested it would be. There

61

should have been a receptionist behind the desk here, but there was no one in sight and Ben assumed she must have been called away.

He waited for a few minutes, but when the receptionist still did not return he became impatient. Lily's room was number thirty-three, on the third floor, one of the best rooms in the clinic, with a spectacular view of the surrounding mountains. As a result of his previous visits he knew where the lift was situated and he decided to wait no longer.

Leaving his luggage beside the desk, he made his way to the lift which was waiting with open doors at the far end of the reception area. Once inside he pressed the button marked 3, the doors closed and the lift began a gentle ascent, gliding to a halt when the indicator showed it had arrived at its destination.

Ben found his heart beating faster as he approached the door to room thirty-three. It had been months since he had last seen Lily, and although he had sent a telegram immediately before leaving London he had not been able to say exactly when he would be arriving.

He knew she would be as excited as he felt at the thought of their meeting. Pausing at the door, he knocked softly. There was no immediate response, and he was about to knock more loudly when he thought that she might be asleep.

Quietly turning the handle, he found the door was unlocked. Pushing it open gently he was startled to discover that the room was empty. Entering, he crossed to the French window that opened out upon the balcony. There was no one there.

Puzzled, he looked about him. The room was immaculate . . . *too* tidy. There was not a personal possession in sight. Crossing to the wardrobe, he opened the door and found it to be empty.

Ruefully, Ben acknowledged that he should have waited for the receptionist to return to her desk. He should have realised that now Lily was fit enough she would have been moved to another room, leaving number thirty-three to be prepared for a new patient to begin his or her recovery in the best room in the clinic. He decided to return to the reception area, find the receptionist and ask where Lily was now.

As he was closing the door he saw a nurse in a spotless uniform coming along the corridor towards him. Seeing him, she appeared surprised, then hurrying towards him she began speaking sharply to him in French.

'I'm sorry, I speak very little French,' he apologised.

'You are English? What were you doing in this room?'

'I was looking for my wife. I thought I would find her here. My name is Retallick.'

'Oh . . . Mr Retallick . . . I am so sorry.' The nurse appeared upset. 'All Mrs Retallick's belongings have been taken to the store room on the ground floor. I will take you there, but . . . you *have* spoken to Dr Bertauld?'

'No. I would like to speak to him later, of course, and we'll arrange for her things to be collected when we leave, but I have only just arrived from England and before I do anything else I want to see my wife. What room is she in now?'

'What room . . . ?' The distress of the nurse was so evident that Ben became alarmed.

63

'What is it?' he demanded. 'Has she taken an unexpected turn for the worse? Where is she?'

'Mr Retallick . . . I am so sorry. So very, very sorry. Your wife died two days ago. She was very popular and we were all delighted that she had made such a splendid recovery, but she suffered a sudden and totally unexpected heart attack . . .'

'I cannot apologise enough for the manner in which you learned of your poor wife's death, Mr Retallick.' Dr Bertauld leaned forward in his chair and touched Ben gently on his arm. 'It must have come as a dreadful shock to you . . . as, indeed, it did to all of us in the clinic. It was her heart. Weakened by such a long and debilitating illness it was unable to cope with the excitement felt by your wife at the thought of returning home after so long. I sent a telegram to you right away, but you must have left England by the time it arrived. The whole of the staff is deeply saddened. We had all grown very fond of your wife during her long stay with us, and we shared her happiness at the thought of returning to you and to England.'

Still unable to accept Lily's death, Ben shook his head in a gesture of defeat. 'We came so close to returning to a normal and happy life,' he said. 'If only I had been able to get here more quickly . . .'

'You must not blame yourself,' Dr Bertauld declared. 'There was no way any of us could have foreseen such a tragic event, and with her heart being so weak her death could have occurred at any time. On the journey home, perhaps. As it is, the only consolation I have to

64

offer you is that she suffered no pain whatsoever and her last days were spent in the happy anticipation of returning to Cornwall.'

Ben acknowledged the doctor's words with a nod, not trusting himself to speak.

Clearing his throat, Dr Bertauld said, 'There is something I need to ask you, Mr Retallick . . . but, of course, I do not expect you to give me a decision right away. Do you wish to take your wife's body back to England, or would you prefer her to be buried in our little cemetery here? It is a quiet and beautiful place, tended lovingly by our staff, and we are able to call upon the services of the Reverend Mr Hawkins, a retired Church of England clergyman who lives nearby. He is a regular visitor to the clinic. Mrs Retallick became a close friend of both him and his wife.'

Ben's immediate reaction was that Lily should be returned home for burial in Cornwall. Then he remembered the chaos of his journey across the Channel and through France. He also recalled seeing the coffins of deceased British officers piled in the rain on the dockside at Boulogne, awaiting shipment home. Despite her illness, Lily had loved the view from the balcony of her room and had declared in many of her letters that the memory would remain with her for always. He decided that this was where she should be laid to rest.

'I have no need to think about it, Dr Bertauld. I would like Lily to be buried here, in this peaceful and beautiful place, surrounded by the mountains of Switzerland.'

III

Travelling through France on the return journey from Switzerland, Ben thought of the decision he had made about Lily's last resting place. He knew he would be reproached by Lily's mother and father for leaving her behind in a foreign country. However, he had arranged for photographs to be taken of the small cemetery and the surrounding mountains. He would show them to her parents and to others in the family, together with the letters in which she expressed her love for the view from her room. When the war ended he would arrange for them to visit Switzerland and see her grave for themselves.

In the meantime he needed to come to terms with the fact that Lily was dead. She had been ill for a very long time and they had spent almost a twelvemonth apart, which went some way towards lessening the impact of her death to a certain extent, but she had been an important part of his life for many years and he had longed for the day when she would return home to Cornwall so that they could take up their happy life together once more.

Twice on the journey from Switzerland to Paris Ben was asked for his papers, once by French police and on another occasion by British military police. The French officials showed both sympathy and understanding when he showed them the letter from Admiral Lord Fisher and explained why Lily was not accompanying him. The British military police did not. True, he was travelling on a train that was crowded with wounded soldiers, but the comments of the sergeant in charge of the small patrol checking the documents of those on board came as a shock when Ben explained why Lily was not with him.

'Well, at least she died in a nice clean bed in comfortable surroundings,' said the NCO callously. 'The poor beggars on this train are all that's left of a whole battalion that was holding a section of the line when the Germans pounded them with artillery before attacking with gun, bayonet . . . and gas. Most of their mates are buried in the mud and muck of the trenches where they died. Few of them will ever be found. It may be small consolation to you, mate, but there are tens of thousands of men out there who would swap their life in the trenches for the luxury of dying in a bed.'

Although the train bound for Paris was already heavily overcrowded, many more wounded men were brought on board as it neared the French capital. Most were victims of a massive gas attack and Ben found the sound of their painful coughing and choking distressing. The gas had affected the eyesight of many of the men too and they needed help with eating, drinking and lighting the inevitable cigarettes.

When the train eventually came to a steam-releasing halt in the Paris railway station wounded men quite literally tumbled out of the carriages. After helping three of the casualties to their feet in quick succession, Ben gave up all thoughts of heading out of the station and assisted an overworked orderly to form those men able to walk into columns, which eventually went on their way with the hand of each casualty resting upon the shoulder of the man in front of him.

Outside the great station building were a number of buses, taxis and ambulances waiting to transport the wounded to various city hospitals, with nurses and doctors moving among them, tending to the more seriously wounded. It was a scene Ben had witnessed before, when the war was no more than a few weeks old and the Germans were knocking on the gates of Paris. Tessa had been driving ambulances then, with Emma, who was now married to Jacob Pengelly, Ben's transport manager, who had also been in Paris at that time. Ben found it difficult to realise that that had been a mere nine months before. The memories of Paris in those early wartime days were still painful.

When the railway station began to show some semblance of order as more and more wounded soldiers were carried away to their various destinations, Ben claimed his luggage and was making his way to the exit when a voice – a woman's voice – called urgently, 'Ben . . . Ben Retallick.'

For a few confused moments, Ben thought it must be a ghost from the past. There could be no one in Paris at this time who knew him. He turned in the direction of the voice . . . and saw Antonia St Anna hurrying towards him.

'What are you doing here?' They both spoke in unison, but while Antonia laughed delightedly, Ben, still caught up in his memories, gave her a smile that lacked mirth.

Antonia was first to give her explanation. 'The London hospital where I am working has prepared two wards to accept soldiers suffering from the effects of gas

68

poisoning. There has been a large-scale battle where gas was extensively used, and I was asked to come to Paris to assist the specialist in charge of the party to bring the wounded men back to London. But what about you, Ben? Why are you in Paris?'

'I am on my way home from Switzerland.'

'But of course! When we met in London you said you were going to fetch Lily home. Where is she?'

'She's not here, Antonia. She had a heart attack and died two days before I reached the clinic.'

'Oh, Ben . . . I am so very, very sorry!' Tears sprang to Antonia's eyes. 'And there was I being so cheerful and happy that we had met. You must feel absolutely devastated.'

'It was a great shock,' he admitted. 'I went to Switzerland expecting to bring her back to Cornwall with me. I had booked the best room in a hotel here, in Paris, where we had stayed on the way to the clinic. I believe the manager has a special meal planned for us. He remembered Lily from last time and knows the doctor who was treating her. He assured me then that she would be cured. He's going to be very unhappy when he learns what has happened.'

At that moment one of the uniformed nurses called to Antonia and she said, 'I must go now, Ben – but I would like to see you later, if you feel you could put up with my company. Where are you staying?'

'The Hotel Crillon,' he replied, 'and I would welcome company . . . make it for dinner.'

The nurse called again, more urgently now, and, reaching out, Antonia gave his arm a sympathetic squeeze before hurrying away to where her colleague was tending one of the few casualties who still remained in the station.

Watching her as she went, Ben wondered whether he should have agreed to meet her that evening. He did not think he would be very good company, although he was relieved he would not have to spend the evening in Paris alone. His memories of the city seemed to be catching up with him.

IV

Contrary to Ben's forebodings, the evening he spent with Antonia proved far more relaxing than he would have believed to be possible. He could not have wished for a more sympathetic companion and she did not allow him to dwell too much upon the past.

Instead, she steered the conversation to thoughts of the future, persuading him to discuss some of the problems the war had brought to the business he had taken over from his grandfather after leaving Africa.

Over dinner he found himself explaining to her the various processes he had needed to learn, the problems he had encountered from his fellow clay works owners, and the current difficulties caused by U-boats which had meant the loss of the important and lucrative overseas markets.

Ben thought he must be boring her with talk of his work but, to his surprise, she said, 'The submarine menace is a problem that might soon be resolved – at least, as far as the ships of neutral countries are concerned.'

'What do you mean?' Ben was puzzled. The Germans were sinking all ships found sailing within British territorial waters, irrespective of their nationalities.

Pausing while a waiter refilled her glass from the bottle keeping cool in the ice bucket beside the table, Antonia said quietly, 'Before leaving London I attended a party with Philippe at the Portuguese embassy. I was with him when some of the diplomats were talking of the sinking of a Portuguese cargo ship carrying coal from Newcastle to Lisbon. The Portuguese government registered a very strong protest, in reply to which the Germans said that their policy of indiscriminate sinking is under review. They declared that although they will still reserve the right to stop and sink a vessel of any nationality if it is carrying a cargo to England that might be used militarily, they will not harm neutral ships carrying cargoes from the British Isles to their own countries.'

'I have heard nothing of this,' Ben said. 'If it is true it could make a great deal of difference to my business.'

'Well, the diplomats were saying the policy is still under review by the Germans – but they seemed in no doubt that it will soon come into effect, especially now the Americans have also lodged a strong protest about the lives of some of their nationals being lost in attacks on neutral ships. Even so, I doubt very much whether the Germans will make a public announcement about it.'

'No, but it means I can start making plans for shipping out my clay the moment it is confirmed by our government – even earlier if some of my previous customers in neutral countries are willing to take a chance on chartering neutral ships.'

Although Antonia was aware that she should not be repeating table talk overheard at an embassy party, she was delighted to have something to take Ben's mind off the death of Lily, even for a short while.

She was able to help him again later that evening when she learned he had not yet made any firm plans for returning to England. A train carrying the wounded troops she had been sent to Paris to tend would be leaving the next day and connecting with a ferry that would transport them from Boulogne to Newhaven.

As had become the norm, the vast number of casualties coming from the battle front meant that the medical services were desperately short of orderlies to help deal with them. Antonia said that if Ben was prepared to help, she could guarantee him a place on both train and cross-Channel ferry.

It was an offer Ben was grateful to accept. It meant he would not meet up with Major Andrews and the officious sergeant and have to explain to them why he was not returning to England with Lily, as his letter of authorisation decreed.

After seeing Antonia off in a taxi that would return her to the hospital where she was staying – the hospital where Tessa had died – Ben had a drink with the manager before going to bed in the hotel that held so many memories for him. He did not expect to be able to sleep; there was far too much to think about and many memories, both good and bad, that had been renewed by his stay in Paris. However, there were also thoughts of the future, cleverly introduced into their conversation by Antonia.

It was not until he was awakened by the sounds of early morning street noises that Ben realised he had slept far more soundly than he had for very many nights.

V

In addition to the victims of the poison gas attack who were being sent to St Thomas's hospital in London, there were wounded men on the crowded train who were destined for many other hospitals. Shortly before the train was due to leave Paris, an additional two carriages were added. Fitted out as hospital wards, they were occupied by seriously wounded officers, few of whom would ever recover sufficiently to take any further part in the war that had injured them.

The officers were fortunate to be given such treatment. There was so dire a shortage of seasoned soldiers that unofficial orders had gone out to senior medical staff that priority was to be given to those men who were less seriously wounded, in order that they might recover and be sent back into battle at the earliest opportunity.

Ben was appalled to learn of such a cynical policy and Antonia confided to him that most doctors felt as he did. Some had gone so far as to suggest that if the generals conducting the war wished to have more men in the trenches they should stop throwing them into battles which invited certain death, or serious injury, for no tangible military advantage.

73

The extra carriages brought only two additional medical staff to assist the already over-stretched nurses, and by the time the wounded men had been transferred from the train to a night-time cross-Channel ferry, from the ferry to a London-bound train, and finally on to the ambulances and coaches bound for their various hospitals, Ben believed he had earned the right to his unpaid journey from Paris to London.

He had only the briefest of opportunities to thank Antonia for arranging the journey home for him. In return she extended the gratitude of the medical staff for the hard work he had performed on the way. On a more personal level, she promised to keep in touch with him during the months ahead.

Meeting Ben once more and sharing with him the task of caring for men suffering from the tragic consequences of war had a strange effect upon Antonia. It took her mind back to Insimo and the days when it was on the fringe of the Boer war.

Antonia had been a young girl then, but not so young that she was unaware of what was going on about her. Her grandmother, Victoria, had been a friend of the Retallicks long before they settled at Insimo, and Therese, the mother of Antonia and Philippe, had been brought up there, enjoying the hospitality of Elvira, mother of Ben, who was herself from a very influential Portuguese Mozambique family.

Even when Therese married and moved to neighbouring Mozambique, she would come to stay at Insimo for long periods of time. It became a second home for

Antonia and her brothers and sisters and she always loved it there, delighting in the company of the Retallick boys and revelling in the freedom it gave her.

It had always been assumed that, in common with most others who met him, Antonia idolised Nat, who had become the leader of the boys after his older brother Wyatt had been killed with his father in a Matabele tribal uprising.

She *did* look up to him, just as any young girl would be attracted to a true hero, especially one to whom she was so close. She was also drawn to Adam, the middle of the three surviving sons.

Wild, unpredictable and handsome, Adam was able to charm most young women who met him. Nevertheless, Antonia realised that he had a dark side to his nature, a ruthlessness and selfishness that was not always evident to those who did not know him well.

The truth was that she had always liked Ben best of the three Retallick boys. The closest to her in age, he had become responsible for controlling the vast lands of Insimo when both his brothers went off to fight for opposing sides in the Boer war. He had held the estate together through drought, tribal disturbances and the conflict that touched it on more than one occasion. Yet, when the war ended, he had handed it back to Nat with no hint of resentment, accepting his status as the junior son, until his grandfather had sent for him to come to England to inherit his china clay holdings. Here, Ben had worked hard to overcome the prejudices of his fellow works owners and had made Ruddlemoor into the largest and most profitable clay company in the county.

It was such qualities that Antonia had recognised and always admired in Ben. She firmly believed that he would have succeeded in whatever he attempted in life. Now she had met him once again at a time when fate had dealt him a severe blow and was deeply concerned for him. She wondered whether there was someone in Cornwall who would be able to take the place of Lily – but she could not decide whether she hoped there was, or was not.

4

I

When Antonia had left the station with her charges, Ben took a taxicab to Paddington and discovered he had an hour to wait before he could catch a Cornwall-bound train. Now, for the first time in more than twenty-four hours, there was no one urgently requiring his attention and the acute awareness that he no longer had Lily once more became uppermost in his thoughts. He knew that in Cornwall he would have to face the grief of her family and friends and the sympathy of those who worked for him at Ruddlemoor.

So far there had been little opportunity for him to fully accept his tragic loss but, given time, he knew he would be able to come to terms with what had happened. The grief and sympathy of others would be less easy to cope with.

However, there was no way he could avoid meeting all those who had known Lily and were still part of his life. He decided that in the time he had on his hands before the departure of his train, he would make a telephone call to Captain Bray at Ruddlemoor and inform him that he would soon be home. Captain Bray could inform Ben's housekeeper, Mrs Rodda, of his imminent arrival and bring Ben up to date on what had been happening at Ruddlemoor during his absence.

Including the time he had spent in Switzerland, Paris and London, Ben had been absent from Ruddlemoor for three weeks. Three personally eventful weeks. Nevertheless, the work routine at Ruddlemoor should not have been unduly affected. His captains were the best in Cornwall, each with many years of experience at producing refined clay. For most of the time Ben was no more than a figurehead for the company, required only to make decisions on major policy issues.

In spite of his confidence in the ability of his captains to continue with their daily work in his absence, Ben found his telephone conversation with Jim Bray vaguely disturbing. As the train sped on its way from London to Cornwall he pondered on what had been said – and even more on what his senior works captain might have left unsaid.

At first, Bray had said all was well. However, Ben detected just the slightest hesitation in the response to his questions and, when pressed, the captain admitted that although production at Ruddlemoor was as high as ever, their sales were falling.

This was not particularly unusual – there was always a certain fluctuation in the demand for their product – but it seemed that Captain Bray's discreet enquiries among his peers indicated that the other clay works were selling more clay than usual. Thus far he had been unable to learn the reason why Ruddlemoor was lagging behind its competitors.

Ben tried to convince himself there was probably nothing particularly sinister in Jim Bray's news, but was unable to do so. Jim Bray had been working clay all his life and was good at his job precisely because he had an instinctive feel for what was going on about him. Ben also recalled the unusually aggressive manner of Brigadier General Sir Robert Grove when Ben had suggested that the industry should reduce the profit made on clay products sold to the government. He had an uneasy feeling that the two matters were somehow linked.

When the train arrived at St Austell the stationmaster was on the platform. He hurried to meet Ben and express the commiserations of himself and the station staff at his tragic loss.

The man's sympathy was genuine and Ben was aware that there were a great many people in the community who had known Lily and would wish to express similar feelings. Many would call at his home when they heard he had returned, and he realised he was faced with the prospect of a depressing few days. However, he decided to call in at the works before returning home to Tregarrick.

Asking the stationmaster to arrange for his luggage to be taken to the house, Ben took a taxicab from the station to Ruddlemoor. Here, after running the gauntlet of sympathisers and tearful office staff, many of whom had known Lily well, Ben finally closeted himself in his office with the works captain.

Jim Bray immediately began apologising for bothering Ben so soon after the death of Lily, but Ben cut him short.

'I know everyone means well, Jim, and I am deeply touched to know how well liked Lily was by all who knew her, but I could easily find myself wallowing in self-pity if I'm not very careful – and that's something I am trying very hard not to do. Lily was proud of the way we built Ruddlemoor up and she contributed in no small way to its success. The finest tribute that could be paid to her would be to ensure that we continue to be the top clay producers in Cornwall. Now, tell me exactly what's been happening while I've been away . . .'

Captain Bray was extremely relieved that Ben intended coming back to work immediately. He had been concerned that he might have been required to run the company until Ben recovered from the grief of Lily's death. Things were happening in the industry that were outside the experience of a practical man like himself.

'As I told you when we spoke on the telephone, Ben, our sales have dropped alarmingly while you've been away, yet those of the other works seem to have risen. After speaking to you I sent for the ledgers and compared sales for the last few weeks with those of previous months – and I've come up with an answer. The bulk of our sales for quite a while now have been to government buyers – yet while you've been away they've taken nothing at all from us. This didn't seem right to me. In view of the way the war's going at the moment I would expect demand to rise, not fall away. Because of this I've spoken to the captains of the other works. To be honest, they were reluctant to talk to me at first, but I eventually learned something that isn't going to please you at all, although I don't know what you'll be able to do about it.'

'Go on, Jim, tell me what it is, then I'll let you know if I think anything can be done.'

Fidgeting uncomfortably in his seat, Captain Bray said, 'Brigadier Grove's behind it all. It seems he's somehow managed to get an exclusive contract with the government to become their sole supplier of china clay.'

'But that's preposterous,' Ben exclaimed incredulously. 'Grove's workings are incapable of producing enough clay to satisfy the government's needs.'

'I know that, Ben, that's why I dug deeper and learned just how devious Grove has been. He's buying from the other works – at his own price, of course. Right now the owners are so desperate they'd sell clay to the devil himself, just to remain in business.'

'But Grove hasn't approached Ruddlemoor to buy our clay?' It was beginning to appear to Ben that the brigadier was making a calculated attempt to bankrupt Ruddlemoor.

'No, Ben – and without a share of that government contract there is no way Ruddlemoor can stay in business.'

'And wouldn't Grove like that?' Ben put the question as much to himself as to the clay works captain.

'I'm sorry, Ben. If I'd learned earlier than I did what

was happening I might have been able to persuade Brigadier Grove to include us in the deal he's made with the others.'

'I doubt it very much, Jim. Do you remember the meeting I had with Grove and the others just before I went to Switzerland? I set out a plan to them that I believed would help all the owners – and the government too. Brigadier Grove was dead set against it. I was very surprised at the time, but now I can see what was behind his objections. He must have already signed the government contract – or been about to. Yes . . . it all makes sense now. My going away played right into his hands. He knew that by the time I returned it would be a *fait accompli*. He must have believed that all he had to do then was sit back and watch me go under.'

'As I said, Ben, I'm sorry to present you with a problem like this, with all that's happened these last couple of weeks. It's the last thing you want just now.'

'No, Jim, you're quite wrong. It's exactly what I *do* need. If this hadn't happened I would have sat around feeling sorry for myself and neglecting Ruddlemoor because I had little heart for work. This has given me something else to think about. Something important. Lily was very proud of Ruddlemoor and what we've achieved here. We'll not only fight Grove at his own game – we'll win. By the time I've finished he'll wish he'd never tried any of his underhand tricks on Ruddlemoor.'

Still not convinced, Jim Bray said, 'Well . . . you know you'll have me and everyone else at Ruddlemoor right behind you, Ben, but, being realistic, what can we do?

It's no use trying to persuade Brigadier Grove to change his mind – he's not even in Cornwall at the moment. He's gone to stay with his son's family, up country. If you ask me, he left Cornwall so he wouldn't have to face you when you came back.'

'I have no intention of going begging to Grove, and the fact that he's away makes what I intend doing much easier.'

'But . . . you know yourself, Ben, that the government is by far our biggest customer now. We need a share of that contract.'

'Perhaps . . . but perhaps not,' Ben said enigmatically. 'I have a few telephone calls to make before I can be certain, but I think Brigadier General Sir Robert Grove might well be in for a very nasty shock.'

On his way home to Tregarrick, Ben called in to see Lily's parents. The meeting with them was as difficult as he had anticipated. Lily's mother, Lottie, was a very strong-willed woman and now she had lost both her son and her daughter to the same illness. However, her son was buried in a Cornish churchyard and she firmly believed it was where her daughter ought to be.

Talking to Lottie and her husband, Jethro, in the front room of their St Austell house, Ben defended his decision to have Lily interred in Switzerland, explaining his reasons and giving them the photographs of her grave and the beautiful countryside surrounding the tiny mountain cemetery. He also promised that as soon as the war in Europe was over he would arrange for Lottie and Jethro to visit Switzerland.

'I don't want to go to any foreign country,' Lottie snapped, 'and I shouldn't need to. A person should be buried in the place where they've been brought up and where they've been happy.'

Lily's father had remained silent since Ben's arrival at the house but, deciding it was time he brought the unhappy exchange to an end, he said, 'I'm quite sure many wives and mothers are saying the same about their soldier husbands and sons, Lottie. Unfortunately far more of them are being buried over in France than in England and a great many parents will never have a grave to visit. I respect Ben's reasons for doing what he did. Our Lily's been laid to rest with just as much love as if she'd been in Cornwall.' Turning to Ben, he went on, 'We both thank you for coming to tell us about the service for Lily, and for bringing us the photographs. At least Lottie and I can console one another to some little extent, but from what I hear you've come home to face a whole lot of new problems at the works. Indeed, there's talk among the men that you're likely to go under. I know you've only just had this mess thrown at you, Ben, but what do you think? Is there any hope of saving Ruddlemoor?'

Jethro was a full-time trade union leader, employed on behalf of the many thousands of men who worked in the Cornish china clay industry.

Before Ben could reply, Lottie said, 'If you men feel it decent and proper to talk business at a time like this then I'll go out to the kitchen and leave you to it. There'll be a cup of tea brewed up in a couple of minutes . . . that's if you feel you can drag your talk away from Ruddlemoor's problems for long enough to drink it.'

The death of her only daughter had hit Lottie very hard, but there had been many tragedies in her life and, realising that she had been unfair to her son-in-law, she drew herself up with a conscious effort. Looking directly at him, she said, 'I'm not forgetting you're grieving too, Ben, and you did everything for her that could be done. You also gave her a good life before she developed the illness that has cursed my family. I'll always be grateful for that . . .'

Suddenly choked with an emotion she could no longer control, Lottie turned to leave the room, but Ben caught up with her before she reached the door. Hugging her to him, he said, 'Thank you for that . . . and I thank both of you for trying to understand why I left Lily in Switzerland instead of bringing her back . . . bringing her home. But Lily loved Ruddlemoor and I intend seeing to it that it continues as a permanent memorial to her.'

II

Ben spent much of the first forty-eight hours after his return to Cornwall speaking on the telephone, many of the calls being made during the dead of night when most of his compatriots were asleep in their beds. He rang London, Lisbon, Paris, New York, Stockholm, Copenhagen . . . and received a great many calls in return. By the end of this period the future of Ruddlemoor had still not been secured, but he was more hopeful than when he had first returned to Cornwall and heard the news of the contract Brigadier Grove had signed with the government.

One of the most important telephone calls had been to the Portuguese embassy in London, where he had a guarded conversation with Philippe St Anna.

When Philippe was told the nature of Ben's enquiry, he became extremely cagey and said he was unable to make any comments – then he went on to hurriedly thank Ben for the invitation he had received to visit him at Tregarrick and said that if it was convenient he and Antonia would be happy to come to stay for the weekend, arriving by train on Friday evening. As Ben had issued no invitation, he realised he had put a sensitive question to Philippe, one he was not prepared to answer over the telephone. However, Ben felt he would be given an answer when they met in the privacy of Tregarrick.

On Friday, before Philippe and Antonia arrived, a deeply concerned Jim Bray brought the sales and production ledgers to Ben's office in order to point out to him that Ruddlemoor's sales had just hit a record low.

'You don't need me to tell you the company is losing money hand over fist, Ben, and the men are aware that things aren't going well for us. The main linhay's full and there's room for less than a week's production in number two store. Now a rumour is going round that we'll be laying off men and going on short time before the month is out.'

'You can scotch the rumours right away,' Ben said firmly. 'There will be no lay-offs and we'll continue with full-time working. As for storage space . . . we've never made use of the old linhays that we took over when we bought up the Varcoe works. Send some of the men over there to clean them out. When there's no more storage space at Ruddlemoor we'll put our clay there.' Giving his works captain a wry grin, Ben added, 'If it does nothing else it will give the other owners pause for thought.'

It was an unsmiling Jim Bray who replied. 'I hope you know what you are doing, Ben. You have more to lose than any of us . . . but I'll tell the men what you've said. It will come as a great relief to them.'

When his works captain had left the office, Ben sat back in his chair and hoped the optimism he had expressed to Jim Bray had not been misplaced. Only he knew that he was gambling the future of Ruddlemoor on a chance remark made by Antonia.

Ben was waiting on St Austell station that evening to greet Philippe and Antonia St Anna on their arrival from London. When the Portuguese brother and sister stepped down from the first class dining car, Antonia's delighted and enthusiastic greeting raised eyebrows among those on the station who knew Ben and were aware of Lily's very recent death. However, most assumed because of their 'foreign' appearance that Philippe and Antonia were probably a married couple from one of the many overseas countries that Ben had visited in the past.

Philippe's greeting was less exuberant but equally warm – and Ben was relieved. Since making his telephone call to the Portuguese attaché he had realised their conversation might have been overheard by the embassy telephone operator and thought that Philippe might be coming to Cornwall to take him to task for his indiscretion.

Ben himself drove his visitors to Tregarrick in his Hotchkiss motor car, which had seen little use since the war began. His chauffeur had enlisted as a military driver as soon as the war began and was currently driving a Rolls-Royce armoured car somewhere in the deserts of the Middle East.

It was a fine early summer evening and Tregarrick and its garden were looking at their very best. After the visitors had been shown to their rooms by Mrs Rodda and had freshened up after their journey, Ben showed them round the house. Antonia, in particular, was enchanted by the old manor.

'Have you lived here for very long, Ben?' she asked, as they gazed out of an upstairs room, across flower beds that were a glorious riot of flowering plants and shrubs.

What she would really have liked to ask was whether he and Lily had chosen the house together. She felt she would like to know a little more about the woman he had married and so recently lost, but it was not a question she could put to him so soon after her death.

However, Ben's reply told her what she wanted to know.

'I've had the house for about ten years now,' he said. 'It belonged to the owner of a clay works adjacent to Ruddlemoor. I bought his works when he retired and fell in love with Tregarrick at the same time. When he died, shortly afterwards, I bought the house too. That was before I was married. Lily was more used to living in a small cottage and the size of Tregarrick frightened her at first. But she soon became used to it and the gardens are largely the result of her planning.'

'They are beautiful,' Antonia said honestly. 'I would like to see round them before it is dark. Why don't you and Philippe enjoy a drink and a chat together while I walk about outside on my own?'

From what she had seen of the gardens from the house, Antonia wished she had come to visit while Lily was alive and living here. She had a feeling she would have liked her.

Ben took Philippe to his study and poured drinks for both of them. Seated in comfortable leather armchairs, with only a small drinks table between them, the men relaxed and Philippe said, 'Your telephone call took me by surprise, Ben. I thought the subject of a U-boat truce for neutral shipping was a well-kept German secret for the time being. It was certainly not something I could discuss over an open line.'

'I'm sorry if I placed you in an embarrassing situation,' Ben apologised. 'I realised immediately I had hung up that I had been less than discreet, but I wouldn't have made such a call to you had it not been important. To be quite honest, the whole future of my company is hanging in the balance at the moment.' Ben told Philippe of Brigadier General Sir Robert Grove's contract with the government and the deal he had made with the other clay owners, to the exclusion of Ruddlemoor.

Philippe was puzzled. 'I am not a businessman, Ben, but this contract . . . should not others have been allowed to tender for it? I thought that was how you did things in this country, especially when government contracts were involved.'

89

'It is certainly the way business is usually conducted here,' Ben agreed, 'and it might be worth my while looking into that aspect of the whole affair, but this is wartime and a lot of usual practices are being bypassed. Brigadier Grove knows a great many people in London who are in positions to help him. If he made a good offer to the right person the deal could have been kept quiet "for security reasons".'

'Such a term might be applied to a great many unusual situations, Ben – including a change in the policy of U-boats sinking neutral ships sailing in British waters.'

Eagerly, Ben leaned forward in his chair. 'Has there been such a change of policy, Philippe? Will ships flying the flag of a neutral country be allowed to come in and pick up cargoes of china clay?'

'I can't give you a definitive answer in respect of specific cargoes, Ben,' Philippe said cautiously, 'but Portugal has been informed by the Germans that ships of neutral countries will no longer be considered legitimate targets merely for being in British waters, or trading with your country. However, I must stress that they refuse to put anything in writing and have said they reserve the right to board ships entering and leaving British ports in order to ascertain the nature of their freight. Should a ship be found to be carrying anything considered to be of a nature that would benefit your war effort then they insist it *will* be sunk. My government requested that the Germans make the policy official, but they insist that they will not do so until it is proved to work. Unfortunately, we have already found that, because it has not been declared to be an official policy, ship owners are reluctant to put it to the test.'

'Oh!' Philippe's final words were a blow to Ben's hopes. But even as they plummeted, he came up with a possible solution, albeit one that would prove disastrously costly should it fail.

'I have an idea, Philippe. One that would prove just how serious the Germans are about this "unofficial policy". If I guarantee to indemnify against the possible loss of his vessel by U-boat action, do you think we could persuade a Portuguese owner to send a ship to Charlestown harbour, here in Cornwall, and carry a cargo of china clay to another neutral country? I have many customers all over Europe – and in America too – all eager to take refined clay if I can get it to them.'

Philippe seemed embarrassed by Ben's question and there was a lengthy silence before he replied, 'Using a Portuguese ship might not be such a good idea, Ben.'

'Why?' Ben persisted. 'You are neutral.'

This time Philippe was silent for so long that Ben felt obliged to prompt him. 'Well, you *are* neutral . . . why is it not a good idea?'

Philippe wrestled with his conscience until, looking directly at Ben, he said, 'Our families have known each other long enough for one to trust the other . . . but what I am going to tell you now must never be repeated outside this room . . . to anyone. Do I have your word on that, Ben?'

'Of course.' Ben was intrigued, wondering what it was he was about to be told.

Hesitating for only a moment more, Philippe said

quietly, 'Yes, Ben, it is quite true that Portugal is neutral . . . at the moment. However, our neutrality is becoming increasingly fragile. Germany is violating our borders in Africa at will and the military in Mozambique – my father, as military commander, in particular – is applying strong pressure upon our government to declare war on Germany. He says the only way to stop them from violating our territory is to cross into German East Africa and eliminate the camps from which the raids originate. Many ministers in our government are in agreement and secret plans are being drawn up for offensive action as soon as war is declared – and it will come soon, Ben, of that I am quite certain.'

Ben topped up both their glasses, trying hard to keep his hand steady. Philippe had just put his career on the line by disclosing the probability of Portugal's declaring war on Germany. It was certainly not information that could possibly have been disclosed over a telephone line.

'I thank you for your trust in me, Philippe. It will not be betrayed. What you have told me will go no further. You are a true friend and you might have saved me from losing so much money that Ruddlemoor would be put out of business. I *will* persuade an owner to risk his ship on my behalf . . . but I'll speak to owners I know in Spain or Scandinavia . . . or perhaps both.'

Leaning across the small table that separated them, he shook hands with Philippe gratefully and, raising his glass, the Portuguese military attaché said, 'You are proposing a bold venture, Ben. I wish you and your company success.'

'I will certainly drink to that,' Ben responded, 'but now let's go and see what Antonia is up to outside in the garden. By leaving her out there on her own for so long I fear I am not being a particularly attentive host.'

'Antonia will welcome an opportunity to be alone for a while,' Philippe replied. 'It has always been very important to her to have time to spend on her own, somewhere quiet. She calls it her "thinking time". There has been very little "thinking time" for her since she began working at St Thomas's hospital. She is there all hours of the day and night. But *you* go and find her. I would like to make use of your telephone, if I may. I am awaiting a rather important message from Lisbon.'

III

Ben found Antonia sitting quite happily on a garden seat surrounded by scented flowers in a secluded walled rose garden that had been one of Lily's favourite spots. He kept this knowledge to himself, not wishing to spoil what was quite obviously a very happy moment.

'It is so wonderfully peaceful here,' she said. 'So far removed from all that is going on in France – and even in London . . . We could be in a different world.'

Sitting down on the seat beside her, Ben said, 'Yes, I often come home from all the noise and clatter at Ruddlemoor and sit here for a while, just to put myself together again. Philippe said that you are working very hard in London with little time to spare to sit somewhere quiet and gather your thoughts.'

He felt guilty when the relaxed expression left her face and she said seriously, 'It is very difficult to think one's own thoughts after spending so many hours among men who are tragically wounded and in pain.'

Reaching out, Ben took her hand for a moment. 'I'm sorry, Antonia. I shouldn't have said anything to remind you of your work.' Standing up, he said, 'I know something that will help you to relax again. There's a small lake on the other side of the house where one of the ducks has hatched out a dozen eggs. We'll call in at the kitchen on the way and take some bread with us to feed them. Their antics are guaranteed to bring a smile to even the most jaded city-dweller.'

Although dusk was approaching, the mother duck brought her brood to the lake's edge and the tiny, fluffy ducklings delighted Antonia by darting around their mother and feeding upon the small pieces of bread being thrown to them. Ben and Antonia remained at the lakeside until the mother duck decided it was too dark for the safety of her large family. The decision made, she set off for the small reed bed where she and her mate had made their nest, the ducklings in line behind her, paddling at great speed in order to keep up.

Watching the delightful family as it swam away from them, Antonia said, 'You have found a very special place here, Ben . . . but then, Insimo is also very special. Do you ever miss Africa?'

'Often,' he declared honestly, surprising himself by the admission. 'Especially lately. As well as having to come to terms with war, during recent years I have lost so many people I loved. Grandfather Josh, Grandmother Miriam, and now Lily . . .'

There had also been Tessa, but this was a private grief that could not be shared with anyone else.

'Have you ever thought of going back to live?' Antonia asked.

'I think about it a great deal,' Ben replied. 'I would like to see Ma again – Insimo too – but I have far too many responsibilities here to seriously contemplate leaving England – leaving Cornwall. Grandfather Josh devoted the last years of his life to Ruddlemoor, and with the help of many dedicated people I have succeeded in building it into the finest china clay works in the country. A great many men and their families depend on me for a living. Besides, apart from Ma there's nothing for me now in Africa. Insimo belongs to Nat and he's making a good job of running it. He wouldn't want me around . . . but that's quite enough talk about me. How do you see your future? Are you planning on returning to Mozambique?'

'I don't know,' Antonia replied. 'That *was* my intention, but there is so much more I can learn in England – and at the moment there is a desperate need for doctors here.' Looking up at Ben as they walked together through the gardens, she smiled uncertainly. 'Life isn't simple, is it, Ben?'

'I don't think it was ever intended it should be,' he replied. 'Never mind, we'll try to sample something of the simple life tomorrow. The weather shows all the signs of giving us a fine warm day. I've asked Mrs Rodda to prepare a picnic for us.'

They were passing through a formal rose garden now and, pausing, he plucked a rose from one of the bushes. Handing it to Antonia, he said, 'Place this in water in one of the small vases you have in your room. The scent will guarantee you have only pleasant dreams during the night.'

Antonia was about to suggest that Ben should take one for himself, but decided it would cast a shadow over what had become an unexpectedly pleasant evening. Instead, she lifted the rose to her nose and said, 'It has an exquisite smell. Thank you.'

They walked on in silence until Antonia suddenly said, 'I can't remember the last time I felt quite so relaxed. Thank you so much for allowing Philippe and me to share your lovely home for the weekend, Ben.'

'It's a very real pleasure,' he said, and meant it. Had she and Philippe not been staying at Tregarrick he would have been contemplating a very gloomy weekend.

As they drew closer to the house they could see the glow of a lighted cigarette at the top of the steps and Ben said, 'It would seem that Philippe has ended his call to London.' After a moment's hesitation, he added, 'Please feel free to use the telephone if there is someone special you would like to call in London – or anywhere else for that matter.'

For a moment Antonia wondered whether Ben's offer might have been his way of ascertaining whether there was anyone special in her life . . . then she decided it was much too soon after Lily's death for him to be entertaining such thoughts.

'Thank you, Ben, but I have been far too busy at St

Thomas's to find time to make any close friends. In fact, that seems to have been the story of my life for the past few years. It is still not easy for a woman to embark upon a career in medicine. I have needed to work hard to prove that I am not only a doctor, but will one day become a very good one.'

Antonia would have been delighted had she known that her reply gave Ben a fleeting moment of pleasure, albeit a slightly guilty one.

IV

The following morning showed all the signs of fulfilling Ben's promise to Antonia that it would be a fine warm day. Loading the picnic basket produced by Mrs Rodda into the Hotchkiss, Ben drove Antonia and Philippe to a spot on a hill overlooking the sea, only a short distance from a magnificent historic house known as Caerhays castle, the home of a landowner and local benefactor named John Williams.

Ben informed the others that the 'castle' and its predecessor had romantic histories. For centuries Caerhays had been the home of the Trevanion family, one of whose daughters was grandmother of the poet, Lord Byron. Unfortunately, the present house, designed by the famous architect John Nash to replace the earlier one which had been pulled down, had crippled the Trevanion family financially. Still unfinished, it had been acquired in the mid-nineteenth century by the Williams family, who had amassed a huge fortune from their mining interests. They not only completed the building, but surrounded it with beautiful gardens containing trees and plants gathered from many parts of the world. A hill between house and sea had also been lowered, allowing a direct view from Caerhays to the cove they owned at Porthluney, immediately beneath the hill on which Ben and his companions were picnicking.

It was an idyllic place to be on a fine summer's day – but they had been enjoying the tranquillity for less than an hour when they received a brutal reminder of the war in which Britain was involved.

Until now the only sounds to be heard in this peaceful spot were the hum of bees exploring the clover growing amongst the grass on the hill, the gentle hush of waves breaking against the foot of the cliffs, and the occasional raucous chorus from scavenging gulls and crows.

Suddenly there was another, alien sound and Antonia said, 'What's that . . . is it thunder?'

'It sounds more like gunfire,' Philippe replied. Even as he spoke there were the sounds of heavier explosions and the trio scrambled to their feet and looked out to sea.

'Look!' Antonia pointed to where a silver, cigar-shaped object hung in the sky, a couple of miles out from where they stood. Below it in the water was a black object of about the same length. As they watched, the silver object turned and began heading towards the spot where they had laid out their picnic.

'It must be an airship!' Ben exclaimed. 'I know we're using them for anti-submarine patrols round the coast, but it's the first one I've actually seen.'

'Then that must be a German U-boat in the water,'

Philippe said excitedly, 'and the sounds we heard were bombs as well as gunfire. I wonder if the airship's attack was successful?'

'It doesn't appear to have caused any serious damage to the U-boat,' Antonia pointed out. 'Look, it's heading out to sea.'

As they were talking the airship had approached closer to the shore and Ben said, 'It looks as though the U-boat came off best. The airship has been damaged. That must be why it broke off the attack.'

It could be seen now that the long, cigar-shaped envelope containing the hydrogen gas which kept the airship airborne was beginning to sag in the centre, causing it to lose its long, streamlined appearance. Slung beneath it was a gondola powered by two push-pull engines and carrying the crew of five naval personnel.

The partial collapse of the airship's central section was causing the gondola to hang at an angle, making control of the machine extremely difficult. Philippe said, 'They are losing height so rapidly they will never be able to clear the cliffs.'

'It looks as though they are trying to guide it into Porthluney cove,' Ben observed. 'Fortunately the tide is well out, so they should be able to make it.'

Antonia said, 'If they have been in a fight it is possible they have wounded men who will need attention. Can we get down to meet them?'

'There's a sheep path zigzagging down that way. We might just make it if we run.'

Leaving their picnic on the ground and with Ben in the lead, the trio began running from the cliff edge, following the path that took an erratic course down the steep hillside to the cove.

By now the airship was close to the safety offered by the sandy cove – but it was even closer to the water and they could see that only the front engine was operating. The rear, pusher propeller had stopped and frequently dipped into the sea with the rear of the gondola.

Suddenly, as the three picnickers reached the cove and began running across the sand to intercept the stricken airship, an armed and uniformed figure came lumbering from the shadow of the cliffs on the far side of the narrow bay and called out to them.

'Halt! Stop where you are!'

It was an army special reservist. Too old to fight in a regular army unit, reservists were employed in coastal counties like Cornwall, to guard against infringements of wartime regulations which forbade such things as photography and sketching. They would also be on the lookout for possible 'spies' who might be signalling to German submarines, or assisting the enemy in other, unspecified ways.

As the surprised trio slowed their pace, the reservist, a man in his sixties, slowed too and advanced towards them carrying a carbine threateningly in front of him. When he was still some paces away, he called breathlessly, 'You . . . who are you? What are you doing here?'

'Who we are doesn't matter right now,' Ben snapped. 'As to what we're doing . . . that should be obvious! There's an airship in trouble and we're going to see what we can do to help.'

'It has been in a battle with a German submarine,' Philippe said. 'It could have wounded men on board.'

Even as he spoke the gondola struck the surface of the sea, very close to the shore now, and bounced up again like a skimmed stone, spilling something into the water that could have been a man, a bomb, or a piece of equipment.

Unfortunately, the army reservist appeared to have no interest in the stricken airship. Raising his gun menacingly, he said, 'You're not English – none of you. Who are you?'

The gondola struck land this time with the sound of splintering wood and as it bounced back into the air Ben could see the men inside clinging desperately to the struts which attached it to the airship's envelope.

'We can sort all that out later,' he said dismissively. 'Just now there are lives to be saved. Come on!'

Ignoring the army reservist he began running towards the stricken airship, which looked as though it was likely to come to rest on the sand of the cove at any moment.

'Stop! That's an order, do you hear?'

The uniformed man threw the butt of the carbine to his shoulder, but it was doubtful whether Ben heard him. The airship was now very close, the gondola scraping on rock and sand and its surviving engine racing as the wooden propeller shattered into matchwood against the ground.

Suddenly there was the sound of a shot and Ben felt a blow as though someone had punched him in the back, just above his left buttock. A moment later his leg collapsed beneath him and he fell to the ground, aware that the engine of the airship had cut out.

The only sound to be heard now was that of Antonia screaming.

V

When the army reservist fired at Ben, Philippe had a moment of disbelief. Then, lunging forward, he seized the barrel of the carbine with his left hand and struck a blow to the man's face with his right fist, knocking him to the ground.

As Antonia ran to where Ben lay on the sand, Philippe, his face contorted with fury, stood over the uniformed man. Pointing the gun at him, he cried, 'I ought to use this on you. Are you mad? Why did you shoot?'

'The gun went off by accident,' pleaded the thoroughly frightened reservist. 'Anyway . . . I called on him to stop.'

By now the airship had settled on the wet sand and lay like a stricken monster giving birth as the crew struggled free from the open gondola, which was buried beneath the silver, rubber-proofed fabric of the airship's envelope. One of the men was being dragged between two of his companions and was obviously hurt. Last to emerge was a naval lieutenant, who struggled free of the envelope to be faced with a totally unexpected and confusing scene.

Less than fifty yards away, a man wearing the uniform of a British soldier lay on the ground with a civilian standing threateningly over him, holding a rifle. Between the two men and the airship another man lay face down on the sand in obvious pain while a young woman kneeled beside him inspecting what appeared to be a bloody wound, exposed between his pulled-up shirt and loosened trousers.

Looking towards him, the woman called out, 'Do you have a first aid box on your airship?'

Noting that she was not English, he replied, 'Yes . . . but what's happening? I have a wounded man here . . .'

'So have I,' Antonia retorted, 'and explanations can wait. I need to stop the bleeding and cover the wound quickly.' When the lieutenant hesitated, she added, 'I am a doctor. Fetch the first aid box quickly and bring your wounded man to me. I'll treat them both as quickly as I can.'

Turning back to Ben, after only the slightest hesitation she ripped off the tail of his shirt and made a pad from it, pressing it over the hole caused by the army reservist's bullet. Ben was conscious but in great pain. Breathing heavily, he said, 'Is it serious, Antonia? It hurts like hell and seems to be affecting the whole of my left leg.'

'I think the bullet might have chipped your pelvis. I can't say what else it might have done until we get you to a hospital and can look at it properly. Try not to move, Ben. I will get one of the crew from the airship to hold this pad in place and while we wait for a first aid box I will have a look at their injured man.'

By a strange coincidence the bullet that had wounded the naval airman had entered his body in a similar place to the one where Ben had been hit. Unfortunately, the sailor's wound was far more serious, the bullet having been fired from a more powerful weapon than the carbine. In addition, as a result of being fired from below, it had travelled up into the man's body and Antonia quickly diagnosed that it had damaged some of his internal organs. His wounds were far more serious than those suffered by Ben.

While she was examining the sailor, a mounted party arrived from nearby Caerhays castle. In the lead was John Williams, owner of Caerhays and of the cove where the airship had crash-landed. With the aid of a telescope which was kept in the study he occupied in a tower of the castle he had watched the action between navy and U-boat and seen the crippled airship limping towards Porthluney cove. Wasting no time, he had rounded up servants and grooms, and as they hurried after him with stretchers and a medical box he had galloped to the scene.

When he arrived he saw Philippe standing guard over the army reservist and demanded angrily, 'What the devil do you think you are doing pointing a gun at Pardoe? He happens to be one of my gamekeepers – and unless I am mistaken that is *his* gun you have. Explain yourself!'

Undaunted by his authoritative manner, Philippe replied, 'I am standing guard over him to prevent him from shooting any more innocent and unarmed people.'

'You are doing what . . . ? Who are you and what are you doing here, on my land? You are certainly not English. Where are you from?'

The gamekeeper, seizing upon his employer's words,

said, 'That's right, Mr Williams. None of them are English. I found them here when the airship was coming in and when one of 'em ran towards it I called on him to stop. When he wouldn't, I . . . I shot him.'

'He was running to see if he could help the crew of the airship. That's why I and my sister are here too.' Speaking to John Williams, Philippe added, 'If this man . . . your gamekeeper . . . was possessed of the slightest grain of sense he would have been doing the same instead of attempting to murder an unarmed man.'

The landowner still viewed Philippe with suspicion, but he had realised from his manner of speaking that he was an educated man – and one with an air of authority. In a slightly less abrasive manner, he said, 'I repeat my question to you, sir. Who are you and your friends, and what are you doing here?'

'I am Captain Philippe St Anna, sir, military attaché at the Portuguese embassy in London. The woman attending the injured men is my sister, Dr Antonia St Anna, who is currently working at a London hospital, treating wounded soldiers. We are here because we were enjoying a picnic with our host, the man who was shot by your gamekeeper. He is Ben Retallick, a lifelong friend of both my sister and myself.'

Philippe's disclosure of his own identity was sufficient to impress the men about him, but it was the mention of Ben which startled the landowner.

'Ben Retallick . . . shot by Pardoe? Ben Retallick of Ruddlemoor?'

When Philippe nodded, grim-faced, John Williams clapped a hand to his forehead and rounded on his gamekeeper, 'Good God, Pardoe, what the devil did you think you were doing?'

Thoroughly alarmed by his employer's reaction, the gamekeeper said, 'I called on him to stop, Mr Williams, but he didn't, and . . . and the gun just went off.'

'As gamekeepers' guns are wont to do, of course.' The sarcastic remark was made by the naval lieutenant, who had been listening to the conversation. Speaking to Philippe with more deference than he had shown hitherto, he said, 'You go and join your sister and your friend, sir. I'll have one of my team stand guard over this man until he can be handed over to the police. No doubt they will have some questions to put to him.'

When Philippe handed over the carbine, John Williams said, 'I'll come with you and see how badly hurt poor Retallick is, then we'll have him and the other wounded man carried to Caerhays and I'll call for an ambulance to take them both to hospital.'

VI

After telephoning to the London hospital where she worked, Antonia was able to remain in Cornwall for two days longer than had been originally planned. Because of her considerable experience in dealing with bullet wounds she was able to give valuable assistance to the surgeon who operated on Ben to remove the bullet that had injured him, and assess the damage it had caused.

As she had initially suspected, it had taken a chip from Ben's pelvis. This in itself was causing a great deal of pain, but, rather more ominously, it seemed it had also damaged a nerve that affected the movement of his left leg. The surgeon feared it might leave him with a permanent limp, although he admitted that at this early stage he was unable to say how serious it might be.

Sadly, the naval airman was less fortunate. The U-boat's bullet had struck his pelvis too, but then travelled upwards, into his stomach. He died before reaching the operating theatre.

When the police came to visit Ben in hospital, he told them it was highly probable that the Caerhays gamekeeper had fired his carbine by mistake. In view of this it was decided that no further action would be taken against the man in respect of the shooting. However, John Williams visited Ben later the same day and informed him that the gamekeeper had been relieved of his duties with the army reserve.

Antonia spent most of her time in Cornwall at the hospital with Ben and she was able to assure him that once the stitches had been removed from his wound he would be able to return to Tregarrick. It was a frustrating time for him because he had a great deal to do if he was to carry out the plans he had made for the future of Ruddlemoor, almost all of which required the use of a telephone. In the meantime, Jim Bray came to the hospital each evening and the two men spent the visits discussing details of the work being done at Ruddlemoor to further Ben's plans.

For Ben, the highlight of each day in the hospital ward was when Antonia came to see him. She would arrive bearing gifts from the Tregarrick kitchen, supplied by Mrs Rodda, who was convinced that hospital fare was inadequate for the needs of her employer. So lavish were her ideas of what was required that many of Ben's fellow patients enjoyed luxuries that rarely found their way to the tables in their own homes.

It was quite apparent to Ben that Mrs Rodda and Antonia were getting on very well, and it surprised him. The housekeeper was ultra-conservative in her outlook and tended to view strangers – especially 'foreign' strangers – with the utmost suspicion. When Ben commented on it, Antonia said, 'She is very fond of you, Ben, and has told me a great deal about you and your life at Tregarrick. She is as proud as any mother about the things you have achieved, but feels that life has dealt you some very hard blows lately. She also believes that you work far too hard. She has accepted me because I was on hand to help you when you were shot – and because she thinks that I am good for you.'

'Well, you certainly brighten my days in here, and the surgeon says that your experience with bullet wounds was invaluable to him in the operating theatre.'

'Mr Hennessey is an excellent surgeon,' Antonia said. 'You are very lucky to have him here in Cornwall. He has introduced me to another exceptional doctor, a Swedish man named Olaf Ericsson who is carrying out pioneering work into the extreme stress caused by the type of warfare being waged on the battlegrounds of Europe. He is deeply concerned that many of the soldiers certified as insane by front-line doctors are really suffering from a serious medical condition. Unfortunately, until its true nature is recognised the authorities seem content to lock them up and forget them. Similarly, he believes that many of those convicted of cowardice have an identifiable illness that requires expert treatment. He is working in the mental hospital in Bodmin, where a number of his patients are soldiers who have been certified insane as a result of their experiences. He says these are probably the lucky ones – but he is very bitter about it. Many soldiers have been court-martialled and shot for behaviour over which they have no control. He showed me round his hospital yesterday. Some of the men are in a pitiful state but he is finding it very difficult to get doctors to come here and help him.'

Something in the way Antonia spoke prompted Ben to ask, 'You're surely not thinking of getting involved with that aspect of doctoring, Antonia? You are far too valuable to St Thomas's.'

'For much of the time that is true, perhaps,' Antonia admitted, 'but how valuable I am depends very much on the surgeon with whom I am working. Some of them – especially military surgeons – have still not accepted that women can also be doctors. They tend to treat us more as nurses. Few, if any, would consider specialising in what is becoming known by more enlightened doctors as "shell-shock".'

'But if this condition . . . shell-shock . . . is not officially recognised where would you carry out your work?'

Antonia avoided looking Ben in the eye. 'That is the rather exciting thing that Olaf and I have been discussing, Ben. He is slowly beginning to gain recognition in more enlightened medical circles for his knowledge of this subject and has suggested that I might consider coming to Cornwall as his assistant and taking on his duties whenever he has an opportunity to go somewhere to discuss his theories at important meetings. He is unable to do it at the moment because there is no one here to continue his work while he is away. He admits there is probably not enough work to keep two doctors occupied full-time just yet, but as more and more wounded soldiers are sent to non-military hospitals there will be an increasing need for doctors to tend them. Indeed, many who have retired are returning to work part-time. I could do that while still working with Olaf.'

Ben thought about what she had said for a while before asking, 'Would it mean working for much of your time in Bodmin if you accepted this Swedish doctor's offer?'

'Yes.' Antonia had no wish to expand on her reply.

Again he thought carefully before speaking. 'Bodmin is so close to St Austell that if you had a small car you could live at Tregarrick and travel each day to Bodmin – or wherever else you were needed.'

It was what Antonia had hoped he might say, but she contained her excitement and, when she made no reply, Ben went on, 'Tregarrick is far too large for just me. You could have your own suite of rooms – or even the whole west wing of the house if you wanted. It's not being used at the moment and I have no plans for doing anything with it.'

'Well, nothing is settled yet, Ben, but I appreciate your offer. If I do decide to come and work with Olaf I would like to stay at Tregarrick. I would like it very much.'

'So would I,' said Ben, and he meant it.

When Antonia had left him, Ben thought about what she had said and decided that having her at Tregarrick would bring the old house to life once more. At the moment it sorely lacked the influence of such a woman.

VII

Nothing more was said about Antonia's possible move to Cornwall before her return to London and she did not mention it in the letter she sent to Ben a few days later. The letter merely told him that she was busy at St Thomas's and expressed the hope that he was progressing well and would soon return home to Tregarrick.

Fourteen days after the operation to remove the bullet from his body he was discharged from the hospital. Jacob Pengelly, the young Ruddlemoor transport manager, drove him to Tregarrick, where he was met by the whole of his small household staff, gathered outside the front entrance to welcome him home.

Mrs Rodda, in particular, fussed over him as he made his way from the car to the house, leaning heavily on a crutch that would hopefully be replaced by a walking stick within a few weeks. She tried to persuade him to go to his bedroom right away for a rest, but, while letting her know he appreciated her concern, Ben told her that a fortnight spent in a hospital bed was quite enough rest for a while. There were things to be done.

Conceding defeat, Mrs Rodda saw him ensconced in his study, occupying a comfortable armchair pushed up close to his desk, with a footstool on which to rest his nerve-damaged leg and the telephone placed close enough for him to make use of it without shifting his position in the chair. Then she brought tea and biscuits in to him and placed them on a small table within easy reach. Not until Ben struggled to his feet and placed a warm kiss on her cheek did his flustered and warmly embarrassed housekeeper depart from the study, leaving him to check the post and prepare himself for the telephone calls he so urgently needed to make.

There was a considerable amount of business mail to be dealt with, together with a number of letters from friends and acquaintances wishing him a speedy recovery, and then he came upon a letter addressed to him from the War Office. Opening it, Ben saw it was from Lieutenant General Carey Hamilton. He read its contents with increasing delight. When he put down the letter, he picked up the telephone and put a call through to Captain Jim Bray, at the Ruddlemoor works office.

'Hello . . . Jim? I'm ringing to say I am back home at Tregarrick and just a telephone call away if you need me.'

The Ruddlemoor captain's relief was evident as he said, 'That's the best news anyone could have given me, Ben. I'll try not to trouble you unless it's for something important.'

'I want you to keep me informed of what's going on at Ruddlemoor, whether you think it's important or not – and whether it is good or bad news. Do you understand me, Jim? It's my leg that's the problem, not my brain. I'll be in to the office as soon as I can fix myself up with a chauffeur. I don't think I'll be driving myself around for quite some time.' Jim Bray made noises that were intended to be sympathetic, but Ben interrupted him. 'One of the first things you can do for me is send someone to Sam Hooper's house. Tell his mother I have some news of Sam and would like to speak to her about it. Ask her to come here, to Tregarrick.' In answer to Captain Bray's immediately concerned question, Ben explained, 'No, Jim, it's not bad news, quite the reverse . . . but I want Mrs Hooper to be the first to be told about it.'

When Betsy Hooper arrived at Tregarrick at six o'clock that evening she was accompanied by Muriel. Jim Bray had sent a messenger to her house as soon as he had ended his telephone call with Ben and, despite the messenger's assurance that Ben did not have any bad news for her, she was not convinced.

Introducing Muriel, she said, 'I hope you didn't mind my bringing her along with me, sir, but she and my Sam are very close and if there's anything wrong I would like her to be here with me to hear it.'

Ben had been waiting for Mrs Hooper in one of Tregarrick's smaller reception rooms, a room usually reserved for close friends and family. Waving the two women to a large and comfortable settee, he said, 'I have nothing but good news for you, Mrs Hooper – but please take a seat.' The two women, Sam's mother in particular, appeared very ill at ease in the large house and he tried to reassure them. 'You'll pardon me for not getting to my feet to greet you but I only left hospital

113

this morning and standing up is still something of a struggle.'

'That's quite all right, Mr Retallick, sir. It was a dreadful thing to happen to you. We were all shocked when we heard about it . . . my Sam would have been too, had he known. But . . . the messenger from Ruddlemoor said you wanted to tell me something about my Sam. Has he written to you from Africa? I haven't had a letter from him yet and neither has Muriel, but I've no doubt you'd be the first to hear from him, seeing as how he's out there on your business.'

Pushing to the back of his mind the guilt he felt for deceiving Sam's mother about Sam's true reason for leaving Cornwall, Ben said, 'My asking you to come here has nothing to do with Sam being in Africa, Mrs Hooper. It's because of what Sam did when he came to London to see me there. When the bomb fell.'

Startled, Betsy Hooper looked from Ben to Muriel, then back to Ben again. 'A bomb, sir? My Sam didn't say anything to me about no bomb. Did he mention it to you, Muriel?'

Muriel had said nothing since entering Tregarrick. Now she shook her head. 'No, he didn't say nothing to me.'

Ben looked at the two women in disbelief. 'You mean . . . he said nothing about being in the street where the bomb fell and going into a burning house to rescue a woman and her three children?'

'Oh . . . my dear soul!' Betsy looked at Ben with an expression that combined disbelief with horror. 'He didn't say a word . . . and I'm not surprised! I'd have likely dropped dead with shock on the spot. You just wait 'til I see him. He'll get an earful for keeping such a thing to himself. All he told me about London was how big it is – oh yes, and he was full of coming back here with a new suit. I told him off about it. The suit he wore up there had hardly any wear in it, for all that it had been bought for our Sam when he wasn't as big as he is now.'

'We had to buy him a new suit,' Ben explained. 'The other one was so badly scorched it couldn't be worn any more.'

'Oh, my dear soul!' Betsy repeated, this time reaching out and clutching Muriel's arm. 'And he didn't say a single word about it to me . . .'

Muriel reached up and gripped Betsy's arm, at the same time saying to Ben, 'I don't think you asked Sam's ma to come here to tell her about what Sam did in London, Mr Retallick. You said you had some good news to tell of him . . . ?'

'That's quite right,' Ben replied. 'But it's to do with what happened that night. We were with some very important people when it happened – one of them an army general. He was so impressed with what Sam did that he recommended him for a bravery award and his recommendation was endorsed by two others who were there – one a military attaché in a London embassy, and the other a doctor. I had a letter today from the general. The award has been confirmed and will be published in the London *Gazette* very soon. Sam has been awarded the Albert medal. It's the highest award for bravery that can be given to a civilian. You should be very, very proud of him. He will be a national hero.'

'Oh my!' Betsy Hooper had no idea what a military attaché was, and very little idea of how prestigious was the Albert medal. All she could think of saying was, 'But how can they give a medal to Sam? He's in Africa.'

'They will wait until he returns,' Ben explained. 'Then the King will present it to him at Buckingham Palace . . . and you will be invited to go there with him.'

Betsy Hooper looked at Ben in bewilderment. 'Buckingham Palace? Me go with Sam to Buckingham Palace . . . to meet the King? Oh my dear soul! Whatever shall I wear?'

Ben smiled. 'Don't worry about that, Mrs Hooper. I am sure we'll be able to find something for you. In the meantime you can expect to be visited by journalists from many of the newspapers who'll want to know all about Sam. I know you will tell them how proud you are of him . . . as I am too. I have no doubt that you'll be even more proud of him when he returns from Africa and tells you about all the things he will have done there . . .'

116

5

I

I

The SS *Tamerlane* left Tilbury docks on 12 June 1915, three days before the ship on which Spicer and the remainder of the expedition to Lake Tanganyika sailed from England.

Despite Acting Commander Spicer's threats, the *Tamerlane* had ample and comfortable accommodation for passengers and was, in fact, carrying only thirteen passengers to South Africa in its twenty passenger cabins. It was a number that made the more superstitious of the sailors uneasy.

In addition to Sam, five of the passengers were nuns, another was the wife of a Nyasaland missionary returning from medical treatment in London, one was a black African nurse and the remainder were four South African women and an Afrikaans predikant – a minister of the Dutch Reformed Church. The last five had been delegated by a Boer action group to travel to London to register a strong protest with the British government about sending captured hardline Boers, who had been fighting on the side of the Germans in South West Africa, to prison camps outside South Africa. Sam and the predikant were the only male passengers.

The ship set off on the late afternoon tide and it was with some apprehension that Sam and his fellow travellers stood at the rails and watched the low-lying land on either side of the Thames estuary recede into the distance as the vessel entered the southernmost waters of the North Sea.

The tension on board increased even further when, hugging the Kent coast, the *Tamerlane* entered the U-boat infested waters of the English Channel. The passengers were reminded of the perils they faced when a seaman was sent aloft to a 'crow's nest' rigged on the forward mast. He would spend the remainder of the daylight hours scanning the sea for mines, or the telltale path of a torpedo heading towards them.

Shortly before dusk there was considerable relief on board when the ship was joined by a Royal Naval destroyer which took up position ahead and slightly to one side of them. Its Aldis lamp clattered out the comforting message that it would be with them throughout the night hours and, in fact, would not leave them until they had passed through the English Channel and reached the more open waters of the Atlantic Ocean.

That evening, as the passengers waited in their lounge for the dinner bell to sound, the South African minister approached Sam and in a very strong Afrikaans accent introduced himself as Predikant de Vries. He asked so many questions about the purpose of Sam's visit to South Africa that the latter became vaguely uneasy. However, when Sam succeeded in convincing him that he was merely travelling to Rhodesia to work on the family farm of his employer, the Afrikaans preacher appeared to lose interest and Sam had the distinct impression that he had been 'written off' as being beneath the predikant's notice. This impression was strengthened when the passengers sat down to eat at a single long table in their dining room, where they were joined by Captain Smith and the officers of the *Tamerlane*. Predikant de Vries ensured that he occupied a seat next to the officers.

There was one vacant place at the long dining table but it had little significance for Sam. He felt uncomfortable in the predominantly feminine gathering, seated, as he was, with the Afrikaner delegation between him and the ship's officers, and the Belgian nuns conversing in their own language on the other side. The only English being spoken was at the head of the table, where the missionary's wife sat with the officers.

Sam excused himself while coffee was being served. Making his way to the upper deck he opened the door from the superstructure and stepped outside, welcoming the fresh night air. He was used to neither the close company of so many women, nor the still unfamiliar etiquette of formal dining.

During the daylight hours Sam had observed that there was a wooden seat tucked between two large steel lockers, adjacent to the ship's superstructure. He believed it would offer a degree of privacy while he would still have the benefit of the breeze generated by the speed of the ship. He made for it now, but when he reached it he was taken aback to find it occupied, although he could make out little of the figure seated there, thanks to the strict blackout enforced on board as a precaution against attack by prowling U-boats.

Murmuring an apology, he had begun to back away when the occupier of the seat said, 'It's all right, I have been here for a while. You can sit down and I will go.'

The voice was that of a young woman. It carried a strong trace of an accent he thought he had heard before, although he could not immediately recall where.

'Thank you,' he said, 'but please don't leave on my account. It's just . . . well, I'm not used to being waited on when I eat – and I find being in the company of so many women when I'm eating a bit overwhelming, especially when none of them are speaking English. I excused myself and came up here.'

There was too little light to see the young woman properly, but he could make out that she had a dark skin and he had seen an African girl wearing the uniform of a nurse walk up the gangway to the ship when they were at Tilbury. He had thought then that she was probably on the medical staff of the port authorities. Then he remembered the empty place at the dinner table in the ship's dining room.

'I didn't see you at dinner . . . weren't you hungry?' he asked.

'I had dinner in my cabin,' the girl replied. 'The purser thought it would be better.'

Puzzled, Sam asked, 'Better? Better for whom . . . and why should he think such a thing?'

The girl looked at him and her teeth gleamed white in the darkness as she smiled. 'You really don't know?'

'No,' he replied honestly.

'It's because I am black,' she said. 'Actually, I am not fully black because I have a white father, but I take after my mother and am black enough to be an embarrassment to the Afrikaans women and their predikant. They are all from families where the only black women that they come in contact with are servants who may be seen but not heard, and would certainly not be allowed to sit down and eat at the same table.'

'You are Portuguese . . . from Mozambique,' Sam said suddenly. It was a statement and not a question.

'That is very astute of you,' the girl said. 'You cannot have met many people from my country in England. My name is Maria, Maria Fernandes . . . and yours?'

'Sam Hooper,' he replied, 'and there's nothing particularly clever in recognising your accent. I met two friends of my employer, a brother and sister from Mozambique, when he and I were in London a few weeks ago. She is a doctor – Dr Antonia St Anna. We all had dinner together.'

'You know Antonia? How wonderful!' cried a delighted Maria. 'We worked together at St Thomas's hospital and became great friends. In fact, she came to the railway station to see me off when I left London. She is a very clever doctor . . . but your employer must be one of the Retallicks whose mother is Portuguese from Mozambique, too. Her father was once the

121

governor there. Antonia found work for one of my brothers on their farm in Rhodesia. She told me a couple of weeks ago that she had dined with one of the family and that he had a friend with him . . . but did you not become involved in the bombing by the Zeppelin that night? Antonia said that Senhor Retallick's friend was very brave and went into a burning house to rescue the woman and her three children who were brought into our hospital that night. Was it you who rescued them?'

Embarrassed by her words, Sam said modestly, 'I did go into the house with Ben Retallick, yes.'

'How wonderful to meet you, Sam, and to know that we have a mutual friend. I was afraid I would spend the whole of the voyage to South Africa sitting in my cabin speaking to no one but the Chinese steward, who speaks very little English – and no Portuguese.'

Sam sat talking to Maria for more than an hour and found her interesting and intelligent company. From her he learned a great deal of what he might expect to come across in Africa and of the power wielded in Rhodesia, and Mozambique too, by the Retallick and St Anna families. She also told him of the frighteningly wide social gap that existed between the various races who shared the vast continent of Africa. It was a gap which was rigidly observed in the parts of Africa dominated by the Boers.

II

For two days Sam ate his meals on the *Tamerlane* in an uncomfortable silence. A nun did try to speak to him on one occasion, but her English was extremely limited and she found his strong Cornish accent incomprehensible.

The Boer women and Predikant de Vries spoke among themselves in Afrikaans and made no attempt to converse with him, behaving as though he did not exist. Had it not been for an occasional exchange of greetings with a ship's officer and what became a regular nightly conversation with Maria, it would have been a very lonely voyage.

Sam was aware that Maria was feeling her own isolation even more keenly than he was, being used to the constant bustle and chatter of a busy city hospital. He thought long and hard about the way she was being treated, and although in Cornwall he had chosen to lead a quiet life, neither making trouble for himself nor becoming involved in the problems of others, he decided that the voyage of the *Tamerlane* was going to be too long to allow the present state of affairs to continue.

Seeking out the purser, he found him poring over papers in his small office and received an abstracted 'Come in' in response to his knock.

The purser greeted him with some surprise. 'Hello, Mr Hooper. What can I do for you?'

'I've called in to tell you that I've decided to take my meals in my cabin in future,' Sam said, in his soft Cornish voice.

Startled, the purser said, 'You'll do *what*? I am sorry, Mr Hooper, but meals can only be served in the ship's dining room. That's the policy on all our company's ships. We don't carry sufficient stewards to enable meals to be served elsewhere.'

'Really? Yet I understand that the Portuguese nurse is taking meals in her cabin.'

Appearing ill at ease, the purser said, 'That is different, Mr Hooper. You see . . . I had a complaint from a number of passengers, as a result of which I discussed the situation with Captain Smith. It was decided that in order to avoid any unpleasantness an exception would be made in this case – but it *is* very much an exception, I can assure you. Miss Fernandes was asked if she would mind eating in her cabin and she agreed.'

'What you are really saying is that the Boer delegation refused to eat their meals with Miss Fernandes for no other reason than that she is black – and you and the captain gave in to them?'

'I realise it is very difficult for anyone who has not been to South Africa to appreciate the strength of feeling about such matters, Mr Hooper. It can run very high, so in the interests of the comfort of the majority of the passengers, the captain decided upon the present arrangement.'

'I believe that the *Tamerlane* is a British ship, Mr Purser, and as such I would expect the captain to put British interests ahead of those of its enemies.'

When the purser appeared puzzled by his words, Sam explained, 'Nurse Fernandes has been working in St Thomas's hospital in London, tending British soldiers who were wounded while fighting the Germans and their allies.'

'That may be so, but . . .'

Sam silenced the purser with an impatient gesture and continued, 'The Boer women, led by the predikant, were in London for a very different reason. They came to petition the British government on behalf of their menfolk who were captured whilst fighting *against* British soldiers. The particular men they represent are so anti-British that they refused to agree not to give the Germans any further support if they were allowed to return home. They belong to the hardcore of anti-British feeling in South Africa.'

It was quite apparent to Sam that the purser had not been aware of the reason why the Boer delegation had been in London. 'Are you quite certain of this, Mr Hooper?' he asked, in disbelief. 'The Boer women have men fighting for the Germans?'

'They had – until the men were captured,' Sam replied.

He was aware his information was second-hand, but it had come from Maria, and she had been quite adamant, explaining that when the information was printed in London newspapers the nurses and wounded soldiers in the hospital were incensed that a delegation had been allowed to come to London to plead the cause of such men.

Aware of the purser's uncertainty, Sam said, 'I understand that public opinion in London is running so high about the whole business that there would have been ugly demonstrations outside your shipping office had it become general knowledge that they are travelling with your shipping line. I have no doubt there would also be a public outcry were it to be reported that a nurse who had come straight from tending wounded British soldiers had been barred from eating with other

125

passengers on your ship because these same pro-Germans objected to her because of her colour. I wouldn't be at all surprised if patriotic dockers went so far as to refuse to load or unload ships belonging to your company.'

The purser knew that Sam was right. Anti-German feelings were running particularly high since the Zeppelin raid on London and the use of poison gas against Allied soldiers in the front-line trenches of Europe – and dockers were a notoriously militant labour force. Nevertheless, he said, 'I doubt whether it will be necessary for anyone in England to go to such extremes, Mr Hooper, but I thank you for bringing the facts to my attention. I will discuss what you have told me with Captain Smith without delay.'

Half an hour before the lunch bell was due to sound, Sam was walking along the companionway in the passenger quarters, on his way to meet Maria on the upper deck, when he met Predikant de Vries coming from the opposite direction.

Instead of brushing past without speaking, as he would usually have done, the South African preacher deliberately stood in Sam's path, bringing him to a surprised halt.

'I believe you have been causing trouble,' de Vries said in his guttural accent. 'I don't know what you hope to gain by your action, but you can expect no gratitude from the Kaffir woman.'

'I presume you are talking about Nurse Fernandes, and the fact that I happened to mention she has been

126

working hard in a London hospital caring for wounded British soldiers? I don't expect any gratitude for that – but I do expect her to be given due recognition for the work she has been doing and treated as befits a member of a highly respected profession.' Sam spoke quietly but firmly.

'She was no doubt being very well paid for whatever she did in London – however she performed her duties. You told me soon after joining the ship that you have never been to Africa. That is quite apparent by your action today. You will learn quickly that you do not take the side of a native against a white man – and you do not sit down at a meal table with them.'

'You may do whatever you please in your own home,' Sam said, 'but this is a British ship and I would be happy to eat with anyone who has been caring for soldiers wounded while fighting for king and country. I would like to believe the captain and his officers feel the same.'

'You won't last long in Africa, young man. And if that Kaffir girl is allowed to eat at the same table on this ship you will not find myself or any of the Afrikaner women in the dining room.'

Sam shrugged indifferently. 'That is a decision for you and the women with you. It will not affect my appetite in any way. Now, if I may pass . . . ?' He pushed past the predikant, aware that the preacher was very angry with him. The only emotion he felt was elation. It would appear his conversation with the purser had borne fruit.

*

Sam was seated in his usual place on the upper deck when Maria appeared from the hatch that led to the passenger quarters. Seeing him, she waved and made her way towards him. Sitting down by his side, she smiled happily and said, 'Guess what, Sam? The purser just came to my cabin and said the captain has learned of the sterling work I have been doing at St Thomas's hospital. It seems that one of his nephews passed through there recently, after being badly wounded in France. The captain insists that I join the other passengers and officers at meal times. What do you think of that?'

'I think it's where you should have been from the first day of the voyage,' Sam replied. 'I am delighted. Perhaps now I'll have someone to chat to while I eat. With five Belgian nuns to my left and six Afrikaans-speaking men and women to my right, I would be wondering whether I was still capable of holding a conversation if it weren't for meeting you here.'

'The predikant and the Afrikaner women are being deliberately rude,' Maria declared. 'They were all chosen for the delegation to London because they *are* able to speak English. They could have included you in their conversations had they wanted to. Mind you, they have probably seen you talking to me. That would be enough to set them against you.'

'I'm not particularly concerned about being included in their conversations,' Sam said, 'but I *am* pleased that you'll be there at meal times, even if we're seated too far apart to do more than smile at each other occasionally.'

'Oh, I have an idea we will manage a little more than that – and I really want to thank you, Sam.'

'Thank me for what?' he asked.

'For making representation to either the captain or the purser on my behalf . . . No, it's no use your trying to deny it,' she added, when he opened his mouth to protest. 'You are the only one on the ship who was aware that I had been working at St Thomas's.' When Sam made no attempt to either confirm or deny his involvement, Maria asked softly, 'Why, Sam? Why have you chosen to involve yourself on my behalf?'

He shrugged, 'I can think of a great many reasons. The first is that I was unhappy about the reason why the Boer women objected to your eating at the same table as everyone else. You have far more breeding and education than any of them – more than me too, come to that. You also have better manners, are kinder, have done far more to help us in a war that doesn't involve your country and, as far as I can see, are leading a far more useful life.' Giving her a sidelong glance, he saw that she was looking at him attentively and he smiled at her before adding, 'Besides, I like you. That alone is reason enough to want to help you.'

Reaching out, she grasped his hand and squeezed it briefly before releasing it again. 'Thank you very much. I think I like that last reason best of all.'

III

Lunch that day on board the *Tamerlane* began as a somewhat strained affair, but Sam's fear that he would have

129

Predikant de Vries and the Afrikaans women between himself and Maria proved groundless. The South African delegation did not put in an appearance and the captain suggested that Sam and the nuns should close up to the officers, the missionary's wife – and Maria.

The result was that Sam found himself in conversation with others at the meal table for the first time since joining the ship. Meanwhile Maria, who was a very attractive and lively girl, swiftly charmed the captain and his officers with her ready wit and intelligent conversation and before long the small group of nuns began practising their limited English vocabulary in the newly relaxed atmosphere that prevailed at the table.

After lunch, as Sam left the dining room, he found himself walking beside the purser and asked if the Boer women were taking the meal in their cabins.

'No,' replied the ship's officer, tight-lipped. 'When I told them that Captain Smith had decided Nurse Fernandes should join us for all meals, they repeated their objections and said if they were not heeded they would eat in their cabins. I told them we possessed neither the facilities nor the stewards to make such an arrangement feasible. They might either eat in the dining room or go hungry – although they are welcome to take advantage of the very limited fare offered by the small shop that is open for the crew for half an hour each evening. It sells mainly biscuits, chocolate and similar snacks.'

'You mean . . . they will not have a proper meal until we arrive in South Africa?' Sam looked at the purser in disbelief.

The purser shrugged nonchalantly. 'It is entirely their own choice. Food will be prepared for them at meal times. If they choose not to eat it . . . then so be it. Besides, we dock at Lisbon in a few days. They can stock up with food there if they still persist in their foolishness.'

By the time the *Tamerlane* berthed at Lisbon two of the Boer women had weakened and were taking meals with the other passengers and the crew, albeit now seated at the opposite end of the table from the captain, separated from him, his crew and Maria by the nuns, the missionary's wife and Sam. The presence of Maria at the same table did nothing to affect their appetites, although they ate in silence and left when coffee was being served and the men lit up their cigars and cigarettes.

The night before the ship was due to dock at Lisbon, Sam was finding sleep difficult. It was hot and his cabin seemed small and stuffy. Reaching out from his bunk he switched on the light and picked up his pocket watch from the locker beside him. It was 1 a.m. He decided he would go to the small passenger lounge that was situated below the bridge. There was only a gentle ocean swell, so he knew all the large windows would be open even though the lounge itself would be in darkness.

It was pleasant sitting alone in the airy lounge and Sam sat there for a long time, smoking a cigarette cupped in his hand and thinking how life had changed for him in just a few weeks. Cornwall – and Muriel – seemed a long way away.

In that time he had been to London and had an adventure, and he was now at sea off the coast of Portugal, heading for the greatest adventure of all. In little more than a fortnight he would be setting foot in Africa, with the prospect of a journey of more than 3,000 miles through that vast and wild continent, and responsibility for two traction engines that were to haul two gunboats through largely uncharted terrain.

Never in his wildest dreams could he have imagined embarking upon such an incredible journey from his small Cornish village. He knew he would encounter many problems along the way, but he would also meet with a great many interesting people. Indeed, he already had. He thought of Lieutenant General Carey Hamilton, Commander Spicer, Antonia St Anna . . . and Maria.

Sam found it difficult to analyse his feelings for the young Portuguese nurse. He found her very attractive and she stirred his emotions in a way that would have broken Muriel's heart had she known. She was also clever – much cleverer than he believed himself to be, and she carried an air of confidence that was at odds with the opinion Predikant de Vries had of her and of others like her.

He thought of Maria for a long time before the air outside began to cool and he decided to return to his cabin. He believed he might be able to sleep now.

He went down the steps to the passageway where all the cabins were situated and had just reached his own when he heard the sound of another door being opened a short distance along the dimly lit passage. He looked towards the noise and was startled to see Jacobus de Vries coming out of a cabin that Sam knew was occupied by one of the ladies of the Boer delegation, the predikant's own cabin being farther along. As the predikant turned in that direction a woman's voice that was little more than a whisper called, 'Jacobus, you left this . . .' Then the occupier of the cabin appeared in the doorway and handed something to de Vries that Sam could not see, but that was not all. Before the predikant went on his way once more, she reached up, touched his cheek and kissed him on his mouth.

At that moment the ship dipped into the trough of a wave, causing Sam to lose his balance and stumble against the bulkhead beside his cabin.

The heads of both the predikant and the woman swung round to look in his direction and Sam knew they must have seen him. The next moment the woman fled inside her cabin and, after only a moment's hesitation, Predikant de Vries hurried off in the direction of his own, leaving Sam to settle down for the second time that night. But now he wore a somewhat bemused smile.

IV

When the *Tamerlane* berthed in the capital of neutral Portugal, early in the morning, Captain Smith informed the passengers that the ship would remain at Lisbon for thirty-six hours. During this time the passengers were free to go ashore and enjoy whatever pleasures the city had to offer them.

Standing near the gangway, Sam stood aside to allow Predikant de Vries and the delegation of Boer women

133

to make their way ashore. De Vries glared at Sam as he passed by, but said nothing. The women did not look at him. Even had they done so, he doubted whether he could have recognised the one who had entertained the predikant in her cabin.

He had not realised the *Tamerlane* would remain at Lisbon for so long and going ashore had not occurred to him. Then he saw Maria heading for the gangway. Reaching him, she said, 'Are you not coming ashore to look round Lisbon, Sam? I carried out my early training here and it is a beautiful city.'

Sheepishly, Sam said, 'Of course, I had forgotten that you are Portuguese. No doubt you will enjoy meeting old friends while you are here.'

'I doubt if there are any of them left in Lisbon, but I will be happy looking round the city again . . . why don't you come with me? I will show you some of the sights.'

Delighted to receive the invitation, Sam replied, 'I would love to come with you. Could you wait a couple of minutes while I tidy myself up a little . . . that's if you really would like me to come with you and are not just being polite?'

'Of course I want you to join me. It will be nice to have your company.'

It was Sam's first glimpse of a foreign city and it was a great help having someone with him who spoke the language. Maria showed him some of the city's famous landmarks such as the cathedral and monastery, but she also introduced him to street cafés where they sat and watched the world go by, and restaurants that sold excellent food but were far more informal than those he had visited with Ben Retallick in London.

She also showed him the hospital where she had received part of her training. It was as they were returning to the more commercial area of the city that Sam suddenly pointed to a man coming down the steps of an impressive building some way ahead of them and said, 'Look! Isn't that Predikant de Vries?'

'Yes, it is,' agreed Maria, 'and that is the German embassy he is coming from.' Grimly, she added, 'It is proof enough, if it were ever needed, just where his sympathies lie.'

When the predikant reached the bottom of the steps he turned away from them, walking in the same direction as themselves. They slowed down so as not to catch up with him and it was not long before he passed out of sight. They discussed what possible reason he could have had for visiting the embassy, but when they reached the heart of the city Maria began telling him of the restaurant she intended taking him to for dinner and the Afrikaner predikant passed from his mind.

The restaurant where they ate was the place where Maria had celebrated special occasions as a student nurse and it was there that they met up with a young doctor and two other nurses who recognised Maria from those days. The reunion quickly became an impromptu party. It was well after midnight when they arrived back on board the *Tamerlane* and both were rather tipsy, making exaggerated 'hush' sounds to each other as they tiptoed past the cabins occupied by the nuns.

Outside Maria's cabin, Sam whispered, 'Thank you,

Maria. That was one of the most enjoyable evenings I have ever spent with anyone.' He meant every word, aware that he had become hopelessly attracted to Maria.

'Yes,' she replied, equally quietly, 'Lisbon is a beautiful city.'

'It's not only the city that I found beautiful, Maria,' he replied; then, aghast at his own temerity, he held his breath as he waited for her reaction, fearing he might have overstepped the mark.

Instead, looking up at him in the dimly lit corridor, she smiled. 'I do believe you are paying me a compliment, Sam.'

'Yes . . . and I mean it,' he declared.

'I know you do, Sam, and that is what makes it special. Thank you.'

She needed only to take a half pace forward in order to kiss him. It began as a brief, affectionate gesture, but when he reached out and pulled her closer to him she responded by clasping her arms about his neck and the kiss lasted until the sound of voices caused them to end the embrace and step back from each other.

In fact, it was only two seamen on the upper deck, making their drunken way to the crew's quarters after spending the evening on shore. But the moment had passed and Maria said, 'I enjoyed the day too, Sam. Thank you again.'

Shakily he made his way to the cabin he occupied. At the door he paused and looked back, but Maria had gone inside her own cabin and the door was closed behind her.

*

The following day at breakfast the purser said to Sam, 'There will be no need to concern yourself any more about Predikant de Vries and his party, Mr Hooper. They have left us and will be taking passage to South Africa in another ship, where they say they will feel more welcome.'

'Perhaps it will be one personally recommended by the German ambassador,' Sam joked. He went on to tell the purser of seeing the predikant leaving the German embassy.

'Are you quite certain it was the German embassy?' the purser queried.

'Yes,' Sam replied. 'Nurse Fernandes was showing me the sights of Lisbon. It's a city she knows well. She saw him too.'

He thought little more about his talk with the purser and went to his cabin to write postcards to post before the *Tamerlane* sailed. There was one for his mother, another to Muriel and a third to Ben Retallick. He smiled as he thought of the thrill it would give the two women to receive them.

There was a knock at the door and the purser entered the cabin. 'I am sorry to trouble you, Mr Hooper,' he said, 'but the captain would like to have a word with you.'

'Me?' Sam queried. 'What about?'

'Captain Smith will tell you,' came the reply. 'I'll take you to his cabin.'

Looking concerned, Captain Smith came straight to the point. 'The purser tells me you think you saw Predikant de Vries coming from the German embassy yesterday.'

137

'I didn't *think* I saw him, Captain, it was definitely him, and he *was* leaving the German embassy. Nurse Fernandes was with me and saw him too. She knows the city well because she trained here.' Remembering his joke to the purser, he added, 'Surely the predikant can't intend taking passage on a German ship? They wouldn't be allowed to dock in South Africa, would they?'

Instead of replying, Captain Smith asked, 'Since we left England has Predikant de Vries ever asked you questions about your business in Africa, or about the two traction engines you have in the hold?'

'He did ask me why I was travelling to South Africa, but when I told him I was going to Rhodesia to do some work on my employer's family farm he seemed to lose interest. The traction engines were never mentioned.' Remembering the mission on which the traction engines would be employed, Sam asked cautiously, 'Is there any particular reason why they should have been?'

Captain Smith and his purser exchanged glances before the *Tamerlane*'s master said, 'There has been a certain amount of speculation about them – but I don't need to know anything. Suffice it to say that whatever the purpose of sending them to Africa, the bill for their transportation is not being settled by your employer, whoever he may be, but by the War Office. I can also tell you – in strict confidence – that we are carrying some very important and sensitive items on behalf of the same source and it has been brought to my attention that Predikant de Vries has been asking my crew a great many questions about what cargo we are carrying in the hold. Far more questions than one would expect from even the most inquisitive passenger. It did not matter too much while he and his delegation were travelling on the same ship with the cargo, but it takes on a new significance when within a few hours of being seen coming from the German embassy he and his party suddenly decide to leave the *Tamerlane*.'

The ship's captain lapsed into deep thought for many moments; then, as though arriving at a sudden decision, he said, 'Thank you very much, Mr Hooper. I trust you will say nothing of this conversation to anyone.'

That lunchtime, Captain Smith announced to the *Tamerlane*'s passengers that the ship would be remaining at Lisbon for approximately twenty-four hours longer than had been originally planned. He offered no explanation for the delay.

Sam wanted to ask Maria to go ashore with him again, but was not certain whether or not she regretted what had happened on their return to the ship the night before. However, as they left the dining room, she fell into step beside him and they walked together to the ship's rail in order to watch an American passenger liner being shepherded out of the dock by a pair of rust-stained but efficient tugs.

On the way to the rail he gave her a couple of side-long glances. She seemed quite unperturbed, but he could eventually contain himself no longer and blurted out, 'I hope I didn't offend you last night . . . when we came back on board.'

'Offend me? How? By telling me that I was beautiful . . . and that you had enjoyed my company?'

'No, of course not . . . I meant it. I wouldn't have said it otherwise.' He had an uneasy feeling that she was teasing him, but he had little experience with women – and none at all with a woman like Maria.

'Then it must be because we kissed,' she said. 'Do you wish now that we had not?'

'Of course I don't. It was . . . it was what I wanted to do.'

'Good . . . and so did I. Is there anything else for which you think you need to apologise?'

Her smile told him for certain that she was teasing him and, slightly abashed, he relaxed and replied, 'No. In fact, as we're to spend another night in Lisbon, I wondered whether we might go ashore together again.'

'I thought you were never going to ask me,' she said, and this time the smile was accompanied by an affectionate squeeze of his arm. 'Give me half an hour to get ready, then you can come to my cabin and call for me.'

When Sam awoke with a start the next morning there was movement beside him in the narrow bunk and Maria said, 'It is about time you woke. I was beginning to feel quite indignant.'

As Sam struggled to sit up in the narrow confines of the bunk, he was aware that both he and Maria were naked.

'I'm sor—'

Her kiss effectively cut off his apology. When she drew back and before he could regain his breath, she said, 'Don't you dare apologise, Sam. Not unless you wish we had not made love. If that is how you feel you can get up and dress and go to your own cabin and pretend it never happened. I will never say anything to anyone.'

It had been late when Sam and Maria returned to the *Tamerlane*, having drunk more than on their previous excursion ashore. When he had kissed her goodnight, as he had on the previous night, she had whispered, 'Shall we go into my cabin? No one can interrupt us there.'

'. . . You have not answered me, Sam. *Do* you wish that nothing had happened between us?'

Leaning heavily on one elbow, he looked down at her and said, 'What will you do if I tell you that you ask a lot of ridiculous questions – and if I refuse to get up and go back to my own cabin?'

Reaching up, she pulled him down to her, and whispered, 'I will think of something . . . especially as we are awake very early. Breakfast will not be ready for another hour and a half . . .'

6

I

When Ben Retallick exchanged the wooden crutch given to him at the hospital for a walking stick, he was able to visit the tiny china clay port of Charlestown in order to witness the first positive result of the many telephone calls he had made while otherwise incapacitated. A small bulk ocean-going cargo ship flying the Spanish flag docked to take on board a cargo of processed china clay – Ruddlemoor clay.

The event provoked great excitement in the area, men, women and children coming from miles around to witness something that had not been seen since the activities of German U-boats had brought the port to a virtual standstill.

Ruddlemoor's fleet of lorries, supplemented by a nose to tail procession of horse-drawn clay wagons, were cheered loudly as they came down the gently sloping road to the port. However, there had been no public intimation from the Germans that they had ceased targeting neutral ships operating in British waters, and many of those watching the loading gloomily predicted that only luck had enabled the ship to sail into Charlestown unmolested. They declared it would almost certainly be sunk when it left fully laden.

For the same reason, the Spanish sailors were feted in the dockside taverns that evening by many who, while welcoming the much needed temporary employment the sailors had brought to the Charlestown dockers, feared they would not survive the U-boat menace on the return voyage.

When the same Spanish vessel returned to Charlestown to take on another cargo nine days later, no one celebrated the occasion with greater fervour than Ben Retallick. There was an extra ten shillings in the wage packet of every one of his workers and the captains of the works and each of the shift captains, together with their wives, joined him at Tregarrick in a celebratory dinner.

Within a month a second Spanish cargo ship had joined the first and then a Swedish ship docked, closely followed by one from Mexico, and the employees of Ruddlemoor and the associated works that Ben owned now needed to work extra hours in order to ensure that they all left Charlestown with full cargo holds.

Ruddlemoor's hitherto flagging profits rose to new heights. The overseas buyers, starved of processed china clay for so long, were willing to pay far more for Ruddlemoor's output than was being received by those owners helping Brigadier Grove to fulfil his contract with the government – and news of Ruddlemoor's soaring profits was not slow in reaching their ears.

Stanley Spargo, owner of one of the smaller companies, was the first to come calling upon Ben, choosing to speak to him at Tregarrick rather than at the Ruddlemoor office. He arrived late on a wet summer evening, having ridden from his home at Lostwithiel, the ancient Cornish stannary town situated some eight miles from Tregarrick. After divesting himself of coat, leggings and hat in the hallway of the house and handing them to a disapproving Mrs Rodda, he was shown into the study where Ben was enjoying an after-dinner brandy.

In typical Cornish fashion, Spargo was slow in broaching the true object of his visit. He first of all commiserated with Ben on his injury, and after expressing a hope that it would soon be fully healed he related the story of a distant relative who had accidently shot himself in the leg with a hunting rifle and eventually needed to have the limb amputated.

When this long and mournful tale came to an end with the untimely death of the relative, Spargo turned to the subject of the weather, but Ben cut him short.

'You haven't ridden all this way in a downpour just to pass the time of day with me, Stanley.' Without rising to his feet Ben poured his visitor a measure of brandy, and slid it across the small table that stood between their chairs. 'Here, drink this. It's from a case brought to me by the captain of one of the Spanish ships that's loading at Charlestown. It should make you forget the weather and remember what you are here to talk about.'

Stanley Spargo took a large swig of the brandy and, when he had recovered his breath, said enviously, 'I haven't tasted brandy like that for a very long time, Ben . . . and the way things are going, I doubt if I will in the near future – if at all. In fact, I'll think myself lucky if I'm able to afford a cup of tea if things don't improve very soon.'

Feigning surprise, Ben said, 'Why is that, Stanley? I thought you and the other owners had teamed up with Brigadier Grove to supply china clay to the government? Mind you, I am only repeating hearsay; Ruddlemoor has never been invited to take part in such a scheme. In fact as I recall, you, Brigadier Grove and the other owners ridiculed such an arrangement when I suggested it at our last meeting.'

Stanley Spargo squirmed unhappily in his seat. 'Yes, I remember that, Ben, but I swear that I was not aware Ruddlemoor had not been included in the arrangement to supply the government when Grove announced he had secured the contract – and by then I and the other owners were becoming desperate. We were all losing money hand over fist.'

'I rather fancy Ruddlemoor was losing more money than all the other companies put together,' Ben retorted unsympathetically, 'yet I was still prepared to offer a scheme that would see us all remaining solvent until the situation improved. Well, it *has* improved, I'm pleased to say. Ruddlemoor is making more profit than ever before.'

Looking pained, Stanley Spargo said, 'Ruddlemoor might be doing well, Ben, but none of the rest of us are.'

'Why not?' Ben asked, again feigning surprise. 'I wouldn't expect you all to become rich men as a result of fulfilling a government contract during wartime, but it should keep you in profit, at least.'

'I have no doubt it is keeping Brigadier Grove and *his* company in profit,' Spargo said, 'but in order for the rest of us to stay in business we have to sell to him at his price. It leaves us with very little profit indeed.'

'I'm sorry, but I fail to see what this has to do with me,' Ben said. 'You and the other owners made it very clear at our last meeting that I am not a Cornishman and, although I too am in the china clay business, I am still an outsider. What's more, you have underlined the fact by reaching an agreement among yourselves that would have put Ruddlemoor out of business had I not gambled my own money by agreeing to compensate any ship owner whose vessel was sunk by a U-boat as a result of coming to Charlestown to load my clay. I would have done the same thing for the benefit of all of us – Brigadier Grove included – had you all dealt fairly and honestly with Ruddlemoor. As it is . . .'

He made a gesture of resignation, then waited for the other man to say something, but Stanley Spargo remained silent, looking unhappily into his almost empty brandy goblet.

When the silence had lasted uncomfortably long, Ben said, 'You have told me of your problems and I have told you what I have done to solve mine. Now perhaps you'll tell me exactly what it was you wanted to discuss with me when you came here tonight?'

Downing the last of his brandy, Spargo said, 'I think

you have answered all the questions I had in mind without my asking them – and I can't blame you for standing back and seeing us all buried in the hole we've dug for ourselves. We haven't played the game with you. For that reason alone we deserve whatever we have coming to us. None of us was happy at Ruddlemoor's not being included in Brigadier Grove's scheme, but he is the one who holds the contract and before you came along he was the clay owners' acknowledged leader. If he said "jump", no one wanted to be the last man seen to do it. When he said he would take our clay no one questioned whether any company was being left out. We all know he is receiving far more money per ton than he gives to us, but that's business. Until now it has been enough to ensure our survival, but times are getting harder and the profit margin has narrowed too much.'

Moved by Stanley Spargo's apparent honesty and sincerity, Ben said, 'I would not be happy to see anyone go under, but surely Grove will give you a little more if you and the others explain your problem? After all, your clay is important to him if he is to meet the terms of his contract with the government.'

As he spoke he was pouring more brandy into Stanley Spargo's glass and the clay works owner gratefully took another large swig before replying. 'The government contract is not for a regular amount, Ben. It isn't even worked out on a monthly basis. The requirements are worked out little more than a week in advance. On a good week they will take all we can produce. At other times they might cut their requirements by as much as sixty per cent. Naturally, when that happens Grove's clay takes priority. If the poor weeks come too often our stock piles become dangerously high and we need to slow production and lay men off. That's not good for us – and it's worse for the men and their families. They never know from one week to the next what money will be coming into the house.'

Ben sipped his own brandy in silence for longer than a minute. When he spoke again, he said, 'As you agreed just now, from Ruddlemoor's point of view you and the other owners deserve all that's happening to you – but the men and their families don't. This war is causing them enough grief and suffering without being forced to lead a hand-to-mouth existence. How much clay can you produce each month?'

Spargo immediately quoted a figure that was no more than a fraction of Ruddlemoor's regular output.

'Very well, I'll take all you can produce.' Ben went on to quote the price he was willing to pay. It would give him a comfortable profit, yet was far in excess of the price being paid to Spargo by Brigadier Grove.

Spargo began to thank him, but he cut him short. 'Before you get too carried away, I have a number of stipulations to make.'

Fearing the worst, Stanley Spargo felt his elation fade. He asked anxiously, 'What are they, Ben? If I can meet them, I will.'

'First of all, my works captain will inspect your clay to ensure that it meets Ruddlemoor standards. Second, for the duration of this arrangement I will take all your production that comes up to the Ruddlemoor standard. That means you will not sell to Grove – or to anyone else – without my written permission. Third, you will sign a contract that I will have drawn up by my solicitor setting out these conditions and making them legally binding. Is that agreed?'

Greatly relieved that Ben's provisos were not more stringent, Spargo agreed readily and the men shook hands to seal their new alliance.

Later that evening, Stanley Spargo left Tregarrick and rode off in the rain somewhat unsteady from the quantity of brandy he had consumed, but far happier than when he had arrived. When he had gone, Ben contemplated the implications of the deal that had been agreed. It made good financial sense for Ruddlemoor, as they would be able to increase their clay exports even more. It also meant that if other clay owners followed Spargo's example Brigadier Grove would find it extremely difficult to fulfil the requirements of his government contract.

It raised some very interesting possibilities.

II

Within two weeks of Stanley Spargo's signing a contract to supply refined china clay to Ben, five other works owners had followed his example on similar terms and rumours began to circulate that Brigadier General Sir Robert Grove's company was having difficulty fulfilling the terms of his government contract.

Ben had successfully turned the tables on his business rival. Although he had no wish to gloat over his success, he could not bring himself to feel any sympathy for the conniving brigadier.

Ships from many neutral countries continued to take on clay at Charlestown, and although two of the vessels were stopped and boarded on the high seas by U-boat crews they had been allowed to continue on their way after no more than a cursory inspection.

Meanwhile, Ben was kept informed by Lieutenant General Carey Hamilton of the progress of the 'Lake Tanganyika Expedition' and the well-being of Sam Hooper. As a result, he was able to tell Mrs Hooper that Sam was well, giving her the impression that his information had been conveyed in telegraphic messages from his family. Betsy Hooper was delighted to be given his up-to-date reports. She was receiving an occasional letter from Sam, but it was always dated weeks before its arrival. She was not to know that in order not to prejudice the security of the expedition all letters were being sent back to South Africa for posting in Cape Town.

Carey Hamilton had informed Ben that, contrary to the expectations of its many sceptics, the expedition was progressing remarkably well, but had not yet reached the area where the power of the huge Ruddlemoor traction engines – and Sam's expertise – would be fully put to the test. The expedition with its two boats would be carried through Africa by rail for the first 2,700 miles, a difficult journey in itself given the primitive state of the railroad and its rolling stock. Once it reached the rail-head at Fungurume, a village which was little more than a name on the unreliable map of the Belgian Congo, the two traction engines would be required to pull the two gunboats 150 miles on improvised trailers, over a moun-

150

tain range and through largely uncharted bush country, to an equally obscure trading post named Sankisia.

From here it was hoped that a narrow-gauge railway would prove capable of carrying the two diminutive warships 15 miles to the Lualaba river. Once at the river, the plan was to return the boats to their natural element. Guided by a small steamboat they would then proceed under their own power for a further 200 miles on their journey towards Lake Tanganyika.

The problem was that between Fungurume and Sankisia, in the daunting mountain range, there were numerous gullies and dried up river beds which could suddenly become raging torrents should there be a storm higher in the mountains. In addition, there were numerous wild and dangerous animals – and it was known to be a breeding ground for the dreaded tsetse fly which carried a parasite which caused an invariably fatal sleeping sickness in humans. Then, of course, as the expedition neared Lake Tanganyika there was always the danger of an attack by the very active and innovative German army, led by a truly brilliant officer, General Paul Emil von Lettow-Vorbeck.

Nevertheless, Carey Hamilton and his fellow officers who had lent their support to the improbable expedition were extremely pleased with the progress it was making.

While the secret expedition made its ponderous way through Africa, Brigadier General Sir Robert Grove returned to Cornwall. It was conveyed to Ben, via Captain Bray and the works captain of the rival company, that he was livid about the defection of so many of his colleagues to Ruddlemoor. Ben realised it was only a question of time before he was subjected to his wrath. In the meantime, he received far more pleasant and exciting news.

He was seated in the study at Tregarrick, writing a letter to his mother in Insimo, when the telephone rang. Picking it up, he was greeted by Antonia's voice.

'Hello, Ben. How is the leg healing?' It was a routine question and one she asked in each of the twice weekly telephone calls she had made to him since his release from hospital.

'It's coming along fine,' he replied. 'I don't think I will ever lose my limp, but I only need to use a stick if I am going to walk any distance. Around the house I can manage without it for much of the time. But how are you? Still as busy as ever with your wounded soldiers?'

'No, there seems to be a lull in the fighting at the moment. If only it would last! But because of the break I am able to do something I have been thinking about ever since I was in Cornwall. If I came to work at Bodmin for a while, does your offer of accommodation still hold good?'

Delighted, Ben said, 'Of course! It would be wonderful to have you here. When do you think you might be coming?'

'Next week, in time for the weekend,' was her surprising news. 'My government has not only given its approval for me to work at Bodmin, but has expressed great interest in the work being carried out by Dr Olaf

152

Ericsson. His research is beginning to achieve world-wide recognition and he is in desperate need of an assistant. It could well become a permanent – and important – post.'

'Then I will feel privileged as well as delighted to have you stay here at Tregarrick. Do you drive?'

Taken by surprise by the question, Antonia said, 'No . . . is it of importance?'

'It will certainly give you a greater degree of independence,' Ben replied. 'I'll make enquiries and see if I can obtain a little motor car for you. If I can't find one immediately I will teach you to drive in the Hotchkiss. It should be fun . . . for both of us!'

'I hope so,' Antonia said, somewhat uncertainly. 'By the way, have you heard from Sam since you sent him to Africa?'

'Yes, I have had a couple of letters from him. Why do you ask?'

'I have had a letter from a friend of mine, Maria, a nurse from Mozambique. She was working with me here in London until recently, but she decided to return home. She travelled to South Africa on the same ship as Sam. She has an African mother and a European father, but she favours her mother. It seems there was also a party of Afrikaners on board who objected so strongly about sharing the dining room with her that she was forced to eat alone, in her cabin – despite the fact that the Afrikaners had been in London to protest about the internment of hardline Boers who had been fighting for the Germans in South West Africa. Sam was outraged and demanded that she be allowed to eat with

153

the others. He won the day, with the result that the Afrikaners left the ship at Lisbon.'

'Good for Sam!' Ben said enthusiastically. 'I recognised some years ago that that quiet manner of his was deceptive and should not be mistaken for weakness. There is something very special about him. The events of recent months have proved me right.'

'Probably more right than we all realise,' Antonia said. 'It seems the ship was carrying an important cargo. When Sam and Maria were ashore together in Lisbon they saw the leader of the Afrikaans delegation leaving the German embassy. When he and the others of his party unexpectedly announced that they were leaving the ship and would find another to take them to South Africa, Sam told the captain what they had seen. The captain felt the information was so important that he delayed the ship's sailing and informed the British admiralty. They sent two destroyers from Gibraltar to escort the ship and after they left Lisbon a U-boat was sighted. The destroyers attacked it and it was probably sunk. At any rate, it was not seen again.'

Aware that the U-boat might have been trying to prevent the arrival of the two traction engines in South Africa, Ben decided he would pass Antonia's news on to Carey Hamilton, but all he said to Antonia was, 'It sounds as though Sam and your friend have been having an exciting time – almost as exciting as having you come to Tregarrick to stay!'

'I am very happy that you are pleased, Ben. I thought you might have just been being polite when you issued the invitation.'

'Certainly not! I am delighted that you are coming here. Mrs Rodda will be, too. She said that when you last visited, Tregarrick came to life again for a while. I can't wait to tell her the news.'

III

Mrs Rodda decided that the arrival of Antonia to stay at Tregarrick should be treated as an occasion to celebrate. For days the servants were kept busy cleaning and preparing the rooms she would occupy in the west wing, and on the morning of her anticipated arrival the housekeeper had the gardener gather armfuls of flowers to fill the rooms with the heady scent of roses and add the colour of a variety of exotic and traditional flowers from garden and greenhouse.

Ben had been busy too. He had managed to acquire a small Warren Lambert two-seater motor car for Antonia. It had been only a few weeks old when its owner went off to war, only to be wounded and taken prisoner on the day his regiment moved up to the front line. His wealthy mother, widowed in the Boer war, was greatly relieved that her son, although wounded, would be relatively safe for the remainder of the war. In selling the vehicle to Ben, she said she did not want the car to be laid up to await his return. Instead, she was selling it now and would buy a new model to celebrate his homecoming, when that happy event occurred.

Ben intended that the vehicle would be a present from himself to welcome Antonia to Cornwall. Although he was still not driving himself, his leg had healed sufficiently for him to accompany Antonia on the road – once she had mastered the elements of driving on the driveways of Tregarrick.

Antonia arrived late on an autumnal afternoon and was delighted with the welcome she received from the servants, who lined up outside the main entrance to the house to greet her. She was also thrilled with her motor car and with the suite of rooms prepared for her in Tregarrick's west wing. She had a break of three days before she needed to assume her new post at the Bodmin hospital and promised Ben that in this time she would master the art of driving the Warren Lambert.

She set about the task with great determination and on the third day ventured out on the lane that passed by Tregarrick. So confident was she that she announced she intended driving herself to Bodmin the next day. However, that evening she persuaded Ben to accompany her on the public highway once more and they were not far from Tregarrick when they encountered a herd of cows being moved along the narrow lane.

Antonia succeeded in stopping the small car, but in so doing she stalled the engine. It was in a very narrow part of the lane and as the cows passed by they jostled the car and it rocked alarmingly, causing Antonia to squeal in alarm. When the last cow had passed by an apprehensive Ben alighted and inspected the motor for damage. Amazingly, it was nothing more serious than a bent mudguard, which Ben was able to straighten with very little effort. Reluctantly, Antonia conceded that she was not yet ready to take to the road on her own, but in retrospect she found the experience amusing rather than frightening and was still laughing happily when they returned to Tregarrick and entered the house together.

Following Antonia to her rooms, Mrs Rodda pointed out a trunk of her belongings, which had arrived while she had been out driving. After ascertaining that Antonia would unpack the trunk herself and did not require the services of a maid, the housekeeper said, 'It has been a very long time since there was such laughter in Tregarrick, Dr St Anna. The servants are absolutely delighted. It was good to hear Mr Retallick laughing too. There has been little humour in his life since poor Mrs Retallick was taken off to Switzerland.'

'Yes, Ben has had a miserable time,' Antonia agreed. 'I am only sorry that I was never able to visit Tregarrick while his wife was alive. I believe she was a very nice woman.' As she had hoped, the statement provoked Mrs Rodda into telling her something about the woman Ben had married and lost.

'Yes, Mistress Lily was both kind and generous, and she thought the world of her husband. He bought this house for her before he had even proposed, you know? When she first came to live at Tregarrick the sheer size of the place terrified her, but she soon settled in. It was she who planned the garden the way you see it today. She came to love the house as much as Mr Retallick does.'

'Was she ill for very long before Ben took her to Switzerland, Mrs Rodda?'

'Yes, for nigh on a couple of years. Although I would never tell Mr Retallick, she once told me that if she ever

157

went away to Switzerland, as all the special doctors said she should, she would never see Tregarrick again.'

Startled, Antonia said, 'She actually said that to you? She believed that if she went away she would never return home?'

'She said far more than that, Dr St Anna. She was so convinced she was going to die that she even spoke to me about what might happen to Mr Retallick when she was gone. She hoped he would meet someone who wanted him for himself and not for what he possessed. There was a young woman who visited Tregarrick about that time who she believed would be absolutely right for him. Because of this she had her here as often as possible. The young woman even met them when they were passing through Paris, on their way to the hospital in Switzerland. Unfortunately, she was one of those "suffragettes".'

Loudly sniffing her disapproval of 'suffragettes' in general, Mrs Rodda continued, 'If you ask me, she was a bit too forward in her ways. Young Emma Cotton, as was, who's now married to Jacob Pengelly, was a companion to Mrs Retallick at the time and knew this suffragette, having been one herself and them both being put in prison together. Anyway, she told me that poor Mrs Retallick did her best to throw Mr Retallick and this young woman together as much as she could, even while she was on her way to the hospital in Switzerland. Emma told me that she thought Mistress Lily had succeeded in what she was trying to do, but I can't make any comment about that.'

Deeply interested, Antonia said, 'This woman . . . has Ben seen anything of her since Lily died?'

Mrs Rodda shook her head. 'No . . . and he won't.

As I've said, I didn't care too much for her myself, but she is no longer with us and I'll not say anything bad about her. The truth is that she died as brave a death as any man who has ever gone off to war.'

'She is dead too?' Antonia's interest was thoroughly aroused by now. 'How did it happen?'

Mrs Rodda enjoyed gossiping, and it was a long time since she had been able to tell this particular story to anyone. 'When the war began, most of the suffragettes stopped all their nonsense in order to show they could serve their country as well as any man. She and Emma were both driving ambulances right up close to the trenches in France to bring wounded soldiers back to hospitals in Paris. One day, while they were up at the front, the Germans shelled their ambulances. The young woman was badly hurt and died in hospital in Paris. Mr Retallick happened to be there at the time, on his way back from a visit to Switzerland. I believe he was with her when she died. He never said anything about it at the time, but I heard him tell Emma once that he felt she should have been given a medal for all that she had done. But there, it's all water under the bridge now. As I said to you earlier, your laughter is like a breath of fresh air in Tregarrick. Perhaps things will start looking up again now.'

When Mrs Rodda had left the room, Antonia stared out of the window across the garden and thought of what had been said. She decided she would like to meet Emma Pengelly sometime and chat to her about the ex-suffragette who had been part of Ben's life, albeit for only a very short time.

She doubted very much whether Ben could ever be persuaded to talk about her.

IV

That evening brought two separate visitors to Tregarrick. The last to arrive was not at all welcome – but Ben could not make his mind up about the other.

The man who provoked his uncertainty was Dr Olaf Ericsson, the medical specialist who was fast becoming the world's leading consultant on the effects upon fighting men of prolonged exposure to the stresses of modern warfare.

Ericsson was much younger than Ben had thought he would be, being probably no more than a couple of years older than Ben himself. He was also tall, blond-haired, possessed of an athletic physique – and extremely handsome.

He greeted Antonia with a familiarity which took Ben by surprise. After he had kissed her on both cheeks and embraced her warmly, Ben was left with the impression that their relationship was based on something a little more personal than a mutual interest in psychological medicine. He found the thought far more disturbing than it should have been.

When Ericsson was introduced to Ben he displayed a pronounced Scandinavian accent – and a charm that matched his appearance.

'I am so pleased to be meeting you, Mr Retallick. It is very kind of you to offer Antonia accommodation in your beautiful house and so enable her to come and help me with my work – but, of course, how could she refuse? I will never know whether it is my work or this house that persuaded her to come to Cornwall. If I had such a wonderful home I would never wish to spend time anywhere else in the world.'

After agreeing that Tregarrick was indeed a very special place, Ben and Antonia escorted the eminent doctor inside, where Mrs Rodda produced tea and a variety of home-made cakes and scones.

Later that evening, while Ben was taking the two doctors on a tour of the gardens, they heard a motor car coming along the driveway to Tregarrick. Apologising to his guests, he left them admiring an enclosed garden that contained some thirty varieties of fuchsias and went to meet the new arrival.

It was Brigadier General Sir Robert Grove and his manner was in sharp contrast to the earlier visitor's. Wasting no time on polite greetings, he said, 'So there you are, Retallick! I doubted whether you would dare show your face to me again after your skulduggery forced me to return to Cornwall before you drove me into bankruptcy.'

'Skulduggery, Sir Robert?' Ben feigned shock. 'Surely not? Business is about making profit – you might remember using those very words to me at our last meeting, when you rejected out of hand any suggestion that we should co-operate to supply the government with our product at the lowest possible price?'

Some of Grove's bluster left him, but only for a moment. Recovering swiftly, he said, 'That was before any of us had thought the matter through properly.

161

When the government came along and offered me a firm contract it was a different matter entirely. I immediately involved all the other clay owners in discussions. Ruddlemoor would have been included too had you not been in France and impossible to get in touch with.'

Ben was aware that this was a blatant lie. Jim Bray had learned from his colleagues in the other works that the contract between Brigadier Grove and the government had been agreed, if not already signed, at the time when Ben was urging co-operation upon the other owners. Grove should have known that secrets did not remain secret for very long in Cornwall, especially in the tightly knit communities in which the clay captains lived.

But he revealed nothing of these thoughts, saying instead, 'I realise that my absence must have made a great difference to you, Brigadier; indeed, your own absence was the reason you were not immediately made aware of my own plans. Such a lack of co-operation might easily have proved disastrous – for both of us. Fortunately, I am able to benefit from my overseas market, while you have your government contract. We will both get by.'

Aware that Ben was being intentionally provocative, Brigadier Grove felt his anger flare up once more. 'Damn you, Retallick, you know full well that I have no chance of fulfilling the government contract without being able to call upon the other owners for clay – and you have seen to it that I am prevented from doing much of that.'

'It's a free market, Brigadier,' Ben said cheerfully. 'If those who haven't signed contracts with me are willing to sell to you – at your price – I will do nothing to prevent them. Neither would I want to see you suffer bankruptcy. I'll tell you what I'll do. If you find you have a shortfall on your quota for the government, I'll make it up with Ruddlemoor clay.'

Astounded by what appeared to be Ben's naive generosity, Brigadier Grove was about to thank him when Ben added, 'Of course, as you have so wisely pointed out in the past, business is business, so I couldn't possibly consider selling Ruddlemoor clay at a loss. You can have as much clay as you want, but I could not sell it for less than . . .'

Ben quoted the exact price he knew Grove was receiving from the government under the terms of his contract with them. There would be no profit for him in such an arrangement. Smiling benignly at his business rival, Ben said, 'I think you will agree that my offer is a generous one – in the circumstances.' Then, rubbing salt into the wound, he added, 'It is far less than I am receiving for the clay I am exporting abroad.'

Brigadier Grove was so angry now that Ben thought he might explode, but he was forced to swallow his pride. So many clay owners had gone over to Ben, or were in the process of doing so, that without Ruddlemoor clay he would be unable to fulfil the requirements of the government contract and as a result would suffer crippling penalties. Knowing he had no alternative, he accepted with bad grace before stalking away muttering to himself. Along the way he brushed angrily past Antonia and Dr Ericsson, ignoring their friendly greeting.

'What a rude man,' Antonia said indignantly, when she and Olaf joined up with Ben. 'Surely he is not one of your friends, Ben?'

Ben smiled. 'No. In fact he is a business rival – and an unscrupulous one. He obtained a contract that was calculated to destroy Ruddlemoor, but I have succeeded in turning the tables on him. Sadly, I doubt whether I have heard the last of the matter. I sometimes think that Brigadier General Sir Robert Grove spends more time scheming to put me out of business than he does on making money for his own company.'

7

I

When the train carrying Sam and the traction engines pulled into Bulawayo railway station, in the heart of Rhodesia's Matabeleland, where Sam had been told he would find Acting Commander Spicer, the leader of the Lake Tanganyika Naval Expedition was on the platform waiting impatiently for his arrival.

With him was a naval officer in his fifties, with dyed blond hair, wearing a monocle and, despite his age, exhibiting the single bar of a lowly sub-lieutenant on his epaulettes. He introduced himself as Sub-lieutenant Tyrer, 'aide-de-camp' to Acting Commander Spicer.

The expedition leader did not come forward to greet Sam, but waited until the latter came to him – and he was in no mood for pleasantries. His first words to Sam carried no greeting.

'What do you mean by bringing the traction engines up here ahead of the boats?' he snapped. 'I gave you no orders to that effect. It is possible you have prejudiced the secrecy of the whole expedition. The Germans have a great many friends in South Africa. Friends who will no doubt tell them about two machines setting off on a mysterious journey to the heart of Africa. Apart from which, word has reached me that you have been consorting with a native woman while in Cape Town. No doubt you have boasted to her of my purpose here?'

Maria and Sam had been parted abruptly when the Portuguese government representative in Cape Town had sent her post haste to a hospital in neighbouring South West Africa where there was a desperate need of medical staff to treat wounded soldiers of the Rhodesian Native Regiment who had been fighting in the German colony. Many of the Rhodesian troops were from a tribe which occupied land straddling the Rhodesia–Mozambique border and Maria was fluent in their language.

Angered by Spicer's description of her, Sam replied, 'The "native woman", as you call her, happens to be a Portuguese nurse who has been tending British soldiers in London – and her astuteness probably saved the traction engines and the ship on which we were travelling from being sunk by a German submarine. As for my being here now . . . you left no orders at all for me in Cape Town. I used my initiative by getting the traction engines out of South Africa and to the place for which they are supposed to be destined – Rhodesia.'

Sam had been hoping that the expedition leader's attitude towards him at their last meeting had been a result of tension, because of the immensity of the daunting task he faced. Now he realised it was Spicer's everyday manner – and it had the same effect upon him as before. He added, 'I suggest that two traction engines will excite a great deal less speculation than the sight of two gunboats being carried to the heart of Africa.'

'You suggest . . . ?' Spicer spluttered. 'You suggest . . . ?' Turning to his monocled ADC, he snapped, 'Have the traction engines off-loaded here, then you can deal with Hooper. I want nothing more to do with him.'

As Spicer turned away, his ADC, seemingly unperturbed by the contretemps he had just witnessed, called after him. 'You have not forgotten that General Edwards has said he wants to see you in his Bulawayo office – with Hooper – immediately upon his arrival?'

'I have forgotten nothing,' Spicer snapped. 'Hopefully, General Edwards has heard of Hooper's disgusting lack of morals and will send him back to England and find me a new engineer.'

'The traction engines belong to Ruddlemoor,' Sam retorted, angered by Spicer's continued denigration of Maria. 'If I go back to Cornwall they go with me, and from what Mr Retallick told me of the country where they are needed you can forget all about your precious expedition without them.'

Ignoring Sam, Spicer turned to Sub-lieutenant Tyrer once more, '*You* take him to General Edwards. I will come there as soon as I have compiled a report on his unsuitability for inclusion on my expedition.'

When Spicer stalked away, Tyrer looked at Sam sympathetically. 'You must not take him too seriously, dear boy; he is simply letting off steam. He has a lot on his mind right now.'

'When times are hard a man needs friends about him, not enemies,' Sam commented. 'Perhaps someone should tell him.'

'Not me, dear boy, and if you take a tip from me, you will not try to tell him either. Lieutenant Commander . . . I beg your pardon, Acting *Commander* Spicer, has been given a chance to make a name for himself after a lifetime of somewhat mediocre naval service. He is determined not to allow such an opportunity to slip from his grasp and neither friendship nor enmity comes into the equation. I do not think Spicer will be in any hurry to get to the army headquarters, so we will make arrangements to have your traction engines unloaded. When they are safely locked away we will pop into the club and have a snifter before going to see General Edwards.'

After securing the traction engines the two men spent an hour in the Bulawayo services club before making their way to army headquarters to see General Edwards, the officer commanding the region. He was in a meeting which did not break up for another half-hour, by which time Spicer had arrived as well.

The three men were ushered into the general's office. He rose to his feet as they entered. After briefly acknowledging the two naval men, he beamed at Sam and advanced towards him, holding out his hand and saying, 'I have been looking forward to meeting you, Hooper. There are not too many occasions, even in the life of a senior army officer, when one has an opportunity to shake hands with a true hero. Please accept my heartiest congratulations.'

168

Thoroughly baffled by the general's effusive greeting, Sam observed that Spicer and Tyrer seemed equally at a loss.

'Congratulations . . . ? For what?' he asked.

Momentarily taken aback, General Edwards said, 'Good gracious . . . are you telling me I am the first to break the news to you? I felt quite certain someone in Cape Town would have told you.' Smiling at Sam, he said, 'You have been awarded an Albert medal, my boy . . . the highest award that can be presented to a civilian, and having read the citation I consider it thoroughly well deserved.'

Still confused, Sam said, 'A medal . . . for what? What am I supposed to have done?'

'There is no *supposed* about it,' General Edwards replied. 'I believe you entered a burning house and rescued a woman and her three children after the first Zeppelin raid on London, did you not?'

'Yes, but . . .'

'There are no buts, Mr Hooper. A report on your actions was sent to the appropriate authorities by Lieutenant General Carey Hamilton – who happens to be a personal friend of mine – and was endorsed by a number of other eye witnesses. I regret that I cannot personally present you with the medal itself, that duty will be performed by His Majesty the King when you return to England, but I have had a very clever local seamstress make up a medal ribbon from coloured silk thread. I am aware that you do not wear uniform, but I have taken the liberty of having the ribbon stitched to a service shirt which I should like you to wear on all suitable occasions.' Turning his attention to Spicer, who appeared stunned by the astonishing turn of events, the general said, 'I suggest that you hold a parade in Hooper's honour when you have all your men together. It should give a welcome boost to their morale. You are fortunate to have such a man on your expedition, Spicer . . . and while we are talking of Hooper and the part he will be playing in your expedition, I would like to congratulate you on having the traction engines sent out of South Africa and brought to Rhodesia. It should allay any unwelcome suspicion and so avoid the possibility of having them wilfully damaged by more militant German supporters, who are unfortunately still active down there. I suggest you get your boats out quickly too, although I understand they are in the naval base at present, and two such vessels will hardly be out of place there. I must say I am impressed with the thought and planning that has gone into the expedition so far. Well done.'

The report Spicer had written about Sam's unsuitability for inclusion on the expedition was burning a hole in his pocket, but he knew he could not possibly deliver it now. Avoiding Sam's eyes, he replied, 'Thank you, sir. I will try to ensure that the remainder of our long journey goes just as smoothly.'

II

The day after his interview with General Edwards was the hottest Sam had experienced since arriving in Africa – and possibly the hottest he had ever known in his

170

young life – yet he felt the traction engines should be run up before being cleaned and greased in preparation for their long journey through Africa.

It was the first opportunity there had been to carry out the work since disembarking from the *Tamerlane*. Stripped to the waist, he had the first of the engines running in a small corral-type area outside the barn where they were garaged and an audience of a couple of dozen Africans had gathered to view the great machines with considerable interest.

Sam had built up a good head of steam in the vehicle's boiler and was making a few adjustments to the various gauges when a tall sun-tanned man in his mid-thirties pushed his way through the Africans. Reaching the wooden rails surrounding the paddock he watched Sam and the traction engine for some minutes. Then, ducking between the rails, he advanced towards them. Sam straightened up and used a forearm to wipe perspiration from his face before towelling oil-blackened hands with a piece of cloth as the uninvited visitor to the cattle pen reached him. Indicating the traction engines, he said, 'They are rather splendid machines.'

Despite a degree of wariness, there was pride in Sam's voice when he replied, 'You won't find finer or more powerful traction engines anywhere in the world.'

'I don't doubt it,' the stranger said. 'Ben would never accept anything but the best.' With a smile, he added, 'I am Nathan Retallick . . . Nat. Ben is my young brother. I understand that you and your machines are officially consigned to my farm at Insimo?'

'Yes . . . and I'm delighted to meet you, sir.' Sam

extended a hand to Nat – and as quickly withdrew it. 'Sorry, but I'm covered in oil.' He looked at the neat, sand-brown shirt and trousers of the other man. 'If you get any of it on your clothes you'll have the devil's own job to get it out.'

'Then we'll consider ourselves as being introduced,' Nat said. 'I already know your name is Sam. I had a hastily written and guarded note from Ben telling me you would be arriving in Rhodesia. Not that your expedition is particularly secret; people here have been talking about it for weeks. They believe it stands no chance of success. Fortunately, the Germans are of the same opinion. They are convinced it's part of an elaborate plot aimed at persuading them to abandon Lake Tanganyika . . . talking of which, unless I am mistaken, here comes the leader of the expedition himself to pay you a visit.'

Acting Commander Spicer, with Sub-lieutenant Tyrer in tow, had come through the barn housing the traction engines and was advancing across the cattle pen towards them. On Spicer's face was the expression that Sam was beginning to believe was especially reserved for him.

Ignoring Nat, Spicer snapped at Sam, 'What do you think you are doing? I gave you no instruction to bring your machines outside and perform to an audience!' Indicating Nat without looking directly at him, he demanded, 'And who is this? Whoever he is, he is on private property and you have no right to allow him to be here.'

Before Sam could reply, Nat said, with deceptive politeness, 'You are quite right, of course, it *is* private

172

property, but as I am the owner I suggest it is *your* presence that might be called into question.'

Momentarily taken aback, Spicer recovered swiftly. 'The ownership of the property is quite irrelevant. It has been commandeered for military use. As such, only authorised personnel are allowed admittance.'

Smiling affably, Nat replied, 'You have a quick mind, Commander, something you will undoubtedly need where you are going, but you will need more than imaginary regulations in order to succeed against General von Lettow.'

'How do you know . . . has Hooper been talking again?' Angrily, Spicer peered more closely at Nat. 'Is that an army uniform you are wearing . . . ?'

'It is,' Nat agreed. 'At least, it's as much of a uniform as most of us choose to wear when we are not on parade, or in action.'

'I don't care what you *choose* to do in this country – or anywhere else for that matter. If you wear the King's uniform then you are subject to all the regulations that come with the honour of wearing that uniform. You are improperly dressed – and you have failed to address a superior officer in a respectful manner. Tyrer . . . arrest him and take him in custody to army headquarters.'

Tyrer was not a physically large man and he looked at Spicer uncertainly. 'Arrest him, sir?'

'That's what I said,' Spicer snapped. 'Immediately.'

Seeming more amused than fearful at the prospect of being arrested, Nat said to the uncertain aide-de-camp, 'You lay a hand on me and you'll end up flat on your back with a bloody nose – and a broken monocle.'

173

Satisfied that Tyrer was unlikely to make any rash move upon him, Nat returned his attention to Spicer. 'As I have already said, *Acting* Commander Spicer, we do not stand on ceremony here in Africa, but since, despite the very unorthodox nature of your expedition, you feel the need to quote the rule book, we will play your game – for a while, at least.'

As he was talking, Nat had been feeling inside a breast pocket of his army-type shirt. Now, pulling out two epaulettes, he attached them to the shoulders of his shirt and Sam observed that each was decorated with a crown and two diamond-shaped 'pips'. Tyrer immediately sprang to attention, while Spicer looked at Nat with disbelief.

The recipient of his look said, 'You will, of course, recognise the insignia of a colonel, *Acting* Commander Spicer – a *full* colonel. Colonel Nathan Retallick, commanding officer of scouts and intelligence for General Edwards. It was he who told me of your expedition. It was a very necessary briefing as it will be my responsibility to ensure there are no Germans in the area of Lake Tanganyika to interfere with your plans . . . whatever they may be. The general and I have also decided that as the two traction engines have been consigned ostensibly for use at Insimo and I happen to have two suitable railway wagons capable of carrying them, it will allay any curiosity about their real purpose if they and Sam are taken to Insimo until you are ready for them to be sent to Fungurume. I understand that is not likely to be until your two gunboats are already there?' Without waiting for Spicer's reply, he added, 'I will have the traction engines loaded and taken to Insimo later today.'

'If you have railway stock capable of carrying traction engines it can be linked to the train carrying my boats and travel with them . . . sir.' The deferential 'sir' was added grudgingly in response to Nat's stern expression and a raised eyebrow.

'The railway line to Insimo is a private narrow-gauge line,' Nat replied. 'Even if this were not so it would take more than one engine to pull a train of such weight and there are no extra engines to spare this far north. Now, if you have nothing more to say I have no doubt you have much to do. You will keep General Edwards informed of your plans and he will pass them on to me. We may or may not meet again in the Lake Tanganyika area, but my men will be there to ensure your safety. It only remains for me to wish you well on a difficult and imaginative task. Succeed and you will have made a significant contribution to the war in Africa. You may carry on now, Acting Commander Spicer.'

As Sam had realised, even before leaving England, Spicer did not take easily to having anyone else make decisions about what he considered to be entirely *his* expedition, but Nat Retallick had left him with no choice about the disposition of the two traction engines. It was also apparent to the commanding officer of the Tanganyika expedition that not only did Nat outrank him, but he was also a man of considerable wealth and influence. There were very few men, whatever their means, who could lay claim to owning their own private railway. He also realised that Nat was close to General Edwards.

Swallowing his damaged pride, Spicer attempted to retrieve what authority he still possessed in the present situation. 'Thank you for your assistance, Colonel Retallick. You can be quite certain I will acquaint the War Office and the Admiralty in London of your co-operation.' Then, with no further acknowledgement of the presence of Sam, Spicer gave Nat a stiff salute before turning away and leaving the cattle pen, closely followed by his aide-de-camp.

When he had passed out of hearing, Nat exclaimed, 'What a pompous little man! But perhaps I am being unduly critical. How do you and the other members of the expedition get along with him?'

'I can't speak for the others,' Sam replied, 'but he and I fell out the first time we met, with the result that I travelled to Africa with the traction engines on a separate ship. Not that I minded – I could keep an eye on the engines, and had a far more enjoyable voyage than had I gone with Spicer. When we met again here we seem to have resumed where we left off.' Looking gratefully at Nat, he said, 'I am very happy to have the opportunity to visit Insimo. A few weeks ago I was in London with Ben . . . Mr Retallick, and with Captain St Anna and Dr Antonia. Much of their talk was of Insimo and I was hoping I might be able to see it for myself while I was in Africa.'

'Ah yes! Antonia and Philippe spent a great deal of their childhood at Insimo – and their grandmother is still living there. She is a remarkable old lady . . . perhaps "indomitable" is a better word. At any rate, she is still a force to be reckoned with. The story of her life would make your hair stand on end.'

176

Casually – perhaps a trifle *too* casually – Nat added, 'Someone else who lives at Insimo is Diego Fernandes. I believe you voyaged from England with one of his many sisters? She wrote to him from Cape Town, telling him a great deal about you. You made quite an impression on her and seem to have had an eventful voyage together!'

'There was an incident on board the ship involving a group of pro-German Afrikaners,' Sam explained. 'They objected to sharing a meal table with Maria and I took her part. She is a very attractive and intelligent woman and has all the good manners that the Afrikaners lacked. I look forward to meeting her brother.'

'He too is a very bright young man,' Nat commented. 'Unfortunately, you will learn that there are many in Rhodesia who share the views of those you met on the ship when it comes to Africans and those of mixed race – and not all such bigots are Afrikaners. We run a school at Insimo for the children of our Matabele workers, but there are times when I wonder whether we are doing them any favours by educating them. There are far too many whites in the country who resent those they refer to as "uppity Kaffirs", and give a very hard time to some of our boys – and girls – when they go out into the world to try to better themselves.'

'Maria has certainly made good use of her education,' Sam said. 'She has been nursing wounded British soldiers in a London hospital and is returning to Portuguese East Africa to help set up a hospital in the country.'

'There is a much narrower gulf between the races in

her country,' Nat admitted. 'And Maria's father is a white man with quite a lot of influence there. He also has five wives!'

Startled, Sam echoed, 'Five wives? Maria mentioned very little about her family. She certainly never hinted that her father kept a harem!'

Nat was amused by Sam's reaction to his revelation. 'Having many wives is an indication of wealth and importance among the tribes and it's a custom that appeals to some Europeans – a number of them right here in Rhodesia. One man I know has more than five wives and has certainly sired more than the twenty-three brothers and sisters that Maria and Diego have.' He turned to more practical issues. 'When you have finished what needs to be done here, we'll get your two machines down to the station. In the meantime I will have the trucks coupled up to an engine and brought alongside the loading platform. We'll need to get to Insimo before dark. There is a large elephant herd on the move in the area and a pair of rhinos have been making a nuisance of themselves along the line. I doubt if Acting Commander Spicer would be too pleased if we allowed anything to happen to Ben's traction engines at this stage. He needs everything to go right for him if he is to get to Lake Tanganyika before the rainy season begins.'

III

The Insimo valley was all that Sam had imagined it would be, and more. The lands owned by the Retallick

178

family extended from the summits of the ranges of hills on either side of the wide, upland valley and took in the whole of its ten-mile length. Within these extensive borders were citrus orchards, fields of tall maize and root vegetables, and vast herds of cattle and horses. There were also at least two large native kraals, laid out in a far neater fashion than any Sam had seen elsewhere.

The railway line ran along the whole length of the valley and, at the far end, just before the land dropped away dramatically to plains that extended as far as the eye could see, were a small number of neat, whitewashed houses, the largest of which nestled among flowering trees and shrubs yet retained panoramic views of the plains.

As the small train, crewed by a cheerful Matabele driver and his fireman, slowed, Sam commented on the tranquillity of the setting.

'It hasn't always been like this,' Nat commented grimly. 'During the war between the Boers and the British, no more than fifteen years ago, a band of Boer guerrillas raided Insimo and put the house to the torch. Earlier there had been a raid by lawless settlers from across the border. They attacked the women, killed a number of the Matabele and kidnapped and later killed the son of one of our friends who was living here. Even farther back in time Matabele war parties would often pass through the valley. It was one of these that speared my father and oldest brother to death. They would have done the same to me had not the same friend who later lost his son seized the reins of my horse and led me to safety.'

When Sam said that it was difficult to imagine such things happening in a seemingly peaceful valley, Nat said, 'Tragically, similar things are happening at this very moment in African countries to the north of us, where the British are battling with Germans and various tribes are fighting with either side whenever an opportunity occurs.'

After a few moments of deep thought, Sam asked, 'Do you really think that Spicer's boats are likely to make any difference to the fighting that's taking place up there?'

'If he succeeds in sinking the German gunboats that have control of the lake at the moment it could have a significant impact on the war in East Africa,' Nat replied seriously, 'but he will need to take the Germans by surprise and we know from some of the prisoners we have taken in the lake area that the Germans have got wind that something is being planned. Fortunately for Spicer they believe we are going to try to build boats at one of the small bases we have been able to retain on our side of the lake. They are confident they will hear about it from tribesmen who live in the area and be able to wreck the boats before they are completed. They have dismissed out of hand the possibility of gunboats being carried up through the heart of Africa and launched on the lake, armed and ready to take them on. They have *heard* that such a plan has been suggested, but laughed it off as being utter nonsense. If Spicer succeeds I think we must all forgive him for any shortcomings he might have.'

'I'll do my best,' Sam promised, 'but I am not finding it very easy at the moment.'

Just then the train came to a bone-juddering halt with a prolonged hiss of escaping steam and Nat said, 'Well, here we are, and in good time. We'll get the traction engines off-loaded and into one of the barns and I'll put a guard on them. We're not likely to be troubled by Germans, but the Matabele youngsters are an inquisitive lot. They would be all over them, inspecting every nut and bolt and going off with anything they found particularly interesting.'

'I'd rather they didn't do that,' Sam said fervently. 'I dread anything going wrong because I have only been able to bring a very limited number of spare parts. Getting any more is likely to be a nightmare.'

'It might not prove as difficult as you think,' Nathan replied. 'Being so far from civilisation we have become masters of improvisation at Insimo. Diego in particular is very clever when it comes to making or repairing parts for the machinery we have here. Come to think of it, he would be a very good man to have with you on the expedition.'

'Do you think he could learn to drive one of the engines?' Sam asked eagerly. 'I desperately need a second driver. I expected to be able to find one in Cape Town but it seems that anyone with mechanical skill goes off to make his fortune on the mines around Johannesburg as soon as he's old enough to be useful.'

'Then it's a good thing I've brought you to Insimo to meet Diego,' Nat said. 'He'll learn whatever you care to teach him in no time at all and, as the engines belong to Ben, you can have him for however long it takes Spicer to do whatever is needed.'

*

Diego did not put in an immediate appearance and one of the Matabele farmhands told Nat that he had gone to a neighbour's farm, about three hours' riding distance away, to help install a wind-powered water pump on a borehole they had recently drilled. Despite the absence of Diego, though, Nat was able to call upon the services of an impressive number of Matabele farmhands to unload the traction engines under Sam's concerned supervision.

The task was almost completed when they were joined by two elderly and very sun-tanned women. One was Elvira Retallick, mother of Nat, Adam and Ben; the other was Victoria, grandmother of Philippe and Antonia St Anna. Elvira explained that Nat's wife, Esme, had remained in the house to supervise dinner preparations for the household and its guest.

The introductions over, Nat said to the women, 'You and Sam will have a great deal to talk about. Shortly before leaving England he and Ben had dinner in London with Philippe and Antonia. He will be able to bring you up to date on how they were all looking when he was with them.'

Sure enough, when the traction engines had been safely installed in a locked barn, the two women bombarded Sam with questions as they all walked together to the house. In return for news of those whom Sam had met in England, Elvira was able to give Sam the startling news of Ben's being shot by the Caerhays gamekeeper and being treated on the spot by Antonia, who was on holiday at Tregarrick at the time. In view of the death of Ben's wife, she was eager to know whether Sam thought he might be finding solace in the company of the girl who had been a friend of the Retallick family since childhood. Both women were disappointed when Sam admitted that such a possibility had never occurred to him.

When they reached the house Sam was shown to his quarters, which were in an annexe beside Victoria's house, but had their own door to the outside. Since they were virtually self-contained, he would need to enter the main house only to take his meals with the others.

After he had been shown round, Sam said to Nat, 'All this seems just too good to be true. I wonder how long Spicer will allow me to remain here enjoying life?'

Nat smiled. 'You need not concern yourself about Spicer. He will find plenty to occupy himself at Fungurume, when he eventually arrives there. It is a desperately primitive place and the going will prove tough from there on. You can count on being at Insimo for at least a fortnight. The gunboats have not even begun their journey from the Cape and things are not done in a hurry here. Just enjoy being at Insimo and take full advantage of all it has to offer. I can promise you will never become bored.'

Sam met Diego Fernandes for the first time at dinner that evening and took a liking to him immediately. Although he was much lighter-skinned than his sister Maria, there was a strong family likeness, together with a similar open-mindedness that greatly appealed to Sam.

Diego was anxious to see the traction engines and

when the meal was over he accompanied Sam and Nat to the barn in which they were housed to inspect them by lantern light. Good-humouredly, Sam resisted Diego's plea to set them running and Maria's brother had to be content with a promise that his instruction on them would begin the following day.

Afterwards, the three men returned to the house where, together with Elvira and Victoria, they sat on the stoep drinking and talking until well into the night. When the impromptu party eventually broke up, Victoria suggested that Sam should see her to the door of her small house, which was only a short distance along a path well lit with lanterns hung from trees. Sam sensed that the suggestion was more in the nature of a command than a request and he wondered why. Not until he agreed to come inside her house and have coffee with her was he given an answer.

A huge kettle of water was simmering on a hob at the side of the fire and as Victoria busied herself making a pot of coffee, she said, 'Diego showed me a letter he received from his sister so that I could see what she had written about my granddaughter Antonia. There was a great deal in the letter about you.'

It was obvious she was expecting a reaction from him and he said, non-committally, 'We enjoyed each other's company, both on the boat and when we went ashore together in Lisbon.'

'Even though she has an African mother and – so I am given to understand – takes after her?'

Stung by her words, Sam replied, 'I can only say that if her mother is as attractive as Maria, I can understand

184

why her father married her – even though he is a white man.'

Giving him a sympathetic look, Victoria said, 'My, you *are* touchy. Things between you must be more serious than I thought. It is as well that you came in for coffee and a chat with me tonight. If you decide to take things any further with Maria you will be encumbering yourself with a burden that will prove very heavy at times, especially if you choose to remain in this part of Africa.' Putting a mug of coffee on the table in front of Sam, she looked him directly in the eyes. 'I *do* know what I'm talking about, Sam. My father was a Sam too. He fell in love with my mother, who was a woman of the Herero tribe, and they married and had me. In those days people were far more tolerant than they are today about marriage between the races, but life was never easy – and it became even harder for me as I grew older. I'm not going to bore you with details of my life, but it would have been very different had I not had the support of the Retallicks and found a refuge here, at Insimo, where I was able to bring up Therese, Antonia's mother, and secure a good marriage for her. Very few mixed-marriage couples have the same good fortune, Sam. Most find themselves outcasts from both their own peoples.'

'Are you telling me I should have nothing to do with Maria? That I should forget her? Is that what you are suggesting?' Sam demanded.

Victoria had sat down at the table close to Sam while she was talking and now she reached across and gripped his wrist tightly. 'No, Sam, that's not what I'm saying at all. To do so would be hypocritical of me. All I'm saying is that you should think very carefully of the consequences for yourself – and for Maria – before you make any firm commitment to each other. You owe it to yourself – and you owe it to her.'

Returning to the annexe later, Sam thought very carefully about his conversation with Victoria. He knew she meant well. He could also guess the reaction of his mother and the small, closely knit community in which they lived if he returned to Cornwall with Maria as his bride – but he was determined not to allow such considerations to change his mind about what he intended to do. Indeed, his chat with Victoria had actually clarified things for him.

He intended to marry Maria and take her back to Cornwall with him when he returned there.

IV

The next few days passed swiftly and happily for Sam. Diego was quick to master the skills needed to drive the giant steam-powered vehicles and displayed an impressive understanding of their mechanics.

On the fifth day of Sam's stay at Insimo, Nat returned from a visit to Bulawayo with news that the two gunboats had still not left Cape Town, and there was no immediate prospect of Sam's being required to leave. As Diego was keeping a promise he had made to complete the installation of the neighbour's water pump, Nat said he would take Sam on a three-day hunting trip to shoot game to help feed the families of his Matabele work force.

It proved a fascinating excursion for Sam. At first he found it difficult to grasp the fact that it was possible to trek for vast distances through bush country that apparently belonged to no one, but he soon began to feel the freedom that came with such a way of life. He had very little experience with firearms, but he discovered that he had a good eye when it came to shooting and he won the delighted applause of the Matabele hunters accompanying Nat and himself when, on the second day, he brought down a kudu, a giant deer that would provide meat for many of the tribesmen's families.

If it had been Nat's intention to give Sam an idea of the 'feel' of Africa, he certainly succeeded. At night Sam would lie awake beneath the vast velvet dark sky, filled with stars as numerous as pebbles on a Cornish beach, listening to the songs of the Matabele hunters as they sat round their camp fires and the many and unfamiliar sounds of the African night.

He learned to recognise the distant trumpeting of elephants and the occasional asthmatic coughing of a prowling leopard that broke in upon the chorus of frogs inhabiting the disjointed string of muddy pools along the bed of a river that would sweep all before it with the advent of the rains. There was a constant and varied noise from myriad insects, and many other alien sounds that he could not identify.

On the last night of the hunting trip, as they lay on their blankets, Nat, aware that his companion was still awake, said, 'Do you think you would enjoy living in Africa, Sam?'

'If life was like this all the time I could easily be tempted,' Sam replied.

'This is the way I remember it when I was a boy,' Nat said. 'It had changed very little from the time when my father came to Africa from Cornwall as a small child with my grandfather and grandmother. They were among the first white people to live among the Matabele.'

'They still talk about your grandfather in Cornwall,' Sam said. 'He was a much respected man there.'

'They still talk about him here in Africa,' Nat replied. 'Many of the older tribesmen say that he and my father were the only two honest white men the Matabele had ever met in the early days – and they haven't fared very much better since then.'

'Have you ever considered moving to England, as Ben did?' Sam asked.

'Never!' Nat said positively. 'I live by the principles taught to me by Father and Grandfather who were both proud of being born in England – or, more accurately, in Cornwall – but it would be a foreign country to me if I were to go there to live. Insimo is my home and the Matabele more my people than any other.'

'And yet, despite this, you are fighting for the British, and General Hamilton said you fought for them in the Boer war too. Why, if you don't consider yourself to be British?'

'That is a very good question,' Nat replied. 'I actually refused to fight for the Brits when the Boer war began because I said it wasn't my war. But then a Boer raiding party attacked Insimo and suddenly it became

188

my war – albeit a personal one. But I never felt I was fighting for any great principle. I was aware of the rights and wrongs of both sides. In fact, when I first met Esme she was actually riding with and fighting for Boer guerrillas.'

Esme, Nat's wife, had impressed Sam as being a particularly gentle woman, although a positive one, and he found it difficult to imagine her being a member of one of the highly successful, hard riding and hard fighting Boer commandos.

'She actually fought against the British army?' he asked. 'But . . . if she did that, and you don't consider yourself to be British, why have you got involved in this war against the Germans?'

'This war is rather different,' Nat explained. 'The Germans were occupying huge territories in South West and East Africa when war began. Had we stood by and done nothing they would have posed a constant threat to all of us here, even had they not actually invaded us – which they most probably would have anyway, especially as they were anticipating strong support from South Africa. We have defeated them in South West Africa, but at the moment they have the upper hand in East Africa. That's why you, Spicer and the expedition to Lake Tanganyika are so important, both to Britain and to all of us living here.'

Sam lay silently mulling over what Nat had said for a long while before asking, 'What do the Africans themselves think about all this? I mean, the tribes who are living in all these countries?'

Nat prefaced his reply with a short laugh which was,

nevertheless, lacking in humour. 'I doubt very much whether anyone, British, German, or Afrikaans, has sought their opinion, but their views will be as diverse as the tribes to which they belong. There are those who will try to gain from the situation by fighting whichever side appears to be weakest at any particular time. Others are showing a quite remarkable loyalty to their colonial overlords. The German askaris, in particular, are a force to be reckoned with, while our Rhodesian Native Regiment is fast becoming respected by both sides. My own native scouts and trackers are also worthy of respect. At this very moment they are scouring the country through which you and Spicer will need to travel, to ensure you do not have any nasty surprises. I will be joining them in a few days' time, so we must make an early start tomorrow, in order to be back at Insimo before dark. I suggest we both try to get some sleep now.'

After his conversation with Nat, Sam lay awake for a long time and had still not gone to sleep when the activity round the Matabele camp fires had died away, leaving the night to the animals, reptiles and insects of the African bush, to whom human intrusion was no more than a fleeting phenomenon. Just before falling asleep, he realised that since coming to Insimo, he had not heard anyone mention the third of the Retallick brothers . . . Adam.

8

I

'Come in.' Ben Retallick's command was in response to
a knock on the door of his study, where he was working
at his desk. When the door opened, he looked up and
was both pleased and surprised to see Antonia come
through the doorway.

'Well, this is a welcome interruption,' he said, rising
to his feet. 'It seems a very long time since we had a
chat together. So long that I thought perhaps I should
ask Mrs Rodda whether you were still at Tregarrick!'
Indicating a comfortable leather armchair, he added,
'Take a seat.'

Ben's comments had been made only partly in jest.
When Antonia had come to live at Tregarrick some
months before, he had hoped they would be able to
spend many evenings catching up on all that had
happened to them both after the childhood days they
had spent together at Insimo. Much had happened in

191

Ben's life since then and he had no doubt the same was true of Antonia. He was aware she was the first woman from Mozambique ever to qualify as a doctor and this in itself was a remarkable achievement for someone with her antecedence.

Her grandmother, Victoria, was the daughter of an English sailor and his native Herero wife and had led an incredibly adventurous life in an Africa that had yet to know law and order. To ensure the survival of herself and her daughter she had been forced to kill more than one man who had taken advantage of them. Antonia's mother, Therese, had been fathered by a *pombeiro*, leader of a small army of bandits in Mozambique, all of whom were of mixed parentage, like himself. His life had ended at the end of a Portuguese rope. Nevertheless, Victoria had seen Therese make a good marriage to the son of a senior Portuguese army officer, ensuring that their two children, Antonia and Philippe, had received good educations. Today there were few people still alive who remembered the colourful background of the elderly woman who lived quietly and happily at Insimo.

Ben had hoped that the link between the St Anna and Retallick families would prove sufficient to forge a bond between himself and Antonia that might help him overcome the emptiness he had felt since the death of Lily. However, Antonia's work with the victims of 'shellshock' had become increasingly important to her and she was working an ever escalating number of hours among them.

'It has been a long time, Ben,' Antonia said apologetically, 'but whenever I managed to get some time off it

192

seemed you were busy trying to sort out the problems involved with running Ruddlemoor in wartime, and whenever *you* had any free time I was always deeply involved in my work with Olaf. Recently we have been checking the case histories of the men who have arrived in Bodmin from France and found a pattern in the way that soldiers – even the bravest of soldiers – react to the effects of being subjected to constant artillery bombardment. It is a very important discovery. Less than a year ago such men were being shot as cowards . . . but we are satisfied that in almost every case it has nothing to do with courage or cowardice. Olaf has worked very hard to have it recognised as a medical condition, and is just beginning to achieve some success. It is a tremendous breakthrough. He and I have long been convinced that such men suffer from a genuine syndrome brought about by being subjected to more than the human mind can cope with, but it has been difficult to persuade some of the more senior army doctors that this is so.'

Antonia's familiarity with the Swedish doctor was apparent by her use of his Christian name, but Ben did not comment. Instead, he said, 'It is very worthwhile work, Antonia. When I was in Paris soon after war began I saw many wounded men who had been brought to the hospitals direct from the battle front. Most had lost all sense of reality. They weren't even aware who they were, let alone how they should be behaving.'

Ben was sincere in his admiration for the work Antonia was doing, but was also honest enough to admit to himself that he would be happier if she were carrying out her work assisting someone less handsome than Dr Olaf Ericsson. At the same time, he conceded that such resentment was totally unreasonable. He had no claim on Antonia, and with Lily's death still a fresh and unhappy memory he had been reluctant to make any advances towards her on the all too few occasions when there might have been an opportunity to do so . . . but Antonia was speaking once more.

'Actually, it's partly Paris that I have come to talk to you about, Ben. Olaf has been asked to go there for a few weeks to see for himself the men of whom you were just talking, soldiers brought to hospital direct from the trenches and suffering the traumatism brought about by trench warfare. He has asked me to go with him. I have accepted, of course, but before we go I said I would ask you to recommend a good hotel, and perhaps a restaurant or two. As you know, I have been to Paris, but while I was there I had no time to get to know the city. I asked Emma Pengelly, the wife of your transport manager, the same questions, knowing she had driven ambulances in Paris, but she had the same story to tell. It seemed the only hotel she stayed in was the one she first went to when she was acting as a companion to Lily, when you were taking her to the clinic in Switzerland. As for restaurants . . . When Emma had any time off all she wanted to do was sleep! She suggested you were the best person to ask . . . so here I am!'

Ben felt it ironic that she should ask his opinion of places to go in Paris, in order that she might enjoy it in the company of another man. Then guilty memories flooded back of the many happy hours he had shared there with Tessa, while he was still married to the ailing Lily.

'I doubt if you'll find a better hotel anywhere than the Crillon. The manager will remember me – and remember Emma too, I am quite sure. She and Jacob had their wedding reception there and spent their wedding night in the bridal suite. It was in recognition of her work and the horrors she had encountered driving ambulances between Paris and the battle front. The wedding briefly lifted the spirits of Parisians too. They had taken the ex-suffragette ambulance drivers to their hearts and made Emma's marriage an occasion to celebrate.'

'Hadn't they also turned out in force as a mark of respect for Emma's friend who died when a shell hit her ambulance? I believe she too was an ex-suffragette . . . was it Tessa?'

It sounded an innocent question but it caused Ben's head to jerk up as though he had been struck on the chin. He was taken off guard by the mention of Tessa and wondered what Emma might have said to Antonia about her . . . and about him.

Ben's reaction to the mention of Tessa's name told Antonia far more than she had learned from Emma. 'Of course, you would have known her too, both of you being in Paris at the same time.'

As casually as he could, Ben said, 'As a matter of fact, Tessa was living in Paris when Emma and I stayed there with Lily, on our way to the Swiss clinic. She showed me round the city.'

'Then she must have shown you something of the

real Paris, the sort of places I would love to see for myself. Is there anywhere special you can recommend, Ben? Perhaps a place to eat that might not be particularly well known to visitors to Paris?'

Ben thought immediately of Henri's, the small establishment on the Left Bank he had sought out on his way to Switzerland in the spring. Tessa had taken him there and when it turned out that the owner had a brother in Rhodesia who knew the Retallicks, Ben had been welcomed as 'family'.

With Antonia's connections, Ben knew she would be made equally welcome. Had *he* been in Paris with her he would have taken her there . . . but he was reluctant for it to be an experience she shared with someone else, even though he found the reason for such reluctance confusing.

'I think you'll find that most of the restaurants I once knew have closed because of the war. However, the manager of the Crillon is a very resourceful and knowledgeable man. He will know the places that are still open and you can trust his recommendations.'

The remainder of a pleasant evening was spent chatting about old times and talking of the many places where Antonia's work was taking her. When she eventually left him and returned to her own part of the house, Ben wondered why he had not been forthcoming with information that might have helped to make her stay in Paris more enjoyable. For her part, Antonia was now entirely convinced that Tessa and Ben's relationship had been much more than a platonic one. She decided that while she was in Paris she would try to learn something more about Tessa.

Later, lying in her bed in the darkness of Tregarrick, she realised it was important to her.

II

Ben had hoped Antonia might return to Tregarrick and spend the Christmas of 1915 there, but she wrote to him early in December to tell him her father would be in Portugal for the festive season. She and her brother intended travelling there to be with him.

Ben was not the only one who would be having a lonely Christmas. On the same day that he received Antonia's letter, he had a visit from Betsy Hooper, mother of Sam, asking hopefully whether her son was likely to be home in time to celebrate the holiday.

In truth, Ben had received no news of Sam for more than a month, although he had been told by Carey Hamilton in a guarded telephone call that both Sam and the traction engines were carrying out the task for which they had gone to Africa. Carey had volunteered no details, and Ben had known better than to ask.

'It will be the first Christmas that our Sam and me haven't spent together,' Betsy said, unhappily. 'We'd plan for weeks what we'd buy for each other and I'd make our Christmas puddings and buy a turkey from Mr Hollis, along at the butcher's. Likely as not, we'd share it with Muriel and her ma, who's a widow too, like me. It's just not going to be the same this year, what with our Sam being away, and I don't feel like doing

197

anything special . . . it hardly seems worth the trouble. I'd just spend the time wondering what Sam was having to eat, out there in Africa.'

'I'm sure he will be eating very well,' Ben said untruthfully, 'and whatever he has, I don't doubt he'll be thinking of you and hoping that you are enjoying the sort of meal he remembers, so we mustn't let him down. I'll have Mrs Rodda order a hamper for you with a turkey, Christmas puddings and a cake, mince tarts and more. I'll make certain there will be more than enough for you to share with Muriel and her mother and commiserate with each other about the absence of Sam. I will also telegraph to my brother in Africa and see if we can't arrange for Sam to telegraph a Christmas message to you. It won't be the same as having him home, of course, but knowing that it was sent only a matter of hours before will bring Sam just that little bit closer for you.'

Betsy Hooper left Tregarrick thrilled by the prospect of receiving a message from Sam that had taken only a matter of hours to reach her. Ben determined that such a message would reach her, even if it was sent in his name by someone else from Insimo.

The telegraph duly arrived for Betsy Hooper and a few days after Christmas she called at Tregarrick to thank Ben, but by then he had other things on his mind. The amount of china clay being received from the other works in the area had been falling in the final weeks of 1915 and Ben had been forced to increase production from Ruddlemoor in order to ensure that the neutral ships leaving Charlestown did so with full cargoes.

There seemed to be no logical explanation for the fall-off in deliveries from the other clay workings. Ruddlemoor was having no difficulty in meeting its production targets and even increasing production when needed. Ben tried to take the matter up with his fellow owners but they proved strangely elusive.

It was not until mid-January 1916 that Jim Bray, Ben's works captain, came to his office early one Monday morning with an explanation.

'The owners are selling their clay to Brigadier Grove, Ben. One of the men from the Spargo works was at my son's house helping him with some decorating and he told him what was going on.'

'Spargo? But he was the first to come to me and sign a contract to say that he would sell his clay to me – and only me. It doesn't make sense. Not only is he breaking the terms of his contract, but he'll also be selling at a loss. Why?'

'Well, first of all, it seems he's found a loophole in the contract, Ben. I believe he has signed to sell only top grade clay to you and is selling clay that hasn't gone through the full process to Grove, leaving him to complete the job. It's clay you wouldn't accept if he offered it to you.'

Ben was puzzled and he expressed his thoughts to the works captain. 'Why should he want to do such a thing? Ruddlemoor is paying a lot more for Spargo clay than he'll get from Grove – especially as he's not selling him a completed first grade product. What's behind it, Jim?'

Looking uncomfortable, Jim Bray said, 'Well, that's

the next thing I was going to tell you, Ben. It seems there are some ugly rumours going around clay country about you.'

'Ugly rumours? What about? As far as I know I've done nothing to warrant anyone's turning against Ruddlemoor.'

Looking even more ill at ease than before, Jim Bray said, 'For some reason word is going round that you are secretly pro-German.' Observing his employer's astonishment, he added hurriedly, 'I know it's not true, as would anyone else who knows you, but somehow that's what's being said. I think a lot of it has to do with that neutral ship from Charlestown the Germans boarded and seized a few weeks ago. It's being said that Germany is desperate for china clay and knew in advance the ship was taking its cargo to France, a country they are at war with. They would have been within their rights to sink it. Instead, they were able to stop it on the high seas and take both the ship and its cargo to Germany.'

'And local people – Cornish people – believe that *I* am the one who informed the Germans the ship was taking its cargo to France? That's absolutely ridiculous. As I said at the time of the inquiry, the bill of lading declared the cargo was destined for Sweden, a neutral country. One to which Ruddlemoor has sent a number of cargoes in recent months. Besides, I have refused to sell any more cargoes to the agent who brokered that sale. If that's enough to have started such a ridiculous rumour . . . !'

'That isn't all, Ben,' Jim Bray said unhappily. 'One of the men said he heard talk in the pub on Saturday night that the two traction engines you sent to Africa weren't intended for your old home there at all. It's being said they will be used by the Germans in East Africa to pull the big guns salvaged from that German cruiser that was sunk by the Navy in some delta along the coast there.'

'A German cruiser, the *Königsberg*, was sunk in the Rufiji delta in German East Africa,' Ben said, 'and I don't doubt the Germans salvaged her guns, but I can assure you that the Ruddlemoor traction engines are very many miles from there.'

Ben wished he could tell Jim Bray exactly what the two machines *were* doing, but there had been no news from Africa for an uncomfortably long time, although if the expedition had been successful the two boats should have reached their destination by now. Rising to his feet and pacing his office, he said to his works captain, 'Who do you think is spreading these rumours, Jim? They are so ridiculous as to be laughable, but when they start to hurt Ruddlemoor it becomes serious. Who would want to see Ruddlemoor suffer in such a way?'

Both men knew the answer to that question, but it was left to the Ruddlemoor works captain to name him.

'Brigadier General Sir Robert Grove!'

'Who else! Not only would he delight in damaging Ruddlemoor, but he would stand to gain more than anyone else if we went out of business.'

'What can be done about it, Ben?'

'At this moment I don't know, Jim. It's no use tackling Grove. He would deny it, and we have no proof that he's the one who started these ridiculous rumours . . . but I'll think of something.'

Five days after Ben's conversation with his works captain, he received news that might have put an end to the malicious rumours about his sympathy with the German cause had he been able to pass it on.

It arrived in a letter, personally delivered by a young army lieutenant, sent to Cornwall from the War Office in London.

The letter was from Carey Hamilton and it contained exciting tidings. With the help of the Ruddlemoor traction engines, the expedition to Lake Tanganyika had proved even more successful than anyone involved had dared hope. Both gunboats had arrived safely at their destination – and had taken part in their first action!

When the boats had been despatched from England, all the information held by the War Office pointed to there being only one German vessel on Lake Tanganyika. However, when the British expedition arrived they quickly learned there were in fact *three* German ships, each of which was considerably larger and carrying heavier armament than the two small British gunboats.

Despite this disadvantage, the British boats had gone into action against one of the German warships, the *Kingani*. After a lengthy engagement one of the diminutive British craft scored a direct hit on its larger adversary, killing the captain and two of his crew, whereupon the survivors promptly surrendered.

A small British crew placed on board the *Kingani* succeeded in bringing the German vessel to shallow water at the shore's edge before it sank. Spicer had high hopes of salvaging the *Kingani* and, flying the white ensign, using it against its former owners.

Carey Hamilton told Ben he was giving him details of the success of the expedition in the strictest confidence. It seemed the action with the *Kingani* had taken place many miles from its base and the Germans were still unaware that two British gunboats were operating on the lake. The War Office wanted them to remain in ignorance. It was hoped that with the element of surprise still very much in their favour, the British gunboats, assisted by the expedition's latest acquisition, would be able to sink or capture the remaining two German vessels and thus assure the British Navy of absolute control of Lake Tanganyika.

The letter contained no information about Sam and the present whereabouts of the two Ruddlemoor traction engines. Ben was worried. It meant he could say nothing to Betsy Hooper, who had expressed her concern that she had received no word from Sam since his brief but welcome telegraphed message at Christmas.

9

I

When Sam returned to Insimo from his hunting foray with Nat Retallick and their Matabele escort, he was both astonished and delighted to discover that Maria was there.

He met her in the entrance hall to the annexe in which he had his room. She had seen him arrive and was waiting for him. So taken aback was he at coming face to face with her that he stood for some moments in disbelief. Then, still not saying a word, he reached out and pulled her to him. When he eventually spoke, it was to ask what she was doing at Insimo.

'The hospital where I was working in South Africa had a great many wounded and sick soldiers of the Rhodesian Native Regiment,' she said. 'When it was decided to repatriate them they needed volunteers to accompany them on the hospital train. As I knew that both you and Diego were at Insimo I thought it was an opportunity too good to be missed. I volunteered, in the hope that you would be pleased to see me . . . but you haven't even kissed me yet.'

Rectifying his omission immediately, Sam hugged her again before saying, 'Having you arrive here so unexpectedly has put the seal on what has been a wonderful time for me at Insimo.'

'Put the seal on . . . ? You are leaving Insimo already? Not today, surely?'

'No,' Sam replied cautiously, Spicer's warning springing to mind, 'I will be leaving in a while, but it's not going to be just yet.'

'Then we will be able to spend a couple of days together . . . and not only the days,' she said boldly. 'I have been given the room next to you, here in the guest annexe – and you and I are the only two guests at Insimo.' Hugging him to her fiercely, she went on, 'I am so glad you are pleased to see me again, Sam. On the way from Bulawayo I began to worry that I might be making a mistake by coming here. That I might prove an embarrassment to you. I will try not to be, if that's what you want.'

'Nothing you do could be an embarrassment,' he said firmly. 'Anyway, the Retallicks think differently about things from the people we met in South Africa – but I am a little surprised they have put us together here, in what is virtually our private suite of rooms.'

'That was Victoria's idea,' Maria explained delightedly. 'Mrs Retallick was going to put me into a small rondavel close to Diego's quarters, but Victoria said she had arranged to have it decorated and insisted I should have the room next to yours, here in the annexe. She said it in such a way that no one would have dared argue with her.'

Sam smiled happily at Maria, then became serious. 'Victoria has first-hand knowledge of the problems faced in Rhodesia and South Africa by couples from different races. She and I have had a number of conversations about it. She is firmly on our side – and a force to be reckoned with.'

Maria looked at Sam for a long while before replying. 'I am afraid it would take a whole army of Victorias to make any difference, Sam. Each race, both black and white, has an ineradicable suspicion of the other that has become increasingly deep-rooted over the years . . . but we only have forty-eight hours before I have to catch a train to Beira, so don't let's waste any of them debating about how we might change the world. Let's just enjoy them.'

The two days Sam and Maria spent in each other's company on the Insimo estate passed all too quickly and Sam tried very hard not to allow his unreasonable resentment at needing to share her with her brother and the others at Insimo during the daylight hours to show. She also held a clinic for the children in one of the villages occupied by Insimo workers, which took away some more of the precious hours they might otherwise have spent together. Fortunately, the time they spent in each other's arms during the night hours more than made up for it, but the time passed all too quickly and it proved difficult for both of them to hide their feelings when it came to parting.

206

Maria was travelling in the Insimo train in company with Nat, who was heading north with his scouts. Spicer and his gunboats were finally on the move and Nat's task would be to ensure they met with none of the enemy along their route.

Maria's instructions were to proceed to the Mozambique port of Beira from where she would be taken to a remote area not very far from the territory's border with German East Africa. Here she would set up a much needed clinic for the benefit of tribes who had come into little contact with European medicines. Also, in due course, the clinic would have facilities to deal with any casualties resulting from border clashes between German and Portuguese troops.

The farewells between Sam and Maria were less than satisfactory until Sam threw discretion to the wind and kissed Maria firmly as she was about to board the narrow-gauge train. The tears she shed as the train pulled away were a combination of sadness at parting and joy that Sam should have made such a public show of his feelings for her.

When the train had steamed out of sight of those who had been seeing her off, and they were walking back to the houses, Victoria fell in beside Sam and said, 'Well! You certainly nailed your colours to the mast when you said farewell to Maria. Have you reached a decision about your future?'

Sam shook his head. 'Maria says she needs time to think about it.'

Victoria made a noise in her throat that expressed disapproval. 'Think about what? There isn't a single person here at Insimo who isn't fully aware of how you two feel about each other.'

'It's more complicated than that,' Sam replied. 'She feels her people in Mozambique need her and she doesn't want to let them down.'

'They might very well need her. Knowing the country there as well as I do, I couldn't argue with that. But she must learn that in this life you look out for yourself first and *then* decide what it is you can do to help others, not the other way round. Besides, not everyone in Mozambique is ready for western medicine yet. She'll find it hard in the place where she's going, and she'll have very little help from older tribesmen.' She shrugged her shoulders. 'But who am I to tell you to pursue a course which can only make more difficulties for both of you? Perhaps it will be just as well and pose fewer problems if you let things go on as they are, meeting whenever you have the opportunity and just making the most of the time you can spend together.'

Sam shook his head. 'No, Victoria. I don't think that would prove satisfactory for either of us. Maria deserves more than that.'

'I wouldn't argue with that,' Victoria agreed, 'but can you think of anything else you can do?'

'I have already done it,' Sam declared. 'Last night I asked Maria to marry me. If she agrees – as I desperately hope she will – I will take her back to Cornwall and we will begin a new life there.'

*

Sam remained at Insimo for another eleven days. During this time one of the traction engines was put to work conveying mining machinery from the Insimo railway to a gold mine owned by the Retallick family. It was an excellent opportunity for Sam to observe how Diego managed when the engine was carrying out the type of work for which it had been designed.

Diego proved that Nat had not exaggerated his skill with all types of machinery. He soon mastered the art of driving the huge locomotives and as quickly grasped an elementary knowledge of their working. Sam was satisfied he had found the best possible second driver for the Ruddlemoor machines. However, although the two men worked well together, Sam felt the very real friendship that had been part of their relationship during his early days at Insimo had disappeared.

One evening, as they were cleaning one of the traction engines after the day's tasks were done, they had been working for almost fifteen minutes without talking when Sam suddenly put down the cloth he was using and turned to his companion.

'Have I done something to offend you, Diego?'

Momentarily startled by Sam's bluntness, Diego recovered quickly. 'No,' he said offhandedly. 'Perhaps there's something on your conscience that *you* feel might have caused me offence.'

'There's absolutely nothing I can think of,' Sam replied. Then, in a moment of inspiration, he asked, 'Does this have anything to do with Maria?'

Diego shrugged. 'Maria's not a little girl any more. She's a woman. She decides for herself how she wants to live her life – but I would hate to see her get hurt. You know she is in love with you?'

'Yes, I do know.' Sam was relieved that the question of his relationship with Maria was about to be brought into the open with Diego. Neither of them had mentioned it before and he realised it had been this that was straining their friendship. 'I feel the same way about her. In fact, the night before she left Insimo I asked her to marry me.'

'You asked her . . . . what did she say?' It was quite apparent to Sam that Maria had said nothing to her brother about his proposal.

'She said she would think about it.'

'What if she says yes? When will you be married, and where will you live? I don't know if you are aware of the strength of ill-feeling there is in this part of the world about mixed marriages. It's easier in the part of the world Maria and I come from, but even there no one would go out of their way to make life easier for you, and unless you spoke the language it would be virtually impossible for you to find work.'

'I've discussed all these problems with Victoria,' Sam said, 'and although I think I could overcome most of them I wouldn't want Maria to be humiliated in any way. I saw how she was treated by the Afrikaners when we were on the ship coming to South Africa. If she agrees to marry me I will take her home to Cornwall. I have a good job there with Ben Retallick and the local hospitals will value Maria's nursing skills. We will have a very happy life.'

It was an over-simplification of the facts, as Sam well knew. His mother would need to get used to the idea of having an African daughter-in-law, but she was a basically kind woman and he was convinced she would come to love Maria as he did. He did have a twinge of conscience about Muriel. It was quite apparent from the letters he had received from her that she viewed their relationship as being much closer than it really was. But he had been away from Cornwall for some months now and would not be returning in the very near future. It was quite possible she would find someone else in his absence.

Sam's conversation with Diego succeeded in clearing the misunderstanding between them. Diego accepted that Sam really did care for Maria, had thought about the problems that were likely to face them in the future and would do whatever was in Maria's best interest. As a result there was a closer bond than ever between them and they were good friends once more.

All too soon, it seemed to Sam, in response to a message from General Edwards, he and Diego took the two traction engines to Bulawayo, in order to be ready to transport them to Fungurume when the wagons that had carried the two gunboats there from Cape Town returned down the line.

Unfortunately, a railway embankment collapsed on the Northern Rhodesia–Belgian Congo border and Sam and Diego were forced to remain in Bulawayo for two full weeks before the line became operational once more.

It was a difficult time, bringing home to Sam the

conversations he had had with both Victoria and Diego. The destination and role of the two Ruddlemoor traction engines was an open secret in the Matabele capital and Sam could have capitalised on his part in the expedition by accepting many invitations that came his way – but Diego was excluded from them and so Sam remained with his second driver in the home of a Portuguese family who lived on the outskirts of the town.

They did once venture to a bar that catered for an African and coloured clientele, but halfway through the evening a group of coloured drinkers became abusive and Sam would have become involved in an ugly brawl had the bar staff and a number of more sober patrons not intervened.

Deeming it wise to leave and return to the house where they were staying, a somewhat bewildered Sam questioned his companion about the motives of the men who had picked on him.

'They had been drinking too much and resented your presence because you were not one of them. There was also the fact that they are not allowed to drink with Europeans and so they resented you drinking in *their* bar,' Diego explained. 'I'm afraid you'll get the same reaction in European bars if you marry Maria. You will never belong anywhere for as long as you remain in Africa. It's sad, but it's the truth, Sam.'

III

Sam had hoped he might receive a letter from Maria before leaving to join Spicer and the Lake Tanganyika expedition at Fungurume, but there had been no news from her by the time the train including the two heavy duty wagons arrived in Bulawayo, the collapsed embankment having been repaired by the Belgians.

Sam carefully inspected the wagons. They had conveyed the two gunboats through from Cape Town to the Belgian Congo safely enough, but he was not entirely satisfied they were capable of carrying the two heavy traction engines. However, when he voiced his misgivings to the Bulawayo stationmaster, he was informed that they were the stoutest rolling stock the railway had to offer and Sam had no alternative but to use them. He had a long conversation with the engine driver, stressing the need to proceed at a slower speed than usual, especially when crossing some of the flimsier bridges, about which Nat had given him a warning. He told the driver to stop and ask his opinion if he had any doubts whatsoever about anything that might possibly result in damage to the heavy machinery. Only when he was entirely satisfied that everything possible had been done to ensure their safe arrival at Fungurume did Sam agree to have the machines loaded and begin the journey.

The journey to Fungurume took twenty days, but when Sam arrived with the traction engines he found that the expedition had expected them to arrive at least ten days before and Spicer had been fuming at what he considered to be an unreasonable delay. Fortunately, he had returned along the railway line to Elisabethville for a meeting with the Belgian commandant of the area, whom he had accused of trying to take over responsibility for the expedition, and in his absence command of the expedition had been temporarily given to a naval officer named Cartwright. He was much more understanding of the reasons for Sam's late arrival than Spicer would have been, and approved the actions Sam had taken to ensure the safety of the two 'land locomotives', as the commander had decided they should be called.

Cartwright was also far more forthcoming than Spicer had been about the role Sam and the Ruddlemoor traction engines were expected to play in the next few weeks. There were 150 miles of rugged country to be traversed before they reached Sankisia, and the travels of the two gunboats would not be over even when the hazardous, shallow and unpredictable Lualaba river was safely negotiated. They would be carried for another 175 miles on yet another section of the Belgian Congo's fragmented railway system before coming to the end of an incredible journey that would have meant travelling more than 9,000 miles since setting out from Great Britain.

The two Ruddlemoor traction engines had been brought to Africa to play their part for only a tiny section of this journey but, as Cartwright stressed to Sam, it was a vital part. Without the two giant 'land locomotives' it was doubtful whether it would be possible to transport the boats over a mountain range that was more than a mile high in some places.

After the traction engines had been off-loaded from the railway wagons, Cartwright said, 'The only way we can keep the commander off your back is to get the boats on their way before he returns. Can you have your machines ready to move off first thing tomorrow morning?'

'If it's likely to put him in a good mood I'll be happy to get under way right now.'

'That won't be necessary.' Cartwright smiled. 'You've had a long and hard journey. Get yourself a good meal and an early night. We'll set off at dawn.'

Cartwright's decision to move off was a sound one – in theory. However, Sam had immediate misgivings about the strength of a log bridge that had been built over a gully just outside the Fungurume camp, which the traction engines and the boats would need to cross.

Cartwright pointed out that the bridge had been approved by Spicer and that if anything went wrong the responsibility would be entirely his. Sam was far more concerned for the safety of the Ruddlemoor traction engines than apportioning blame for any mishap but, having registered his misgivings, he agreed to put the bridge to the test.

With the first of the gunboats on a trailer behind the land locomotive, Sam drove gingerly on to the bridge and began crossing at a snail's pace. He was almost halfway across when there was a sudden sound as though a giant rifle had been fired and the logs beneath the steam vehicle and its load gave way. The traction engine tilted to one side alarmingly. So too did the boat and trailer.

'Quick . . . jump and run!' Sam shouted at Diego, who was riding on the traction engine with him. Changing his mind immediately, he said, '*No!* Get wires

215

on to the trailer and attach them to the other traction engine to save the boat – then get ropes on to this one with as many natives as can be found to hold on to the other end of them.'

In the next few minutes the sailors of the expedition worked frantically to secure a wire hawser from Diego's traction engine to the boat and trailer while Sam supervised the attachment of a number of stout ropes to his vehicle, which was tilting at an alarming angle over the side of the log bridge. The ropes succeeded in preventing the land locomotive from tilting any more and disappearing into the gully far below. Meanwhile, Diego began the tricky task of edging the trailer and its valuable load inch by inch to safety back on solid ground. The movement caused more logs to shift and break but the Africans holding the ropes succeeded in keeping Sam's traction engine more or less upright.

There was a huge cheer when the trailer with its precious load reached safety, but another movement of the log bridge almost caused Sam and his traction engine to slip into the gully. Observing what was happening, Cartwright shouted, 'Jump, Sam! Jump!'

When the bridge collapsed, Sam had turned off the steam valves. Now he began turning them on again. 'There's no way I can go back, but get the wire hawser, attach it to my engine, then nip across the bridge and take it round that tree on the other side – the largest one, dead ahead – then bring it back to Diego . . . with him pulling I'll use what power I can and with luck I'll make it to the other side – but hurry! More logs could give way at any moment.'

Aware of the danger Sam was in and of what it would mean to the expedition to lose one of the land locomotives, Cartwright joined his men in doing what Sam had directed. When the hawser had been taken round the tree and secured to the second traction engine, all the sailors hurried off the bridge before turning to watch what happened.

Cautiously, Diego inched his machine away from the bridge, and as the hawser tightened and took the weight of the stranded engine every one of the watching men held their breath.

Almost imperceptibly at first, Sam's traction engine began to move forward. Then, as logs fell into the gully behind it, he succeeded in guiding it to the centre of the bridge. Diego increased speed, and, after what seemed an age to the watching men, the front wheels of Sam's machine reached solid land. He opened the steam valves, and the huge rear wheels drove it up the slope to safety.

The cheer that went up from the sailors and the African helpers was even louder than it had been when the gunboat trailer was pulled back off the bridge, and a hugely relieved Sam turned and waved in acknowledgement.

For the remainder of that hot day everyone worked without respite to build a new bridge farther along the gully where it was wider, but lower. Fortunately there was no shortage of trees in the area and, before nightfall, the expedition tried, successfully this time, to move forward once more. By the time the sun disappeared at their backs, both traction engines and the boats were safely on the far side of the gully and the long trek over the mountains had begun.

The bridge episode was repeated more than once during the course of the nightmare journey across the mountains. Then, for a while, they could find no water for the thirsty engines and it seemed the expedition was doomed to failure, until, quite unexpectedly, a Belgian official appeared, accompanied by a small army of women, each carrying a jar of water on her head. They had carried their loads from a village eight miles away – and they repeated the journey on a number of occasions in the following few days.

It was not only bridges that collapsed. The trailers carrying the boats did so too and the traction engines were forced to sacrifice their log fuel carrying trailers, which were then adapted to carry the weight of the boats. In addition the members of the expedition had to contend with hordes of death-dealing tsetse flies and a constant threat from wild animals, snakes and mosquitoes.

Despite all these tribulations, forty-four days after setting off from the railhead at Fungurume, the Ruddlemoor traction engines steamed into the tiny Belgian trading post of Sankisia with their precious loads intact on trailers behind them. The traction engines had successfully completed the task for which they had been brought to Africa. As a result, the naval expedition to Lake Tanganyika was still on course for success.

10

I

'Mr Retallick, there are two gentlemen in the office who say they wish to speak to you.' The message was given to Ben by an agitated young girl clerk from the Ruddlemoor general office.

Deeply involved in an important meeting with Jim Bray and his shift captains to discuss the reasons behind the fall-off in the sale of Ruddlemoor china clay, Ben was annoyed by the interruption.

Frowning, he asked, 'Who are they, Alice? No, it doesn't matter who they are, I'm busy right now. If they want to speak to me tell them to make an appointment.'

He had hardly finished talking when the first of two men pushed past the office clerk and the older of them said, 'If you are Benjamin Retallick then the business I have with you takes precedence over whatever is going on here. I am Superintendent Buchanan and this is Sergeant Callaghan. We are both attached to the Special

Branch of the National Security Service at Scotland Yard. There are a few questions I would like to put to you and I think they would be best discussed in private.'

'Special Branch . . . questions . . . ? Really, Superintendent, you have interrupted a very important meeting – and with no possible good cause that I can think of, however urgent you may consider your business to be. I feel a telephone call to arrange a meeting would not have come amiss.'

'We would both appear to be busy men, Mr Retallick, so I suggest we do not waste time arguing about what should or should not have been done. If you would prefer it we could carry out the interview at your local police station.'

'That won't be necessary.' Aware that he could not win an argument with the police superintendent, Ben said to his Ruddlemoor captains, 'It seems our meeting will need to be brought to an end for the time being, gentlemen. I am no wiser than you are about the reason for this interruption and what it is that can be so important to our Security Service. When I do know I will tell you. Jim . . . and gentlemen . . . think over what we have talked about so far and let me have your thoughts in due course. Thank you.'

As the men filed from the office, Ben resumed his seat behind his desk and said to the two Special Branch policemen, 'Choose your seats, and then you can tell me the reason for your disruptive visit.'

The superintendent chose a seat that faced Ben across the width of his office desk, while his sergeant sat with a vacant chair between himself and Superintendent

Buchanan. He drew pencil and notebook from a pocket and prepared to record what was about to be said.

The superintendent was the first to speak. 'I am here on a very serious matter, Mr Retallick. There has been an allegation that you are involved in activities that are prejudicial to the state. In view of the fact that we are at war, such actions would constitute a capital offence. Indeed, a convicted spy was executed by firing squad in the Tower of London this very morning.'

Ben was horrified by the image the superintendent's words conjured up, but in a moment of bravado he said, 'I trust he was convicted on more than a malicious allegation. May I ask who has laid such a ludicrous charge against me?'

'You may ask, Mr Retallick, but I regret that I am unable to enlighten you. Suffice it to say that it comes from a very credible source.'

'Or from someone with friends in high places,' Ben retorted, 'and unless I am mistaken he is also an unscrupulous business rival who once held a senior rank in the army.'

'You may speculate all you like, Mr Retallick, but we are here to verify or reject the claims that have been made against you.'

The superintendent had given no hint that Ben's description of his accuser was accurate, but Ben had seen the sergeant's momentary start of surprise and knew his surmise was correct. The false allegation had originated from Brigadier General Sir Robert Grove.

'Do you intend to arrest me?' he asked.

'If I think it necessary,' was the reply, 'but for now I

am here to ask you a few questions in respect of the allegations that have been made against you.'

'And what are these allegations?'

Instead of replying, Superintendent Buchanan nodded to his sergeant who immediately consulted his notebook and, holding it open in front of his face, read from it.

'The first allegation is that you delivered a cargo of china clay to the Swedish steamship *Eva*, knowing it would be intercepted on the high seas and the ship and its cargo taken to Germany, a country with which Great Britain is at war.'

'The answer to that allegation may be found in both the Ruddlemoor and Department of Trade files,' Ben replied. 'The buyer was a Swedish dealer who has been a Ruddlemoor customer for many years. His bill of lading stated that the cargo was destined for Sweden – a neutral country. It was only after the ship was seized by the Germans that I learned the captain was in fact taking the cargo to France. There was nothing wrong with that, France is an ally of Great Britain, but it did mean that when the Germans stopped and boarded the ship they were quite within their rights under international law to confiscate both ship and cargo. It was sheer stupidity on the part of the ship's captain and the buyer. As a result I have refused to sell any more clay to him.'

'Very commendable,' said the superintendent with more than a hint of sarcasm in his voice, 'but I believe the Germans were in sore need of china clay. Can you tell me how they knew which ship to board in order to have a legitimate excuse to confiscate it?'

'It was most probably a stroke of luck on their part,' Ben declared. 'The *Eva* wasn't the first ship they have stopped and boarded, but the others were bound for neutral countries and were allowed to sail on to their destinations.'

'Is it not true that the Germans were sinking even neutral ships if they were sailing in British waters? At least, they were until your company started loading neutral ships with your product, when suddenly and inexplicably there were no more sinkings of such vessels.'

'That's perfectly true,' Ben admitted. He was aware that the superintendent was waiting for more, but he had no intention of revealing the true source of his information about the change in German naval policy. Instead, he said, 'When I was on my way to visit my late wife, who was in a Swiss clinic, I learned from a friend that there would be no more sinking of neutral ships.'

'Ah yes, your late wife . . . you have my sympathy for your sad loss, Mr Retallick. She was in Dr Bertauld's clinic for a very long time, I believe. You were no doubt aware that another patient in the same clinic was the wife of a German naval *Kommodore* – Commodore Korber? According to our intelligence sources he was a frequent visitor to his wife. You probably met . . . and it would be perfectly natural in such circumstances for two men whose wives shared a serious illness in common to sympathise with each other, despite their countries' being at war with each other. And who better than such a senior officer to inform you of changes in German naval policy?' Abruptly leaning forward in his

223

chair to bring his face closer to Ben's, Superintendent Buchanan added, 'Of course, such information would be of such great benefit to your business that Korber would quite naturally expect something from you in return. Perhaps a shipment of material that, while not directly aiding the German war effort, would be very welcome to them. Is that how it worked, Mr Retallick?'

Meeting the police superintendent's direct look and carefully controlling the anger he felt at the accusation, Ben said, 'I met no Germans during the occasions when I was visiting the Swiss clinic, Superintendent. Neither patients, nor visitors. Since your intelligence sources are so efficient, they will no doubt have informed you that when I arrived at the clinic on that last occasion I was given the news that my wife had died unexpectedly. It was hardly an occasion to exchange confidences with an enemy, even had I been so inclined.'

Making no comment on Ben's statement, Buchanan demanded, 'Then where *did* you learn about the change in German U-boat policy, if not from Commodore Korber?'

'I am afraid I cannot answer that question without prejudicing the man who told me, Superintendent – but if you check with the intelligence sources you are so fond of quoting, you will learn that as a result of very strong protests from a great many neutral governments about the sinking of their ships, they received an assurance from the German government that such actions would cease. Through my business connections in very many countries I learned of the German assurance and acted accordingly.'

Ben thought it to be close enough to the truth without implicating Philippe St Anna. He hoped it would be sufficient to satisfy Superintendent Buchanan, but now it was the turn of the sergeant to question him.

'I believe you were somewhere near at hand when a U-boat was sighted just off the Cornish coast by a Royal Navy airship? In fact, I understand you were shot by an army reservist performing coast watch duties because you were in the company of two aliens in the area and behaving suspiciously.'

'Behaving suspiciously?' This time Ben allowed his anger to show. 'I was running to the aid of the crew of the airship. It had been hit by gunfire from the U-boat and was in danger of crashing into the sea. The reservist could see that for himself but felt that his damn-fool order to me to stop running towards the airship was more important than helping to save the crew. In fact, one of them *did* die.'

'Tell me about the two people you were with, and what you were doing on the coast at that time,' the sergeant persisted, ignoring Ben's anger.

'They are Portuguese with whom I have been friends since childhood and we were having a picnic. If you need more details you can contact one of them. He is Captain Philippe St Anna from Mozambique, military attaché at the Portuguese embassy in London. He was visiting me with his sister, Dr Antonia St Anna, who at the time was working among wounded British soldiers in a London hospital. She later moved to Cornwall to carry out research into a pioneer treatment for soldiers suffering mental problems as a result of their experiences in the trenches. Speaking to her might prove more difficult, as she is currently in Paris treating soldiers brought straight from the front.' Suddenly losing patience with his questioners, Ben stood up. 'Now, if that is all, perhaps you will be kind enough to allow me to get on with some work. Ruddlemoor is going through a difficult patch at the moment and I need to work to turn round its fortunes if we are to survive.'

'It is not quite all, I'm afraid, Mr Retallick. There are two more points I would like to have cleared up before I decide what action I am to take in respect of the allegations that have been made against you.' It was Superintendent Buchanan talking once more. 'You have mentioned your business, and that brings me to another question. You say your company is having difficulties, yet you sent two traction engines to Africa . . . machines that I am told could not really be spared. Rumours are circulating that the traction engines are now in the hands of the German army and are being used in East Africa to haul heavy artillery in support of their troops. I must stress this is based purely on rumour – but, as the saying goes, there is seldom smoke without fire. Perhaps you would care to comment?'

Ben was in a predicament. The superintendent was a government official, but information about the Tanganyika expedition was still classified as 'top secret'. He could not tell the two men the true use to which the traction engines were being put.

Deciding that attack was the best means of defence, he said, 'So far you have put allegations to me based purely on speculation and circumstantial evidence of a flimsy and distorted nature. Now you are quoting rumour as grounds for your information. Really, Superintendent, if this was not so serious for my reputation and the reputation of my company it would be laughable.'

'Very well, Mr Retallick,' said the superintendent, apparently unperturbed by Ben's outburst, 'then let us deal in facts. I believe you still have a brother living in Africa?'

'No,' Ben retorted, 'I have *two* brothers there.'

'I am concerned with only one . . . Adam Retallick?'

'Yes, he is my brother,' Ben replied, wondering why Adam should have been brought into the conversation. 'He is farming in South Africa and has nothing to do with your farcical investigation.'

'I agree that it is something of a peripheral matter, Mr Retallick, South Africa being outside my jurisdiction, but – and again I admit this is no more than rumour – I have heard that he has been taken prisoner while fighting for the Germans in South West Africa . . .'

11

I

Word that war had been declared between Great Britain and Germany had been slow in reaching Adam Retallick's farm, which was situated in the Lichtenburg district of South Africa's Transvaal. By the time the news arrived, fighting was already taking place in the neighbouring German colony of South West Africa between South African troops loyal to the Crown and German soldiers supported by dissident Boers.

News of the war reached Adam's remote farm in typical African fashion. It was carried by a Boer *voortrekker* passing through the sparsely populated area with his native African wife and their numerous children. Riding on an ox-wagon containing all his worldly possessions, the man was seeking an even more remote area of the Transvaal, where he could build a primitive homestead and eke out a meagre existence away from the censure of those to whom union between the two races was anathema.

228

The *voortrekker* was both uneducated and somewhat simple-minded. While his wife filled an animal-skin water bag from the farm well, assisted by older members of their large family, he pulled a crumpled piece of paper from a pouch. After displaying his illiteracy by holding it upside down and pretending to read it, he handed it to Adam and, speaking in Afrikaans, asked, 'Is your name on this?'

Adam took the piece of paper, on which were pencilled about thirty names, some familiar to him, others unknown. His name was third on the list. Puzzled, he said, 'Yes, my name is here. What does it mean?'

The *voortrekker* shrugged indifferently. 'I was given it by someone named Van Klerk. He wrote the names and said I would find most of you living up this way. I was to tell you that there's a war going on between Germans and Rooineks over in South West.'

He used the Afrikaans word meaning 'red-neck' which had been used in a derogatory manner to describe British soldiers during the Boer war, adding, 'Van Klerk's collecting an army together and wants anyone on the list to come and join him.'

Matthias Van Klerk was one of the commando leaders with whom Adam had served during the Boer war. He was a man whom Adam would follow anywhere if he went to war, but the *voortrekker's* information was sketchy, to say the least.

'Join him where?' he demanded.

'I didn't ask,' came the reply. 'I wouldn't have even spoken to him if one of the axles on my wagon hadn't broken. Some of his men helped me to fix it. I reckoned

I owed him a favour. We would have been stranded for a long time if he and his men hadn't come along when they did.'

'Where did this happen?' Adam asked, becoming exasperated by the *voortrekker*'s failure to be more specific. 'And how long ago?'

'It was this side of the Vaal river. As for when . . . time doesn't mean very much to me. Might have been three weeks . . . could have been five. I'd ask the woman, but it wouldn't be no use. Most of the time she couldn't even tell you what day it is.'

When the *voortrekker* and his family had left the farm, replenished with water, bread and a number of pies baked by Johanna, Adam's wife, Adam stood for a long time staring after the slow-moving ox-wagon. Then, climbing the half-dozen steps to the stoep, he cuffed the ear of one of two children brawling in the doorway before entering the single living room. Striding to the fireplace he took down a heavy calibre hunting rifle hanging above it.

'What are you doing with that?' Johanna asked as she entered the room from the kitchen.

'The *voortrekker* had a list of names written by Matthias Van Klerk and a message from him for those he had named. My name is on the list.'

Suddenly tense, Johanna queried, 'Oh . . . and what was the message?'

'England and Germany have gone to war with each other. Matthias is raising an army. He wants me to go and fight with him.'

'Why? What does a war between England and

Germany have to do with you?' Johanna demanded. 'What has it to do with Matthias, come to that?'

'He is obviously someone important now – and he's asked for my help. He wouldn't do that unless he needed me.'

'Needs you for what?' Johanna asked. 'Who will you be fighting?'

The question took Adam aback. It was something he had not even thought about.

His hesitation was not lost on Johanna. 'You don't even know, do you? You get a vague message from someone you haven't seen for nigh on fifteen years and on the strength of that you'd up and leave your farm and family and go to fight for a cause you know nothing about – and don't even know what you're fighting for – or who you are fighting against! What sort of fool would do that?'

'The sort of fool who is loyal to his friends,' Adam retorted, stung by her words. 'And if my memory serves me right he was once your friend too, just in case you have forgotten.'

'I've forgotten nothing,' Johanna said, her anger rising. 'I seem to remember that under the leadership of Matthias Van Klerk and others like him we *lost* the war – but we have won the peace. It is an honourable peace, one that has given us self-respect and virtual self-government. Would you risk all that by fighting against the British again, knowing there is no more chance of winning now than there was before?'

'As you said just now, we don't know we *are* fighting the British. It could be that Matthias feels as you do,

231

and that we are fighting with the British against the Germans.'

'*Could* be?' Johanna said scornfully. 'The truth is that you don't really care what side you are on, do you? You have never settled down to farming, even after all these years of raising a family and seeing the farm gradually recovering from the last war in which we were involved. You believe that unless a man has a gun in his hands he is less than a whole man. Well, you're wrong. A true man is one who devotes his life to improving the world around him and building a life for himself, his family and his friends and neighbours, not destroying it for no other reason than he enjoys killing. That's not strength, Adam, it's a weakness.'

Her words were no more than a variation on a theme she had repeated many times since she and Adam had taken over the Viljoen family farm after the Boer war had claimed the lives of her father and brother.

Both Adam and Johanna had been active participants in that war, with Johanna being as ruthless as any man in the pursuit of independence from the yoke of colonialism which had been placed by the British about the necks of the independent settlers of Dutch descent. However, once the war had ended in far from ignominious defeat for the Boers, she had settled down to the life of a working wife on the remote Transvaal farm and raised three boys.

It had been a hard life, but a satisfying one. At least, it had been for Johanna, but she had become increasingly aware that the farm and she and the boys had not given Adam the same satisfaction. During the Boer war

Adam had been regarded as a daring, if occasionally reckless, fighting man, and his inherent powers of leadership meant that others would follow him willingly. Nothing Adam had done since those days had earned for him the same degree of respect he had known then. Over the years he had become increasingly restless, and he had taken to going away for lone 'hunting trips', their duration becoming longer on each occasion.

Johanna was aware that she was unable to change things. War, with its thrills and constant dangers, had provided a strong bond between them. Peace had offered nothing to take its place. Johanna knew this, but now she waited for Adam to say something that might prove her wrong.

The words she wanted to hear did not come. Resigned to the inevitable, she asked, 'When will you be leaving?'

'Tomorrow morning,' he replied. 'You'll manage well enough until I come back. There is nothing around the farm that Uiys can't cope with, and old Pieter Pretorius is always happy to come and lend a hand.'

Uiys was their fourteen-year-old son, who had inherited a love of farming from his maternal grandfather. It was a love that Adam lacked. Pieter was an old homesteader who lived alone in a shack on the fringe of the farm. As Adam had said, he enjoyed being allowed to carry out tasks about the farm.

'Then I suppose I had better make sure you have all the things you will need to take away with you,' Johanna said, in a matter-of-fact tone that successfully hid the deep unhappiness knotted inside her.

Although she could think of nothing she might have

done differently, she felt she had failed both as a wife and as a partner to the man she still loved as much as she had when they had set out on a life together.

II

For Adam, riding along with a heavy-bore rifle in a saddle holster, a belt of bullets worn as a bandolier and the prospect of action against an enemy at the end of the ride, it was a return to the days when he had belonged to a wide-ranging Boer commando. The only difference was that in his current situation he was searching for an army that he was not certain existed, anticipating action against an as yet unidentified enemy and travelling through country that was entirely unknown to him.

Adam had been travelling south in the hope of learning something of Matthias Van Klerk's movements when he met up with an itinerant predikant who was able to tell him that Van Klerk had passed through the area more than a month before, at the head of over a hundred armed and mounted men, heading for the border with German South West Africa.

It was the first information of Matthias Adam had received and he was duly grateful. He was about to ride on when he remembered what could prove to be an important factor in the war in which he was about to become involved.

Calling out to the departing predikant, he asked, 'Do you know which side Van Klerk was fighting for?'

Taken aback by the question, the predikant said, 'I

am a preacher, not a fighting man. I can only say that we have been neighbours of the Germans for a very long time and shared each other's problems for as long as I can remember. Anyone here who has taken up arms has been sympathetic to the German cause – which I consider to be a just one. I cannot see your friend coming through here if he did not support them too.'

As a result of his conversation with the predikant, Adam turned off the north to south road and headed east across the bush country towards the border with South West Africa, urging his horse to a canter. He hoped he might meet up with his old friend before the latter saw too much action without him. Adam had always enjoyed leading men and it would be more difficult staking his claim to promotion if others had already proved themselves in battle.

The country through which he was passing now was largely unoccupied. There were farms and smallholdings, but they were few and far between, occupied by Boers who preferred to live with only the company of their immediate family, and were quite likely to move on if other settlers built a homestead within a day's ride of their own remote farmhouse. Many of them were men who had fought against the British during the Anglo-Boer war and had been unable to swallow the bitter pill of defeat. They wanted nothing to do with the British and for this reason alone Adam, as a former Boer commando, was given food and shelter in households where news of the war between Britain and Germany was received with little interest. Their sympathies lay with the Germans, but they felt they owed no allegiance to either side and intended taking no part in the conflict.

There was nothing to tell Adam when and where it was that he crossed the unmarked border into German South West Africa, and although there were signs that the land had once been occupied by African tribes, he had met with no other human beings for more than a week when he made camp for the night beside a river bed.

By digging a hole in the surface-dry mud he was able to obtain sufficient water to meet his immediate needs; then, gathering large quantities of thorn bushes of a type used by the natives to protect their kraals against predators, he built himself an impenetrable space in which to tether his horse, light his fire and set out a blanket.

The night was relatively quiet, although he reached for his rifle when he smelled the distinctive and pungent odour of a hyena, circling the thorn barrier in the vain hope of finding a way into the camp. When he woke in the morning it was about an hour after sunrise and time to be on his way.

He had knocked out only one of his boots in order to ensure it was clear of scorpions, or other unwanted creatures that might have taken refuge in his footwear during the night, when a voice called out 'Good morning' in Afrikaans. The greeting was not to prove appropriate for Adam.

In the same language, the speaker added hurriedly, 'No . . . do not reach for your rifle or we will have no compunction in killing you.'

The man, who held a revolver which was pointed at

236

Adam, wore a pith helmet and army uniform, complete with knee-high boots. With him were about a dozen other Europeans who wore a variety of uniforms that gave no indication of their nationality or allegiance.

'Remove some of those thorn bushes – but keep well away from your gun. While you work you can tell us who you are and what you are doing in South West Africa.'

While the apparent leader of the armed men was talking, two of his men were speaking to each other in a language Adam recognised as German. Cautiously beginning to clear the temporary but effective fencing, he said, 'My name is Adam Retallick and I am here looking for Matthias Van Klerk. He sent a message asking me to join him in South West Africa.'

'Retallick? You are English?'

'No, I am from Matabeleland. My family were living there before the British came to the country. In fact, I fought against them in the Boer war. So too did Matthias Van Klerk and he'll be doing the same now, I have no doubt.'

The man who appeared to be in charge said something in German to his companions and there was much shaking of heads among them before the leader turned back to Adam.

'No one here has ever heard of Van Klerk. We'll take you to Captain Wahle, the military commandant of this region. Perhaps he will know the man you seek.'

When enough of the thorn bush stockade had been removed, Adam's captors took his guns and ammunition belt from him. They were on foot, so would not allow him to ride, but despite this they were quite sociable and chatted amiably to him as they headed for a very small township about two hours' walk away.

Adam learned that the men were Germans, but not professional soldiers. They were, in fact, part-time members of the German South West African defence force – the *Schutztruppe*. His fire had been spotted by one of their number whilst the latter was out on a reconnaissance patrol and he had returned to the township for backup before investigating further.

The township of Heinrichburg gave the appearance of having been shaken from a giant hand, each of the fifty or so bungalow-type houses deposited in a haphazard manner and left where they fell upon the flat and arid land. There was a spoil heap indicating that at some time there had been mining activity at the edge of the township, but the small size of the mound of waste and the present state of the houses indicated that it had been neither successful nor prosperous.

One of the larger but equally tired-looking houses was occupied by Captain Wahle, who, despite his bleak surroundings, was a very different manner of man from the part-time soldiers of the *Schutztruppe*. A regular army officer, he was past retirement age, but had been retained in South West Africa because of the outbreak of war. He listened scornfully to Adam's story as related by the senior member of the *Schutztruppe*, before addressing their prisoner.

'You, an Englishman, have been captured in German territory and give a fanciful story about coming to fight for us. Do you take us for fools, eh?'

Aware of the very real danger he was in, Adam said, 'If I took you for fools I wouldn't have come here to fight for you and, as I told your men, I am *not* English. I am from Matabeleland and was born there before the English – or the Germans – came to this part of Africa. I am in South West Africa because I had a message to join a man with whom I had fought the British in the Boer war. It was for this reason I left my farm in the Transvaal and came here to find him. That is the truth.'

It was apparent to Adam that Captain Wahle did not believe him. 'This man you came looking for . . . what is his name?'

'Matthias Van Klerk.'

'Matthias Van Klerk,' Captain Wahle echoed incredulously. 'You came here to fight for Colonel Van Klerk?'

'I wasn't aware of his rank,' Adam replied, relieved that the German officer knew of him, 'but I am not surprised. He was an excellent soldier.'

'Not too good, I hope,' Captain Wahle replied. Standing up abruptly and resting both hands on the desk in front of him, he glared at Adam angrily. 'Colonel Van Klerk is not fighting *for* Germany, but against us!'

While Adam was digesting the sudden alarming turn his fortunes had taken, Captain Wahle addressed the leader of the men who had brought him into the township.

'Take him away and throw him into the gaol. Tomorrow I will decide whether he will be shot as an enemy spy.'

*

The following morning, lying on the bare-board bunk that was the only item of furniture in his tiny, spartan cell, Adam was awakened from a poor night's sleep by the sound of small arms gunfire. It seemed to be coming from both inside and outside the township.

There was no one in the gaol whom he might ask what was happening and, frustrated that he could not reach the bars of a tiny, glassless window high up in a corner of the wall, Adam could only pace up and down his narrow cell, occasionally calling for attention when he thought he heard voices outside the gaol building.

At first, he thought the township must be under attack from the British, but the firing lacked the discipline to be expected from a professional fighting force. Sporadic in nature, it appeared to be coming from a great many directions at once. At one point there was a great deal of shouting, although he could make nothing of it. Then, more ominously, he heard the sound of a woman screaming, and his frustration at not knowing what was happening increased even more.

Eventually, when the fighting appeared to have died down a little, there was the sound of the outer door of the small gaol house being opened. A few moments later a key turned in the solid cell door and it swung open to reveal one of the men who had captured him the day before.

'What's going on?' Adam demanded. 'Are the British attacking?'

'No,' the German replied. 'We are being attacked by the Herero. They are taking advantage of the war to settle old scores with the settlers. They know things are going badly for us Germans. We are outnumbered by at least fifty to one and the Hereros have already taken one of the houses on the outskirts of Heinrichburg. We need every man and woman who can handle a rifle. If the township is taken not a man will be left alive, whether he supports England or Germany. As for our women and children . . .'

He had no need to complete the sentence and Adam said, 'Where is my rifle and ammunition?'

'Here, in the gaol office. Bring it with you. We have put all the women and children in the church and are defending the houses in a rough square round it – but we are hard pressed.'

They were in the gaol office now and Adam took up his rifle and ammunition bandolier from a corner of the room, where they had been placed together with his saddle, pack and bedroll.

'How many men do we have?' he asked.

'We started the battle with thirty, plus seven women who can shoot,' he was told, 'but two men have been killed and five are wounded, including two of the women, although they are still able to handle a gun.'

'What about the Herero . . . they can't all have guns?'

'No,' the German replied. 'They probably have no more than a hundred in all . . . and I doubt if there is a single marksman among them, thank God. But there seems to be no shortage of ammunition and they all have weapons of one sort or another. Our men who died

241

were both killed by spears. We have shot scores of Herero and they have been driven back for a while, but the lull cannot last . . .'

Even as he spoke there was an outbreak of shooting from the far side of the wooden-spired church.

The German militiaman said, 'That's the most vulnerable part of our defensive perimeter. The houses held by the Herero are so close to ours that if they attack in sufficient numbers they will be upon us before we can kill enough of them to bring them to a halt.'

'Then let's get there before they break through.'

Even as he was speaking Adam had broken into a run. Bypassing the church they saw a whole host of Herero tribesmen running towards the small bungalows that formed a defence line on this side of the square. The defenders inside the small houses were firing as fast as they could and each shot found a target but it seemed they would be overwhelmed – until Adam began firing as he ran.

His weapon was a pump action repeating rifle which was able to fire fifteen shots before needing to be reloaded, and each bullet fired from it downed a tribesman. It was the equivalent of having an extra fourteen men armed with single-shot rifles. His unexpected intervention caused the entire Herero attack to falter, during which time the defenders inside the beleaguered houses continued to shoot, giving Adam time to fumble bullets free from his bandolier and reload the chamber of his rifle.

He completed the task just as the tribesmen gathered themselves sufficiently to press home their attack yet again – but it was too late. Adam was firing once more and now he was close enough for his companion to bring his .45 calibre revolver into action. Within the space of two minutes they downed almost twenty Hereros and the attack broke.

Reaching the defended houses, Adam cut short the congratulations of the grateful men of the German *Schutztruppe*. 'There is no sense staying here and waiting for them to regroup and attack again. They are on the run now, so let's keep it that way. Load your guns and follow me. If we apply enough pressure we can drive them back to the edge of the township.' Before anyone could argue, he spoke to one of the three women who were in the house he had just entered. 'What are you doing?'

'Loading rifles,' she replied.

'You can leave that for a while,' Adam declared. 'When we go out to attack, you follow and pick up the rifles that have been dropped by the Herero. There must be almost twenty. They can ill afford to lose them and it will give us increased firepower. Bring them back here and load them ready for our return.'

The commander of the group which had captured Adam was in charge of the defences in this particular house, but he made no attempt to contradict his orders and Adam continued, 'We must not remain on the defensive. Sooner or later the Herero will realise they have only to hold off until nightfall, then they can come in and overwhelm us by sheer weight of numbers. We need to force them to draw back and lick their wounds instead of planning a final attack. Come, let's go – and call on the men in the other houses to come with us. Hurry now, before the tribesmen recover from the shock we've given them.'

Minutes later the men with Adam broke from the house and charged towards the houses to which the Herero had retreated, shouting wildly for the men of the *Schutztruppe* in the other houses to come with them. There were a few hurried shots fired at them, but Adam's bold plan succeeded in taking the tribesmen by surprise and they fled, pursued by a hail of bullets as the Germans fanned out, clearing the houses on either side of those occupied by their late attackers.

Within an hour the Herero had been driven to the outskirts of the small township, while behind the German women and children feverishly raised defences round the church in anticipation of a night attack.

The efficacy of their efforts was never put to the test. Late that afternoon, when most of the *Schutztruppe* had returned to assist the women and children, a shout went up that the Herero could be seen withdrawing to the east of the township.

The withdrawal mystified the beleaguered defenders of Heinrichburg, but the reason soon became apparent. A column of British soldiers came into view to the west of the township, headed by a detachment of Royal Naval Rolls-Royce armoured cars armed with formidable machine guns.

The siege of the Heinrichburg was over and its tiny garrison surrendered to the vastly superior British force with almost rapturous relief.

*

With the arrival of the British soldiers, Adam thought his captivity was at an end, but his hopes were dashed by the corporal of the relieving force who was taking details of the men who had surrendered their weapons before removing them in custody to the prisoner-of-war camp which had been set up in the rear of the main British force advancing through the territory some miles to the south of Heinrichburg.

When asked to give his name, Adam said, 'It's Adam Retallick – but I am not one of the *Schutztruppe*.'

The corporal looked up from the book in which he was entering details of the prisoners. 'Oh! Then why were you fighting alongside them . . . and don't say that you weren't. I myself saw you hand in a rifle and bandolier of ammunition when we disarmed you all.'

'I was captured and put in the town gaol when I was on my way to join up with Matthias Van Klerk . . . *Colonel* Van Klerk. The Germans only let me out because they needed every man they could muster to fight the Herero. If you check my gun you'll find that it's a hunting rifle and not a regular German issue.'

The corporal was anxious to complete the task he had been given and rejoin his unit in anticipation of seeing action against a large German force which was believed to be in the area. 'You can tell your story to the officer in charge of the prison camp. He'll have more time to listen to you than I have.'

'But I've told you . . . I'm not one of them. They had thrown me into gaol . . .'

'With a name like Retallick you'll be lucky if you're treated as leniently when you get to the prison camp.

245

If you're found to be English the commander-in-chief is likely to have you shot as a traitor. Now, get over with the others. I have to finish this list of names and submit it to headquarters before I can get back to my own company – and I've wasted enough time on you.'

12

I

Three days after Ben had been visited by Superintendent
Buchanan and Sergeant Callaghan of Scotland Yard's
Special Branch, Antonia St Anna made an unexpected
return to Tregarrick from Paris.

Despite his anxiety over the seriousness of the allegations being investigated by the two police officers and
his inability to produce evidence to immediately refute
them, Ben was delighted to see Antonia again – even
when he learned that she too had problems.

When he asked whether her work in Paris had 'borne
fruit', she looked unhappy and said, 'That is an English
expression that might have proved to be only too apt if
Olaf had gathered the harvest he was anticipating.'

Hoping he was mistaken in what he was thinking,
Ben asked, 'What exactly do you mean? Did something
go wrong?'

'Yes . . . at least, it did for Olaf. It seems I did not

show him the gratitude he expected of me for being allowed to share in his pioneering work.'

Aghast, Ben demanded, 'He . . . he didn't actually try to *do* anything . . . ? I mean . . .'

'I know what you mean, Ben and, no, he didn't physically attack me, although there was one particularly nasty incident at the hotel when he came to my room after he had been drinking. That might have been a whole lot worse had a maid not heard the commotion and knocked at the door. Even then I might have forgiven him had he apologised the next morning. I was aware how hard he was working and knew he was under a great strain. But he chose to ignore me and hardly said a word to me during the remainder of the time I was in Paris. It was no way to behave when we were both trying to learn something of great medical importance. I decided I should leave, and . . . well, here I am,' she ended lamely.

Antonia looked so unhappy and vulnerable that Ben felt an almost overwhelming urge to take her in his arms and comfort her. However, in view of the experience she had just related to him he felt it would be inappropriate. Instead, he said, 'That was an unforgivable way for him to behave, Antonia. Shouldn't you report it to someone?'

She shook her head vigorously. 'The work he is doing is far too important to have something like that bring it to an end. Thanks to the French maid nothing serious occurred.'

'All the same . . .' Ben began, but Antonia silenced him with a dismissive gesture of her hand.

248

'No, Ben. I thank you for your concern for me, but I decided the incident would be best forgotten.'

'That's all very well,' Ben persisted, 'but what will you do now? Your own career should not have to suffer because of something he did.'

'I am not sure yet,' Antonia replied. 'I could go back to Bodmin and carry on working there, but that could prove difficult when Olaf returns – as he will in due course. But I do not have to make up my mind immediately. I spoke on the telephone to Philippe a couple of days ago. He has been promoted and will be returning to active duties in Mozambique. I thought I would go to London and discuss things with him. I might even go home with him.'

Ben was genuinely dismayed. 'Don't do anything too hastily, Antonia. Think about it carefully first. Why don't you stay at Tregarrick and rest for a while? It will give you an opportunity to think things over without being subjected to any kind of pressure.'

'I promise I will not make any hasty decisions, Ben, but I want to see Philippe before he leaves, so I will need to do my thinking in London.' She looked at Ben speculatively. 'Why don't you come up to London for a few days? You look tired too. You would benefit from a break. Philippe would like to see you again before he leaves the country and you and I could explore some of the sights of London together. While I was working there I never had time to visit many of the places I was hoping to see.'

It was an offer that Ben would have accepted with alacrity had it come a few weeks earlier. As it was, circumstances forced him to decline and he hastened to explain. 'I'm sorry, Antonia – I can think of nothing I would enjoy more, but, unfortunately, I am under house arrest and not allowed to leave the St Austell area.'

'Under house arrest?' Antonia looked at him in disbelief. 'Why? What have you done?'

Ben told her of the visit he had received from the two Scotland Yard policemen. Before leaving Ruddlemoor, Superintendent Buchanan had told Ben that the allegations that had been made against him provided him with sufficient grounds for taking him into custody. However, in view of Ben's standing in the community and his vehement protestations of innocence, the superintendent was allowing him to remain at large while further inquiries were carried out. But he must not leave the St Austell area. Should he not comply with this restriction he would be immediately arrested and placed in custody in an aliens' detention centre pending the result of the Special Branch policeman's inquiries.

Antonia listened to Ben's story with utter disbelief. 'But . . . the allegations against you are absolutely preposterous, Ben. No one in their right mind would believe them!'

'Thank you,' Ben said. 'Unfortunately the evidence against me appears extremely strong – albeit almost entirely circumstantial. Superintendent Buchanan is being very generous by allowing me to enjoy the freedom I have. He could have arrested me and kept me in custody while he carried out his inquiries, however long they took. Had he done so nobody would have criticised him.'

Antonia had great difficulty in accepting what Ben

had told her. Her observation had led her to believe that Ben was a much respected businessman in Cornwall, and a pillar of local society. 'What has gone wrong for you, Ben? Who could have made such absurd allegations against you?'

'Superintendent Buchanan won't tell me,' Ben replied, 'but for them to be taken so seriously means it must be someone of importance who dislikes me enough to want me put away – or even shot! There is only one person I can think of who fits into both these categories . . . Brigadier General Sir Robert Grove.'

'Is he the very rude man who came to Tregarrick when Olaf was here?'

When Ben nodded, Antonia said, 'He is certainly a rude and bad-tempered man, but would he go so far to harm you?'

'I wish I could say no, but he has tried very seriously to put Ruddlemoor out of business in the past and he was absolutely furious on the last occasion when I succeeded in turning the tables on him and he was forced to buy clay from me and accept the terms I offered him. He also has a reputation for being utterly ruthless in business matters.'

Suddenly thoughtful, Antonia said, 'Do you think it would help if I spoke to Philippe and persuaded him to tell this policeman that he was the one who told you about the truce the Germans called with ships of neutral countries trading with Britain? He and I could also write letters confirming that we were with you when the airship crashed and you were merely intent on rescuing the British sailors on board.'

'Your confirmation of what we were all doing at Caerhays on that day would be appreciated,' Ben replied, 'but you mustn't say that Philippe gave me information that he gained as a result of his work at the embassy. It would not only get him into serious trouble, but permanently damage his career. No, we will stick to the story I told Buchanan. The truth will eventually come out to refute the other allegations. It must . . .'

Suddenly, and it was as much of a surprise to Antonia as it was to Ben, tears sprang to her eyes as she said, 'I am so sorry, Ben. You had to listen to me complaining that my world was coming to an end just because someone made a pass at me and yet you said nothing at the time about something that is not only affecting the whole of your business, but could even put your life in jeopardy. I am so sorry, Ben . . . I really am.'

It was another moment when Ben might have taken Antonia in his arms and assured her that everything would eventually be all right. He knew it – and so did Antonia.

She actually held her breath as she waited for him to react to her emotional outburst . . . and then there was a sudden knock on the door and Mrs Rodda appeared to say that dinner was about to be placed on the table.

II

The 'few days' Antonia had intended spending at Tregarrick before going on to London to be with her brother stretched to ten and for Ben they were the happiest he had enjoyed for a very long time. During

252

the daytime spent in Antonia's company he was able to push the thought of Superintendent Buchanan and his inquiries to the back of his mind. It was only at night, in the darkness of his bedroom, that thoughts of what might happen to him returned and made sleep difficult. However, as the days passed without further word from the Special Branch superintendent, the whole nightmare of the accusations made against him assumed an air of unreality.

He had written to his brother Nat at Insimo and, without giving him any details of his troubles, had asked for news of Adam, enquiring whether he had involved himself in the war that seemed to be sucking men in from all corners of the world. He did not want to be more specific, aware that if Nat was away from Insimo his mother would recognise the handwriting of her youngest son and might open the letter.

During the time Antonia was at Tregarrick, she enjoyed Ben's company quite as much as he enjoyed hers, and was aware that they were discovering they had far more in common than a childhood spent together in a little known corner of Africa. She was disappointed that he never tried to move their relationship on, even though she gave him every opportunity to do so. It was not that he did not think enough of her, he made that clear in many little ways, but Antonia thought it might have something to do with the guilt he felt about having an affair with Tessa while Lily was still alive. She believed he had managed to convince himself that he had no right to happiness . . . at least, not yet.

Somehow she needed to persuade Ben this was not

so, but her experiences with the shell-shocked men who had suffered trauma in the trenches had illustrated to her that the human mind was extremely complex and perhaps only time would be able to solve the problem for her. At all events, she and Ben had become much closer to each other since her return from France, and when she heard from Philippe, to say that his passage to Mozambique had been booked and he would be departing from England in a few days' time, she was unhappy to leave Ben in order to go to London to say farewell to her brother.

Ben too was unhappy that she was leaving Tregarrick, if only for a few days, but Antonia and Philippe had always been close to each other and he knew she had to go to him.

On the day of her departure he arranged for one of the Tregarrick servants to go to the station to purchase a ticket for her and, after loading her suitcases and a trunk into his Hotchkiss, he took her to St Austell to catch a London-bound train.

At the station he received an unwelcome reminder that he was the subject of a serious investigation into his alleged pro-German sympathies.

He and Antonia were seated in the waiting room when two men entered. Making straight for Ben, one of the two said, 'Mr Retallick? I would like a word with you in private. Perhaps we could go outside, on to the platform?'

Taken by surprise, Ben asked, 'Why? What do you want with me?'

There were a number of other travellers in the waiting

254

room, some of whom were aware who Ben was, and they were taking a considerable interest in the conversation.

'I think it best if we discuss the matter outside,' the stranger repeated and Ben realised the men must have some connection with Superintendent Buchanan and that he had been under surveillance. Apologising to Antonia, he assured her he would not be away long and followed the two men from the waiting room.

When they were on the platform the man who had spoken to Ben confirmed that he was a plainclothes policeman and said, 'You are aware that Superintendent Buchanan has left instructions that you are not to leave the St Austell area?'

'I am,' Ben replied curtly.

'Then what you are doing here, at the railway station – and with a considerable amount of baggage, if I may say so?'

'I have *no* baggage,' Ben retorted angrily. 'I am here to see off Dr St Anna who is travelling to the Portuguese embassy in London in order to say goodbye to her brother, a senior member of the embassy staff who is being recalled for duties elsewhere.'

Ben's reply was not what the policeman had been expecting and he was momentarily lost for words. It was left to his companion to say, 'I am afraid we need proof that you are telling the truth, Mr Retallick.'

'Then I suggest you speak to Dr St Anna. She is aware of the ridiculous allegations that have been made against me and will confirm what I have told you.'

'I am sorry, but for all we know she may be involved

255

too.' This from the first policeman. 'We need to be satisfied you are telling us the truth.' Turning to his companion, he said, 'Will you ask the woman to come out here? We will need to search through the luggage – whoever it belongs to.'

'This has now gone beyond a joke!' Ben declared angrily. 'I can hear the train coming along the line. Dr St Anna needs to be on it if she is to get to London. She is being met at Paddington by staff from the Portuguese embassy. I can assure you that if she fails to turn up there will be repercussions at a diplomatic level – especially if it's as a result of your idiotic decision to search her baggage.'

'I think you're protesting too much,' said the policeman. 'It makes me more determined than ever to carry out my duty.'

Antonia added her protests to Ben's when she accompanied the second policeman from the waiting room, but they were lost in the noise from the engine of the London-bound train which was just pulling into the station.

There was a great deal of interest from the passengers and their friends who emerged from the waiting room at the same time, especially when the porter who was about to put Antonia's luggage on the train was told to take it instead to the stationmaster's office.

Here, Antonia unlocked the trunk and suitcases, asking the two policemen to hurry, in order that she did not miss her train. Initially, they ignored her, but as they rummaged through her bags and it became apparent that there was nothing but her clothes in them, they began

256

to respond to the increasing sense of urgency in her voice. Eventually, the man who had first spoken to Ben, noticeably less confident now, said to her, 'I am sorry to have caused you any inconvenience, Dr St Anna, but we were only carrying out our duty. I will see that the train waits until you and your luggage are safely on board . . .'

Even as he spoke there was the shrill sound of the stationmaster's whistle and, seconds later, a short blast on the engine's whistle was followed by the breathless sound of escaping steam as the engine began to draw the train out of the station. Startled, the policeman ran out of the office and those inside could hear him shouting for the stationmaster to 'Stop the train!'

His demands were to no avail and when he and the stationmaster returned to the office the railway official was saying, 'You should have said something to me earlier and I would have held the train up for a few minutes – even though I would have probably been reprimanded for it. I've known Mr Retallick for a long time. He's an important man in these parts and has put a lot of business in the way of the railway. But there's no way I can stop the train once it's been signalled to go. Any fool should know that.'

Distraught, Antonia said, 'What can I do now, Ben? Philippe is expecting me, but there are no more trains leaving for London today. We will have very little time together now.'

She was close to tears. Ignoring the apologies of the policemen, Ben spoke to the stationmaster. 'Will you have Dr St Anna's luggage put in my motor car as quickly as you can, please?'

'Of course, Mr Retallick. Right away. I am very sorry that the doctor missed the train.'

'It's not your fault. She missed it because of these two officious idiots here,' Ben said angrily. He was aware that the two policemen could hear him, but he no longer cared. 'I will take that up with the proper authorities as soon as I have made the necessary arrangements for Dr St Anna. Do you have a train timetable you could let me have?'

'Of course.'

'Thank you. Bring it out to the car, will you? I'll hurry the man who is loading the doctor's luggage.'

Outside the station the luggage was secured in the back of the Hotchkiss and Ben had Antonia seated and the engine started by the time the stationmaster came hurrying out to hand him a timetable. Not until now did the policemen react. Suddenly suspicious, the first of them said to Ben, 'What are you going to do with that, Retallick? I hope you are not thinking of doing anything foolish.'

'All the foolishness has already been done, by you and your companion. I am going to see what can be done to undo it.' As the Hotchkiss moved off, Ben called out, 'I am taking Dr St Anna to Plymouth, to catch her train from there.'

III

When Ben returned to Tregarrick that afternoon he found two motor cars parked outside the entrance to the house. Leaving the Hotchkiss alongside them, he made his way

258

to the main door to find his way barred by a uniformed policeman.

'I'm sorry, sir, but no visitors are allowed inside just at the moment.'

'I am not a visitor,' Ben retorted, 'I live here. What are you doing here? You aren't from St Austell.'

He went to push past the constable but an outstretched arm barred the way. Ben's reply had temporarily nonplussed the constable, but he had been given his instructions by a very senior policeman – from London, no less – and he would obey them to the letter.

'I am sorry, sir, but I have my orders.'

'Orders from whom?' Ben demanded, although he already knew the answer.

'Superintendent Buchanan of Scotland Yard.'

'Is Buchanan inside?' Ben asked angrily. 'If he is, you had better go and find him quickly. I'll not be prevented from entry to my own home by him, you . . . or anyone else.'

Ben's uncompromising attitude posed a problem for the constable. He had been told not to allow anyone inside the house and if he left his post at the front door he was in no doubt that Ben *would* enter. On the other hand, if the angry man confronting him *was* the owner of the house . . .

He was saved from being forced to make a decision by the arrival of Superintendent Buchanan in the hall behind him. He had been in the study and seen Ben's arrival – and it was to him he spoke now.

'I believe you have behaved in a very foolish manner and broken the terms of the parole I allowed you, Mr

Retallick. Do you mind telling me where you have been?'

'You know very well where I have been,' Ben retorted. 'Thanks to the high-handed actions of the men you obviously had watching the house, the friend I took to St Austell railway station missed her train to London. It is important that she should arrive there today and there were no more trains from St Austell, so I took her to Plymouth.'

'This "friend" . . . you told the officer at the station that she was a doctor and she told him she was Portuguese. Is this the same woman who was with you when the airship crashed on the coast near here?'

'That's right. She is on her way to London to bid farewell to her brother who is returning to Mozambique.'

'Ah yes, Mozambique was mentioned in our earlier conversation. I looked it up in an atlas and saw that it borders on *German* East Africa,' said the superintendent. 'Very interesting . . . very interesting indeed.'

Ben looked at Superintendent Buchanan with an expression of incredulity. 'Are you suggesting there is something significant in that? If you studied the atlas you will have observed that Mozambique also has borders with the British colonies of North and South Rhodesia and Nyasaland – and South Africa.'

'The significance is that if I correctly recall what you told me when I interviewed you, your friend's brother is currently the military attaché at the Portuguese embassy in London. During his time there he will no doubt have gathered a great deal of information about British military matters. Come to that, his sister – your doctor friend – would have done the same in the course of her work with British soldiers both here and more recently in Paris. The Germans would consider the information possessed by both these friends of yours of considerable interest.'

Ben found it difficult to hide the anger he felt at the implication of the superintendent's words. 'Are you suggesting that Philippe and Antonia might be passing on information to the Germans? I took you for a misguided man, Superintendent, but not a foolish one. If you have looked into the backgrounds of both the St Annas – as I am sure you have – you will be aware that their father is commander-in-chief of the army in Mozambique and that Portugal is particularly sympathetic to the British cause. It has also complained very strongly to Germany about the constant violation of the borders of their colony in East Africa by German troops. It is to back up such protests that Philippe St Anna has been promoted and is returning to Mozambique to take an active part in preventing such incursions. As for Antonia . . . she has worked as hard as any British doctor treating our troops wounded in this war – indeed, she has probably worked harder. She has been instrumental in pioneering a new approach to those who are suffering from the results of German barbarism.' Thoroughly aroused by now, Ben did nothing to disguise the disdain he felt for Buchanan. 'Dr St Anna telephoned the Portuguese embassy from Plymouth station to register a formal complaint about the actions of your men. When I tell her what you have insinuated about her and her brother I have no doubt there will be a formal complaint from the Portuguese authorities at a much higher governmental level.'

Superintendent Buchanan had been stung by Ben's words, especially as they had been uttered in the presence of two of the uniformed policemen who had accompanied the senior Special Branch officer to Tregarrick. Now, he said, 'You will be saying nothing to Dr St Anna – or to anyone else – for quite some time, Mr Retallick. In view of your breach of the parole I granted to you when I first began investigations into the allegations made against you, I am placing you under arrest and you will remain in police custody until you are either charged with knowingly assisting an enemy of the state, or are taken into detention pending the end of the war with Germany in a centre for those who are considered to be a threat to the security of Great Britain.'

IV

When Superintendent Buchanan told Ben that he would not be allowed to speak to anyone after being taken into custody he meant exactly what he said. Ben was taken away from Tregarrick to a cell in the police headquarters in Bodmin and, despite his protests, was not allowed to speak to Mrs Rodda or leave her with instructions on what to do in what might well prove to be a very long absence.

That evening, when Antonia telephoned Tregarrick to tell Ben she had arrived safely in London and was with Philippe, she was horrified to learn the news of Ben's arrest. Mrs Rodda was deeply upset at what had happened to her employer and was also fearful that trouble would erupt at Tregarrick. Jim Bray had telephoned to say there had been an anti-Ben demonstration outside the entrance to the Ruddlemoor clay works and, only a few minutes before Antonia's call, one of the maids had left the house saying that both of her brothers were in France serving with the army and she was not prepared to work for a man who supported the country's enemies. The housekeeper was quick to stress, however, that the housemaid had not been employed at Tregarrick for very long. She was confident that all the other servants and employees would remain steadfastly loyal to Ben.

Nevertheless, despite Mrs Rodda's unswerving loyalty to Ben, she was not a young woman and Antonia sensed that she had been badly shaken by the events of the day, keenly aware that responsibility for Tregarrick now rested squarely upon her shoulders. After informing the stalwart housekeeper that she would be returning to Tregarrick in a couple of days' time to help her cope with the many problems caused by Ben's arrest, Antonia added that Ben had some very influential friends in London. She promised to contact them immediately, adding hopefully that it was possible Ben might be free to meet her upon her return to Cornwall.

When Antonia put down the telephone she held a brief conversation with Philippe, telling him what had happened, and then, at his suggestion, made a telephone call to the War Office and asked to speak to Lieutenant General Carey Hamilton.

Much later that evening a grumbling Tregarrick house-keeper, complete with muslin nightcap hiding her curling rags and wearing a high-necked nightgown and felt slippers, made her way down the staircase to the hall in response to the insistent ringing of the telephone.

The call was from a jubilant Antonia. 'I have wonderful news for you, Mrs Rodda. I have spoken to General Hamilton, the senior army officer who called at Tregarrick last year. He said he has just received impor-tant news that will ensure Ben's . . . Mr Retallick's release from police custody. It should also put a stop to all these ridiculous rumours about his being pro-German. General Hamilton has spoken to his brother-in-law, Lord Dudley, who is a minister at the Home Office. He can do nothing tonight but will order Ben's release first thing tomorrow. He should be home at Tregarrick by lunchtime. 'I'm sorry I am ringing you so late, but it took a long time to find General Hamilton and he has only just rung me back with the news. I hope I did not wake you.'

'I was in bed,' Mrs Rodda admitted, 'but sleep was out of the question. There was far too much on my mind . . . and now I am so relieved and excited too that I doubt if I will sleep . . . Just a minute. One of the house-maids is coming down the stairs. She must have heard the telephone ring. I will give her the good news and she can pass it on to the other servants, and then we will all have a cup of tea before going back to our beds much happier knowing that all is going to be well for poor Mr Retallick. I doubt if he will be sleeping tonight, but I will make certain that Cook has something special

264

waiting for him when he returns. Thank you, Dr Antonia, thank you very much indeed for ringing to put my mind at rest.'

It was late the following morning when Ben heard voices in the corridor outside the cell in the Bodmin police headquarters. Then a key was turned in the lock of the heavy iron door. Moments later the door swung open on protesting hinges and, removing the key, a uniformed police sergeant stood back to allow Superintendent Buchanan and Sergeant Callaghan to enter the cell.

The superintendent was the first to speak. 'Good morning, Mr Retallick. I trust the station sergeant and his officers have attended to your needs?'

Ben had passed a cold and sleepless night and, although he had been given a jug of cold water and a bowl in which to wash, he had not shaved or cleaned his teeth and was in no mood for civilities. 'Whatever it is you want, I have nothing to say to you or to anyone else until you come to your senses and let me out of here.'

'Then you may talk to your heart's content,' said the superintendent with feigned casualness. 'You are free to go.'

It took a few moments for the policeman's words to sink in. When they had, Ben snapped, 'It is a pity you did not accept twenty-four hours ago that the allegations against me are without foundation. It would have avoided a great deal of unpleasantness for a number of people.'

'I said nothing about accepting that the allegations

265

are untrue,' retorted Superintendent Buchanan, 'only that you are free to go. My orders to release you come from the War Office, via the Home Secretary. However, although you may have friends in high places, it will not prevent me from carrying out my duty. The investigations into your activities will continue and the outcome will be decided in a court of law, not in the leather-seated lounge of a gentlemen's club in London.'

Ben was almost as surprised as Superintendent Buchanan had been at learning of the source of his release, but he remembered that Carey Hamilton's sister was married to Lord Dudley, Minister of State at the Home Office – and Thomasina, Lady Dudley, had spent time at Insimo. Carey must have made Thomasina and her politician husband aware of his predicament – and there was only one person who would have appealed to him for help.

Ben believed that the person he had to thank for his unexpected freedom was . . . Antonia.

V

After dark in the late evening of the day following Ben's release from police custody, Antonia returned to Cornwall, having seen her brother set off on the long journey which would first take him to Lisbon for talks with the Portuguese military authorities. He would then travel on to Mozambique, where he had been appointed to the post of military commander of a region which bordered the German East African territory.

Acting on the advice of a concerned Jim Bray, Ben

had not been to Ruddlemoor since he left the Bodmin police headquarters. Word of his arrest had spread rapidly, due in the main to reports of the allegations against him being published in the *Cornish Telegraph*, a newspaper which covered the whole of Cornwall. It also carried a speculative and largely inaccurate editorial listing Ben's so-called 'pro-German activities'.

The reports had resulted in a crowd gathering outside the gates of the Ruddlemoor works, exhibiting banners and placards demanding that Ben be brought to trial. The demonstrators jeered and vilified Ruddlemoor workers as they arrived for work, or left to go home at the end of their shift. A few of them were close relatives or friends of soldiers who had lost their lives in the fighting in France or Belgium, or who had loved ones there, but they were greatly outnumbered by others who had no other motive than to cause a nuisance. Jim Bray reported to Ben that he had been able to keep the protesters outside the gates, but felt that if Ben were to put in an appearance, more serious trouble was likely to erupt.

It was against this background that Ben telephoned Antonia before she left London and urged her to catch a motor taxicab from St Austell in order to avoid any unpleasantness that might occur should Ben come to meet her at the railway station and be recognised.

Ben's welcome for Antonia contained all the warmth she could have wished for and neither his kiss, nor the embrace that accompanied it, was feigned. Not only was Ben grateful to Antonia for securing his freedom, but seeing her again made him realise, perhaps for the first time, just how much he had missed her company. He was reluctant to let her go and Mrs Rodda, entering the hall with the intention of greeting Antonia and expressing her own gratitude to her for securing Ben's release so promptly, tactfully decided to postpone her welcome and withdrew silently from the hallway.

Eventually, releasing his hold on Antonia, Ben said, 'I will have your luggage taken up to your room in a few minutes, but first come to the drawing room and tell me how you succeeded in persuading everyone that I am not the traitor that Superintendent Buchanan still believes me to be.'

'You have General Hamilton to thank for that,' Antonia replied. 'He never doubted your patriotism and once he grasped what had happened he left no one else in any doubt either. He would have telephoned you himself today, but after working for much of the night on your behalf he had to leave early this morning to accompany the King on a visit to France. But I feel quite certain you will approve of the results of his efforts . . .'

Producing a newspaper, she handed it to him, saying, 'Here is the *London Evening Standard*. The Tanganyika expedition is front page news and you, Sam Hooper and the Ruddlemoor traction engines are featured prominently in the item. There are also a number of articles connected to the main story. One is about Sam's Albert medal, together with details of your part in the incident. Another describes how you were shot when you were going to the rescue of the stricken airship. It also praises your business acumen when, as it says here, you "received information, whilst abroad on the Continent, of Germany's intention to stop sinking neutral ships carrying non-military cargoes in British waters". General Hamilton and Philippe had a long conversation over the telephone and together they tried to produce a press release that would counter most of the allegations made against you. I believe they have largely succeeded. Read it for yourself and see if you agree with me. I hope you do because the same article will be in every national newspaper tomorrow morning!'

Taking the newspaper from her, Ben began reading it. Halfway through the front page he glanced at Antonia; then, without speaking, he took the newspaper to an armchair and, sitting down, resumed reading.

The report was mainly about what it described as 'an incredible journey' by Commander Spicer (the promotion had now been confirmed by the Admiralty, his seniority dating from the day of the first action on Lake Tanganyika) with the gunboats which had been given the incongruous names of *Mimi* and *Toutou*.

Not only had Spicer successfully conveyed the two gunboats overland for a distance of more than three thousand miles, he had then succeeded in capturing one armed German vessel and sinking another, both of which were considerably superior in size and armament to his own diminutive craft. By so doing he had wrested control of Lake Tanganyika from Germany.

It was a truly remarkable achievement and one which the press, accustomed to reporting depressing news from the bloody debacle in Europe, was delighted to seize upon. Suddenly, Commander Spicer was a national hero

269

and everyone who had helped to make the expedition such a resounding success was included in the glory of his victory. The part played by the Ruddlemoor traction engines was given considerable prominence, thanks to General Carey Hamilton, and both Ben and Sam Hooper came in for unstinting praise, with separate articles on the part each had played in the successful mission and detailing events in their lives which were intended to show that they were both citizens of whom Britain could be proud.

When Ben finished reading the newspaper reports he put the paper aside and said, 'How can I possibly thank you for all you have done for me, Antonia? I owe you not only my freedom, but also the whole future of Ruddlemoor. You have worked a miracle.'

'I am happy to have been able to help you,' Antonia said, delighted with his praise, 'but it would not have been possible without Carey Hamilton. He was outraged to learn of your arrest. Had he not been able to secure your release by any other means I think he might have brought a regiment of soldiers to Cornwall and stormed the gaol where you were being held!'

'I will thank Carey when he is back in the country,' Ben said, 'but for now . . .' Standing up, he held out his arms to her. 'Antonia . . . come here . . . please.'

She came to him eagerly and, when he was holding her, he said, 'You know, you are the best thing to happen to me for longer than I can remember. I should have recognised it and done something about it many months ago.'

*

VI

Early the next morning Ben had difficulty persuading Antonia not to accompany him to Ruddlemoor. Leaving her at Tregarrick to worry about him, he set off in his Hotchkiss. On the way he stopped at a newspaper wholesaler in St Austell where he bought bundles of national newspapers. With these on the seat beside him he drove along the valley that led to his clay works.

Prior to setting off he had telephoned Jim Bray to tell him his plans, and when the works captain heard the sound of the Hotchkiss approaching some thirty of the burliest Ruddlemoor employees emerged from the works in time to surround the vehicle when it reached the gates, keeping the noisy, jeering pickets at bay.

Much to the surprise of the protesters, instead of driving inside, Ben stopped his car and, standing up in it, eventually succeeded in silencing them sufficiently for what he had to say to them to be heard.

'Have any of you seen a newspaper this morning?' he demanded.

The majority of those who deigned to reply shouted a 'No!' but one voice was heard to call, 'What have the newspapers got to do with anything?'

'If you come into Ruddlemoor you can find out,' Ben replied. 'I am calling a meeting of all my employees to tell them what the newspapers have to say. Come and join them and then you can each have a newspaper to take home as a souvenir of a truly remarkable British victory.'

271

There were murmurs from a few of the protesters that it was 'some kind of trick', but Ben's actions had taken the majority of them by surprise and they were curious to hear what he had to say. When the first of their number followed the Hotchkiss into Ruddlemoor, the others trooped after them.

All work had ceased and Jim Bray had assembled every man and woman employed at Ruddlemoor in the great linhay where the refined clay was stored prior to being shipped. A number of the off-duty shift workers who lived close to Ruddlemoor had also heard that Ben was to make an 'announcement' to his employees and had hurried in to learn what it was about. In view of the rumours that had been circulating concerning Ben's own future, they feared he might be informing them that he was closing the works, and they had brought along their wives to hear the news at first hand.

When Ben climbed the steps to a platform at one end of the linhay, where there was a weighing machine and bundles of sacks, a hush fell over the assembly. Even the protesters from outside the works gates, usually so vociferous, remained quiet.

After thanking his employees for remaining loyal during what he was aware had been a difficult time, Ben said he would like to read a lengthy news item that had made the headlines in all the national newspapers.

First, he held up one of the newspapers which carried the banner headline, INCREDIBLE VICTORY BY NAVY'S WARSHIPS – MORE THAN 600 MILES FROM THE SEA!

Ben read aloud from the report on the incredible overland journey of *Mimi* and *Toutou*, which had lasted almost six months before they were launched on Lake Tanganyika. The newspaper gave graphic accounts of the battles between the British and German warships which secured the lake for Great Britain and its allies.

Ben's listeners found news of the battle exciting and cheered patriotically when he relayed details of the gunboats' second victory – but they were puzzled. Why should he have stopped all work at Ruddlemoor and assembled his employees in order to relay such an item of news to them . . . albeit a remarkable one?

It was left to one of the protesters, bolder than his companions, to voice the general bemusement.

'This is great news,' he declared loudly, 'but what does it have to do with you and your sympathies with the Germans?'

His words brought an angry response from the Ruddlemoor workers and the defiant protester looked about him fearfully until Ben's voice rose above the din, calling for quiet.

When the noise had died down to a low grumbling murmur, Ben said, 'If you will allow me to continue with the newspaper report you will learn exactly what it has to do with me – and the ridiculous accusations made against me of being pro-German. You will also realise how Ruddlemoor – and Sam Hooper in particular – has played a not insignificant part in the success of the Lake Tanganyika expedition.'

His surprising announcement caused another outbreak of sound, but this time it was interest and not anger that was being expressed. All the Ruddlemoor employees, and many of the protesters too, knew Sam Hooper.

When the noise had died down once more, Ben continued reading from the newspaper, telling his increasingly excited audience of the part played by Sam Hooper and the two Ruddlemoor traction engines and explaining why it had been so necessary to keep all details of the operation secret, even when it led to such serious consequences for Ben himself. It was apparent to Ben that the newspaper report had been written by Carey Hamilton, who had used every opportunity to discount all rumours about Ben being sympathetic to Germany.

There was a separate article giving details of Ben's own background, saying that he had obtained details of the proposed cessation of German hostilities against neutral shipping from a friendly foreign 'diplomatic source' and praising his entrepreneurial actions in risking his own money to persuade neutral ships to come to Charlestown again, bringing work and money back to the hard-hit port and those families who depended upon it for their survival.

There was much more in a similar vein, but Ben cut it short by saying that his listeners could take a newspaper home with them and read it for themselves. He ended by calling for three cheers for Sam Hooper and the part he had played in the successful Lake Tanganyika expedition.

These were given readily; then, as Ben was about to make his way from the platform, the booming voice of one of his shift captains rose above the now excited buzz of voices in the linhay and called for 'Three cheers for Ben Retallick'.

The response must have been heard in St Austell, and those who had earlier been protesting outside the gates of Ruddlemoor shouted as loud as anyone else. Ben waved a hand somewhat sardonically in acknowledgement as he left the platform and made his way to the Ruddlemoor office, the good wishes of his employees ringing in his ears.

That evening, at Tregarrick, Ben called all his household staff together and, after thanking them for their loyalty during the recent difficult weeks, had champagne brought from the cellar in order that they might all celebrate the success of the Tanganyika naval expedition.

During the celebrations, Ben called for a special toast in honour of Antonia, who had done so much to secure his release from police custody. The household was still celebrating when the doorbell rang. One of the housemaids went to answer it and returned looking flustered, closely followed by Betsy Hooper.

With a guilty start, Ben realised that with all that had been going on in his own life he had quite forgotten to inform Betsy Hooper of what had been happening to Sam in Africa. He hoped that Sam might somehow have been able to keep in touch with her, but Betsy's first words proved that this was not so.

'Mr Retallick . . . I'm sorry to break in on your celebration, sir, but what's this folk are telling me about my Sam? I thought he was safe and well in your family's home in Africa, but people are saying that he's been mixed up in some fighting there. I haven't heard from him for some weeks now, Mr Retallick. What's he been getting up to . . . and when is he coming back home?'

13

I

Soon after reaching Sankisia, the Tanganyika Lake naval expedition embarked with *Mimi* and *Toutou* on a narrow-gauge railway that would take them to another trading post, this time on the banks of the Lualaba river. From here the two boats would be launched and the white ensign would fly for the first time on a river in the very heart of Africa, setting out on what it was hoped would be the penultimate leg of their incredible journey.

It would be another month before they reached Lake Tanganyika, but the naval men were jubilant. Once the boats were in the water their destinies would be in the hands of sailors, confident in their own skills and not reliant upon others.

The traction engines had successfully carried out the task for which they had been brought all the way from Cornwall, but now it had been completed it seemed the expedition leader was no longer interested in them, or their drivers. Sam and Diego were left behind in Sankisia with their charges – and no instructions about what they were expected to do now.

Sam had erroneously assumed that Spicer had made arrangements with the drunken Belgian trader in charge of the trading post to provide native porters who would find water for the two machines on their return journey across the mountains, but the trader declared that Spicer had made no such request of him. Besides, all the available porters had been sent on ahead with stores for the expedition.

Sam hoped that the absence of orders for the traction engines and their drivers was no more than another example of the lack of communication between Spicer and himself and that the commander would send a sufficient number of porters back to enable him to make the return journey over the mountains, once the boats had been launched on the Lualaba river. However, when the days of waiting had become a week, it was apparent that no porters were forthcoming, and Sam realised that he and Diego had been left to solve their own problems.

Fortunately, there was no shortage of food. Sam estimated that the wagonload of supplies left behind by the naval expedition would last him and Diego for at least three months – but he had no intention of remaining at the trading post for such a length of time. The two trailers which had come with the traction engines and were designed to carry log fuel for them had been adapted to carry the two gunboats, but, no longer required, they had been left behind too and could easily be returned to their original state.

Unfortunately, none of this would solve the problem that had bedevilled the expedition on its hard-fought trek across the mountains – finding water to fill the boilers of the two steam-powered 'land locomotives'. Without water, and with no labour force to cut timber to use as fuel, Sam decided that a return journey across the mountains was out of the question – but his knowledge of the geography of the country in which they now found themselves was decidedly sketchy.

The alcoholic Belgian in charge of the trading post had promised to draw a map by which they could find their way back to the railway that would carry them southward to Rhodesia, but he was never sober enough to complete such a document. It was probably just as well, because Sam soon discovered that the Belgian was not as familiar with the country in which he lived as he claimed to be. It was necessary to think of another means of escape before the rainy season arrived.

Sam felt that if he could only get his charges to Rhodesia, General Edwards would be able to make arrangements for them to be returned to Ruddlemoor. Even if the general was not available, Sam knew help would be forthcoming from the Retallicks at Insimo. He should probably take the traction engines to Insimo anyway and leave them there while he made his way to Mozambique to find Maria and hopefully persuade her to return to Cornwall with him.

In the meantime, while he tried to find a solution to his problems, Sam and Diego worked on readying the huge machines for whatever lay ahead. They had been worked hard on the six-week journey across the mountains and required a major service.

Work on the two traction engines took longer than Sam had anticipated. A further six weeks after the departure of Acting Commander Spicer and the members of his expedition, Sam and Diego were still putting the finishing touches to the overhaul of their charges – and Sam was no closer to a solution to the problem of how to return them to the United Kingdom.

For Diego, the enforced stay at Sankisia was not a particular hardship. He had no ties and the bold and handsome young African women from the village surrounding the trading post found him attractive. One evening, when he was setting off to the trading store where a bout of drinking would precede another amorous encounter, he suggested that Sam accompany him.

It was the first time he had asked Sam to go with him but Sam declined, saying, 'No, thanks, I have things to do. There is an old locomotive boiler down by the railway sheds. It needs a bit of work done on it, but if it can be made watertight and fitted with wheels I want to work out whether that, together with one traction engine topped up with water and towed by the other, will get us across the mountains.'

'I doubt it very much,' said Diego. 'It will take far more water than that. Besides, I too have looked at the locomotive boiler and it's so badly rusted you'd need to completely rebuild it to make it hold water. There are neither the tools nor the material here to carry out the work that's needed. No, forget it for one night and come out and enjoy yourself.' Giving Sam a sly look, he added, 'I wouldn't tell Maria, if that's what's stopping you. Anyway, she's made you no promises yet so she can't expect you to live like a monk while she's making up her mind.'

'Maria has nothing to do with my not wanting to go out drinking at the trading post,' Sam said, 'and it isn't the only thing that stops me from enjoying the company of the local women. It isn't so long ago since Arab slavers were in this part of Africa buying or stealing women. When they passed through it wasn't only sorrow they spread. I respect my body and wouldn't want to expose it to any of the diseases they have left behind. I certainly wouldn't want to pass them on to anyone else.'

Diego stared at Sam in silence for a while, then he shrugged. 'You only have one life, Sam. You should make the most of it – I do.' With that he left the dilapidated bungalow that had once been the residence of a Belgian district commissioner when Sankisia was of far more importance than it was today, and went off into the night.

When he had gone, Sam worked on the calculations he was making about the maximum amount of water that could be carried by all the means available to him. So far, no matter how hard he had tried, the result had always been the same. It would not be enough and there seemed to be nothing he could do to solve the problem. During the journey across the mountains he had kept a detailed diary which itemised the performances of both traction engines and listed places where they had been able to obtain water. He had already studied it closely, but now he went through it again, bringing the capacity of the second locomotive's boiler into the equation.

He was still checking his calculations a couple of hours later when the front door to the bungalow slammed shut and a hot and dishevelled Diego burst into the room. Startled, Sam began to question him about his appearance and the reason for his abrupt entry, but Diego cut him short. 'I'll explain everything to you later, Sam, but if anyone comes looking for me, say I have been working on the traction engines and have just gone back to the engine sheds.'

'What . . . ? Who is likely to come looking for you?'

'I'll explain later. I'm going to my room, but remember, if anyone comes looking for me, I have been working on the traction engines and have gone back to the engine sheds.'

'Who is likely to come looking for you?' Sam demanded once more, but his flustered housemate turned and hurried away, and Sam realised he was not alone. There had been someone with him when he entered the house and he had left her – and Sam had no doubt at all that it was a woman – in the hallway.

Sam rose to his feet to follow Diego and demand an explanation, only to hear the key turn in the lock of Diego's door. He was still standing on the threshold of the room where he had been working when there was a fierce hammering on the front door of the house and a man began shouting in a language Sam recognised as 'Belgian French'. He could not understand what was being shouted, but the noise outside left him in no doubt about the unseen man's anger. He made his way to the door, picking up the loaded rifle that was standing in a corner of his room as he went.

Keeping a loaded weapon close at hand was a precaution observed by most settlers in the country in these uncertain times. There was always the possibility of a raid by German troops from across Lake Tanganyika, as well as the constant threat of violence from the Congolese natives who bitterly resented the presence of their colonial overlords.

Sam opened the door cautiously, and had he not been prepared he would have been bowled over by the angry man who had been banging on it. As it was, he was able to catch the would-be intruder off balance and heave him backwards. His arms flailing wildly, the man staggered back before falling off the covered-in veranda and landing heavily on the hard ground in front of the bungalow. He leaped to his feet immediately and there was the glint of metal in his hand.

Sam kicked the door open wide so that the light from a lamp in the hallway fell upon the rifle he was pointing in the direction of the other man. The latter came to a halt, but he continued to shout at Sam.

'Unless you can speak English, you are wasting your breath,' Sam said, hoping his voice did not betray the nervousness he felt.

The man outside the bungalow was still angry. Breathing heavily, he said in halting English, 'With you I have no quarrel – but I kill Diego.'

The light from the hallway was not particularly

strong, but it was sufficient for Sam to see that the man, like Diego, was of mixed African and European blood. His next words indicated that this was not the only thing they had in common.

'Diego . . . he has taken my woman.'

Sam had already guessed that a woman was at the root of the quarrel the angry visitor had with his house-mate. But the Insimo employee was his friend, as well as being essential for the safe return of the Ruddlemoor traction engines to their owner.

'I doubt it very much,' he said. 'He has spent most of the day working on our two machines. In fact, I think he is still in the engine shed with them right now.'

'He is not in your house?'

'No,' Sam lied, relieved that the other man seemed to have accepted his story. 'If he returns before you find him, who shall I say called?'

It was a facetious question, and instead of replying the man turned on his heel and hurried away into the night.

Only now did Sam become aware that the hand that had been resting on the rifle's trigger guard was trembling. Stepping back inside the hallway he shut the door and, as an afterthought, shot home the two bolts that secured it on the inside. There were heavy shutters fitted to each of the windows. If the angry stranger decided to return to the bungalow when he found the engine shed firmly padlocked, he would not be able to gain entry.

With the door secured, Sam strode purposefully to Diego's bedroom and knocked heavily on the door with his clenched fist. 'You can come out now. The man who came looking for you has gone – for the time being, at least.'

There was movement in the room, but when the door remained unopened Sam knocked on it once more, louder this time. 'Do you hear me, Diego? Come out and give me an explanation of why I needed to keep a caller at bay with a loaded rifle.'

There was the sound of whispering in the room, then the key turned in the lock and a sheepish-looking Diego appeared. His room was in darkness, but Sam said, 'The woman who is with you can come out too. She seems to be at the root of all the trouble.'

Turning back into the bedroom, Diego said something in a language that was as unfamiliar to Sam as the stranger's Belgian-French had been, but not the same. It sounded as though it might be an African native language, but it had the result Sam had requested. Diego stepped aside to allow the woman at the centre of the dispute to show herself.

She was African, but Sam was startled to see that she was very young . . . probably no more than sixteen years of age. She was also strikingly beautiful – and very, very frightened.

By way of introduction, Diego said, 'Sam, this is Mumbi. She is from Mozambique and speaks no English.'

'She also seems to be another man's wife,' Sam said accusingly, 'and that makes her trouble. Trouble we can do without.'

'Trouble she may be, Sam,' Diego admitted reluctantly,

'but she is nobody's wife. Certainly not Louis Jadot's. He bought her from her stepfather, in Mozambique, and is taking her north to the Sudan. He has been boasting that he will make a handsome profit when he sells her on to an Arab trader he knows there.'

Sam looked from Diego to the girl, then back again. 'Is this the truth?' he asked suspiciously. 'Or is it a story you have just made up to get yourself out of trouble?'

'It's the truth,' Diego declared. 'Ask Andre in the store tomorrow. If he's sober enough he will verify that Louis Jadot trades between Mozambique and the Sudan regularly, buying and selling as he goes along – but most of his money comes from slaving.'

Still suspicious, Sam said, 'Slavery was stopped many years ago. It's banned everywhere in the world.'

'Tell that to the other half-dozen Africans Jadot has chained in a wagon hidden outside Sankisia,' Diego retorted. 'In a couple of months' time they will be working for a rich Arab on the other side of the Red Sea – working for no pay and with the prospect of a beating if they don't do what they're told quickly enough.'

'If these so-called slaves are kept chained, how did you manage to rescue Mumbi?' Sam was still not convinced of the veracity of Diego's story.

'Jadot brought her to the trading post to show her off,' Diego explained. 'I think he half hoped that Andre might offer to buy her, to join the other girls he has working at the trading post, but some Belgian officials take slavery very seriously and Andre wasn't drunk enough to take up his offer. Then, when Jadot ordered her to tell Andre her name, he spoke in Portuguese. I butted in and spoke to her in the native dialect spoken by my mother, asking what she was doing with Jadot – and she replied in the same language. Jadot became very angry because he didn't understand what we were saying. After threatening to knife me, he dragged Mumbi away to the camp where he had left his wagon. I followed them without being seen. After giving her a good slapping for talking to me, as a punishment he left her standing beneath a tree with her hands chained to a branch above her head. Then he returned to the trading post to continue drinking with Andre. I came back to the engine shed, took the bolt cutters from your toolbox, went to Jadot's camp and cut her free. The bolt cutters are still in the hall, where I left them when I came in with Mumbi. Unfortunately, Jadot returned to the camp earlier than I had expected and nearly caught us. It was too dark for him to see it was me, but it wouldn't have taken much figuring out. He must have gone straight back to the trading post and found out where I was staying.' Giving Sam a nervous, lop-sided grin, Diego added, 'It was a good job you were here when Jadot arrived. Had you been out he would have kicked the door down, I would be dead and Mumbi would have taken the beating of her life when he got her back to his camp.'

Sam had seen the bolt cutters in the hallway and wondered what they were doing there. Convinced now that Diego was telling the truth, he said, 'I think we should pay a call on Jadot – and we will both go armed.'

'I will be very happy to do that, Sam,' Diego replied, 'but not tonight. He has a number of Sudanese bearers

287

with him and our guns wouldn't help us much in the darkness. It will be far better if we tackle him in daylight – in the morning.'

There was sense in Diego's suggestion and Sam agreed, but he asked, 'What do we do with Mumbi until then? We only have two bedrooms – and two beds.'

'She won't feel safe unless I am with her,' Diego said. 'I am the only one she can talk to who can keep her informed about what is going on. She will stay in my room for the night.'

Sam did not speak Mumbi's language, but it did not require words to understand that she regarded Diego as her saviour, and would not easily be separated from him.

'All right. We will talk about her future tomorrow – after we have dealt with Jadot.'

II

The next morning, when Sam and Diego arrived at the site where Louis Jadot had been camping with his wagon, they found he had already gone. The embers of a fire were still smouldering and there were other signs that he and his party had made a hasty departure.

Diego's first thought was that Jadot might be making another attempt to recapture Mumbi, who had been left locked in the bungalow with strict orders to open the door to no one, and he and Sam ran all the way back to the trading post. Much to their relief, they discovered that Mumbi had not been disturbed during their absence.

'He must have guessed what we would do and

decided to accept the loss of Mumbi and make good his escape,' said a jubilant Diego.

Sam was less convinced. 'Jadot was very determined to get her back last night,' he said, 'and he was quite ready to attempt it on his own. You say he has a number of Sudanese to back him up if he decides to try again – and I am convinced he will. I think we had better keep a close watch on Mumbi at all times and make quite certain we are armed wherever we go.'

Both Sam and Diego were quite wrong in their assumptions about Jadot's reasons for breaking camp in such a hurry, and the likelihood of his making another attempt to reclaim Mumbi.

Diego went to the trading store for a few provisions later that morning and came hurrying back with some exciting news. Late the previous night a mounted Rhodesian army scout had come to the trading store enquiring whether Sam and his traction engines were still at Sankisia. He had been sent on ahead of a sizeable Rhodesian army unit, which was accompanied by a small Belgian cavalry troop. Some of the Sudanese traders had been drinking in the store at the time and, hurrying back to their camp, had warned Jadot of the Belgian army's presence. Had Louis Jadot been discovered with his African slaves, he and all those with him would have been arrested and most certainly given lengthy jail sentences.

Sam was excited by the news that he was being sought by Rhodesian soldiers. He hoped it meant that his concerns about getting his traction engines back to Insimo were about to be resolved.

*

The Rhodesians arrived in the late afternoon that day. They were a large force of heavily armed and mounted men, a number of white army scouts and some forty Africans. All the latter were excellent trackers of both men and animals and, much to Sam's delight, they were led by Colonel Nat Retallick.

Nat was accompanied by a short, stocky army officer who, like himself, wore the insignia of a full colonel. Before making introductions, Nat shook hands with Sam and said, 'I'm glad I have found you here, Sam, and would like to be the first to congratulate you on the important part you, Diego and your traction engines played in the success of the naval expedition to Lake Tanganyika. Spicer and his men have proved themselves, against all the odds. I hope he was sufficiently grateful to you.'

'If he was, he didn't show it to me. Did he say anything to you, Diego?'

When Diego shook his head, Nat said, 'Well, whether he showed it or not, you have good cause to be proud of your efforts. Thanks to you, Spicer has done battle with a German gunboat, killing the captain and forcing the crew to surrender to him. He is now lying in wait for a still larger prize, the *Hedwig von Wissmann*. I don't doubt he'll take that too, despite the fact that it's more than ten times the size of his own gunboats.'

Sam was impressed by the news of Spicer's epic victory, despite his dislike of the expedition's leader. He had successfully achieved what he had set out to do and Sam admired him for that. Nodding his approval, he said, 'Spicer has done what most of those who knew about the expedition declared couldn't be done. He deserves respect for that. But what are you doing here? Can you help me get the traction engines back to Ruddlemoor? I have been having nightmares about being stranded here and watching them rust away!'

Nat smiled. 'I wouldn't have allowed that to happen. Diego is far too useful to me at Insimo . . . but I am hoping you are not in a desperate hurry to return to Cornwall because I have a proposition to put to you.'

'I am in no particular hurry to get back to England,' Sam replied cautiously, 'but I was hoping to pay a visit to Mozambique in the near future.'

Nat and his army companion exchanged meaningful glances before Nat said, 'Then what I have to say might suit you very well, Sam.' Indicating his fellow officer, he said, 'This is Colonel Murray. He is leading a column of Southern Rhodesia Volunteers and British South Africa Police – employed by the British South Africa Company. He and his men have been ordered to make their way to Mozambique as speedily as possible . . . but I'll let Colonel Murray explain the situation to you.'

Colonel Ronald Murray was a thick-set, dark-haired man with a heavy moustache, and Sam would learn that he was also a courageous soldier whose men would follow him wherever he led them.

Shaking hands with Sam, he came straight to the point. 'I am glad we have found you, Mr Hooper. My column has urgent need of one of your traction engines. We have long been at a considerable disadvantage to the Germans in having no artillery, as they possess heavy guns salvaged from a sunken cruiser, the *Königsberg*, and have adapted them to make formidable artillery pieces. We were recently lucky enough to capture one of these guns, together with a great deal of ammunition. Unfortunately, because of its weight and bulk we are unable to take it along with us. This is where one of your traction engines would prove invaluable. I realise that their owner is Colonel Retallick's brother and he has made you responsible for them, but Colonel Retallick has telegraphed him seeking permission for one of them to be made available for military use. He is confident he will give his consent.'

'He will,' Sam agreed. 'Especially as it will be helping a Rhodesian force. But where is the gun now – and what about the other traction engine? What will happen to that?'

'The gun is being manhandled over the mountains by a whole army of porters,' replied Murray, 'but I can't take them along with me. As for the other engine . . .' He looked to Nat to provide an answer to Sam's question.

'I will have it taken back to Insimo until you are ready to return to Ruddlemoor,' Nat said. 'Diego will make certain that it is kept in tip-top condition.'

'If you agree to come with us, we will of course regularise your situation,' Colonel Murray said to Sam. 'You will be given a commission as a lieutenant in the British South Africa Police – and be paid by the company as such. It means you will be subject to Company regulations, as opposed to those of the army, but it will regularise your position should you be unfortunate enough to be taken prisoner by the Germans . . . although you

292

have my assurance that we will do our best to ensure that does not happen.'

After a lengthening silence, during which Sam mulled over what had been said, Nat asked, 'Well, what do you say, Sam? Would you be happy to join the Rhodesians in their fight against Germany, or would you prefer to return to Cornwall and go off to war with a British force? And you would, because conscription has just been brought in there.'

'I will be very happy to join Colonel Murray's column,' Sam replied, 'but why should it be heading for Mozambique? Portugal is not at war with Germany.'

'It wasn't when we left Insimo,' said Colonel Murray, 'but the Portuguese government has informed us they are about to declare war on Germany and they would like us to be there when they do, in order to counter the attacks that are bound to come from across the border with German East Africa.'

Suddenly remembering Mumbi, Sam said, 'Going to Mozambique could solve another problem that has just come up for Diego and me . . .'

He gave Nat and Colonel Murray brief details of the events of the previous evening, adding, 'If the column is heading for Mozambique we could probably take Mumbi along with us and return her to her home.'

Colonel Murray shook his head vigorously. 'I'm leading a column of hard riding, hard living and hard fighting men. There's no way I could take a woman along with us, whatever the circumstances.'

Before Sam could reply, Diego said, 'Mumbi wouldn't want to go back to Mozambique. If she did, her stepfather would merely sell her to the next slaver who came along – and they will come along, as they always have. I've got a better idea.' Speaking to Colonel Murray, he said, 'If Colonel Retallick agrees, sir, and you would let me have some of your porters to help get the traction engine back over the mountains, I would like to take Mumbi back to Insimo with me.' Looking pleadingly at Nat, he said, 'She would fit in well there, I know she would . . . and I would take full responsibility for her.'

Looking quizzically at Diego, Nat said, 'Would I be right in thinking this Mumbi is quite attractive?'

'She is *very* attractive,' Sam said, 'and also extremely grateful to Diego for saving her from Jadot. But he is right – after what's happened I don't think she would want to go back to her home.'

'Then I suppose she had better go to Insimo.' Nat smiled wryly at Diego. 'She will feel quite at home with Victoria – and my mother too, of course – but she will remain your responsibility for as long as she is there.'

'Thank you . . . thank you very much.' Diego was finding difficulty in containing his delight as he said, 'If you don't mind, I'll go back to the bungalow and tell Mumbi what is happening.'

When Diego had hurried away, almost running in his eagerness, Nat commented, 'Diego has always been known to have a great fondness for the ladies, but I don't think I have ever seen him quite so smitten before.'

'I think Mumbi probably feels the same way about Diego,' Sam said. 'He is her idea of the complete hero.

I don't think it will be long before there is a wedding at Insimo.'

'I am sure they will both be very happy,' said Colonel Murray curtly, 'but may we get down to business now? If I have Hooper sworn in as a lieutenant in my force, do you think it will be possible to move out with the traction engine this afternoon? I want to reach Mozambique before von Lettow and his army – and I would like to have the artillery piece with me . . .'

14

I

'I am going to have to return home to Mozambique, Ben. I am needed there.'

Seated in the lounge at Tregarrick, Antonia put down the letter she had been reading and spoke almost tearfully to Ben who, until that moment, had been seated nearby feeling relaxed and at peace with the world.

Startled by her words, he said, 'Is it bad news about your family?'

The letter she had been reading had been placed on top of the post waiting for her on a small table in the hall and he had noticed it was from Mozambique.

'No, it's from Maria, the nurse from Mozambique with whom I worked in London,' Antonia replied, adding, 'She is the girl who was on the ship to South Africa with Sam.'

Mention of Sam made Ben feel guilty, remembering how unhappy Betsy Hooper had been when she came to Tregarrick having learned of the part played by Sam in the successful naval expedition to Lake Tanganyika. He had been able to mollify her then, but it had taken Antonia's gentle bedside manner to comfort her when news reached Cornwall that Sam and one of the Ruddlemoor traction engines were now part of a Rhodesian fighting unit.

Antonia had pointed out that the theatre of war in Africa covered such a vast area that the combatants would often not come together in battle for weeks at a time and then, more often than not, engage in only sporadic exchanges of fire. It was a gross understatement of the situation there, but she was able to convince Betsy that had Sam not been in Africa he would have been conscripted into the army and rushed to Europe where the slaughter of tens of thousands of young men continued unabated.

Sam's letters to his mother were few, infrequent and so lacking in details of what he was doing that they did little to reassure her . . . but it was Maria's letter to Antonia that was the subject of Ben's consternation today.

'What has Maria said that has made you feel you need to return to Mozambique?' he asked anxiously.

'She is single-handedly running a clinic in a remote area close to the border with German East Africa,' Antonia replied. 'That is difficult enough in itself in normal times, but there have recently been clashes between Portuguese troops and Germans as a result of which casualties have been brought to the clinic. Most have been treated by army doctors before they arrive, but as the doctors need to remain with the main body of fighting men, she is left to cope with wounded men by herself. She says there is a desperate need for a doctor to work at her clinic. She is as good as begging for my help, Ben. I know Maria well. She is a dedicated and very competent nurse and would not ask for assistance unless she was really desperate.'

Ben had always known that Antonia was likely to return to Mozambique one day – she had said so when they had met for the first time in many years in the London restaurant – but she had become so involved with the research she was carrying out into shell-shock at the Bodmin hospital that he had deliberately pushed the knowledge to the back of his mind.

It was of her research that he now spoke. 'What about the work you are doing at Bodmin? That is very important too . . . even your own government says so.'

'It is important,' Antonia agreed, 'but I don't doubt that Olaf can find someone else to carry on the work being done there.'

She struggled with her emotions for some moments and when she spoke again appeared to have them under control. But her distress had nothing to do with the need to leave her work at Bodmin. She was upset at the thought of leaving Ben.

They had become very close in the months that had passed since her return from Paris and she believed she had succeeded in banishing the ghosts of the past that had been haunting him since the death of Lily, although he had been frustratingly tardy in putting into words his feelings for her.

'I can't ignore Maria's plea, Ben,' she continued. 'The authorities in my country were wonderful in supporting me during the years when I was studying to become a doctor. I owe it to them to do something positive to show my gratitude – and now they need me. This is the way I can repay them.'

Ben had come to know Antonia well enough to accept that, once she had arrived at a decision on such an important matter, he would not be able to persuade her to change her mind. Nor would he attempt to. He was aware of how important the subject was to her.

Then something she had said returned to him. 'The fighting that Maria mentions . . . I don't suppose she said whether any Rhodesian troops were involved?'

Aware of his concern for Sam, Antonia said, 'No . . . at least, not specifically – she says she has not seen Sam. She was expecting him to be in Mozambique by now. When she last heard from him he said he would be heading that way very soon, so he might be somewhere in the area.'

When Ben asked 'I wonder whether I should tell Sam's mother what Maria says about him?' Antonia thought he must have dismissed the thought of her leaving Tregarrick from his mind. It hurt, but she replied to his question.

'As far as I know, Sam has made no mention of Maria to his mother, so neither should you. If it is a serious relationship I think he should be the one to tell her. If it is not serious there is no reason for her to know anything. I have been in Cornwall long enough to learn that marrying a girl from another village is an occasion for head-shaking and predictions of dire consequences. Having her son take up with a girl from Africa – a *black* girl – would horrify her. I am quite certain she still expects him to return home and marry his childhood sweetheart . . . Muriel, is that her name? No, Ben, don't become involved in any way. Say you have heard that he is on his way to Mozambique, if you feel you need to, although I doubt if it will mean much to Betsy, but let Sam tell her about Maria, if that is what he wants to do.'

Suddenly and unexpectedly, Ben returned to the subject of Antonia's leaving Tregarrick. 'Talking of marrying girls from Africa . . . how do you think your going away will affect our future, Antonia . . . you and me?'

Astonished, Antonia asked, 'What do you mean, Ben . . . you and me? Marriage has never even been mentioned.'

'I am mentioning it now.' Ben spoke more arrogantly than had been his intention. He had just decided to bring up the subject that he had shied away from for far too long. It was not that he was at all unsure of the way he felt about Antonia – but he was not absolutely certain that she felt the same way about him. Had he proposed and been turned down it would have made it very difficult for her to remain at Tregarrick – and that was the last thing he wanted to happen. Her work, too, had been a reason for saying nothing. He believed it to be so important to her that he had hesitated to broach the subject of their relationship, believing the right occasion would present itself in due course.

300

But now the letter from Maria, and Antonia's reaction to it, had changed everything. If she returned to Mozambique he might not see her again for many years – and in that time she could meet someone else. If he was going to tell her of his feelings it had to be now – but it might already be too late. Returning to Mozambique was obviously very important to her – it had to be for her to forsake the work she was engaged in at Bodmin: work she felt to be worthwhile and professionally rewarding. He knew he should have spoken a long time before.

'Why have you suddenly decided to talk of marriage now, Ben?'

Antonia was confused – and she was suddenly unreasonably angry, as well. If he really loved her, why had he not said anything until she had announced that she was going to leave Tregarrick – and leave England too? There had been no lack of opportunities. Why had he waited until now to broach the subject – and in such an arrogant and almost casual manner? Goaded by her anger, she wondered whether there might be another reason why he wanted her to remain at Tregarrick . . .

'Do you *really* want to marry me, Ben . . . or is it somehow *comfortable* having me around? Is what you have in mind something along the lines of a "marriage of convenience"? A friend to talk to when there are problems, but for whom you need to take no responsibility and who doesn't tie you in any way? We have always been friends, Ben . . . very good friends, but I expect more than that from a marriage.'

When Ben did not reply immediately, Antonia felt

deeply hurt by his failure to say what she was hoping to hear. To refute her accusations. Her own emotions were in such a turmoil that she felt almost as though she was in a state of shock. Trying to pull herself together, she said sharply, 'Anyway, whatever either of us feels makes no difference now. I have a duty towards my country – and I am going back to Mozambique.'

She suddenly felt close to tears. Maintaining control of herself with great difficulty, she said, 'I am going to my own rooms now to telephone to my embassy in London and ask them to arrange a passage for me.'

Not trusting herself to say more, she turned and fled from the room.

II

'Tregarrick is not going to be the same without her, and that's a fact. Dr Antonia has won the hearts of all the staff while she's been here.'

'I shall miss her too, Mrs Rodda.'

Ben and his housekeeper were talking in the hallway, watching through a window as one of the handymen employed at Tregarrick carried the last of Antonia's luggage from her wing of the house to Ben's Hotchkiss which was parked outside the main entrance.

'Have you told *her* how much you're going to miss her?' the housekeeper asked.

'There hasn't been much time to speak to her about anything,' Ben replied. 'It's only been two days since she received the letter from the nurse in Mozambique, and she's spent almost all that time either at the hospital

302

in Bodmin, or going out of her way to avoid me. Now, without giving me an opportunity to talk to her, she is leaving for London to take passage on a Dutch liner bound for South Africa.'

'It's never too late to tell someone how you feel about them if you really want them to know,' Mrs Rodda said unsympathetically. 'It's always been a great comfort to me that Mr Rodda found time to say how much I meant to him before he made his last voyage.'

Mrs Rodda's husband had been second officer on a cargo ship that set off on a voyage to South America and was never seen or heard of again.

Expressing his sympathy, Ben said, 'How old were you then, Mrs Rodda?'

'About the same age as Dr Antonia – and Mr Rodda was much the same age as you. It was a long time ago, but the heartache is still there.'

'You think I should have tried to stop Dr Antonia from returning to Mozambique, don't you?' Ben said.

Mrs Rodda shook her head. 'I don't think anyone could have stopped her from doing what she feels is her duty . . . but if the right words have been said by the time she leaves we can all look forward to having her back here at Tregarrick, one day.'

When Antonia left her wing of the house all the servants gathered in the hallway to say goodbye to her, but the farewells were hurried along by Ben, and when she made a mild protest he said, 'We need to be at the station early. You have a lot of luggage to be stowed in the guard's van.'

When Antonia was safely seated on the passenger's seat of the Hotchkiss, Ben set off. As they passed out through the gates of Tregarrick she turned for a final wave to the servants who were crowded in a small group outside the main door of the house. When they passed from sight, she said emotionally, 'You are very lucky to have such a pleasant and loyal staff. I shall miss them all.'

'I know,' Ben agreed. 'And Mrs Rodda has told me how much they are going to miss *you* – just as I am.'

They drove on in silence for a few minutes before Antonia said suddenly, 'What are you doing, Ben? This is not the way to the station.'

'It is,' Ben replied, 'although it's not the quickest route. I need to talk to you, Antonia.'

'If you intend trying to persuade me to change my mind about going to Mozambique it's far too late, Ben.'

'I wouldn't ask you to change your mind, Antonia . . . however much I wish I could. You feel it is your duty to return home and I respect you for that. No, what I have to say is of a far more personal nature and is something I should have said . . . something I *wanted* to say to you a long time ago, but, like the fool that I am, I've left it too late.'

They had reached a spot in the narrow lane where a level grass verge was overhung by the branches of an ancient and impressive oak tree. Here, Ben turned the Hotchkiss off the road and switched off the engine.

When Antonia began protesting that she would miss her train, Ben silenced her by touching her lips with a finger. 'We have lots of time. I made certain that we left the house early. Please listen to what I have to say, and then I will take you to the station. It's important, Antonia . . . at least, it is to me.'

Antonia bit back a retort about the importance to *her* of catching the train, and sat back in her seat, staring straight ahead.

Ben began, 'When we were talking about Sam and Maria, a few days ago, I made a very clumsy reference to marriage between you and me. I realised as soon as I said it that it had come out all wrong . . . despite all the many hours I've spent deciding what I was going to say when an opportunity arose. I got it so wrong because it was suddenly brought home to me that the right opportunity might never occur. That I might never be able to tell you how I feel about you and what my hopes were for a future together.'

While Ben was talking, Antonia had turned towards him, studying his face, and now she asked, 'What are these hopes and feelings, Ben – or am I to go away never to know?'

'I love you, Antonia. I think I have loved you since I first saw you walk into the restaurant in London when I was dining with Sam and Carey.'

Ben's admission left Antonia dumbfounded. Trying to gather her thoughts together, she said, 'But . . . if you have felt so strongly for all this time, why have you said nothing about it to me while I've been staying at Tregarrick? Why leave it until now, when you know I am going away . . . perhaps for ever?'

'I can give you any number of reasons,' Ben replied miserably, 'but I doubt whether any of them will make more sense to you than they do to me now.'

'Try me, Ben,' Antonia persisted. 'I want to understand.'

Hesitantly at first, but gaining confidence as he spoke, Ben said, 'When we met in London after so many years, I thought you were the most beautiful woman I had ever seen. I still believe that, but then I had Lily and felt guilty that I could look at another woman with such feelings . . .'

As Ben hesitated, Antonia thought that some of his guilt was probably because he had found solace with Tessa while Lily was still alive, but she said nothing and he continued, 'Then when you first came to Tregarrick you were heavily involved with your research into shell-shock and also, I believed, with Dr Olaf Ericsson. I felt I had no right to attempt to come between you and a man of whom you seemed to be very fond, and who could do a great deal to further your professional career.'

'I never looked upon Olaf as anything other than a brilliant doctor who is pioneering a new way of treating soldiers suffering the horrific effects of a new kind of warfare.' Antonia spoke passionately, but the fire went out of her voice as she said, 'And yet *you* believed I was enamoured of him . . . and he believed the same! I must have been sending out the wrong signals to everyone. I am so sorry, Ben, but after I returned from France surely I made it clear to you that I had no romantic feelings for Olaf? Indeed, I believed that you and I were becoming very much closer. Didn't you realise that? Why did you say nothing then?'

'For the very reason that Olaf mistook the way you

306

felt about him,' Ben said miserably. 'I thought I might be deluding myself. I enjoyed having you at Tregarrick . . . I enjoyed it very much, and didn't want to make the same mistake as Olaf and say or do something that would make you feel you needed to go away. I decided to let things carry on as they were, either until an opportunity arose when I could tell you how I felt about you without frightening you away, or until I could be certain you felt the same way about me.' He made a gesture of resignation. 'Now it doesn't matter . . . nothing matters any more. You are returning to Africa, we will probably never see each other again, and I will spend the rest of my life regretting what might have been.' He smiled briefly. 'And now I had better get you to the station.'

'No, Ben,' Antonia said quickly. 'We still have a few more minutes – and this is important. Very important.'

Ben's hands were gripping the steering wheel of the Hotchkiss as though he was afraid that it too might escape from him, and Antonia rested a hand on the outstretched arm nearest to her. Speaking softly, she said, 'I can't change my mind about going away, Ben . . . not now, but it doesn't have to be goodbye for ever if you really feel about me the way you say you do.'

It took a few moments for the meaning of her words to sink in. Then, trying not to jump to the wrong conclusion, he said, 'You mean . . . you think you might one day feel the same way about me?'

'Oh, Ben! You are a fool,' Antonia said huskily. 'We both are. I have probably loved you since the time when we were children together at Insimo.'

Ben looked at her in disbelief. 'Since Insimo . . . but Nat was your hero then. He was everyone's hero.'

'That's right, he was *everyone's* hero, and that included me, but it was you I loved, not Nat.' Antonia was tearful at the thought of the mistakes they had made, and, seeing her face screwed up in misery, Ben kissed her.

The kiss lasted a long time . . . . too long. Suddenly pulling away from him, Antonia said, 'Ben . . . the train!'

'You can catch a later one,' he said, reaching for her again, but this time she resisted.

'No, I can't. I'm expected at the Portuguese embassy this afternoon to collect some papers that I must complete while I am at the hotel tonight. I really must go, Ben . . . I am so sorry.'

'When does your boat leave?'

'It sails from London docks the day after tomorrow.'

'Then I'll catch the night train to London tonight and we will have as much of tomorrow together as we can manage. We have things to talk about, Antonia . . . wonderful things . . . and plans to make.'

'Yes, Ben.' Antonia was still tearful, but also excited too, now. 'Come to London tomorrow, but . . . the train!'

Starting the engine of the Hotchkiss, Ben found time to kiss Antonia once more, but briefly this time. Then, putting the vehicle into gear, he drove back on to the road, the misery of only a few minutes earlier replaced by a feeling that everything was going to be all right. Tomorrow he and Antonia would lay plans for the future . . . together.

*

III

'You make quite certain you say the right things to Dr Antonia when you get to London. Don't you let her go on her way without knowing *exactly* how you feel about her, and how much you and everyone else at Tregarrick want her back here as soon as possible.'

The Tregarrick housekeeper was giving her instructions to Ben as she packed the clothes he was to take with him on the overnight sleeping-car train to Paddington. She had been overjoyed when he told her he was going to spend the day with Antonia before she embarked on the ship that would take her to South Africa, and that they would be making provisional plans for a future together. Within a very short time the news had been passed on to the household staff and was received with great joy by all of them.

'I have already made my feelings quite clear to her, Mrs Rodda, but I will ensure she is in no doubt at all about how much we all love her.'

The Portuguese embassy had booked a room for Antonia at the St Ermin's hotel, just outside the busy centre of London, but not very far from the embassy itself. When Ben arrived in a motorised taxicab from Paddington station it was too early in the day to book into a room, and after depositing his luggage with the hall porter he went in search of Antonia.

He found her in the dining room, and her delight at seeing him dispelled all the doubts that had bedevilled him during the night. They enjoyed a relaxed breakfast together before Antonia went to her room to ready herself for the day ahead.

Ben decided to walk with her to the embassy and Antonia displayed a girlish delight in walking through the London streets with a firm grip upon Ben's arm. 'I love London,' she said, after they had weaved their way across a street that was so busy that all traffic, motorised and horse-drawn, had been brought to a halt. 'It's so alive and vibrant, even now, in wartime.'

Not all women in London were as happy as Antonia. One, wearing a sash with lettering on it that had become unreadable due to the creasing of the material on which it was printed, stood at a corner of the main road handing out white chicken feathers to men who were not in uniform.

The white feathers were a recognised symbol of cowardice. Some of the recipients appeared embarrassed, while others accepted the feathers and immediately threw them into the gutter. Many simply brushed the woman's hand aside and went on their way, ignoring the accusations of cowardice – or worse – she hurled at them. She had a feather ready for Ben, but hesitated at the last moment when she realised he was walking with a limp. However, she was determined he should not pass her unchallenged.

'Have you been examined by a doctor and officially declared unfit for military service?' she demanded.

'Madam,' Ben replied, 'my limp is the result of a bullet wound, so stand aside, if you please.'

Obeying him immediately, the woman said, 'Please accept my apologies, sir – and God bless you for a brave man.'

When they were out of hearing, Ben said to Antonia, 'I wonder what she would have said had she known the bullet was fired from a rifle held by a man in British army uniform?'

Antonia giggled. 'She would probably have fallen to the ground in a faint.' Suddenly serious, she said, 'Actually, I should have suggested that instead of standing on a London street corner handing out white feathers to men of whose background she knows absolutely nothing, she should put together a first aid bag and take it to the battle front in France and do something worthwhile. A few days there and she would not be quite so keen to send young men out there to be killed or maimed.'

Gripping his arm more tightly and resting her head on his shoulder for a moment, she said, 'I love you, Ben, and I so enjoy being with you like this. Why couldn't we have told each other how we felt when we first met in London? We have wasted so much time.'

'Yes, we have,' he agreed, 'but at least we have managed to put things right before you leave. It would have been tragic for both of us had you left before we discovered the truth.'

'That's very true,' she said, 'but I wish I had not been so keen to volunteer to return to Mozambique.'

'I certainly wouldn't argue with that. But there was nothing else you could do once you had received Maria's letter.'

'I'm glad you understand, Ben. I promise I will hurry back to you as soon as I feel I'm no longer needed there.'

'That's what I wanted to hear more than anything

else,' Ben declared. 'Here's your embassy. Shall I wait for you?'

Antonia shook her head. 'I'm to be briefed by a number of embassy officials, and the ambassador and his wife have invited me to have lunch with them. I met them on a number of occasions when Philippe was military attaché and I had accepted before I knew you were coming to London.'

Ben was disappointed that he would not be spending more of the day with Antonia, but he said, 'That's all right. There are a number of things I want to do while I'm here. I'll return to the hotel after lunch and wait for you there.'

When Antonia entered the embassy, Ben hailed a taxicab and told the driver to take him to Regent Street. Here he browsed among the numerous jewellers until he discovered what he was seeking in the window of a shop that proudly displayed the royal coat of arms, above a gold-lettered sign proclaiming that its wares had been bought by members of the British royal family.

He left the shop after a while with a velvet-lined leather box in his pocket. Inside was a diamond ring, the price of which would have paid the wages of the Ruddlemoor work force for a whole week. He had been forced to guess at the size, aided by the personal observation and long experience of the shop's manager, who declared that the little finger of a man's left hand was usually a trustworthy guide to the third finger of a woman of average build.

Returning to the hotel, Ben ate lunch, then waited in

the lounge until the early evening before Antonia put in an appearance. Spotting him as he rose to his feet to attract her attention, she hurried to him and giving him a brief but warm kiss of greeting apologised profusely for not returning earlier.

'It was mainly the fault of the secretary, who should have had my journey planned in detail. He seemed to know nothing of the geography of Africa and would have had me going backwards and forwards across much of the continent in order to reach my destination. I eventually persuaded him to route me through Rhodesia, so that I can spend a couple of days at Insimo with Grandmother Victoria and your mother before going on by rail to Beira. I also asked him to send a telegraph message to my father, asking him to arrange to have me met and taken on from there. Hopefully he will be there to meet me personally. We haven't seen each other for a long time.'

'I am very pleased that you will be going to Insimo. I have something I think they will be delighted to see – but first you need to assure me that you have not changed your mind and will marry me as soon as circumstances allow.'

'Ben, I would marry you today if it were possible . . . but in a way I am glad it's not. I want to have time to enjoy being married to you, not have to hurry away from you in a matter of hours. But what am I to take to Insimo that is going to please everyone so much?'

'This.' Removing the boxed ring from his pocket, Ben placed it on the low table that separated their two armchairs.

Antonia gave a small gasp of surprise. Picking up the

313

box, she opened it and her jaw dropped, her expression becoming one of total disbelief. Looking up at him, it was some moments before she was able to speak. Then: 'Ben! This is so beautiful! But . . . the diamond is *huge*! It must have cost an absolute fortune. It is insanely extravagant.'

'I will never ever buy another for anyone else, Antonia, so let it be a once in a lifetime extravagance for us. I happen to believe you are worth it – and far, far more. But does it fit? That thought has been worrying me all day.'

As excited as Ben had ever seen her, Antonia said, 'Put it on for me, Ben. I daren't try to do it for myself.'

Taking the ring from the box, Ben slid it on to the third finger of her left hand. There was the slightest resistance from the second joint of the finger – then it was in place and Antonia was holding it out in front of her face, her expression one of sheer joy.

'Ben . . . it is absolutely *wonderful* – I do love you so very, very much.' She was so excited that her voice carried to the farthest corner of the lounge. Then, rising from her armchair, Antonia dropped to her knees and threw her arms round him, giving him a kiss that provoked reactions from the occupants of the hotel lounge that ranged from scandalised disapproval to envy, depending upon the age and sex of the observer.

The lounge waiter, who had witnessed only Antonia's reaction, was quickly on the scene, but before he could admonish her Antonia held up her hand to show the ring and said ecstatically, 'Look. We have just become officially engaged.'

The waiter discreetly backed away as the lounge erupted with applause and good wishes.

Later that evening, when Ben and Antonia were at their table in the hotel dining room, the waiter brought a bottle of champagne to their table, explaining that it came with the compliments of an anonymous guest who had been in the hotel lounge when Ben presented the engagement ring to Antonia. The kind act set the seal on a happy occasion, marred only by the knowledge that within a matter of hours they would be parted for a period that might be counted in months, or could prove to be years. However, neither dwelled upon this thought, determined to enjoy to the full the time that was left to them.

They had almost completed their meal when Ben glanced towards the door and started in surprise, his pleasure dissipating.

'Ben . . . what is it?' Antonia was alarmed at the change in his expression. Following his glance, she saw two men at the doorway waiting to be shown to a table. At that moment one of them looked in their direction and his reaction mirrored that of Ben.

Saying something to his companion, the man left him and crossed the room to their table. After acknowledging Antonia's presence with a brief nod, he spoke to Ben. 'Good evening, Mr Retallick. You are probably the last person I expected to see here this evening.'

'I could say the same thing, Superintendent Buchanan. I wasn't aware that policemen frequented such establishments as the St Ermin's.'

'Few policemen do,' agreed Buchanan amiably. 'However, much of my work is carried out at the Home Office, which is just round the corner from here, and the hotel restaurant is most convenient – as well as offering special rates for my colleagues and myself.'

Pointing to the champagne bottle protruding from an ice bucket beside Ben and Antonia's table, he added, 'I can see you are having a private celebration, so I will not interrupt you further, except to say that I am very pleased indeed that your little problem has been satisfactorily resolved. Good evening to you – and to you, miss.'

The police superintendent turned to go, then suddenly turned back to address Ben once more. 'I think you should know that I recently received information from the same source as before, suggesting that I should look more closely into the activities and affiliations of a certain Adam Retallick. I declined to take any action because, as I think I once informed you, the person named is outside my jurisdiction. I also happen to believe that no one should be a subject of suspicion because of the actions of another member of his family. However, in view of the mischief this informant has done to you in the past, I feel it only fair to warn you – after all, there are always those who are ready to believe gossip.'

Ben's heart sank at the superintendent's words. The last thing he wanted was more trouble affecting Ruddlemoor, but, suspicious of Buchanan's motives, he asked, 'Why are you telling me this, Superintendent?'

'Because I believe that your assessment of the reason why the earlier allegations were made is perfectly correct

– and I do not like being used by someone who has an ulterior motive for making such a complaint. Forewarned is forearmed, Mr Retallick. Do with the information what you will; it will certainly not be the subject of a police investigation. I wish you a good evening once more.'

15

I

Sam Hooper's first meeting with Adam Retallick came in the summer of 1916. During the preceding months Sam had seldom been far from Ben's other brother, Nat.

Nat's scouts formed a watchful, if rarely seen, screen round the combined column of Rhodesian volunteers and the Special Service Company of British South Africa Police as they advanced through difficult bush country. The men frequently made their way through elephant grass so tall and dense that it was difficult enough for someone in the file to see the colleague in front of him, let alone spot an enemy ambush. On one occasion German and Rhodesian columns, hundreds strong, actually passed within a hundred and fifty yards of the other, each oblivious of the presence of the enemy.

Sam had joined the Rhodesian column with the Ruddlemoor traction engine in the expectation of heading for Mozambique where he hoped to meet Maria, but soon after the column set out from the small Belgian trading post orders had been received from the commanding officer of the operational area which changed their plans.

The German East African army had split into a number of smaller, but potentially extremely dangerous, fighting units. One such unit had crossed the vaguely defined border between German East Africa and Northern Rhodesia and was already creating havoc, particularly along the railway line from the south that was vital to the very existence of the British colony. Since joining the column Sam had been involved in a number of sharp skirmishes between the two opposing fighting units and, although the captured German gun had been brought into action on only one occasion, it had proved highly effective, causing great consternation among the German askaris, who had never before been subjected to shellfire.

However, after being involved in one skirmish which involved an exchange of machine-gun fire, Sam realised that the boiler of the traction engine was vulnerable to such attacks and he insisted that the column head for one of the railway repair depots. Here he fitted steel plates to his 'land locomotive', angled in order to deflect German bullets. As an afterthought he added low steel plates to the exposed driving platform as partial protection for himself.

It was while Sam was at the railway depot that he received news of the Lake Tanganyika naval expedition from one of its members who was travelling on a train which halted at the depot. It seemed that after the initial successes with his diminutive gunboats, which had brought the expedition awards, promotions and a telegram of congratulation from King George V, Spicer had been reluctant to risk his reputation – and his small flotilla – by taking them into action again.

When an opportunity arose to engage the Germans' sole remaining Lake Tanganyika warship in battle, Spicer refused to heed the pleas from his own officers to give battle to the enemy. Since then his vessels had been used only to ferry stores to some of the British lakeside communities and the morale of his sailors was understandably low.

When Murray's column was in camp at the southern end of Lake Tanganyika, Sam took the traction engine out with a wood-cutting party and an escort party, to gather fuel for the wood-burning vehicle. There was a sudden stir among the Africans and, on the driving platform, Sam looked up to see a rider coming towards them.

Dressed in army uniform, he wore a bush hat, the brim turned up on one side, crossed ammunition belts, and a holstered revolver. In a scabbard beside the saddle of his horse he carried a rifle.

Sam was the only European in his small party and, seeing him, the stranger waved a hand and turned his horse towards him. When he was close enough he called a greeting in a language Sam recognised as Afrikaans, the first language of a number of men in Murray's column.

'I'm sorry,' he called back, 'I speak only English, I'm afraid.'

'Don't worry. I'll try not to hold that against you,' said the newcomer drily, as he brought his horse to a halt. 'Are you with the column led by Colonel Murray?'

'Yes,' Sam replied. 'If you are looking for him, I will take you there. We have just about as much fuel as the trailer will take now.'

'That's a very fine machine you have there,' said the stranger. 'I hardly expected to find anything like it here, in bushveld country.'

'I brought it out from England to help bring a couple of gunboats up from Cape Town to Lake Tanganyika,' Sam replied. 'The engine actually belongs to Ruddlemoor, a Cornish clay works.'

The news appeared to startle the stranger. 'Ruddlemoor? Isn't that owned by Ben . . . Ben Retallick?'

Now it was Sam's turn to be taken aback. 'Yes, I work for him. Do you know him?'

The stranger smiled. 'I should do, even though we haven't seen each other for some years.' Reaching out to the driving platform from the saddle of his horse, he explained, 'I am Adam Retallick. Ben's brother.'

Shaking Adam's hand enthusiastically, Sam replied, 'My name is Sam Hooper. I am very pleased to meet you, Mr Retallick.'

'And I you,' Adam said, 'but what are you doing here now? I would have thought your work was done once you had brought the boats to Lake Tanganyika.'

'Colonel Murray's column captured a German gun, but needed something powerful to pull it around the veld. They asked me if I would accept a commission in the British South Africa Police and stay on to help them.

Your other brother, Nat, took responsibility for informing Ben, and so here I am.'

'You know Nat too?' Adam was delighted. 'I haven't seen him for years either. How is he?'

'You will be able to see for yourself,' Sam replied. 'He is at the camp no more than a mile away, with Colonel Murray. We're ready to go now – but you had better move away while I get the traction engine under way. The noise tends to frighten horses.'

II

The meeting between the two Retallick brothers was as warm as it was unexpected. It cooled slightly when Nat enquired after Johanna and the family Adam had left behind when he set off to go to war. Adam was forced to admit he had heard nothing from them, and had not written to Johanna since leaving their Transvaal farm.

Fortunately, Adam's story of being interned by the British because they believed him to be fighting with the Germans restored the good humour. Adam had been taken to the main internment camp with the others, but here the German commandant had told the truth about Adam's part in the desperate fight against the Herero tribesmen, and when some of the South African officers of Colonel Matthias Van Klerk, who were in the area, vouched for Adam he was released.

Sam was included in the conversation between Adam, Nat and Colonel Murray because the Ruddlemoor traction engine would play an important part in ensuring that the captured German gun would be available to take a part in the plans they were making. When the talks began, he was surprised to learn that Adam not only held the rank of major in the South African army, but was also a staff officer to General Jan Smuts, a prominent Afrikaans politician, lawyer and Boer war leader, who had recently, and somewhat surprisingly, been appointed commander-in-chief of British forces in East Africa. He had taken over from a series of inept professional British soldiers and upon his arrival in East Africa had begun a vigorous campaign against the German army of General von Lettow-Vorbeck.

Adam's arrival in the camp of Colonel Murray was in furtherance of this campaign. General Smuts wanted the colonel to strike at the fortified German base at Bismarckburg, at the southern end of Lake Tanganyika. He was to be given naval support by Commander Spicer and his flotilla of small gunboats.

'But I have had no contact with Spicer,' Murray said. 'I don't even know where to find him.'

'He will find *you*,' Adam said. 'I have been to see him and told him to be at Kituta in four days' time to meet you there and discuss your tactics. You will find it a reasonable place to make your camp.'

Kituta was a small lakeside community in Northern Rhodesia that Murray had visited a couple of times before with his force, but it was not this that caught his attention. There was something in Adam's manner that made the colonel ask, 'This Commander Spicer . . . what sort of man is he?'

Adam hesitated for a few moments before saying, 'I have a feeling that you will not find him your type of

323

man, Colonel. He is pompous, dismissive and full of his own importance.'

After digesting what Adam had told him, Murray said, 'And yet he brought two gunboats all the way overland from South Africa and succeeded in sinking two of the German boats that were controlling the lake. He has some claim to self-importance, surely?'

'I can't argue with that, Colonel Murray, but since then he has refused to take out the small flotilla he now commands to tackle the last remaining armed German craft . . . even though his own officers begged him to take action when an opportunity arose. I found his men, who ought to be feeling very proud of themselves, totally demoralised.' Pausing a moment, perhaps to gain maximum effect, Adam added, 'Oh, by the way, he has now taken to wearing a skirt.'

Startled, Murray said, 'A skirt? You mean a kilt?'

Trying hard to keep a straight face, Adam said, 'No, Colonel, I mean a skirt – and it is of a somewhat immodest length, ending just above the knee. He told me he designed it himself and seems to be extremely proud of it. He said it is ideal for wear in the tropics.'

Murray muttered, 'A skirt . . . ? What sort of man would wear a *skirt*?' Turning abruptly to Sam, he said, 'You travelled out from England with him. What's he like . . . and did he wear this damned skirt along the way?'

Shaking his head, Sam replied, 'I really wouldn't know, sir. Commander Spicer and I fell out before leaving England, as a result of which he travelled with the rest of his party on a passenger liner while I came to Africa on a cargo-passenger ship with the two Ruddlemoor traction engines. Since arriving in Africa he has avoided speaking to me – unless it was to complain about something I'd done, or not done. His orders usually came through someone else.'

'So as well as all his other shortcomings it sounds as though he is also easily offended? Well, so am I, so he had better prove himself to be the sort of man I need to support me and my column, otherwise I'll have his guts for garters . . . . skirt or no bloody skirt.'

Commander Spicer, complete with skirt, duly arrived at Kituta and, as Adam had predicted, he and Colonel Murray found they had little in common. As a result, Murray decided he would carry out the attack on Bismarckburg without Spicer's assistance.

It was Nat who persuaded the Rhodesian commander to change his mind. He had taken some of his scouts to the vicinity of the German base and made a detailed survey of the area. Bismarckburg boasted a fort which would be difficult to take without a stiff fight – unless the captured German gun was used to bombard it from the land side, assisted by naval guns from Spicer's flotilla on the lake. In order to reach the fort Murray's men would also need to cross a deep gorge, and here too naval fire power would be required.

There was another very important consideration. There were a number of very large dhows and canoes in Bismarckburg harbour: enough to evacuate the whole garrison, if the need arose – and this was what the Germans would most certainly attempt to do if defeat seemed inevitable. By their daring and initiative the Germans were able to capture guns, ammunition and even provisions – but they could not replace their fighting men.

The great distance of East Africa from the Fatherland, together with the fact that they were surrounded on all sides by enemy territory and the almost impenetrable blockade maintained on the German East African coastline, meant that no reinforcements could reach von Lettow from outside the country. This was the main reason why he avoided set battles. He could not afford to sustain casualties on a large scale.

Colonel Murray wanted to capture Bismarckburg – but he was also anxious to take its garrison prisoner. He agreed with Nat and sent a messenger asking Spicer to provide firepower for the attack and, of equal importance, to ensure that the dhows and canoes were put out of action, so they could not assist any of the garrison to escape.

The Rhodesian column advanced upon the fortified lakeside community and Sam brought the gun and ammunition as close as he dared to the base before taking the traction engines out of range of the German fort's artillery. Nat and Adam were scanning the lake for Spicer – but without success.

'Where the hell is the man?' Adam asked angrily. 'He should have been close enough to give his support.'

'He is probably lying off the coast, out of sight,' Nat said, 'no doubt trying to lure the dhows out of harbour so that he might sink them – preferably when they are fully loaded.'

'He had better be,' Adam growled, 'but he should have been here to support Colonel Murray when he was crossing the ravine. Murray has suffered casualties, and one of the reasons his men are so loyal to him is because, although he does whatever is required of him, he tries to do it with the minimum danger to the men he commands. He is not going to be happy with Commander Spicer.'

When morning came and Colonel Murray ordered his men to make the final assault on the fort, he had even more reason to be unhappy with Commander Spicer. The fort was empty and the dhows were gone from the harbour. The whole garrison had escaped during the night, despite the fort's being surrounded, on the land side at least, by the Rhodesians of Murray's column.

The following day, Spicer brought his flotilla from the harbour farther up the lake where they had been for the last five days. They had approached Bismarckburg, but when he saw the fort Spicer decided that it would be too dangerous for his craft to attempt to destroy the dhows in the harbour, just in case the Germans had guns capable of damaging his gunboats. He had ignored the pleas of his officers to attempt to put the dhows out of action using only one of the boats, or even none at all and taking a landing party ashore.

When the British gunboats entered the empty harbour, there were derisory calls from the Rhodesians and demands to know where the navy had been while the German garrison was escaping. It was not long before a messenger arrived, ordering Spicer to go ashore and

327

explain his actions – or the lack of them – to Adam and the commanding officer of the Rhodesian column.

Spicer stepped ashore accompanied by two of his officers. He was wearing smart uniform above the waist, and stockings and shoes beneath. In between was his skirt.

His appearance brought catcalls and laughter from the Rhodesian soldiers. Trying to maintain at least a semblance of dignity, Spicer approached a junior officer and demanded to know where he would find Colonel Murray. Instead of offering to take him there, the officer merely jerked a thumb in the direction of the fort and told him to find it for himself.

The fury felt by Spicer was plain to all who saw him, but there was worse to come. As he passed through the crowds of soldiers there were wolf whistles and many remarks that might have been made had a woman of easy virtue walked through such a gathering. By the time the commander arrived at the fort, which Murray had made his headquarters, he was absolutely furious, and he entered the office commandeered by the leader of the Rhodesian column determined to take him to task for the lack of discipline among his troops.

Less than ten minutes later Spicer emerged from Murray's office looking like a man in a state of deep shock. He stumbled as he walked and seemed hardly aware of where he was, or what he was doing.

What was said to him by the furious and down-to-earth Rhodesian army commander was never disclosed, but it mentally destroyed the naval expedition leader. He would never again set sail with his flotilla and two months later he returned to England, being declared unfit to continue active service.

Knowing that Spicer's inaction had robbed the Rhodesians of a well-deserved victory, and seeing the state of the naval commander when he came out of Colonel Murray's office, Sam thought it was an ignominious conclusion to the remarkable exploits of the Lake Tanganyika naval expedition.

III

While Murray's column was still at Bismarckburg they were joined by a company of the Rhodesia Native Regiment, in which only the officers were European.

It was a newly formed infantry company which had not yet seen action, and after discussion with Adam it was agreed that in view of the latest tactics of the Germans, splitting their forces into small fast-moving units and fighting what was rapidly becoming a guerrilla-type campaign, Murray's column should adopt a similar approach.

It meant dispensing with the traction engine and the artillery piece. An inexperienced infantry company would also hamper the newly formed units and it was decided that while Murray's column moved deeper into German East Africa in search of an elusive enemy, the Rhodesian African troops, supported by a small unit of artillerymen and the captured German gun, would make for the Portuguese colony of Mozambique to assist their allies. Nat and half his scouts would accompany the Rhodesian Africans, with the remainder scouting for

Colonel Murray. Meanwhile, Adam returned to East Africa, to report to General Smuts on what was happening in the more remote areas of his command.

The new arrangement suited Sam very well. Mozambique had been where he had thought he was heading when he had agreed to accompany Murray.

It was another six weeks before Sam and the soldiers of the Rhodesia Native Regiment arrived in northern Mozambique and linked up with Portuguese troops at a spot not far from the country's border with German East Africa.

The Portuguese soldiers were in a state of great excitement. A small body of askaris, led by German officers, were in the area. So far they had attacked and destroyed a regional police station and set fire to a village which contained a government store and administration centre. When asked whether they had given battle to the askaris the Portuguese soldiers gave many different versions of what had happened, but it was evident that they had all fled, many leaving their weapons behind to be taken by the Germans.

Sam could not help feeling sorry for them. The soldier in charge of the men was of equivalent rank to an English corporal and far too inexperienced to have been given such responsibility. The officers attached to the unit had abandoned their men, preferring the comforts of a town almost fifty miles from the place where the soldiers were camped. Further questioning revealed that none of the officers had visited the troops for almost a fortnight.

While the Rhodesians set up camp a short distance

from the Portuguese soldiers and cleaned their weapons in preparation for battle, Nat set off with his scouts to locate the German raiding party.

Sam was checking the traction engine later that evening when a large body of Portuguese soldiers rode into camp. With them were the missing officers and the regional commander – Major Philippe St Anna.

Philippe did not immediately recognise Sam, but when realisation came he embraced him, and slapping him on the back looked him up and down, saying, 'Antonia told me you were with the Rhodesian army somewhere in Africa, but I see you have a commission now. Congratulations!'

'Antonia told you . . . ? You mean, she wrote to you?'

'No,' came the surprising reply, 'she told me. She is in charge of a small hospital that has been set up in a village not too far from here. She is there with someone who I believe is a very good friend of yours. Maria Fernandes.'

'Maria is near here? Where?' Sam was unable to contain his excitement. After trying for so long to reach Mozambique in order to see her again, he had almost given up hope that it would happen.

'The village is called Manchemba . . . but I regret your reunion must wait for a while longer. There has been a raid here by German soldiers. I want to locate and destroy them before they cause more damage in the region for which I am responsible. Such a task should already have been carried out by the dolts who dare to call themselves army officers. I sent them here especially to thwart just such a raid. First of all I must try to find

331

out whether anyone knows in which direction the Germans have gone.'

'Colonel Nat Retallick has gone out to try to locate them,' Sam said. 'As soon as he has found them he will return. We have a company of the Rhodesia Native Regiment and a heavy artillery piece with us, ready to take on the Germans.'

'Nat is here with you?' Philippe's pleasure was unfeigned. 'That is very good news indeed. We have not met for some years but I will never forget how proud I was to know him when I was a boy and he was chief of scouts for the British during the Boer war. Between us we will teach the Germans the folly of making a raid into my country.'

'Nat is in charge of scouts once more,' Sam said, 'but the Rhodesian troops are commanded by Captain Tim MacAllen. He is a good soldier and I think you will get along with him. I can see him coming to meet you now. I will introduce you.'

Captain MacAllen and Major St Anna greeted each other cordially enough, but each was somewhat wary of the other. Along the route from Lake Tanganyika there had been an occasion when the European officers of the Rhodesia Native Regiment were airing their views on the quality of Portuguese soldiers. A number of derogatory remarks were made about their prowess until Nat remarked casually that his mother was Portuguese and that his maternal grandfather had been Governor of Mozambique and, as such, commander-in-chief of the Portuguese army there.

The criticism of Portuguese soldiers had been effectively silenced, but it left Sam in no doubt about the way the Rhodesian officers felt about their Portuguese allies.

Despite Philippe's declared delight at the presence of the Rhodesian troops, he too was wary of the men from Mozambique's neighbour and ally. His father was now a general and in command of the Portuguese armies in Mozambique, but as a young officer he had been seriously wounded by British soldiers during a dispute over the border between the two adjacent colonies. There was still a strong feeling among certain residents of the Portuguese colony that Britain coveted at least a portion of Mozambique in order to obtain access to the sea.

Nevertheless, the two men realised that now they were both at war with Germany they would need to work together if they were to defeat their mutual enemy, and Philippe accepted an invitation to dine with MacAllen and his officers that evening.

The meal passed without any unpleasantness between Philippe and his hosts, and as it was ending Nat returned to the camp. Entering the mess tent, he greeted Philippe with a warmth that displayed the great friendship that had always existed between their two families. However, there would be no pleasant reminiscing over dinner for the two friends that evening. Their greeting over, Nat announced to the officers, who had risen to their feet in deference to his senior rank, 'I trust you have all dined well, gentlemen? I fear there is going to be no time to allow it to digest. I and my scouts have found the Germans who have been causing all the problems in the area. There are approximately a hundred and fifty askaris, with perhaps fifteen German officers and NCOs, and they are camped no more than ten miles from here. For those of you who are unused to the tactics of these German guerrilla groups, I can tell you that they are in the habit of moving off at dawn from wherever they happen to be camped, so we will need to be in position to attack them at first light. I suggest you give the orders for the men to prepare to move off, while we discuss our tactics.'

IV

At the meeting between the Rhodesian and Portuguese officers, it was suggested that the sound of the traction engine in the still night air might destroy the essential element of surprise if it was decided to make use of the captured gun from the *Königsberg*, but Nat had already thought of that.

'The gun has a range of some six or seven miles and the veld around there is pretty dense,' he explained. 'We will take it to within three miles of the German camp and they will not hear a thing. We can site it on a low hill that is in just the right spot. If we cut up one of the white tents that you have, I will have my scouts attach the pieces to the tops of trees in a straight line between the gun and the camp, the last piece being, as close as can be measured, exactly a quarter of a mile from the camp. That way, the gun crew will have a direct line of fire and know how far the German camp is from the final marker.'

Cutting short the approbation that greeted his ingenuity, Nat added, 'The bombardment will need to begin as soon as it is light enough to see the markers. By then your men should be in position to cut off the German escape. I will leave it to your own officers to organise how that is done – saying only, in conclusion, that on no account should you underestimate the ingenuity and fighting ability of the Germans and their askaris. They are expert in the type of warfare they have chosen to adopt.'

Despite Colonel Nat Retallick's cautionary warning, there was an air of great excitement among the Rhodesian officers when they went off to prepare their men for the night march and the fight that would come at the end of it.

The artillery piece and the soldiers of the two allied colonies were in position long before dawn and Nat and his scouts formed a loose outer ring to warn of any of the enemy who succeeded in escaping from the trap that had been set for them.

The artillerymen were as excited as the infantrymen, and when their gun was positioned so that it was pointing in the general direction of the German camp, they sat around talking quietly among themselves. Some followed the example of Sam, who was on the driving platform of the traction engine, and tried to doze off until it was light enough to line their gun up on the markers. When the artilleryman in charge was satisfied that it was accurately homed in on the unsuspecting target he would order the first shot to be fired. It would be the signal for what it was hoped would be a brief and one-sided battle.

Long before the sun put in an appearance over the eastern horizon Sam realised he was able to see the outlines of the trees around him. The artillerymen were aware of it too and they gathered round their gun, ready to align it more accurately as soon as the tent-cloth markers were sighted.

'There's one!' The low call came from one of the more sure-sighted soldiers and the gun was immediately man-handled into a more accurate position.

'There's another!'

The gun's alignment was altered slightly once more and very soon all the markers could be seen. Some were slightly off-line, but the gunner in charge of the artillerymen was satisfied that the line of fire was as accurate as it possibly could be.

When the last marker was plain to see and the elevation of the gun barrel had been checked and re-checked, the order for which the gun's crew had been waiting was given.

'Fire!'

At the order the artillerymen, who had been crouching as though in a game of charades, sprang into action, and seconds later a thirty-pound shell was sent hurtling through the air towards the camp of the German raiding party. Before it reached its target the shell case had been ejected and another shell was loaded and ready to follow the first.

Nat's scouts and the artillerymen had carried out their duties admirably and the very first shell landed on the edge of the German camp, causing consternation as well as a number of casualties. But these were seasoned soldiers, led by experienced officers. Mustering the men to one side of their camp, out of the line of the shelling, they made a swift assessment of their situation. It was quite evident that the enemy knew exactly where they were and had been able to take ample time to make their preparations. The German commander assumed, correctly, that the bombardment was intended to panic them into fleeing away from the source of the firing in an attempt to get out of range. This was what they would have been expected to do and the commander of the attacking force would have laid his plans accordingly.

'Very well,' declared the German leader, 'we will confound the enemy and flee not *from* the source of the bombardment but *towards* it.'

It was a clever tactic. By doing so they might not only make good their escape, but also succeed in putting the artillery piece out of action and thus turn defeat into victory.

To the Germans, beleaguered as they were by land and sea, every single item of equipment was irreplaceable. They would leave nothing behind. So it was that the Rhodesian artillerymen, still labouring to keep their gun firing at the known camp of the Germans, were taken by surprise when fire was opened upon them by a German manned machine gun.

A number of the gunners and their guard of Portuguese and Rhodesian Native troops were hit by the machine-gun bullets, but they instinctively dropped

337

to the ground and once the initial shock was over they recovered sufficiently to return the fire.

Sam was on the driving platform of the traction engine when the firing began and, being higher than the men manning the artillery piece, could see immediately where the machine gun was sited. Grabbing his rifle, he kneeled behind the low armour plate surrounding the platform and, aiming carefully, picked off two of the three-man machine-gun team, bringing the firing to an immediate halt. He was able to prevent others from taking their place, but in doing so he drew angry fire from the remainder of the attacking German force and bullets ricocheted in all directions off the armour plate protecting the traction engine.

However, his efforts gained the respite needed by the Rhodesian and Portuguese troops guarding the gun and they took full advantage of it to return the enemy's fire. The Germans, aware that the force besieging the camp they had so hastily evacuated would realise what was happening and hurry to the aid of their countrymen, gathered up the machine gun and the weapons of their dead and wounded comrades and vanished into the dense bushveld, firing as they went in an attempt to deter anyone from following them.

It was unfortunate that Nat, realising what the Germans were doing, had gathered a number of his mounted scouts and galloped back in an attempt to cut off the escape of the fleeing Germans.

They ran into each other less than half a mile from where the captured *Königsberg* gun was sited, and Nat and his scouts were heavily outnumbered. They fired at the Germans, but their fire was returned and many of the saddles of the scouts' horses were quickly emptied.

One of the first to fall was Nat. As he lay on the ground, one of the German askaris ran to him and plunged a bayonet deep into his body. He was about to repeat his action when one of the scouts who was still mounted saw what was happening and shot the German dead.

The next few minutes were confused as gun and bayonet were brought into use by both sides. Then, as the shouts of the pursuing Rhodesian and Portuguese troops were heard approaching, the Germans quickly disappeared into the tall elephant grass, leaving their opponents to tend their own and the German wounded.

V

The sight of Colonel Nat Retallick lying on the ground seriously wounded caused consternation among Rhodesians, Portuguese and African scouts alike. As well as being very well liked by all the men who served with him, the loss of his great experience of scouting in an African environment would be a devastating blow to the troops fighting von Lettow.

The news that Nat was a casualty was brought to Sam by a very concerned Philippe. In answer to Sam's anxious question, the Portuguese area commander replied, 'His wounds are very serious indeed. They were dressed by one of our medical orderlies, but he believes that if Nat is not seen by a doctor very soon he will die.'

'Where can we find the nearest doctor?' Sam demanded.

'At Manchemba . . . Antonia is there,' replied a distraught Philippe, 'but that is thirty miles away. He might be dead by the time his men get him there.'

'No he won't,' Sam said positively. 'Get your men and the Rhodesian Africans to unload the logs from the traction engine's trailer – leave me just enough for the journey to Manchemba. At the same time tell them to unlimber the gun and ammunition carriage . . . and cut elephant grass to make a bed on the trailer. We'll take *all* the wounded to Manchemba – but make certain Nat is made particularly comfortable. In the meantime I'll be getting up steam.'

The journey to Manchemba was accomplished in four and a half hours. There was a narrow track that served as a road and Sam kept to this, flattening all but the sturdiest trees in his path and doing his best to make the ride as smooth as was possible in the circumstances.

He had judged the fuel the machine would require with an expert eye. When they eventually steamed into Manchemba, there were two logs remaining on the trailer – but Nat and all but one of the other wounded men were still alive.

The sound of the traction engine brought everyone out of their homes – among them Antonia and Maria.

Maria was both delighted and astonished to see Sam, but there was no time to enjoy the sort of reunion Sam had looked forward to. In a few words he explained to Antonia that Nat was among the wounded on the trailer, and that he was gravely ill. Maria realised immediately that this was no time to talk to Sam about their future. She and Antonia set about having the men transferred from the trailer to a small, and still rather primitive, hospital.

The locally recruited African 'nurses' had received as much training as possible from Maria, and while they were dealing with the majority of the casualties, Antonia, aware that Nat was the most seriously hurt of them all, examined his wounds.

Her examination over, she said to Sam and Philippe, 'I can operate on the bayonet wound and am confident of making good any damage it has caused, but I have no X-ray machine here and in his present state I am not prepared to cut him open and probe for a bullet. Hopefully, my work will staunch the bleeding that threatens his life right now, but there is a bullet somewhere inside him and we need to know exactly where it is in order to remove it and guarantee a full recovery.' Aware that her prognosis was not as reassuring as it might have been, she added, 'Getting him here as quickly as you did undoubtedly saved his life, Sam. Now we must make certain that we keep him alive. I will do everything humanly possible for him, but he will be in God's hands for at least twenty-four hours – less if that bullet is lodged close to a vital organ. Now, while he is being prepared for surgery, I will have a look at some of the others . . .'

It was close to midnight that night before Maria and Antonia had dealt with all the casualties. Antonia was satisfied that in Nat's case she had stopped the internal bleeding that had been caused by the askari's bayonet,

341

and had transfused blood from some compatible volunteers among his scouts and artillerymen to make up for the large amount he had lost, but she was still concerned about the bullet that was somewhere inside his body.

Sam was waiting in Maria's hut and was having difficulty remaining awake. Suddenly, the door opened and she came in. His weariness disappeared immediately when she rushed to him and embraced him fiercely. When they both paused for breath, she said, 'I was beginning to think I would never see you again, Sam, and that you might have regretted all the things you said to me before you went off to join Spicer's expedition. Have you received all the letters I have sent to you?'

'Not one. I was beginning to believe that *you* might be having second thoughts about us.'

Her vehement 'No, Sam . . . *never*! Not for a moment!' was the signal for another embrace that aroused the passion in both of them, and for a while they were able to shut out the world outside the primitive mud and grass hut.

Later, lying in her arms in the narrow bed, Sam asked, 'What did you say in the letters that never arrived, Maria? Have you decided whether you will marry me?'

'I said that if you still felt the same when we met again, I *would* marry you . . .' When Sam showed his delight by kissing her again and again, she eventually managed to add, '. . . but not immediately, Sam.'

'What do you mean? Why not now . . . here?'

'Because when we are married I want to be a full wife to you . . . in every sense of the word. I want to devote the whole of my life to you and for us to be together all the time. That just isn't possible right now. You have seen what has happened today. There have been other days like it . . . and there will be many more in the future. Days – sometimes weeks when all my thoughts and energy need to be given to wounded men . . . men like poor Nat Retallick. If I deserted them now I would feel guilty for the rest of my life . . . and I don't want to feel guilt where you are concerned, Sam, not about anything.'

'But we could still be married and enjoy married life whenever possible . . .'

'No, Sam. I am more than happy to give myself to you when the opportunity arises – and I will make as many opportunities as is humanly possible – but when we are married I want to be able to give you far more. I want to make a home for you . . . children . . . a settled life for both of us. This war won't last for ever. When it is over we can be married and I will be the happiest woman in the whole world and be able to do my very best to make you the happiest man. Will you wait until then, Sam?'

'It seems I have no alternative,' he said ruefully.

'That is not the answer I was hoping for,' she said quietly.

'Of course I will wait,' he replied. 'I don't want to, but you and Antonia are doing a wonderful job here, something truly worthwhile, and you are not the only one who would feel guilty if I tried to persuade you to give it up and come away with me. In fact, if it were at all possible I could love you all the more for having such a strong sense of where your duty lies. I don't

really think it's possible for me to love you any more
than I do right now, but I'll try . . .'

VI

'We have to find that bullet, Sam. Unless we do, Nat is
going to die . . . but if I go into his body without knowing
precisely where it is, it will be me, not the bullet, that
kills him.'

It was the morning after the arrival of the wounded
men in Manchemba and Sam felt desperately sorry for
Antonia. Nat had been her hero from the time she had
been a young girl. Her family and his were close friends
and she would be marrying his brother as soon as the
war ended – Maria had told him that she carried the
engagement ring Ben had given her on a cord about her
neck, not being able to wear it while she carried out
operations and afraid of losing it if she left it anywhere.
Yet if she operated on Nat in his present state, she was
likely to put an end to the life of her future husband's
much loved eldest brother.

In an effort to reassure her, Sam said, 'Everyone will
know – and that includes Ben – that whatever happens
you will have done all that you possibly can to help
Nat, Antonia. Is there anything that anyone else can do?
This X-ray machine you were talking about earlier, that
can look inside people and find things like bullets, where
is the nearest one?'

'Probably South Africa,' Antonia replied. 'We do not
have one in Mozambique yet, but Philippe has sent wireless messages to everyone he believes might be able to

help, British, Belgians, Rhodesians, South Africans . . . He has even sent a message to General Smuts, telling him what has happened and asking for his help.'

'I'll go over to see him and find out whether he has had any replies,' Sam said. He was as concerned as everyone else. He admired Nat and regarded him as a friend. He was also aware just how important he was in the fight against the Germans in this part of Africa.

He found Philippe pacing the floor in the wireless office that was attached to his headquarters in the building that had been taken over from the Portuguese district administrator. When Sam asked whether there had been any encouraging replies to his appeals for help, Philippe replied, 'None. The nearest X-ray machine would appear to be in a South African hospital – except for one on board a hospital ship that is on its way to Mombasa, in British East Africa. It will be passing the coast of Mozambique tomorrow, but there is no way we can get Nat there in time to be taken off.'

'Why not?' Sam demanded. 'How far is the sea from here?'

'To Palma? About sixty miles, perhaps more,' Philippe replied, 'but it is not flat country as it was from the scene of yesterday's battle. There are hills, and rough country.'

'Is there a road?'

'Not as such,' Philippe said. 'It is more of a track – used by camels. I know what you are thinking, but even if we were able to clear the way for your traction engine the going would be so rough that Nat would never survive the journey.'

'Leave me to deal with that,' Sam said. 'You arrange

for as many men as possible to set off along this track – now! Let them look at the traction engine first and see what clearance it has. Then they are to clear the sides of the track sufficiently to allow me and a trailer to pass through. Meanwhile I will have a sling set up on the trailer to hold Nat and soften the effect of the rough ground. Antonia can accompany us and do whatever is needed for him along the way. In the meantime, send a wireless message to whoever is responsible for the hospital ship. Tell them to send a boat ashore to Palma to take Nat on board and find this bullet that's causing all the trouble. I will go and make the traction engine ready for the journey. If need be we will travel all night – but I don't think it will be necessary. What *is* certain is that we will have Nat on board the hospital ship tomorrow and find that bullet.'

Nat's scouts took charge of the Portuguese Africans who were sent along the track to Palma to clear the way for Sam's traction engine. By alternately cajoling and threatening the work force, they were three-quarters of the way to the coastal village of Palma before Sam caught up with them with Nat on the trailer in a hammock slung on flexible branches attached to two supports. Alongside him, ensuring that he was not shaken up too much, was Antonia. They had travelled until darkness fell, then rested until dawn broke. Providing a concerned escort were more of Nat's scouts.

The party reached Palma at ten o'clock in the morning, two hours before they were scheduled to meet a boat sent ashore from the hospital ship *Maine*. As it happened, the *Maine* was early too. Their boat was on its way ashore with a doctor on board as the Ruddlemoor traction engine and its escort arrived at the short, rickety jetty with Nat. He would be the hospital ship's only patient until the vessel arrived at Mombasa to embark the many wounded men taking passage back to the United Kingdom, via Cape Town.

Nat had stood up well to the journey from Manchemba and, watching the boat carrying him ploughing through the water on the way to the *Maine*, both Sam and Antonia were convinced that he was well on the road to full recovery. They could make their way back to the border hospital well satisfied with what they had been able to achieve.

On the return journey to Manchemba a steam pipe on the traction engine fractured and it took Sam three hours to repair it. As a result they were forced to stay at a tiny Portuguese settlement along the way instead of completing the return journey that night. It was mid-morning when they steamed into the hospital compound – and they found it in a state of uproar. Antonia hurried into the hospital to learn the cause of the disturbance, and returned pale-faced.

There had been no sign of Maria. Deeply concerned and with a frightening premonition that she was at the heart of the consternation, Sam ran to meet Antonia.

'What is happening?' he demanded. 'Does it have something to do with Maria? Where is she?'

'A company of the Rhodesian Native Regiment met up with the German raiders yesterday and there was a battle,' Antonia explained, deeply distressed. 'There were many wounded on both sides. Most were brought here, but Maria went out to tend to those most seriously hurt, who could not be moved.'

'Of course, she would,' Sam said. 'But where is she now? Why hasn't she come out to meet us? Is she still with the wounded men?'

'She isn't here, Sam. She did not return. She and the hospital staff with her were ambushed on their way to the scene of the battle. All the men were either killed or wounded.'

Deeply alarmed, Sam demanded, 'What of Maria? Was she among the wounded?' When Antonia did not reply immediately, Sam was frantic. 'She's not . . . she wasn't killed?'

'No, Sam,' Antonia replied, even more distressed than before. 'She was taken prisoner . . . by German askaris.'

VII

Sam wasted no time in gathering all the available scouts who had been to the coast with him, and finding fresh horses for them and one for himself. Then, pushing his horse hard, he set off for the scene of the ambush where Maria had been taken prisoner.

It was not difficult to find. The undergrowth was dense here and, although the Germans had buried all the dead they could see, they had been in a hurry to move on and some had been missed. Sam and the scouts were guided to the spot by the vultures circling over-head.

348

Sam sent off most of the scouts to find the direction taken by the Germans. He had ascertained that they were on foot and had hopes that he would be able to catch up with them, even though they had almost twenty-four hours' start.

Following the path indicated by the scouts, Sam must have been riding for four hours after leaving the scene of Maria's capture when two of the African trackers reported back to him. The Germans had made camp close to a small river, no more than another half-hour's ride ahead. Surprisingly, they seemed to be perfectly relaxed and taking things easy.

It sounded so unlike the actions of a German guerrilla group that Sam thought it must be a trap, set for anyone who might be following. However, one of the two European scouts who had remained with Sam explained that German intelligence was second to none, especially in areas close to the German East African border, where the native tribes favoured the Germans more than they did the Portuguese. The Germans would know that the Rhodesian troops in the area were pursuing the main German force with whom they had fought and were far to the west. There were a number of Portuguese troops in forts scattered about the area, but the Germans had a very low opinion of them and treated them with disdain. They felt they could afford to take the rare opportunity to rest for twenty-four hours.

'Will it be possible to attack the Germans and take them by surprise?' Sam asked the scouts who had located the enemy camp.

Their reply was translated by one of the two

Europeans. 'No. There are more than two hundred askaris in the camp. They are all seasoned fighting men and have sentries posted with machine guns. Even were that not so, we would still be outnumbered by more than ten to one.'

It would be suicidal to attempt an attack upon the Germans, but Sam was determined that Maria should not remain in their hands. 'If there is no way of defeating them by force, then I am going to have to go in there on my own, under a white flag,' he said.

The idea did not appeal to the European scouts and one of them said, 'German askaris do not have a good record of recognising the significance of a white flag. Besides, why should they release their prisoner just because you want her back?'

'I will have to hope I am spotted first by a German and not an askari,' Sam retorted grimly. 'As for releasing Maria . . . she is a nurse and is desperately needed at Manchemba – and not just for our own wounded. There are almost as many Germans as our own men in the hospital. If the German officer in command has any compassion for his own men, he will release Maria.'

The Rhodesian scout remained sceptical, but Sam was already trying to find material with which to make a white flag. It was not easy. White material was not something that was carried about with them by men at war.

The problem was solved when one of the scouts who doubled as a medical orderly produced a large role of medical lint. Using this, and with the aid of a needle and catgut from the same source, Sam was able to cobble together a passable white flag, which he secured to a stick cut from a nearby tree.

One of the European scouts offered to accompany him into the German camp, but he felt it would be better if he went in alone, and unarmed. Guided to within a short distance of his destination, Sam handed over rifle and side arm, together with his ammunition belts, and then, displaying the white flag to the best possible advantage, rode slowly in the direction of the camp.

It was doubtful whether the white flag would have offered him any protection had a German officer not been inspecting the sentries at a machine-gun post as Sam approached. An askari saw him first and ran to the machine gun shouting a warning. Fortunately, the German officer recognised the white flag for what it was and kicked over the machine gun before the askari could curl his finger about the trigger. Soundly cursing the African soldier, the officer climbed from the depression in the ground that was the site for the machine gun and, drawing his revolver, advanced towards Sam.

When the two men were still some distance apart, the German pointed his revolver and called for Sam to halt. He spoke in German, and although Sam did not understand the words the meaning was quite clear.

Bringing his horse to a halt, Sam indicated the empty rifle scabbard beside the saddle and said, 'I have no weapons. I have come to speak to whoever is in command here.'

It was evident that the German did not understand him, but he motioned for Sam to dismount, then walked round the horse suspiciously before making it clear that he wanted Sam to lead the animal into the camp while he followed close behind.

Sam's arrival caused an immediate stir in the camp and two German officers emerged from one of only three tents that were pitched in the clearing. Sam guessed correctly that the older of the two was the officer in charge. The other was younger and, surprisingly, wore German naval uniform. Although Sam was not aware of the fact at the time, the officer was from the wrecked German warship the *Königsberg*, the vessel from which came the captured gun he had been towing around the African countryside. All the surviving crew members had been integrated into von Lettow's East African army.

The naval officer spoke perfect English, having received part of his education at an English university. Introducing himself with formal politeness as Lieutenant Max Wenig, he asked the purpose of Sam's visit to the German camp under the protection of a white flag.

'I have come to ask for the return of the nurse captured by your men yesterday when she and a medical party on its way to help the men wounded in a battle between our forces were ambushed some miles to the west of here.'

The young naval officer translated Sam's words to the German commander and the other officers standing nearby and they all made replies accompanied by the shaking of heads.

'We know of the battle,' said Wenig, speaking to Sam, 'and also of the ambush of the smaller party, although we were not aware it was a medical party. However, we took no prisoners, men or woman. But, even if we had, why should we return her to you?'

352

'Because her work is vital,' Sam explained. 'She and a woman doctor are the only qualified medical staff in a hospital where there are as many wounded German soldiers as British. Without her, many soldiers will die – your men as well as ours.'

Again there was a discussion among the German officers, and when Wenig spoke to Sam again he repeated what he had said before. No prisoners had been taken, but he added, 'The medical party was ambushed by a platoon of our askaris, led by one of their own non-commissioned officers. We are sending for him and will ask if he knows anything of a nurse. In the meantime, please, join us for a cup of tea.'

Sam's arrival had caused considerable interest among the German and African troops in the camp and by the time the messenger returned with the askari NCO there was a considerable crowd round the commanding officer's tent. The officer put a question to the askari and, although he shook his head, there was something about his manner that made Sam doubt that he was telling the truth.

The German officer too was not convinced and his voice was raised angrily when he questioned the askari once more. Suddenly there was a great deal of excited questioning and answering, with many of the German officers joining in.

Then Lieutenant Wenig said, 'The askari was less than honest. A woman *was* taken prisoner, but she was African, not European.'

Sam did not know whether to be jubilant or dismayed. Maria had been in the hands of the askaris for twenty-four hours – without the knowledge of the German officers. 'She has an African mother, but her father is an important Portuguese businessman. She has only recently returned from nursing in London, where she also treated soldiers from all armies. Her name is Maria Fernandes.'

The naval officer had been studying Sam closely as he was speaking and now he said, 'Pardon me if I am wrong, but it would seem that this woman is more than just a nurse to you.'

Sam met the other man's unswerving gaze and said, 'I have asked her to marry me and she has agreed – but not until this war is over and there are no more wounded to be treated.'

Lieutenant Wenig translated to his fellow German officers what Sam had said and there was a mixture of reactions, some contemptuous, but most sympathetic.

The German naval officer turned upon the askari once again and this time his questioning was accompanied by a couple of hard cuffs to the face. Then two German soldiers were called forward, and after a brief discussion with Wenig and their commanding officer they hurried away with the askari.

'Most of our askaris are camped in the veld, outside the main camp, with their womenfolk,' he explained. 'That is why your nurse was not noticed before. She will be brought to us here.'

After waiting for fifteen long minutes Sam was becoming worried when he saw the two soldiers who had been sent off returning, closely followed by a large crowd of noisy askaris. With the two European soldiers was

354

Maria – but this was not the neat and clean nurse he had left behind at Manchemba when he had gone off with Nat and Antonia. She was unkempt and dirty and there was a swelling on the side of her face that indicated a beating.

Deeply concerned, Sam called, 'Maria! Are you all right?'

He would have hurried to her, but the German naval officer reached out and stopped him, saying, 'Wait.'

When Maria reached them, Sam became even more concerned. With the two German soldiers flanking her, she stopped short of Sam and the German officers but did not look at any of them. Instead, her gaze remained upon the ground at her feet. Even when the German commanding officer spoke to her, she said nothing and did not look up. It could have been that she did not understand what he was saying, but then another of the officers spoke to her in what Sam recognised as Portuguese – and still she remained silent.

Eventually, after a discussion among the German officers, Lieutenant Wenig said to Sam, 'Major Schönfeld wishes me to convey to you his apologies and assure you that we do not make prisoners of women. The askaris involved will be punished. You and your nurse may go now.'

Sam stepped forward and took Maria by the arm. 'It's all right, Maria, you are safe now. We can go back to Manchemba.'

Maria did not speak, but when she turned her face up to his the look in her eyes frightened him. However, explanations could wait. The main thing was to get her back to safety as quickly as possible.

One of the askaris had been holding Sam's horse and now he passed the reins back to him. With one hand holding the reins and the other about Maria's shoulders, Sam set off away from the camp, aware as he did so of angry voices among the askaris who had followed Maria and her escort to the commanding officer's tent.

The sound did not die away as Sam walked farther away and then, suddenly, there was the crack of a rifle shot from behind them. Maria's head snapped back and, letting out what sounded like a great sigh, she sagged beneath his arm – and slumped face down to the ground.

'Maria!' Dropping to his knees beside the prone body, Sam turned her over and held her in his arms. Blood . . . a great deal of blood . . . was oozing from her mouth, which opened and closed as though she was trying to speak as she looked up at him. Then her head dropped sideways and he knew she was dead.

From behind him in the German camp there was another shot. This time he recognised it as a pistol shot, and, suddenly, something in Sam snapped. Leaving Maria lying on the ground, he leaped into the saddle of his horse and galloped to where he knew the two Rhodesian scouts were waiting.

Reaching them, he shouted, 'Give me my gun . . . quickly!'

'Wait a minute, Sam . . . what are you going to do?'

Without replying, Sam leaped from his horse, seized his rifle from where it leaned against a tree, buckled on his holstered revolver and slung one of the ammunition belts across his shoulder. He was about to leap back into the saddle when the butt of a rifle, wielded by one of the scouts, struck him hard on the side of his head and he collapsed to the ground, unconscious.

Expressionless, the scout who had wielded the rifle looked down at Sam on the ground and his companion said, 'What about the nurse? We've been to all this trouble finding her; we can't just ride away and leave her lying dead where she was shot.'

'True,' agreed the first scout. Indicating Sam he added, 'Especially as he was ready to give his life for her. Use the remainder of that lint to make another white flag. We'll make a litter to pull behind one of the horses and take her back to Manchemba with us.'

As the two scouts approached Maria's body, Lieutenant Wenig came to meet them from the German camp. In his hand he held an ivory-handled Mauser pistol.

Pointing to the weapon, the first Rhodesian scout said, 'You won't need that. We've come to pick up the murdered body of Nurse Fernandes, that's all.'

'Where is the young English officer?' Wenig asked.

'He lost his head, took up his rifle and was coming to take on the whole German East African army because the nurse had been shot. I had to knock him unconscious.'

'I thought something like that might have happened,' said the German naval officer sympathetically. 'Her death is a matter of deep sorrow to us also. It is a stain upon our honour. Unfortunately, the askari who took her prisoner looked upon her as his own property. He was deeply aggrieved when we handed her over to the Englishman. It was he who fired the shot that killed her.'

Holding out the ornate Mauser towards the scout, Wenig said, 'When the Englishman recovers, please give him this. It belonged to my commanding officer. He had the askari brought to him, and when he admitted shooting the nurse he was executed on the spot with this weapon. My commanding officer wishes the Englishman to have it, and sends with it his deepest apologies for this most regrettable incident.'

16

I

Ten o'clock on a Friday morning was an unusual time for Ben Retallick to be languishing in bed, but he was recovering from a bout of influenza and had been in no state to argue with his housekeeper when, two days before, she had insisted that he take to his bed until he was in a fit state to take up the reins at Ruddlemoor once more. He was actually feeling better this morning, but had decided that one more day would see him fully fit again. Besides, Ruddlemoor seemed to be coping well enough without him. At least, no disasters had been reported.

There was a knock on the door and, sitting up and adjusting his pillows, he called, 'Come in!'

The door opened and, expecting a maid to enter the room, Ben was surprised when Mrs Rodda came in with a newspaper tucked beneath her arm and bearing a tray upon which were tea, toast and marmalade, together with a small pile of letters.

'I wasn't expecting to have you waiting on me, Mrs Rodda,' Ben said as the housekeeper slid the stand of a sick-bed table beneath the bed and placed the tray upon the table. 'Is the maid sick too?'

'No, sir,' she replied, 'but I thought I would come up myself and see how you are feeling.'

'I am much improved, thank you, Mrs Rodda.'

'Good. There is a letter here from Mozambique. Hopefully it is from Dr Antonia and will make you feel even better.'

Eagerly, Ben located Antonia's letter and tore it open before starting on his breakfast. Then, as he read, his expression changed from one of delight to disbelief and then outright dismay.

Alarmed, Mrs Rodda asked, 'What is it, sir? Is something wrong with Dr Antonia?'

'No, thank God!' Ben said fervently. 'But everything else seems to have been going wrong out there . . . *very* wrong. My oldest brother, Nat, has been seriously wounded in a clash with a German raiding party. It seems he was both shot and bayoneted. She says that if it hadn't been for Sam Hooper he couldn't have survived. She dealt with the bayonet wound, but was unable to find the bullet that was still inside him. By using the Ruddlemoor traction engine, Sam managed to get Nat to the coast and have him ferried out to a hospital ship, where they found and removed the bullet. Her brother – the Portuguese officer who was with her when she visited Tregarrick for the first time – has had a wireless message to say that Nat is recovering in hospital in Kenya, which was the hospital ship's destination.'

'Well, at least *that* is good news, sir,' said Mrs Rodda.

'Yes, it would be – if that was all,' Ben said, reading on, 'but it seems that a young Portuguese nurse was captured by the Germans in an ambush not very far from the hospital – and once again it was Sam who went to her rescue, finding where the Germans were and going into their camp under a flag of truce. He got her back only to see her shot dead by one of the German African soldiers who had captured her in the first place. It seems that Sam was so upset that he has abandoned the traction engine and joined up with a column of Rhodesian soldiers in order to fight the Germans.'

'Oh my!' Mrs Rodda was aghast. 'Will you be telling Betsy Hooper, sir? She'll worry herself sick if you do.'

'I can't *not* tell her,' Ben replied unhappily. 'It wouldn't be fair, especially if something were to happen to him – and it certainly sounds as though he is in the thick of whatever is going on there. I will say this for him – and I have said it before – Sam is certainly not lacking in courage. Betsy Hooper can be very proud of him. When he returns I must find some way of thanking him for what he did for Nat.'

'Ah yes, your brother . . .'

The way Mrs Rodda said it made Ben look at her sharply.

'I believe you have another brother?' she said.

'That's right. Adam. There was a fourth brother, Wyatt . . . he was the eldest, but he died with my father when the Matabele rose in rebellion against the whites who had settled in their country.'

Mrs Rodda knew nothing about the Matabele, but

that did not matter for the moment. Taking the newspaper from beneath her arm, she said, 'There is something in here I think you should see, sir, before someone else tells you about it. I don't like showing it to you on top of all the other bad news you have had, but it's about the other brother . . . Adam. It says here that he has been taken prisoner, sir . . . while fighting for the Germans.'

When Ben rose from his bed, leaving his breakfast untouched, he discovered he was not as well as he had thought. He felt queasy and off balance, but he was determined to do something about the report in the weekly newspaper that was printed beneath the headline NO SMOKE WITHOUT FIRE? It was a scurrilous article full of innuendo and re-reporting the rumours that had led to Ben's arrest months before and for which the same newspaper, the *Cornish Telegraph*, had been obliged to print an apology, albeit a grudging one.

The newspaper announced that it now felt its duty was to report that it had obtained 'irrefutable evidence' that another of the Retallick family was a proven enemy of Great Britain and had been captured while fighting for Germany against British soldiers in South West Africa. The article went on to add that this was not the first occasion on which Adam had taken part in anti-British activities, and described many battles during the Anglo-Boer war in which he was supposed to have fought the British army.

Ben knew that many of the battles reported by the newspaper had indeed been fought between British and

Boer armies – but he also knew that Adam had taken part in few, if any, of them. Adam *had* fought for the Boers, but it was because he supported their cause, rather than because he was anti-British.

The *Cornish Telegraph* article ended by saying that the information it was printing had been received from 'an impeccable source'.

Not surprisingly, perhaps, by the time he had finished reading the article Ben had developed a severe headache in addition to his other symptoms. Nevertheless, he telephoned the newspaper and demanded to speak to the editor, only to be told he was not available. When Ben asked that a message be passed to the editor telling of his intention to instruct his solicitor to take action against him and his newspaper, he was told, insolently, 'It's a free country, you can do what you like.'

Ben's next telephone call was to his solicitor, who agreed to write a letter to the editor notifying him of Ben's intention to take action against him for libel if a full apology was not printed in the next issue of the newspaper. However, the solicitor warned Ben that he would need to be able to prove the article was untrue if action was to be taken.

The solicitor's warning left Ben in a quandary. In other circumstances his first action would be to telegraph Nat at Insimo, asking for news of Adam – but Nat had been seriously wounded and was in a hospital in British East Africa and their mother would have enough to worry about without taking on an inquiry of this nature.

Ben decided he would write to Adam's Transvaal

home. If he was not there, his wife Johanna should be able to inform him of what Adam was doing.

Ben's day had been a long and exhausting one and his influenza seemed to have returned. After making numerous telephone calls, he had sent for Betsy Hooper. Although he did not tell her of Sam's involvement in the war in East Africa, he did tell her how he had saved Nat's life and that he was now part of an active service unit. Despite his efforts to play down Sam's activities, it was a tearful Betsy Hooper who left Tregarrick to return to her small cottage close to Ruddlemoor.

When Mrs Rodda came to the study where Ben was enjoying a well-earned drink, she sympathised with him for having such a difficult day and told him he did not look at all well.

'I am concerned for Antonia, for Sam – and for my brother Nat too, Mrs Rodda. I could do without this report in the newspaper. I really don't know why they should be running what can only be called a vendetta against me, but they seem determined to find something that will seriously affect my business.'

'I have been thinking about that, sir, and I remembered that some years ago, certainly before you came to Tregarrick, there was a very strong rumour going around that the *Cornish Telegraph* was on the verge of becoming bankrupt. Then someone came along and put money into the newspaper in order to save it. I never took very much notice of what was going on at the time, and it was only today, when I got to thinking about things, that I remembered the name of the man who was

364

rumoured to have put the money up. It was Brigadier General Sir Robert Grove.'

II

By Monday, Ben had succeeded in throwing off the fever and the nagging headache that had been symptomatic of the bout of influenza from which he had been suffering and was thinking more clearly about the numerous problems with which he had been faced before the weekend.

The first telephone call he made was to Lieutenant General Carey Hamilton, at the War Office in London, to tell him about Nat.

Carey was extremely concerned about his long-time friend and promised to have a wireless message relayed to General Jan Smuts, the South African statesman and ex-guerrilla leader who was commander-in-chief of the army in East Africa, requesting information about him.

A reply was received three days later. It appeared that Nat's recovery had been so satisfactory that he had been returned to another hospital ship for the journey south and put off at Beira, from where he had been able to take a train to Rhodesia, in order that he might convalesce at Insimo. The report added that Nat was not expected to be fit enough to resume active duties for at least twelve months.

The news that Nat was on the road to recovery came as an enormous relief to Ben and helped provide the impetus he needed to tackle the problem of the *Cornish Telegraph*'s smear campaign against him. Now that there was little doubt that Brigadier Grove's influence was behind it, Ben decided it was time to take the initiative in the business rivalry that existed between their two china clay companies – rivalry that had also been instigated by Grove.

Calling a meeting of the owners of all the various companies with whom he had drawn up contracts to supply Ruddlemoor with their refined clay, he told them he was aware they had been supplying Grove's company with clay that had not been fully refined, in order to circumvent the terms of the contract. In future, Ruddlemoor would refuse to accept clay from any company that did business with Grove.

His announcement brought protests from the owners, who declared that such a decision would add to the difficulties they were already experiencing. As one explained, 'We are making little enough profit from the clay we sell to the Grove works – but it is still profit and we are being forced to operate on the narrowest margin any of us can remember.'

His words were greeted with agreement from every owner present and Ben said, 'I am aware of your problems, but I regret that the time has come when you have to decide whether you run with the fox or with the hounds. Some of you will know already why I am taking such a drastic step. The others soon will. Now, I have recently made a number of new contacts in neutral countries. I will take all the fine clay you produce . . . at the agreed price. But don't think you can hold me to ransom by threatening to cut off your supply if you are not allowed to sell to Grove. I can increase Ruddlemoor production to meet any demands that are made on the company. I can also afford to buy out any clay company that goes out of business. I don't want that to happen, but for the first time since I came to England to take over Ruddlemoor from my grandfather, I am putting my own interests above all other considerations. That is all I have to say. Thank you for coming here today, gentlemen.'

The owners left the Ruddlemoor office talking angrily among themselves at being dictated to in such a manner by a man who not only was the youngest owner of a Cornish china clay company, but had come into the business from abroad. Those who were not aware of who was behind the campaign being waged against Ben in the *Cornish Telegraph* were saying bitterly that perhaps the newspaper was right and that Ben was intent upon closing the china clay companies down because their production was aiding the war effort. Others, aware of the reason why Ben had given them such an ultimatum, remained silent.

All the owners were aware of the quandary they were in. It had now become an all-out battle for supremacy in the Cornish china clay industry between Ben Retallick and Brigadier General Sir Robert Grove. It would end only when one of the two was forced out of business – and the owner who chose to throw in his lot with the wrong man would go out of business with him . . .

Almost three months passed and although the newspaper campaign continued against Ben, it became more sporadic and Ben began to believe that it would soon die away.

367

In the meantime, all but one of the owners who had signed contracts with Ben to supply him with refined china clay had cut their ties with Brigadier Grove and were reaping increased profits as a result.

The same could not be said of the Grove works. In the beginning the brigadier had a very large stockpile of clay bought from the other owners before Ben issued his ultimatum which had not been through the final stage of refining, but as 1916 drew towards its close Brigadier Grove realised he would not have enough clay to meet his commitments to the government.

He appealed to the other owners, offering them a more generous price for their produce, but none would risk incurring Ben's wrath and having him make good his promise to stop buying from them.

The *Cornish Telegraph* suddenly seemed to lose all interest in the war being waged in East Africa and those whom it believed to be supporting the Germans there. At the same time, an approach was made to the Ruddlemoor works captain from his opposite number in the Grove works. It was an offer to purchase clay from the company which was its acknowledged rival, at the going market rate.

'What did you tell him, Jim?' Ben asked, when he was told of the approach.

'I said I thought you would rather give our clay away than sell it to the Grove works,' declared the Ruddlemoor captain.

'And what did he say to that?' Ben asked.

'He had obviously been sent to see me by Grove himself,' Jim Bray replied. 'He said he knew that would be the answer he would get, but he had to try, not just for Grove, but for all the men who would lose their jobs if the company folded.'

'If that happened I would put in an offer for the Grove works,' Ben said. 'I probably wouldn't pay as much as it is worth, but if things reach that stage then Grove will be glad to take any offer. He has pared his profits so much by starting this stupid feud with Ruddlemoor that he will have little space for manoeuvre. If I took it over the men would stay on and we would dominate the clay business in Cornwall. We could set the prices for everyone and the business would be assured for a great many years to come. I believe that is what Grove has been hoping to do for his own profit. We will have to see what he does now.'

Brigadier Sir Robert Grove paid an evening call upon Ben at Tregarrick two days later. Ben led him to the study and politely invited him to seat himself before pouring a large brandy for the choleric ex-army man. Then Ben sat down saying absolutely nothing, waiting for Grove to broach the subject for which he knew he had come.

After taking two large draughts from his brandy goblet, Grove cleared his throat and said, 'Look here, Retallick, I have come to ask you to call off this stupid embargo you have put on those owners who have contracts with you, forcing them to stop selling dried clay to me.'

'I am not stopping them from selling clay to you, Brigadier, merely telling them that they must choose to whom they sell their clay. To you, or to me.'

'That's the same thing, and you know it. I have a contract to fulfil . . . a government contract, that has me selling my clay at a rock-bottom price. I've made damn little profit out of it and can't afford to pay the penalties that will be incurred if I don't meet my commitments.'

'Perhaps you should have thought of all that before taking the contract, Brigadier. Surely that would have been good business practice?'

For a moment it seemed to Ben that Brigadier Grove might explode. Instead, he said, 'Damn it, Retallick! I have not come here to be lectured on business practices . . .'

Interrupting him, Ben said, 'Why *have* you come here, Brigadier? To ask my help? To ask the help of someone you have done your best to brand as pro-German – in order to fulfil a British government contract? Don't you see a certain irony in such a situation?'

'Are you accusing me of being behind the revelations about you, Retallick? That is downright slanderous.'

'Slander . . . libel . . . you and I will probably be settling such matters in court, Brigadier, so perhaps we should not pursue this conversation any further.'

Brigadier Grove stood up, but not before he had downed the remainder of the brandy in his goblet. 'I knew it would be futile coming here to ask you to see sense, Retallick, but I had to try – for the sake of the men who depend on me for their daily bread. However, I will not remain to have you gloat over my misfortune.'

'I am not gloating. Brigadier Grove. My feelings are more of sorrow than anything else. I have always tried hard to deal fairly with my fellow clay owners. I regret you have not done the same by me. Sadly, I have learned my lesson and am now playing the game according to your rules.'

'You will regret this, Retallick. You feel aggrieved to think you have been wrongly accused of being pro-German? You have not experienced the half of it yet. By the time I have finished with you, you will be drummed out of the county – and good riddance too!' With that, Brigadier Sir Robert Grove stormed out of Tregarrick, roughly brushing aside the maidservant who was hurrying to open the entrance door for him.

III

A few days after the stormy meeting between Ben and the brigadier, the *Cornish Telegraph* began publishing a new series of articles about the conflict that had taken place in South West Africa in 1915, which it described as 'The Forgotten War'.

In the first article the newspaper succeeded in bringing in a number of references to the Anglo-Boer war that had taken place some fifteen years or so before and the significant part played in both by a certain Adam Retallick, 'brother of a well-known Cornish businessman whose loyalty to his adopted country was investigated by Special Branch police some months ago'.

While Ben was still digesting the article, which came very close to libelling him, he received an unexpected telephone call from Carey Hamilton at the War Office.

After exchanging the usual pleasantries, Carey said,

'I have had a telegraph message from Philippe St Anna. Your man in East Africa has contacted him and asked him to arrange for the traction engine currently at Manchemba to be sent to Insimo. Once there it can be serviced by the young man who accompanied Hooper on the Lake Tanganyika naval expedition, before both machines are returned to you at Ruddlemoor.'

'Thank you. I think Nat will probably be well enough to reply to a letter by now. I will write to him and make sure he has no use for either engine before having them shipped back to Cornwall. If he has, he might as well keep one or both of them. I have already bought a new one. It will not set me back too much to buy another from the same maker. However, I wish Sam could be persuaded to return to Ruddlemoor, with or without the traction engines. I could use his expertise here at the moment.'

'Your wish might well be granted sooner than you think, Ben – but I wouldn't like to say whether he will be fit to return to work for you right away. At the moment he is in hospital in Mombasa, where he has been since suffering a severe bout of malaria. When I learned of it I knew you would be concerned so I had a wireless message sent through army channels, asking for details of his condition. It seems he is expected to recover in due course, but will not be fit enough for further service in the East African campaign. He will be sent home as soon as a berth can be obtained for him in a hospital ship. I don't know when that is likely to be – the medical people are quite rightly giving preference to wounded men who need specialist treatment back in this country.'

Ben was alarmed at the news of Sam's illness. Neither he nor Betsy Hooper had heard from him since before the tragic affair of the Portuguese East African nurse. He would need to tell Betsy this latest bad news, while at the same time trying to impress upon her that Sam was definitely on the mend and would be home with her before too long.

'I hope Sam will be well enough to attend his investiture at Buckingham Palace,' Ben said. 'I will need to mention that if I am to take his mother's mind off the fact that he has been seriously ill without anyone informing her.'

'Talking of investitures . . .' Carey Hamilton said. 'I don't suppose you were told by anyone that the Portuguese authorities presented him with one of their most prestigious awards for his courage in securing the release of the unfortunate nurse? Our commander-in-chief in East Africa, General Smuts, personally congratulated him. Young Sam Hooper has certainly made his mark out there . . . but, as you and I are aware, he has never been lacking in courage.'

The telephone conversation continued on more general subjects before Carey Hamilton said, 'I trust all that silly nonsense about your loyalty to the country has gone away for good now?'

Had such a question been put to him on any other day, Ben would have said nothing, but the latest article to be published in the *Cornish Telegraph* was still fresh in his mind, and it rankled.

'As a matter of fact it has started up again only today,' he said. 'I believe it is being stirred up by Brigadier

General Sir Robert Grove, a retired army officer who is the owner of a rival china clay company here in Cornwall. We had a rather acrimonious exchange the other day and I have recently learned that he is part owner of the newspaper involved.'

'Sir Robert Grove?' Carey Hamilton queried. 'His name cropped up in conversation the other day in the club. One of the officers here at the War Office served with him and they are great friends, apparently. Come to think of it, this officer served in an administration post in the South West African campaign . . . It probably has nothing to do with your problem, Ben, but I will look into it all the same. Leave it with me.'

Five days later Carey Hamilton telephoned Ben again, and he was quite excited. 'I have made a few discreet enquiries and ascertained that the officer I mentioned as knowing Brigadier Grove *was* in South West Africa and would have made a great many contacts there. He is also in the habit of going back over the files on that campaign, which he has recently been drawing from our records office here . . . but you have no need to concern yourself with that for the time being. I have just received some news that is very exciting and should enable you to bring these scurrilous insinuations against you to an end once and for all. In fact, if you decide to proceed against the offending newspaper in court, I have no doubt you will be awarded substantial costs against them.'

When Ben tried to question Carey further, the lieutenant general said, 'I am sorry, Ben, I can say nothing more for the moment. You will just have to trust me and be patient, but you need be in no doubt about it. Your problems are at an end.'

In spite of the assurances he had received from Carey Hamilton, Ben was not entirely convinced, and when two weeks had passed and two more articles on South West Africa had appeared in the *Cornish Telegraph*, each with more references to the part played by the Retallick family in that little-known conflict, he began to despair of ever being able to put an end to the virulent campaign.

He was in the study of Tregarrick that evening, penning a letter to Antonia, when the telephone rang. Mrs Rodda had just put her head round the door, telling Ben she was on her way to visit her sister. Before Ben could reach the study extension, she picked up the hall telephone as she passed by.

Ben heard her voice speaking to whoever had called, before asking, 'May I ask who is speaking?'

Moments later he heard her hurrying from the hall along the corridor to the study door. He had asked her to leave it slightly ajar, as he was expecting Jim Bray to come round for a chat and wanted to hear him when he arrived, and now she pushed the door open without knocking.

'Who is it, Mrs Rodda? Is it Jim Bray to say he has been delayed?'

'No, sir.' In moments of stress, or great excitement, Mrs Rodda was apt to forget the refined accent she had deliberately acquired over the years and slip back into the broad Cornish dialect she had spoken as a girl. This was one such moment. ''Tis your brother, sir. 'Tis Adam Retallick.'

17

I

When he re-joined General Jan Smuts, Adam accompanied the East African commander-in-chief in pursuit of the elusive German commander, General von Lettow. In so doing, he proved he had forgotten none of the lessons he had learned as a guerrilla fighter during the Anglo-Boer war. During that conflict, Adam had served for a while in the Boer force led by Smuts and had made himself conversant with the way the man thought and the tactics he deemed necessary in the hit-and-run battles he fought against the British. That fact, together with Adam's understanding of von Lettow's aims and the problems of fighting a guerrilla-style conflict in a very difficult environment, prompted General Smuts to appoint Adam as one of his most valued staff officers.

It was for these reasons, too, that when in late 1916 Smuts was ordered to send an experienced senior officer to London to represent him at a War Office conference, convened to discuss the future conduct of the war in East Africa, the commander-in-chief chose Adam to be his representative.

Informing Adam of his decision, the slightly built general added, 'I think I should promote you to lieutenant colonel, too. I can't have you outranked by some British officer who believes that if we dig a trench in the bush von Lettow will obligingly come and build another facing us. You will have your work cut out to convince them that we are fighting a new and unconventional type of war, Adam – and one which is being conducted for the enemy by a man who has no equal in this type of warfare. The only way I can beat von Lettow is by being given sufficient men to block his every move, as well as having troops capable of surviving the rigours of bush warfare. That means seasoned troops, not raw conscripts. Make quite certain they understand that.'

En route to the United Kingdom, Adam called at Beira for an arranged meeting with the Portuguese army's commander-in-chief, General Carlos St Anna, father of Philippe and Antonia. General St Anna's wife Therese was in Beira with him and, much to Adam's delight, so too was Antonia.

Adam dined with them that evening, and when they were all talking of old times spent together at Insimo he told them that he intended calling there to check on Nat's progress and spend a couple of days with his mother before travelling on to South Africa to take passage for the United Kingdom.

'When are you going?' asked Therese.

'I am taking tomorrow's train.'

'Then you will be able to escort Antonia,' said a delighted Therese. 'She too is returning to England soon, but is going to Insimo to see her grandmother first. I was concerned about her travelling all that way on her own, especially after what happened to that poor nurse from her hospital. I am so glad Antonia is no longer there. I am able to sleep much better at night.'

'You have left Manchemba for good?' Adam asked Antonia in surprise. A lot of money and effort had gone into providing such a modern, well-equipped hospital close to what was likely to become a battleground in the not too distant future.

'After poor Maria was killed, Father decided that Manchemba was far too dangerous for a woman,' Antonia replied. 'I do not agree with him, but he is a general and I am only a humble doctor. I was overruled.'

'Does that mean there is no longer a hospital at Manchemba?' Adam was aware that its closure could affect the long-term planning of General Smuts's campaign.

'No.' The reply came from General St Anna himself. 'I have sent two male doctors to Manchemba to take Antonia's place. In fact we are extending the hospital. It will be ready to take a large number of military casualties, should they occur. In the meantime it will cater for the needs of the natives. Manchemba is at the heart of one of the unhealthiest provinces in the country. It will do much good . . . but the reason Antonia is leaving is not only because of the dangers she would face there.'

There was pride in General St Anna's voice when he said, 'Tell him the main reason, Antonia.'

Smiling at her father, Antonia said, 'In England I was working with a Dr Ericsson who is the world's expert on what has become known as shell-shock. It is a traumatic condition suffered by men who are forced to endure constant bombardment and attack in the appalling conditions found in the front-line trenches of Europe. Dr Ericsson has been given a great deal of money by the Americans to go to the United States to continue his research over there. He approached the Portuguese government and asked them to release me from my work here in order that I might take over from him in England . . . in Cornwall, to be exact.'

'And, of course, Cornwall is where Ben is,' said Adam knowingly. He had been told of Antonia's engagement to the youngest Retallick brother. 'He is a very lucky man.'

'No, *I* am the lucky one,' Antonia declared. 'Ben is a very special man and I will be living in his wonderful house when we are married.' Holding out her left hand, on which the ring Ben had bought for her was once more being worn, she said, 'I hope that soon after I am back in England there will be a wedding ring on this finger, too.'

II

The sun had just slipped beneath the crests of the surrounding hills when Adam and Antonia reached Insimo on the estate's narrow-gauge railway train. Adam

380

had telephoned a few days earlier to tell his mother when they would be leaving Beira. Consequently, when the train came to a halt they were met by a party which included Elvira Retallick, Victoria, Diego Fernandes, Esme, and a pale and stooped Nat.

Elvira shed tears as she hugged the son she had not seen for many years, while Victoria embraced her grand-daughter before standing back to admire her and tell her that she must be the most beautiful doctor in the whole of the medical profession.

There was a hug too for Diego from Antonia when she commiserated with him on the loss of his sister. She added, 'Poor Sam was devastated by her death. He would have taken on the whole German force that had crossed into Mozambique, had not one of Nat's scouts prevented him by clubbing him with a rifle butt and knocking him unconscious.'

'Sam never made any secret of the way he felt about Maria,' Diego said. 'No matter where he was, or who he was talking to. He would have been a good husband to her.'

'Talking of good husbands . . . I think you should hurry on ahead to the house, Adam,' Elvira said mean-ingfully. 'There is someone there waiting for you. I believe she has been waiting for a very long time.'

Adam looked at her in consternation, 'You don't mean . . . Johanna and the children are here . . . at Insimo?'

'The children are not here, but Johanna is.'

'Why . . . ? What is she doing here . . . and where are the children?' Adam was confused.

'Those are questions you will need to ask her yourself,' Elvira said, 'but from what she has said to me since she arrived at Insimo, you had better have answers as well as questions for her.'

When an apprehensive Adam reached the house that had been his childhood home, he found Johanna seated in shadow on the stoep.

He was expecting her to rise and greet him and tell him how good it was to see him. In truth, he would be delighted to be reunited with her. When not actively pursuing the enemy, he actually did miss her – and the children too. He had intended to write to her on many occasions, but something . . . the war, meetings, planning . . . always seemed to get in the way of his good intentions.

Breaking the silence that hung heavily between them, he said, 'Johanna . . . when Ma told me you were here, I hurried straight to the house ahead of everyone else. This is a great surprise!'

'I don't doubt it,' came the terse reply – and nothing else.

Adam waited for her to say more. When she did not, he said, 'Aren't you even going to stand up and let me give you a kiss and a hug?'

'No,' she said bluntly. 'I – and the children – have managed without so much as a message from you for getting on for two years now. We have learned to do without anything from you.'

'Is it as long as that?' Adam was floundering for something to say that would excuse his failure to communicate with her for so long. 'I . . . I never realised.

I always meant to write, but something always seemed to come up. I'm sorry . . .'

'Are you?' she retorted coldly. 'I doubt it very much. From what I hear, you have done very well without us. We have probably not done quite so well without you, but we have managed. Yes, we have all become very good at managing.'

They both heard the sound of voices along the path that led from the railway to the house. Adam said, 'Look . . . I've said I'm sorry. Let's not have an argument in front of the others. We will talk about it tonight . . . in private.'

'No we will not,' Johanna said vehemently. 'Not unless you intend shouting out all you have to say to me for everyone at Insimo to hear. *You* are sleeping here, in your old room. *I* have a bed in Victoria's house, sharing the annexe with Antonia.'

Adam would have protested strongly about the sleeping arrangements, but the others had reached the house and they began seating themselves on the stoep, around Adam and Johanna, as Elvira called for the Matabele servants to come and serve them drinks.

Johanna never said a word to Adam during the whole of that evening, and when the two Retallick brothers went off to Nat's room to chart the progress of the East African campaign on the maps that Nat kept there, Elvira managed to take her to one side and express her concern about what appeared to be a serious breakdown in their marriage.

'Don't worry about it,' Johanna said reassuringly. 'It won't hurt Adam to be kept at arm's length for a while.

As a colonel and staff officer in Jan Smuts's army he is used to having everyone do exactly what he wants, when he wants it. That may be all right for the army, but it doesn't work in a marriage.' Aware that Elvira was seriously concerned, she added, 'It will be all right, I promise you. I knew what Adam was like when I married him. He was never meant to be a farmer and I give him credit for sticking at it for so many years. He is back doing what he does best now and, because of it, is feeling guilty about his family. I have a few ideas about how we can work things out for the future. I'll discuss them with him before he leaves Insimo.'

Johanna's attitude towards her husband did not thaw until the evening before he was to leave Insimo. She realised just how important he was to the British war effort when a rider arrived to deliver a message that had been received and decoded for him in the military wireless office in Bulawayo. The message instructed Adam that he was to leave at the earliest opportunity for Cape Town, where a destroyer had been placed at his disposal and was waiting to convey him to England for his meeting with senior officers at the War Office in London.

When Adam pleaded with Johanna to talk to him before he left, she eventually – and with a feigned show of reluctance – agreed. It was a great relief to Elvira to see them walking in the Insimo garden deep in conversation. It pleased her even more when Johanna spent that night in Adam's room and not in Victoria's quarters.

The following day, as Elvira and Johanna walked back

384

to the house after they had waved Adam out of sight on the Insimo train taking him to Bulawayo, Elvira asked her daughter-in-law if she and Adam had reached agreement about the future.

'Yes, and I think it will work,' Johanna replied. 'As I said to you the evening Adam arrived, I have known for a long time that Adam's heart has never been in farming and I was wrong to expect him to be happy there. Now, seeing what he has achieved since he went off to war, I realise that soldiering is what he does best.'

'That's all very well,' Elvira said, 'but the war won't last for ever. What will he do when it's over if he gives up farming?'

'I asked the same question,' Johanna said, 'and Adam had an answer. It seems that both Jan Smuts and Louis Botha think very highly of him' – Louis Botha had also been a leader of Boer forces during the Anglo-Boer war but was now President of South Africa – 'and Botha has suggested that he takes a high military post in the South African army when the war comes to an end. Adam says the war is not likely to end for another couple of years and by then Uiys will be eighteen and old enough to take over the running of the farm. He has been doing it anyway, since Adam went off to war. He has a man to help him and my ma will be there to take care of him until he finds himself a wife.'

'What about you and the other two children?' Elvira asked.

'Adam says the army will find a house for us in Pretoria, or wherever else he is sent. He also agrees that I – or all of us – can return to the farm for as long as we wish, whenever we feel like it. It will be a good life, Elvira. Certainly better than becoming old before my time by working all hours of the day trying to keep the farm going, as I have been doing for these last couple of years.'

Elvira remained thoughtfully silent for a long time before saying, 'I think everything could work out very well for you all, Johanna. I hope Adam realises just how lucky he is to have you as his wife.' Turning to her daughter-in-law, she gave her a warm embrace, and as they resumed walking along the path she said, 'That's you and Adam settled. Nat is well on the road to recovery and he and Esme are very happy together. I will be glad when Antonia is back in England and she and Ben are married. He is not having a particularly happy time at the moment but when Antonia is there once more he will at least have someone with whom he can talk over all the problems that have come his way as a result of his success in the business he took over from his grand-father.'

'You mean those insinuations that he is pro-German?' Johanna said. 'Antonia has spoken to Adam about them and I believe they have formed some sort of plan together. Once Adam is in Britain he will of course contact Ben and Antonia seems to think he will be able to silence Ben's critics. Given a few weeks, all your sons will be able to look forward to a happy and successful future. I hope I will one day be able to say the same about my three sons!'

tell them not to go to too much trouble with her rooms.

18

I

Ben had a lengthy conversation with Adam on the telephone, and when he hung up the handset he was in a
jubilant mood. Mrs Rodda had lingered in the hope of
learning something of what effect a telephone call from
the apparently errant Retallick brother would have upon
Ben. She was taken entirely by surprise when Ben rushed
out of his study, swooped her up in his arms and whirled
her around in the hall.

'Mr Retallick . . . sir! Whatever are you doing?'

'I am expressing sheer joy, Mrs Rodda. That was my
brother, the one who has also been the subject of the
scurrilous articles in the *Cornish Telegraph*. He is in
London, but before leaving Africa he met Antonia. She
is returning to England on the next hospital ship available from Cape Town and will most probably be home
sometime in the next couple of weeks! Isn't that
absolutely wonderful? Adam also mentioned the

problems I am having with the *Cornish Telegraph*. He had dinner last night with General Hamilton and they discussed them. Adam says he has an answer to every one of their accusations and that we have all we need to nail the newspaper – and Brigadier Sir Robert Grove with it. I am on top of the world, Mrs Rodda.'

Straightening her clothes, but looking pleasurably flustered, Mrs Rodda said, 'It is very good news indeed, sir. You won't mind if I tell the staff now that Dr Antonia will soon be back with us? It will give them very great pleasure to begin making ready for her return.'

'Go ahead and let them get started, Mrs Rodda – but tell them not to go to too much trouble with her rooms. I intend that Antonia will marry me and move into the main house just as soon as I can organise it after her return.'

Adam arrived at Tregarrick two days later and almost immediately he and Ben set off for a pre-arranged interview with the editor of the *West Country Clarion*, rival newspaper to the *Cornish Telegraph*.

After two hours, during which a secretary scribbled frantically, filling page after page with shorthand, the editor said, 'You have given us some remarkable material for a series of articles, Mr Retallick, but can all the incidents you relate be verified?'

'Every single one of them,' Adam assured him. 'In fact, if you contact the men whose names and addresses I have written out for you, I have no doubt they will remember many more incidents with which to fill the pages of your newspaper. Africa is a different world from that known to your readers. You only have to look at me! Two years ago I was scratching a living on a drought-stricken farm in the Transvaal and here I am, a lieutenant colonel and staff officer to General Jan Smuts – who also fought for the Boers in the Anglo-Boer war, yet is now one of Britain's most loyal soldiers. I am the subject of scurrilous accusations, yet, having had a Royal Navy warship put at my disposal to bring me to England from Southern Africa, I have come here to talk to you direct from a meeting with the top officers in the British army at the War Office in London, at which the future direction of the war in East Africa was decided. It is quite likely that this time next month I will once more be deep in the African bushveld, stalking the armies of General von Lettow in country where mosquitoes and tsetse flies claim more victims than the enemy. Your rival newspaper has run a vindictive campaign against the Retallick family, based on falsehood and innuendo. I have given you a true picture of the war in Africa, and the part played in it by all the members of my family. I trust you will make good use of the information.'

'Rest assured that the people of the west country will soon be able to read about the not inconsiderable part played by the Retallick family against the enemy,' said the jubilant editor of the *West Country Clarion*. 'Furthermore, if you and Mr Ben Retallick pursue your claims for libel against the *Cornish Telegraph* we are likely to be the only newspaper bringing the truth to this corner of Great Britain.'

*

When the first article about Adam and his family was published it created a considerable stir in Cornwall, and such was the demand for the second week's instalment that it was sold out by noon and the newspaper was forced to go into a second printing.

In sharp contrast, sales of the *Cornish Telegraph* were at an all-time low. And when a writ for libel was served on the editor by Ben's solicitor, on behalf of Ben and Adam Retallick, the newspaper's joint owners convened an emergency meeting with their own solicitors present to discuss the situation.

It was a long meeting, during which their solicitor made the gravity of the alleged offence clear. If they were found guilty, the judge would take a particularly serious view of the matter, since in the recent articles the *Cornish Telegraph* had repeated the substance of allegations for which they had previously printed an apology because they were aware the allegations were unfounded.

The solicitor also pointed out that he had read the articles complained of and had compared them with the articles in the *West Country Clarion*. If the latter could be substantiated – and he pointed out that they most probably could – then the *Cornish Telegraph* could expect to be ordered to pay very heavy damages to the two brothers, together with significant costs. The case would need to be heard in the High Court, which meant engaging barristers – and doubtless the Retallicks would employ the very best, and most expensive – for which the losers in the trial would pick up the bill.

'Is there any advice you can offer that might help us out of this most unwelcome mess, Mr Button?'

The question was put to the solicitor by Brigadier Grove's co-director, a wealthy Cornish landowner with a great many business interests in and outside the county.

'As I see it, the only way out would be to persuade the Retallicks to withdraw their writ and agree to an out of court settlement, but in order to do that someone will need to eat a great deal of humble pie.' The solicitor offered his solution to the matter without once looking at Brigadier Grove, but everyone in the room was aware that the 'someone' to whom he referred was Brigadier Grove.

The brigadier was aware of it too and he said, irascibly, 'Well, I'm damned if I am going to grovel before Retallick and beg him not to take us to court and dispute something that everyone knows is perfectly true.'

'Not *everyone*, Sir Robert,' retorted his co-director. 'As I recall, the series of articles published by the *Cornish Telegraph* was compiled at your insistence, from material provided by you. I had misgivings at the time – you will find my comments recorded in the minutes of an earlier meeting on the subject held in this very office. However, publication went ahead and so I must bear a share of the responsibility for that. If it costs me money, then so be it. A man usually has to pay for his mistakes.'

'That may be all right for you,' Brigadier Grove said bitterly, 'you can afford to pay. Thanks to Ben Retallick, the Grove china clay works is already losing more money than at any time in its history.'

'Then you should have made your peace with Retallick instead of instigating a vendetta through the pages of the *Cornish Telegraph*, based not on fact but on personal malice,' retorted his co-director. 'Now, if you gentlemen will excuse me, I have more important business matters to attend to. Mr Button has given us his considered opinion about the means by which the problems facing the *Cornish Telegraph* might – and I repeat, just *might* – be solved. It is entirely up to you whether or not you take his advice, Sir Robert. For my part, when the time comes I will apologise to the court for my very minor input in the libellous articles printed in the newspaper and express my willingness to pay whatever amount the court apportions to me.'

'Look here, Retallick, I have apologised to you on behalf of the *Cornish Telegraph* for printing stories about you which have turned out to be untrue – although it was believed at the time that they were accurate and were published in all good faith. What more can I do?'

'You *could* tell the truth and say, "I persuaded the editor of the newspaper to publish the stories I gave him about you because I wanted to see Ruddlemoor go out of business." Had you said that to me I would respect you a great deal more. As it is, I suggest you save any pleas for understanding for your court appearance – although I doubt whether it will influence the judge and jury.'

'You know damn well that if this business goes to court and a ruling goes against me, I will be a ruined man.'

'Yes, Brigadier, I do know that, and there was a time when it would have mattered to me, but, to use one of your own favourite words, I don't give a damn what happens to you now. You deliberately set out to discredit me and put Ruddlemoor out of business. Well, the plan has backfired and now it's you who are likely to go out of business as a result. I won't say I am happy about it, but it is no more than you deserve.'

Clutching at what he believed to be a slight softening in Ben's attitude, Brigadier Grove said, 'All right, so I deserve to be taken to task for using unethical tactics in order to steal a march on a business rival. I am not the first, and certainly won't be the last to employ such methods, but I will not suffer alone. If the Grove works is forced to close, hundreds of men will be put out of work and their wives and children will suffer as a result. Is that what you want?'

'No, it is not what I want,' Ben admitted, 'but if you really care about them I am willing to come to an agreement to ensure it does not happen.'

'You mean . . . you will consider an apology – a full apology – as sufficient to drop your libel action?'

'No, Brigadier. An apology from you would be utterly meaningless, but I have spoken to Adam and he agrees with me that there is a way you can come out of this situation with your reputation intact, and still remain solvent.'

'If it is a reasonable solution, you have my word that I will do whatever it is you want,' Brigadier Grove said eagerly. 'What is it?'

'Sell the Grove works to me and I will drop the libel action. In fact, I have Adam's retraction, duly signed and witnessed and ready to be produced to the court. It is locked away in my safe, here in Tregarrick.'

Brigadier Grove stood up abruptly and the look he gave Ben was venomous. 'Sell the Grove works to you? *Never!* I would rather die first.'

II

When the telephone rang in the Tregarrick main hall at seven o'clock in the morning, Ben was shaving.

It was an unusually early time of day for anyone to telephone, unless there was an emergency at Ruddlemoor, and Ben opened the door of the bathroom in order to listen as one of the housemaids lifted the receiver from its cradle and held it to her ear. As he stood, razor in hand, he heard the maid say, 'Yes, of course . . . I'll go and find him right away.'

Moving swiftly to the top of the stairs, Ben called, 'I am here, Dorothy. Is it Ruddlemoor?'

'No, sir,' the maid called up to him, 'it's Dr Antonia.'

Ben almost fell down the stairs in his haste to reach the telephone. Snatching up the receiver and putting it to his ear, he shouted into the mouthpiece, 'Antonia . . . is it really you? Where are you?'

'I am at the Royal Naval Hospital in Portsmouth, Ben, and . . . oh, it is wonderful to hear your voice again. How are you?'

'I am absolutely fine! Adam was at Tregarrick a few weeks ago and told me you would be returning to England on a hospital ship. When did you arrive . . . and when will you be coming to Tregarrick? I know . . . I will come to Portsmouth and fetch you. I can be there by early evening . . .'

There was the sound of happy laughter from the other end of the telephone line and Antonia said, 'There will be no need to fetch me, Ben. I am catching a train very soon now. It will arrive at Plymouth a few minutes after two o'clock. I have not yet found out the time of a connection to St Austell . . .'

'Forget a connection!' Ben was beside himself with excitement. 'I will bring the Hotchkiss and meet you at Plymouth.'

'Are you quite sure, Ben? It *would* be marvellous to see you that much sooner than if I came on to St Austell.'

'Am I sure? I would have driven all the way to Mozambique had you asked me to.'

Echoing his enthusiasm, Antonia said, 'I am so happy that you sound so pleased that I am back in England, Ben. There were times when I feared you might have changed your mind about me.'

'Changed my mind?' Ben sounded shocked. 'Antonia, I am so happy to know you are back in England that I might hurry off to see the vicar and arrange a wedding date before coming to Plymouth. Perhaps he could perform the ceremony today . . . if we get home in time.'

Once again there was the sound of delighted laughter in Ben's ear, but suddenly Antonia became serious. 'By the way, Ben, there is someone with me who would also appreciate a lift to St Austell.'

'Someone else?' Ben realised he seemed to be echoing much of what Antonia was saying to him, but he was too excited to care. 'Philippe hasn't returned to England with you?'

'No, not Philippe, but a young man who was on the

395

same hospital ship, and who looks very handsome in the uniform of a lieutenant in the British South Africa Company Police.'

'You mean Sam? You came home with Sam?'

'Yes. He has been a very sick man, but he is much better now and the senior doctor on the ship declared him fit enough to return home to Cornwall with me.'

'Betsy Hooper is going to be absolutely ecstatic,' Ben said. 'I will go and tell her right away – and I'll bring her to Plymouth with me.'

'That will be wonderful, Ben . . . but I must give up the telephone now. There are a lot of impatient men waiting to use it.'

'Of course, but . . . I love you.'

'I love you too, Ben. I hope we can arrange that wedding very soon.'

When Ben replaced the telephone receiver, he found that Mrs Rodda was standing in the hall, with two of the housemaids in the passageway behind her. It seemed that the maid who had first taken Antonia's call had wasted no time in spreading the news.

Still in a state of high excitement, Ben said, 'I am going to see Betsy Hooper right away, Mrs Rodda. Antonia is in England – and young Sam Hooper is with her. I am going to Plymouth to meet them off a train at two o'clock today.'

'The news will delight a great many people, sir . . . but may I suggest you finish shaving before you go out . . . and try not to cut yourself,' she called after him as he ran up the stairs from the hall.

*

Betsy Hooper was every bit as excited at the news of her son's return as Ben had anticipated she would be. Receiving no reply when he rapped his knuckles on the front door of the Hooper cottage, he went to the back door and found her in the kitchen, wiping up the plate and utensils from her breakfast.

She was so excited that she put a plate on the shelf, took it off again and replaced it three times, not fully knowing what she was doing.

After the fourth 'Oh, my dear soul!' she turned to Ben in a state of distress. 'But . . . what can I give him to eat? I have barely enough food in the house for one. Oh, my dear soul . . .'

'Mrs Hooper, it wouldn't matter what you cooked for him. Sam will just be delighted to be back with you. But think of Sam's favourite meal and tell me what it is. I'll have Mrs Rodda buy all the ingredients while we are in Plymouth and we'll pick them up on the way home.'

It seemed that Sam's favourite food was the pasty. Ben said he would have the Tregarrick cook make a few and Mrs Rodda would provide all the trimmings to go with them. Then he excused himself by saying he needed to tell Jim Bray he would not be at Ruddlemoor that day, but he promised to return for her at 11 a.m.

It was difficult to know whether it was Ben or Betsy Hooper who was the more excited when the train pulled slowly into Plymouth station before coming to a halt in a cloud of hissing steam.

There was a brief moment of panic when all the carriage doors opened and a flood of people poured on to the platform without a sign of Antonia or Sam. Then, as the passengers converged upon the exit stairs, two figures emerged from a carriage at the far end of the train, one wearing a sand-brown uniform.

Ben ran along the platform to greet them, but the plump Betsy Hooper was hardly any slower. Then Ben was embracing Antonia while Betsy shed tears on the shoulder of her son, who was still looking tanned, but decidedly fragile.

The first moments of emotion over, Ben clasped Sam's hand and told him how pleased he was to see him, and what a wonderful job he had done in Africa.

'Thank you,' Sam said, 'but I hope you are not angry that I left the two traction engines behind at Insimo.'

'Sam, if that was the price that needed to be paid to have you home safely, you could have sunk them both in Lake Tanganyika. As it is, I have heard from Nat and they will be put to good use at Insimo. But today I don't care what is happening in the rest of the world. I have Antonia and your ma has you, so let's get a porter to bring all the luggage and we'll get you back where you belong – in Cornwall.'

III

It was not long before Antonia and Sam were both feeling at home in Cornwall once more, Antonia working at the hospital in Bodmin, and Sam putting in an increasing amount of time at Ruddlemoor, in spite of Ben's directive that he was to enjoy fully paid sick leave until he was once more a hundred per cent fit.

Worried that Sam was doing far too much before he had fully recovered from the serious bout of malaria which had brought about the end of his brief career as an officer in the military arm of the British South Africa Company Police, Ben voiced his misgivings to Antonia when they were relaxing after dinner at Tregarrick.

'He is by no means fully fit yet,' Antonia agreed, 'but he really did love Maria. It was her tragic death that drove him to become a fighting man in Africa. He has still not recovered from her death, but now he can no longer fight Germans he needs something else to take his mind off what happened in Mozambique. One day, I have no doubt that some really nice young girl will come along to help him to forget the past. I just hope it might be sooner rather than later.'

Soon after this conversation, Ben hit upon the idea of making Sam the Ruddlemoor chief engineer, with responsibility for all the vehicles and steam machinery at the clay works. By doing so he ensured that Sam spent his time supervising others when they worked on machinery, instead of doing it himself.

Meanwhile, during her off-duty hours Antonia was rediscovering the gardens and the many pleasures of country life at Tregarrick – but there were all too few leisure hours. The war in Europe had become ever more inhumane, taking a very heavy toll on the minds and bodies of soldiers forced to endure the horrors of trench warfare, and she was kept extremely busy at the hospital.

Nevertheless, she and Ben had decided that they would be married as soon as the libel case against the *Cornish Telegraph* was brought to a conclusion. Then, less than two months after Antonia's return, something occurred which made Ben think very hard about what he was doing.

It happened during the week in which Sam had been informed that he was to be presented with his Albert medal by King George V at an investiture at Buckingham Palace. The invitation informed Sam that he could invite two guests to accompany him to the palace.

With the letter in his hand, Sam said to his mother, 'You will be coming with me, of course, Ma, but who else do you think I should invite? I wonder whether I ought to invite Ben Retallick?'

'Certainly not,' Betsy replied firmly. 'I know he has been very good to you, and to me too, but this is a family occasion and I need someone I can depend upon to support me while you are up there talking to the King. I think you should invite Muriel.'

Remembering the plain and rather plump girl with whom he had grown up – and who was so unlike Maria – Sam baulked at the idea, but then he thought of his mother, whose only venture outside Cornwall during the whole of her lifetime had been when Ben took her to Plymouth on his return to England. This was going to be a very special occasion for her.

A few months before Sam's homecoming Muriel had been persuaded by one of her customers at the hair-dressing salon to join the Women's Royal Naval Service. The customer, wife of a senior naval officer, was herself in the service. Although not yet formally recognised, the WRNS was rapidly increasing in numbers, its members carrying out a great many non-combatant duties.

'Perhaps Muriel won't be able to get leave to come with us to the palace,' he said, hopefully.

'Of course she will,' Betsy said confidently. 'She was going to get leave to be here when you got home, but you surprised us all by arriving without any warning. Besides, when they hear that she's going to Buckingham Palace to see you given your medal from the King, they'll be more than happy to let her off.'

And so it was decided. Sam wrote to confirm his presence at the investiture and nominated his mother and Muriel as the guests who would accompany him.

On the day after Sam sent off his letter, Ben arrived at Ruddlemoor to be met by a solemn Jim Bray. Taking Ben to one side, the works captain said, 'I know there is no love lost between you and Brigadier Grove, Ben, but I thought you ought to know that he received a telegram yesterday to say that his son has been killed on the Somme. Word is that Grove is totally bereft. He idolised his son and was so proud when he was given a commission in his old regiment. I thought that, despite all that has happened, you might want to send a message of condolence to him.'

Ben felt a moment of deep sorrow for his business rival. He too was aware of Brigadier Grove's feelings for his son. 'Thank you for telling me, Jim. You're quite right, he and I have never got on, but this is something I would not wish upon anyone.'

Whatever Ben did that morning, his thoughts kept to returning to Brigadier Grove and the grief he must be feeling. Shortly before noon, he left Ruddlemoor, but instead of returning to Tregarrick for lunch he drove to Grove House, which was close to the small port of Charlestown. He was met by a manservant, who said, 'Sir Robert is not receiving visitors today, Mr Retallick . . . you have heard the tragic news about his son?'

'Yes,' said Ben. 'It is very sad indeed, and I am here to offer my condolences, which I hope to be able to express in more than mere words. Will you ask him if he will see me, please?'

The servant went away to convey the message to his employer and a few minutes later the brigadier came into the hall. Ben was shocked by his appearance. He looked ten years older and had the air of a defeated man – but his manner had not changed. 'What is it, Retallick? I don't know what you have to say, but this is not a time to bring up anything that might come out in court. Besides, I don't really care what happens any more.'

'I am aware how you must be feeling just now, Brigadier, and would like to express my deepest sympathy. I also want to tell you that at such a time I do not intend to add to your very real grief. As a mark of respect for your son I am instructing my solicitor to withdraw the libel action. I will give him the letter written by my brother which conveys the same instructions, for I know he will be in full agreement with me. I will leave you now, but you have my deepest sympathy, sir.'

Ben did not wait for Brigadier Grove's reaction to his decision, but turned and left the house.

That evening, when he told Antonia what he had

402

done, she said, 'I am proud of you, Ben. You behaved exactly as I would have wished in such circumstances. It is exactly the decision I would have hoped the man I am going to marry would make.'

IV

Sam and Betsy Hooper were waiting at St Austell station three days before the investiture was due to take place in London. Sam had been regretting his decision to invite Muriel to accompany them to Buckingham Palace. He felt that 'the girl next door' would not be at her ease in the big city and subject to the attention of the press that he had been warned the whole party could expect.

When the train came to a halt in the station only two passengers alighted. Both were women and both were in uniform. One wore the uniform of the Women's Royal Naval Service, the other was in khaki. Neither was Muriel – or so he believed.

Not until the young woman in WRNS uniform came up to him and his mother and said, 'Hello, Sam. Thank you for inviting me to come to Buckingham Palace with you and your ma,' did he realise that it was Muriel.

Sam looked at her in open-mouthed astonishment. This was not the Muriel he had left behind when he set off on his journey to Africa. This assured young woman was far slimmer than the younger Muriel had been and no longer was she shy and tongue-tied. The woman standing before him had an air of worldliness about her that Sam found disconcerting.

'It . . . it's my pleasure,' he eventually managed to

say, 'but . . . you've changed, Muriel. If we had met unexpectedly somewhere, I'm not sure I would have recognised you.'

She smiled at him. 'It wouldn't have mattered, Sam, I would have recognised you, even though you've lost some weight. You must have seen and done a great many things that we never dreamed of before we both left Cornwall and went off into the big wide world. I have too – but sometime you must tell me all about Africa and the things you saw and did there.'

'Of course,' Sam replied, not yet fully recovered from the shock of Muriel's transition from the somewhat gauche girl he had left behind to this self-assured and worldly young woman, who would probably be more at home in London than he would.

The day after the investiture, when Sam, Muriel and his mother were still in London celebrating his award, Ben had a visitor at Ruddlemoor. It was Brigadier Grove's solicitor.

When he was ushered into his office, Ben shook his hand and said, 'What can I do for you? If it's about the libel action, I have already told the brigadier that I am dropping it – and my own solicitor is doing all that is necessary.'

'Yes, indeed. Your solicitor has already been in communication with me about the matter. It is a very generous and Christian gesture on your part in view of the brigadier's tragic loss . . . but the tragedy is partly the reason why I am here. Sir Robert had always intended that the Grove works would be passed on as a profitable company to his son. Now, sadly, the incentive for him to remain in business has gone and he wishes to sell the company. I understand you have offered to purchase it – at a price to be agreed between your respective accountants, of course. Brigadier Sir Robert has asked me to come here to tell you he is ready to sell to you on those terms . . .'

That night, when Ben told Antonia the news, she was jubilant. 'That's wonderful, Ben. It means that you will now virtually control the china clay industry in Cornwall and no one will be able to make things difficult for you. You must be very happy, despite the circumstances that have brought it about.' Then, apparently changing the subject, she said, 'Have you seen a national newspaper today?'

When he admitted he had not, she said, 'I have one in my room that I bought in Bodmin. It has a photograph of the investiture in London and shows Sam with Muriel at Buckingham Palace.' Looking suddenly coy, she asked, 'Did you mean what you said to me when I returned from Africa? That you would marry me when the libel issue against the *Cornish Telegraph* was settled?'

'Yes . . . and, of course, now it is – but what has that to do with Sam and Muriel?'

'I will go and find the paper and you can see for yourself how they are are looking at each other,' she replied. 'I am convinced that, unless you want Sam and Muriel to be married before we are, it is going to be necessary to begin making our arrangements right away . . . unless you have changed your mind?'

Neither Ben nor Antonia heard the door of the study open a few minutes later when Mrs Rodda came to see if there was anything they needed before she went to bed. Backing away quickly, she closed the door quietly behind her without saying anything.

When the discreet housekeeper reached her own room she opened her wardrobe door and studied her clothes with a critical eye. She decided that on her next afternoon off work she would walk into St Austell and look in the shops there with a view to choosing an outfit suitable for her to wear at her employer's wedding. It was apparent to her that it would be taking place in the very near future.

TOMORROW IS
FOR EVER

E. V. Thompson

For Alan Carter the greatest personal sacrifice of the
Great War of 1914–18 is being called-up after only one
week of marriage. Leaving his new bride is even more
painful than the wound that, months later, interrupts
his war at sea and sends him to Cornwall to convalesce.
For, there, he has time to think about Dora and about
the career as a writer that he secretly nurtures. A career
that seems possible when he finds himself accepted by
the established colony of Newlin artists.

There is one artist in particular – Vicky Hazleton – who
encourages Alan's leanings towards the arts. And she
stirs other feelings: inappropriate and impossible ones.
For Vicky and her set inhabit a different world from
Alan. He, as one of Vicky's friends makes clear, belongs
to London's East End – and to Dora . . .

ISBN 978-0-7515-4552-4

THE VAGRANT KING

E. V. Thompson

Cornish farmer Joseph Moyle's loyalty to the crown goes well rewarded – his stepson Ralf is appointed page to the future Charles II. And when Ralf takes up his post, Britain is in the midst of its most tumultuous period ever – the war between the Royalists and the Parliamentarians and the dawning of an entirely new era . . .

Ralf's duties oblige him to follow the heir to the throne through the western counties, where he experiences not only court intrigue and the constant threat of Cromwell's armies, but also romance. As Charles begins the first of many affairs, Ralf also falls in love. But this first love is a dangerous one. Brighid is an Irish Catholic and complicit in an attempt to kidnap Charles – a fact that Ralf discovers when he foils the plot . . .

ISBN 978-0-7515-4502-9

Other bestselling titles available by mail